13

to the

Gallows

13
to the
Gallows

John Dickson Carr

and

Val Gielgud

Edited by
Tony Medawar

Crippen & Landru Publishers
Norfolk, Virginia
2008

Cover design by Deborah Miller

Crippen & Landru logo by Eric D. Greene

ISBN (limited clothbound edition): 978-1-932009-58-3
ISBN (trade softcover edition): 978-1-932009-59-0

FIRST EDITION

Printed in the United States of America on recycled, acid-free paper

Crippen & Landru Publishers
P. O. Box 9315
Norfolk, VA 23505
USA
www.crippenlandru.com   Info@crippenlandru.com

Contents

Suspense on Stage

"This whole show was designed as a series of traps for the witnesses. There was probably a trick in half the things they saw ... If we could find out exactly what they saw, or thought they saw ..."

John Dickson Carr, *The Black Spectacles*

In his masterful biography, *John Dickson Carr, The Man Who Explained Miracles*, Professor Douglas Greene disclosed that John Dickson Carr's interest in the theatre began at a young age, with *Arms and the God*, a play co-authored around 1925 with a school friend Sheldon Dick. Carr's second play, written in 1926 while at Haverford College, was a musical parody of *The Student Prince*, the famous operetta, which had opened in 1924 in New York. From its title, *The Stewed Prince of Haverburg* would appear to have been filled with puns as well as what Greene describes as "topical references to Haverford events and professors."[1] But like *Arms and the God*, Carr's only venture into what might loosely be termed light operetta is lost.

As far as we know, it was not until the advent of the Second World War that Carr once again turned his hand to the art of writing for the stage, producing the four plays that comprise this volume. Two were written in collaboration with Val Gielgud, at the time Director of Drama at the British Broadcasting Corporation, then as now the major broadcaster of radio and television drama in the United Kingdom. Gielgud and Carr first met in 1939, it would appear in the context of a Detection Club function to which Carr had invited Gielgud. They quickly forged a strong friendship, a friendship that led to the two collaborations for the stage, published for the first time in this volume, and which perhaps grew out of

---

[1] *John Dickson Carr: The Man Who Explained Miracles.* New York: Otto Penzler Books/Simon & Schuster, 1995.

their shared interest in detective stories and fencing.

The first of these plays was *Inspector Silence Takes the Air*, a mystery set against the background of an outside broadcast by the BBC. The genesis and division of the writing of *Inspector Silence Takes the Air* is unclear but it is certain that Gielgud was responsible for the authentic detail about the vicissitudes of live radio and likely that Carr provided the bulk of the mystery. The stage play was in fact effectively a sequel to two radio plays. Chief Inspector Jack Silence[2] had made his first appearance in *Death Comes to the Hibiscus*, a serial written for radio by Val Gielgud and 'Nicholas Vane,' a pen name for the mystery writer Francis Durbridge who created the celebrated radio sleuth Paul Temple. In this serial, broadcast weekly between November 28, 1941 and February 20, 1942, Silence investigates a series of murders in and around the Hibiscus night-club in London. The culprit seems clear, "a marvellous pianist" named, curiously, Mr Bizarre. But evidence is hard to come by and frustratingly the final episodes of the serial appear lost so there is no record of whether Silence caught his man. This seems likely however as he next appeared in one of Carr's earliest radio plays, *Inspector Silence Takes the Underground*, which was written specially for its star, the veteran actor Leon M. Lion.[3]

Inspector Silence Takes the Underground was broadcast on the BBC on March 25, 1942. Despite its title, the play is set on the New York subway. An unidentified criminal, tagged by the press as "False Face" for his curious habit of wearing a mask, is wanted for a series of apparently motiveless attacks on a number of women. Silence, now retired from the Yard, is in New York to stay with a friend. Shortly after the start of the play he boards a subway car at the precise moment that it is surrounded by police, who are certain that False Face is on board, as proves to be the case. The play lasted only twenty minutes and it is therefore unsurprising that the mystery was not particularly complicated. Interestingly, in its set-

---

[2] Silence's first name was not disclosed until *Inspector Silence Takes the Underground*. He may be related to John Silence, the detective of the supernatural created by Algernon Blackwood. In *Death Comes to the Hibiscus*, Silence was played by Godfrey Baseley, who went on to become a producer and created *The Archers*, the world's longest-running radio series.

[3] Lion and Carr may already have known each other as they were both members of the London's Savage Club.

up and solution, the play prefigures a celebrated short story by Edmund Crispin (1921-1978). Crispin, whose real name was Bruce Montgomery, was a tremendous Carr enthusiast and his own sleuth, Gervase Fen, was clearly inspired by Carr's Gideon Fell. It is therefore not too fanciful to imagine that Crispin might have been in some way influenced by Carr's radio play when it came to writing "Beware of the Trains," Crispin's response to the classic challenge of the vanishing man.

While the sequel to *Inspector Silence Takes the Underground,* initially entitled *Murder Takes the Air,* was being considered as a stage play by the impresario Firth Shephard, Val Gielgud received a proposal that he or Carr should restructure the play into a serial for *Answers* magazine but this never transpired. Shephard lost interest and it fell to E.G. Norman, managing director of St Martin's Theatre, London, to take on the presentation of the play — now entitled *Inspector Silence Takes the Air* — with the intention of mounting it in London after a tour in what were then described as "the provinces." As well as organising the venues of the tour, Norman had to acquire the license that was required before any stage production could be put on. The licensing authority was the Lord Chamberlain's Examiners of Plays, who could block a production or require changes to the script; Norman was obliged to make two minor changes, both of which are noted in the Afterword to the play and will seem wholly unnecessary to twenty-first century eyes.

Duly licensed and described in advance publicity as "a new comedy thriller of broadcasting by Val Gielgud and John Dixon-Carr (sic)," *Inspector Silence Takes the Air* was first performed at the long since demolished Pavilion Theatre, located at the end of the pier in the Welsh seaside town of Llandudno. As with *Inspector Silence Takes the Underground,* Leon M. Lion starred as Silence, who has on this occasion been invited to take part in *Murderers' Row,* a BBC programme not unlike those in which Carr would himself take part in later years. The rest of the cast was drawn from the BBC's Repertory Company. Carr and Gielgud attended the opening night and Gielgud made "a neat speech of appreciation at the reception accorded the play."[4] Although Carr was unimpressed with Llandudno — describing it to Anthony Boucher as a

---

[4] *Llandudno Advertiser,* April 25, 1942.

"godforsaken town,"[5] Llandudno was very impressed with *Inspector Silence Takes the Air* — with one local newspaper praising it as "undoubtedly the best play of its kind we have had during the war."[6] Most critics found the thriller element more successful than the comedy but the run was short, less than six weeks and the planned run in London did not transpire. Many years later, an enthusiast of Carr's work, the late Derek Smith, asked Val Gielgud why the play had had such a short run. According to Smith, Gielgud told him that "the production had been a shambles, and best forgotten. Apparently Leon M. Lion could never remember his lines, even those he had insisted upon writing himself!"[7] Gielgud also confirmed that the character of Julian Caird was "a rather mocking self portrait," carried over from his performance in *Death at Broadcasting House*, a murder mystery set at the BBC's headquarters based on a script by Gielgud and Holt Marvell and published as a novel some years earlier. Certainly, when Derek Smith eventually had the opportunity to read the script of the production he had been thinking about "for nearly fifty years," he felt that Gielgud "materialised out of the pages" in the part of Julian Caird.

In late 1943 and despite — or perhaps because of — the limited success of *Inspector Silence Takes the Air*, Carr and Gielgud embarked on a second play. As with their first collaboration, Carr clearly contributed the mystery and Gielgud the authentic details of broadcasting for *Thirteen to the Gallows* which, like *Inspector Silence Takes the Air*, takes place during a live outside broadcast of a multilocational episode of *In Town Tonight*. In reality, *In Town Tonight* was one of the BBC's most popular programmes and it ran for many years, presenting each week an extraordinary range of national and local personalities.[8] Carr and Gielgud have great fun blending a poetry recital by "the youngest munitions factory beauty queen in England" and memorable performances by "the only

---

[5] Carr to Anthony Boucher, March 14, 1942.

[6] *North Wales Pioneer*, April 23, 1942.

[7] Letter to Tony Medawar, November 21, 1990.

[8] Some of the more unusual guests on *In Town Tonight* over the years were a fire-eater Signor Stromboli, a 90 year old town crier from Suffolk, a flea trainer, a one-armed parachutist and the Crime Reporter for the *Daily Mall*, a British newspaper.

school bell-ringer in the Midlands who plays the flute" and Sandoz and his sea-lions with an impromptu discussion of what is billed as "the most famous unsolved murder mystery of recent years."

After an initial week of performances in April 1944, the production was pulled for reasons that are now unclear but which may lie in the fact that the play does not appear to have been submitted for licensing. It did not resurface for eighteen months when Leon M. Lion, the star of *Inspector Silence Takes the Air*, took over the starring role of Sir Henry Bryce.[9] When the play was submitted for licensing purposes in 1945, under the title *Out of Town Tonight*, the Lord Chamberlain's Examiner was the poet Geoffrey Dearmer, who would himself work for the BBC in later years. Dearmer saw no need to wield the blue pencil, commenting drily that "there are one or two emotionally justified 'God's' but nothing exceptional in the way of expletives; the characters being a respectable lot."[10] Dearmer concluded that the play was "a good job of work" with a "satisfying" denouement but it is apparent from contemporary reviews that *Thirteen to the Gallows* did not play well.

Lion must have been very impressed with the script for he put up a quarter of the finance for the play in exchange for half of the profits.[11] He was to be sorely disappointed by the return for the changes to the cast were not enough to save the play and a month later the second, somewhat episodic, run of *Thirteen to the Gallows* came to an end.

It is difficult to be certain why the play failed. At least on paper, it is a better play than *Inspector Silence Takes the Air*, with a more baffling problem and considerably more effective comedy in the "mechanicals." Perhaps Val Gielgud's memories, described above, related to *Thirteen to the Gallows* rather than *Inspector Silence Takes the Air* as it hard to understand why Lion would have been cast in another mystery if his performance in the earlier play had been so unreliable. Then again, the play does have a complex solution and, as some reviews pointed out, the

---

[9] Given the similarity in name, it is possible that Carr might originally have conceived the play as a vehicle for Sir Henry Merrivale, the hero of many of the novels written under his "Carter Dickson" pseudonym.

[10] "Reader's Report," 9 April 1944. British Library: *Lord Chamberlain's Plays, Manuscripts Collection, Folder No. 5484.*

[11] Undated letter Leon M. Lion to Elem Ltd. University of Rochester Library.

array of suspects is difficult to credit.

It was to be the last play on which Carr and Gielgud would collaborate for, around this time, something happened — exactly what is unclear. In Carr's words to Gielgud five years later "a slight crack got into our old friendship."[12] The cause of that crack is not known but Gielgud later described it to Carr as "that extremely stupid and tactless affair of the royal broadcast,"[13] a reference whose meaning may one day become apparent.

There would be some minor "cracks" in later years too but the men remained on good terms, at least while Carr was living in Britain and writing for BBC radio, albeit more and more infrequently over the years.[14]

Notwithstanding the comparative failure of both of the plays he had written with Gielgud, Carr was not deterred and he next turned his hand to producing a version for the stage of his famous BBC series *Appointment with Fear.*

It is easy to underestimate the significance of *Appointment with Fear* to British mystery fans of a certain vintage. First broadcast in 1943, and drawing very heavily on Carr's work for the CBS series *Suspense, Appointment with Fear* was a great success, described in the advance publicity for the stage version as "the enormously popular BBC feature, to which over ten million people have listened in each week."[15] As in *Suspense,* if not more so, a key role was played by the narrator who, for *Appointment with Fear,* was played by Valentine Dyall. In Dyall's words, the narrator's role was simple — to ensure that every programme started

---

[12] Carr to Gielgud, September 15, 1949. BBC Archives.

[13] Gielgud to Carr September 20, 1949. BBC Archives.

[14] In 1956, Gielgud sponsored Carr's application for British citizenship. Carr's other sponsors were Dorothy L. Sayers and R. L. Jackson, the then Assistant Commissioner at Scotland Yard.

[15] Gordon West, the male protagonist of *Night at the Mocking Widow* (1950), written as by "Carter Dickson," wrote what he described as a very popular "weekly terror play for the BBC." In an unpublished biographical note, written in 1954, Carr said that *Appointment with Fear* "swept everything else off the board for popularity."

"on a note of tension from the word 'go,' like all good thrillers."[16]

The stage production of *Appointment with Fear*, written by Carr and produced by Martyn C. Webster, who directed the radio series, had been commissioned by William Watt, with an eye to a tour around Britain followed by a London run. It was to include three short plays. Carr developed two of the scripts, one inspired by a problem he had set and solved in a novel ten years earlier and the other drawing on one of his earliest radio plays. Watt requested that the plays not be "horrific" and in the programmes explained that they "must not be compared for example with the "Grand Guignol" type of plays which had a vogue in England years ago." *Intruding Shadow* is a domestic murder mystery, with a limited number of suspects. The second play, *She Slept Lightly*, is set in Napoleonic France, a period that held some fascination for Carr,[17] possibly through his having read Conan Doyle's stories of Brigadier Gerard, an effete braggart who recounts various improbable and unconvicing deeds of heroism in the face of dastardly European villainy.

On stage as on radio the plays would be introduced by the sepulchral tones of Valentine Dyall and, to lighten the tension, Watt arranged for *Prize Onions*, an inoffensive "comedy of village life" by the little known E Eynon Evans, to play between Carr's dramas.[18] All three plays survived the licensing stage unscathed, though in that Watt was fortunate because the licensing application was not submitted until March 27, 1945, only days before the plays were due to open.

The stage production of *Appointment with Fear* ran three months, which was quite respectable in the circumstances. It did not transfer to London and, while there is no evidence that this is so, one cannot help but suspect that audiences declined after the declaration of the end of the

---

[16]Valentine Dyall. "Appointment with Fear." *Radio & Television Annual.* London: Sampson Low, Marston & Co (1947).

[17] James E Keirans, "A Fascination with Napoleon: John Dickson Carr and the Emperor." *CADS* 23, May 1994.

[18]*Prize Onions* was dropped after three weeks. The reasons are unclear but it is likely that, in the light of the reviews and audience response, the concept of a comic intermission between two tense melodramas simply did not work. When *Prize Onions* was cut from the programme, Carr expanded *Intruding Shadow* and *She Slept Lightly* and it is the full length versions that are published in this volume.

Second World War and that the play's management might have felt the nature of the play to be at odds with the jubilation that was sweeping the country. But eventually the idea of a new stage version of *Appointment with Fear* was mooted; Val Gielgud told Carr the following Summer that "our old friend *Appointment with Fear* has again cropped up as a possible touring dramatic proposition."[19] As Gielgud had anticipated, Carr was not interested principally because he was at that time working on the script for a film. Although Carr urged Gielgud to commission Francis Durbridge to work on a script, there was no new stage play but the "man in black," still played by Valentine Dyall, made his next appearance in a film of that name and in three short films based on three of Carr's radioscripts.[20] The radio broadcasts of *Appointment with Fear* also continued, with new thrillers as well as adaptations of ghost stories by the masters of the genre, M. R. James and E. F. Benson, and a final series by Carr in 1955. But, while he wrote many other radio plays[21] too, on both sides of the Atlantic, and scripted some short plays for private performances by and for the Mystery Writers of America, he wrote no more for the commercial stage. That phase of John Dickson Carr's prodigious career was over.

As always thanks are due to various people for their help in making this volume possibly, especially the late Derek Smith who first conceived of this collection, describing it, we hope accurately, as "a magnificent treat," Geoff Bradley, editor of *CADS* magazine where details of the plays in this volume were first published, June Whitfield CBE for her memories of *She Slept Lightly,* and locating the only known photograph of any of the plays, regrettably too indistinct to be reproduced in this volume, And thanks are also due to Doug Greene, staff of the British Library and BBC Written Archives for having the foresight to retain copies of the relevant scripts, Denis Gifford whose book *The Golden Age of Radio* is an invaluable guide to wartime radio in Britain, Arthur Vidro for catching errors in the proofing, and finally numerous librarians in the United

---

[19] Gielgud to Carr, 29 August 1946. BBC Archives.

[20] "The Clock Strikes Eight," "The Gong Cried Murder" and "The House in Rue Rapp," which was based on "The Silver Curtain"; the scripts were adapted by Roy Clark. The films were distributed in England by Twentieth Century Fox but no prints are known to have survived.

[21] It is possible that other propaganda scripts by Carr have yet to be discovered.

Kingdom and the United States for their help in tracing reviews and other ephemera.

*

Agatha Christie, who knew a little about the art of the crime and detection genre, once called Carr the King of Misdirection and his skills in that respect are reflected in full measure in his work for the stage. In the four plays in this volume, you will find vanishing weapons and invisible hands, murderers that manage to be in two places at once and a young woman who manages to cheat death, even at the moment of her execution. For your maximum enjoyment, we ask you to settle into an easy chair and make yourself comfortable.

And do be sure to comply with the request included in the programme for *Intruding Shadow* and *She Slept Lightly* — "In the interests of future patrons, please do not divulge the solutions to these plays."

Tony Medawar
St Katharine Dock, London

Inspector Silence Takes the Air

A Play in Three Acts

by

John Dickson Carr
and
Val Gielgud

Inspector Silence Takes the Air

The Characters

Chief-Inspector Silence	Formerly of Scotland Yard
Antony Barran	A BBC producer
Elliott Vandeleur	An Actor
Jennifer Sloane	His wife, an actress
Lanyon Kelsey	An actor
May Matheson	An elderly actress
Julian Caird	Dramatic Director BBC
Helen Searle	His secretary
Herbert Pope	Programme Engineer
George Sloane	Junior Programme Engineer
Edna Nasmith	Junior Programme Engineer
Basil Cheston	A BBC announcer
Croker	Studio attendant

ACT I

The scene of the play is an underground vault or cellar below a large country-house on the outskirts of a provincial town. The building has been taken over by the BBC as an emergency security set of studios, and this particular basement has recently been fitted up for use in broadcasting plays.

The room is hung round with dull grey "drapes" for acoustic reasons. In fact only the sham Gothic outline of the door upstage left (facing the audience) reveals its original appearance. This door leads to the staircase connecting with the ground floor of the house.

About two-thirds of the back of the stage, and about eight feet of its depth, are taken up by the Listening Room. This room contains a mixing-unit for the producer, and a gramophone turntable unit — four tables — for the programme engineers. Little of this gear is visible, though people in the room are clearly seen by the audience through a glass panel, which separates it from the studio proper. A solid wooden door at the side of the glass panel opens into the Listening Room. When opened a loudspeaker can be seen facing it. The Listening Room should accommodate in comfort at least four people with the necessary indications of gear.

The Studio itself is pretty bare. In the centre of the Stage is a slung microphone. A green cue-light is attached to the latter. Over both doors are two lights, green and red. Just below the line of the front is the Listening Room, and between the corner of the latter and the door up left, is a miscellaneous collection of "Effects": a tin bath, a roller skate, a cushioned chair, water carafe and glasses, and other appropriate gadgets. Slanting along the wall left is a grand piano, with a small settee below it, leather and chromium. A second settee of similar type but longer, runs along wall right from the wall of the Listening Room. At the corner next to this settee a pane of the glass panel is made practicable for opening. Anywhere where it will not be in the way there should be a second loudspeaker in the studio itself. The stand microphone connected with the latter can be seen on the producer's mixing unit desk in the Listening Room.

After the theatre darkens, but before the curtain rises, a voice is heard through the loudspeaker.

Vandeleur: So you've been sleeping with my wife, eh, you swine!

Then follows the sound of four pistol-shots.

The curtain then rises. Elliott Vandeleur, Jennifer Sloane, his wife, Lanyon Kelsey and May Matheson are grouped at the microphone. In the Listening Room are Antony Barran, the producer, with two Programme Engineers — Herbert Pope and a girl. George Sloane stands amidst his "'ffects"'gear, his right hand in the air holding a cane with which he has been beating the seat of a chair. Ex-Chief-Inspector

Silence, and Basil Cheston, an Announcer, sit on the settee below the piano.

Barran, long, lean and untidy of hair, flings open the door of the Listening Room and emerges wrathfully.

May Matheson (*sotto voce*): Here comes His Nibs again!

Miss Matheson is fifty, fattish, garrulous and very much of the old "pro."

Barran (*agonised*): No, no, no!

May Matheson: What is it this time, Mr Barran?

Barran (*ignoring her*): You, Elliott! Not all that much furious surprise, old boy! Don't say it as though you'd found it out that minute! You dam' well know he's been sleeping with your wife!

Vandeleur: Do I?

Kelsey (*grinning*): I rather fear you do.

Jennifer, blonde, pretty and fluffy looks quickly from the rather elegant though elderly and slow-moving figure of her husband to the slim and sallow good looks of Kelsey.

Barran: You've constructed this whole elaborate plot just to kill him and get away with it. You want to register satisfaction. This is the moment of your revenge, old boy.

Vandeleur: Right you are. It's the timing I find tricky.

May Matheson: I don't think I've really got the development of the character, Mr Barran.

Barran: If we run through once more —

Jennifer: Tony, we've been rehearsing this little bit for hours. Can't we have a break to get something to eat?

Barran (*urgently*): Just a minute, Jennifer. (*To Vandeleur*) This is where you show him where he gets off. (*With a slow, horrible leer*) 'So you've been sleeping with my wife, eh?' And then — bam, bam, bam!

Vandeleur: I quite see what you mean, old man. I'll make a note of it.

Kelsey (*sardonically*): Have you a pencil?

Vandeleur: Yes, thanks.

Kelsey: I only wondered.

Barran (*whirling round*): And you, Lanyon!

Kelsey: At your service.

Barran (*reasoning with him*): Now you've had more microphone experience than that. You don't have to stand here after you've said your last speech. You only get in others' way. When you've said your

last line, go over and sit down.
Kelsey crosses to the sofa and sits down.
Kelsey: Anything to oblige.
Barran: You're dead, see? You've been pumped full of ... wait a minute!
   (*Turning to Sloane*) George! How many shots did you give me then?
Sloane: Four shots, Mr Barran. (*Illustrates.*)
Barran: I said five shots.
Sloane: No, Mr Barran; you said —
Barran: I distinctly said five shots. Who is producing this play, me or the
   Junior Programme Engineer? I want five shots: bam, bam, bam,
   bam, bam!
Kelsey (*lazily*): Why not use all six, and make sure of polishing me off?
Vandeleur: Not a bad idea.
Jennifer: Tony, couldn't we go and get some coffee now?
Barran: Listen. You're all on edge, and I want you to come off it! You're
   on edge, and I'm on edge — and it won't do! I know this isn't Broad-
   casting House. I know it's been tiresome for you, that you've had a
   foul journey to the other end of nowhere. But I don't control the
   BBC. I'm just a poor bloody producer. And if they choose to stick us
   in a condemned set of wine-cellars under a condemned ex-stately
   home of England three miles outside the dullest provincial town in the
   British Isles I can't help it. It just shows you how much your lives are
   valued!
Jennifer: Do they have sirens out here, Tony, if there's a raid?
   *Door opens. Enter Croker. With a grave and intent face he walks
   across, pushes Jennifer aside, moves the microphone back, looks
   round, goes to a sand-filled bucket under Listening Room panel, lifts
   it, puts it down, shakes his head despondently, and returns to door
   while they all stare at him.*
Croker (*sepulchrally*): You ought to be ashamed of yourselves!
   He goes out. Pause.
Silence: Was that Mr Priestley, by any chance?[1]

---

[1]The lugubrious J.B. Priestley was a regular broadcaster on the BBC,
winning lasting fame for his Sunday evening broadcasts during the Second
World War. Priestley lived near Carr in London and, as recorded in Doug
Greene's biography of Carr, the two men were good friends and explored the

Barran wakes up. He goes to door and calls out of it.

Barran: Hey! You! Oi!

Croker (*offstage*): Yessir?

Barran: What's the game? What do you think you're doing, butting into a rehearsal like that?

Croker: I'm protecting this 'ere studio, that's what I'm doing! Air raid warning light's gone yellow.

Jennifer: Tony! Does that mean ...?

Barran closes the door.

Barran: No, Jennifer. You won't hear anything down here, even if there is a raid.

Vandeleur (*thoughtfully*): Not even the noise of firing.

Barran: Now listen to me, everybody! We're starting a new series of true crime-plays. We've got a distinguished guest, Chief Inspector Silence ...

Vandeleur: That's all right, Tony. But it's tricky —

Barran: Don't I know it?

Vandeleur: Did you get that gun to help me with my timing?

Jennifer: Don't pander to him, Tony. It's sheer affectation.

Vandeleur: It's nothing of the kind. It helps no end to have something in your hand —

Kelsey: I can lend you a pipe.

May Matheson: I've a propelling pencil in my bag —

Vandeleur: Have you got the gun, Tony?

Barran: Oddly enough, I have.

He goes into the listening room and comes out with a .22 pistol which he hands to Vandeleur.

Jennifer: I still think it's nonsense.

May Matheson: I hope you've made sure it's not loaded.

Barran: Oddly enough, I have.

Vandeleur: Thanks.

He takes position by the microphone, and gripping the pistol menacingly repeats his line, clicking the trigger rapidly at the end of it.

---

possibility of collaboration on more than one occasion. They also shared an admiration for the Marx Brothers. In a memorable and oft-quoted review of one of Carr's books, Priestley said that he had "a sense of the macabre that lifts him high above the average run of detective story writers."

So you've been sleeping with my wife, eh, you swine?

Barran: Yes, that's better. But you mustn't click the trigger. It'll come over.

Vandeleur: I'll remember. Queer, how much difference it makes — the feel of a gun in one's hand.

Kelsey: Does it?

Jennifer: I don't like it, Elliott. I wish you wouldn't.

Vandeleur: I can assure you and Miss Matheson that it is not loaded.

May Matheson: O — er — Chief — Inspector —

Silence: Retired, madam. Just mister for short.

Silence is about fifty, with a deep bass voice and spectacles.

May Matheson: I'm sure you can help me over the characterization. After all the story was true wasn't it?

Silence: Very true. I hanged the criminal.

May Matheson: There you are, then. You must know. Do tell me what the mother-in-law was really like. If I'm to do anything with such a small part I really must know as much about the character as I can.

Silence: Well, madam, she was fat and fifty. She wore a red wig and false teeth. And she never stopped talking.

May Matheson: She doesn't sound a particularly *pleasant* character.

Silence: It's my private opinion it was his mother-in-law's tongue, and not his wife's infidelity that drove the poor devil I hanged to his crime.

May Matheson: Well, of course, that alters the whole conception of the part. Mr Barran, I must really ask you to let me run over my scene again, if I'm to do justice —

Barran: Sorry, Miss Matheson. Time.

May Matheson: What do you mean? There's plenty of time.

Barran: There's just half an hour. We overran five minutes. The News waits for no man, least of all a dramatic producer. I'm sorry, Miss Matheson, but we shall have to cut that scene.

May Matheson: Cut it!

Barran: Sorry.

Jennifer: Oh that is hard lines!

Kelsey: You can cut *me* about if you like — so long as you don't cut my fee.

Barran: I'm sorry. There's no alternative. We must keep the bones of the big situation. It's tough on you, Miss Matheson, but the part is just padding you know. Curse the author, if you like!

May Matheson: Padding! An artist of my reputation! It's outrageous!

Barran: I'm sorry.

May Matheson: You've given me no help at rehearsal from the start, Mr Barran. And. now you treat me like this. I shall write to the Director General —

Barran: He'll be delighted, I'm sure.

May Matheson: It's so unfair! (*She becomes tearful.*)

Vandeleur: Come along, May. It happens to the best of us.

May Matheson: I always said the BBC was run by a lot of amateurs!

Jennifer: Tony, can't you really — ?

Barran: No, Jennifer, I can't. Let's get on.

May Matheson: I'm getting out.

Barran: What?

May Matheson: You don't think I'll stay here a moment longer?

Barran: I'm afraid you must. There's no car to take you back until after the show.

May Matheson: Then I'll walk!

Jennifer: But suppose there's a raid, May. It's three miles.

May Matheson: I'd still walk if there were three raids and it was three hundred miles!

She flounces out.

Barran: Whew! Sorry.

Jennifer: I think you were rather mean to her, Tony.

Barran: I couldn't help it, I tell you.

Kelsey: Poor old cow.

Jennifer: Lanyon — don't.

Vandeleur: Are we doing it again, or not?

Barran: We are, if you'll all pull yourselves together.

Kelsey: If anyone's on edge, Barran, I suggest that you are.

Barran: Of course I am. Wouldn't you be?

Kelsey: I'm just an actor. I wouldn't know.

Jennifer: I wish it was all over. I'm sure something —

Vandeleur: Not another of your premonitions, please, darling.

Jennifer: Well, you read Lyndoe too.[2] Don't you think he's wonderful?

---

[2] Edward Lyndoe, author of *Complete Practical Astrology* (1938), *Lyndoe's Year Book* (1940 and after), etc.

Barran (*drily*): Remarkable. Can we get going? *You're* all right, Mr
   Silence, aren't you?

Silence: No.

Barran: What's wrong?

Silence: I *was* all right. Years ago. Before I came down here. Something's happened to me since then. I feel like a Depression over
   Iceland. My throat's dry. My legs are shaky. And every time I look at
   that dam' thing, I feel I'm being hypnotized.

Jennifer: Just microphone fright, Mr Silence. I've had it. You'll get over
   it.

Silence: Never.

Vandeleur: Of course you will. Take my own case. Why, once I had to
   say the line 'I wish I could wash my hands of this,' and actually I found
   myself saying 'I wash I could wish — '

Jennifer: Must you, Elliott?

Silence: Don't put that sort of thing into my head! My wife is at home,
   waiting to listen. So are all her relations, like vultures sitting above a
   carcass! Waiting for me to give them a family joke for the next seven
   years —

He fumbles for and brings out a packet of cigarettes.

Barran: Sorry, Mr Silence. Sedatives are out.

*He points to a NO SMOKING notice hung prominently on the
Listening Room door. Silence puts his cigarettes away, looking
miserable. Cheston snores sharply.*

Silence: Oh — just one thing.

Barran: Yes?

Silence: I've met most of you. I knew Mr Vandeleur and Miss Sloane
   before, of course, by reputation —

Jennifer: Thank you, Mr Silence.

Vandeleur: Then you know Miss Sloane and I are married.

Kelsey: Very much married. Preservation of the maiden name — an old
   theatrical custom, even for the most married of wives.

Vandeleur: Some old customs might with advantage be done away with.

Kelsey: Including this one?

Jennifer: What do you mean, Elliott?

Vandeleur: Nothing.

Silence: Who is this bloke who snores? (*He points to Cheston.*)

Barran: He is the News, and that is Basil Cheston reading it. I won't wake

him up, if you don't mind. Now, look! We'll just run through the
final two minutes and the shooting. Green light for the shots, George.
And, Jennifer — try to sound as though you meant it.
He goes towards the Listening Room.
Silence: Oi! What about me?
Barran: We won't trouble you, Mr Silence. Yours is only explanatory
reading at the beginning.
 Silence has again taken out his cigarettes; and Barran again repeats his
 sad head-shake and indication of the NO SMOKING sign before
 going into the Listening Room.
Jennifer (*nervously*): I *know* we're going to have a raid tonight. Every-
 where *I* go, there's trouble.
Vandeleur: I can well believe that, my dear.
Kelsey: And so can I. Remember, Jennifer: try to sound as though you
 meant it.
Vandeleur (*suddenly furious*): Mr Kelsey, once and for all —
 Barran's voice is heard through the loudspeaker.
Barran: All right; let's go.
Vandeleur: "So you've been sleeping with my wife, eh, you swine?"
 The green light flashes; George Sloane, with the stick in his right hand,
 strikes the cushion five times.
 'What a pleasure this is! What a complete pleasure!'
Jennifer (*from a distance back*): "Tommy! Tommy!"
Vandeleur: "Yes, my dear ?"
Jennifer (*approaching the microphone*): "What was that n— *Oh!*"
Vandeleur: "Yes, my dear?"
Jennifer: "What have you done to him?"
Vandeleur: "I've done to him precisely what he deserved; no more, and
 no less."
Jennifer: "That revolver ..."
Vandeleur (*mockingly*): "Oh, the revolver is only a blind. You mustn't
 believe everything you see. Why don't you go closer, and look at
 him? Or don't you dare look at your lover like that?"
Jennifer: "His head's back! He doesn't move! There's blood all over his
 chest."
Vandeleur: "Yes. He's not a pretty sight."
Jennifer: "They'll hang you for this!"
Vandeleur: "No, I think not. As I explained to him before he left us, I

have devised a way to commit murder and be perfectly safe. Ring up the police! By all means ring up the police. But you will find, I feel sure, that no blame can possibly be attached to me."

Pause

Barran (*through the loudspeaker*): All right. That's all.

Cheston instantly wakes up. He is a smooth-haired young man with an old-school tie. Taking one of the several scripts in his lap, he strides to the microphone.

Cheston (*breezily*): You have been listening to an address by Very Reverend the Dean of Bellchester, speaking on the subject of ....

Barran (*through the loudspeaker*): NO! NO! NO!

Cheston (*contrite*): I say, I'm terribly sorry. I must have been looking at the wrong script.

Barran hurls open the Listening Room door.

Barran: Look, Basil. This is only a rehearsal. You don't have to announce it. But for God's sweet sake get it right when we're on the air!

Cheston: I'm sorry. I wasn't sure whether you were the pig noises or the Very Reverend the Dean of Bellchester.

Barran: Pig noises?

Cheston: That's right, old chap.

Barran: You mean big noises, don't you?

Cheston: No, old chap. Pig noises. Placid Porkers of Britain. Honk, honk, honk. Then the Dean of Bellchester. Then the Augmented Welsh Choir selection, "Silent Now the Drowsy Bird."

Barran (*with restraint*): Look, Basil!

Cheston: Yes, old chap?

Barran: We're not either of 'em — any of 'em!

Cheston: I know that. I just got the scripts mixed. (*Thoughtfully*) You know, Tony, I've often wondered about that.

Barran: About what?

Cheston: About that title "Very Reverend." Is an ordinary Reverend only partly reverend; and, if so, what's wrong with his morals?

Barran: Basil.

Cheston: Yes, old chap?

Barran (*firmly*): Sit down.

Cheston (*cheerfully*): Right-ho.

The door to the stairs, right, opens. Croker, a suspicious-looking man in studio attendant's uniform, pokes his head in and makes a sinister hissing sound to attract attention.

Croker: Mr Barran! *S-s-ssss-st!*

Barran: Yes? What is it?

Croker: There's a gent upstairs oo's been *tryin'* to see you for a long time. *I've* taken care of 'im, though!

Barran: Who is he?

Croker: Well! He *says* he's the Drama Director of the BBC.[3]

Barran: Oh, God! And you've been keeping him out of here?

Croker (*darkly*): These Jerries is awful clever, Mr Barran.

Barran: He's got a BBC card, hasn't he?

Croker (*not to be hoodwinked*): Yus, 'e's got that; but these Jerries is a-a-a-wful clever!

Barran: Let him in, you idiot!

Croker disappears.

Now what's he doing here? (*Waking up*) That's all for the rest of you, thanks. Come back in (*looking at wrist-watch*) in twenty minutes, and we're on just before the nine o'clock news.

Cheston takes his overcoat from the piano and goes out. Jennifer, Vandeleur, and Kelsey drift towards the piano, where their coats are lying. George Sloane goes to the Listening Room; as he passes Jennifer she presses his arm and they exchange smiles. As Jennifer, Vandeleur, Kelsey, and Silence put on their coats before going out, it is during the following:

Kelsey: I hope we can get a drink at this canteen.

Silence (*glumly*): You can't. I tried it coming down.

Kelsey (*faintly insolent*): It must be very embarrassing when a police-officer can't get a drink.

Silence: I'm not a copper; I'm an ex-copper and beginning to wish I'd never been one.

Vandeleur: Still frightened?

Silence: It's getting worse. Look here: suppose I walloped out and said something terrible in front of that microphone? Like this Freudian business, you know.

Kelsey: Keep thinking about it, and you will. — Coming with me, Jennifer?

---

[3] Val Gielgud had precisely this title between 1945 and 1948.

Vandeleur: Coming with *me*, Jennifer?

Jennifer: I'm going with Mr Silence. He really has got it rather badly.
   Now there's nothing to worry about! Honestly there isn't! All you
   have to remember ....

   They leave. Barran is left in the centre of the stage.

Barran (*looking toward the Listening Room*): George!

   *Before the Listening Room door opens, Barran takes a .22 revolver
   out of his side pocket, and weighs it in his hand. George comes out of
   the Listening Room.*

Sloane: Did you call me?

Barran (*not looking round*): I wanted to tell you about a little change in
   the arrangements.

Sloane: Yes?

Barran: I want you to .... (*slips the gun into his pocket and whirls round*)
   Never mind! There's somebody coming. See me before you go.

Sloane: All right. Whatever you say.

   *Sloane goes back into the Listening Room and closes the door. After
   some commotion, the door to the stairs opens. Croker brings in
   Julian Caird, a tall bland man of forty or so, carrying a brief-case. He
   takes off hat but not overcoat. He is followed by Helen Searle, his
   secretary, dark and attractive but with a worried expression.*

Croker: Very sorry, I'm sure, sir.

Caird: Not at all, Cerberus, not at all. England expects the BBC will do
   its duty. Good evening, Tony.

Barran: Hullo, Julian. Come to look for the body?

Caird: I get around. Rather like an excuse for a little country air. Want
   to see you, too.

Barran: Oh — why?

Caird: It'll keep.

Croker: Sorry, miss, but I've strict orders —

Helen: Mr Caird!

Caird: This, my good Cerberus, is Miss Searle — my secretary. She is not
   a parachutist. She does not belong to the Fifth Column. And she
   would acutely resent being searched.

Helen: Mr Caird!

Caird: Satisfied, Cerberus?

Croker: Sorry, sir. But there'll be an air-raid tonight. You'll see.

   Croker withdraws.

Barran: Why *have* you come down, Julian?

Caird: I wanted to see the first of *Murderers' Row*. It was a good idea getting hold of Silence. You ought to make a job of it. Thank the Lord I go back tomorrow. What a god-forsaken bit of nowhere this is!

Helen: There's nothing wrong with this part of the world, Mr Caird!

Caird: You sound very positive, Miss Searle.

Helen: I am. This is my home town.

Caird: I'm sorry.

Helen: You needn't be. All it needs is a little better climate, and up-to-date water supply.

Caird: That, Miss Searle, is all hell needs! Everything as it should be, Tony?

Barran: I think so.

Caird: You could be a little more enthusiastic. Trouble at rehearsal?

Barran: A little.

Caird: Well?

Barran: I had to cut old May Matheson's part out. She flounced out in a huff. She said she was going to write to the D.G. about it.

Caird: That'll cost her twopence halfpenny and won't hurt me much. All the same —

Barran: What?

Caird: I wish you wouldn't make these mistakes. It only means more care about your preliminary timings. I hate putting actors' backs up.

Barran (*angrily*): If you knew what things were like down here —

Caird: Simmer down. Miss Searle!

Helen: Yes, Mr Caird.

Caird: I want to talk to Mr Barran. Run away and play with the knobs in the Listening Room, there's a good girl.

Helen: Very well.

Caird: Tony, I'm going to talk to you seriously for once. What the devil's the matter with you?

Barran: Not a thing.

Caird: Come on. We've known each other quite a while. Come clean, Tony.

Barran: I tell you there's nothing. I haven't touched a drink for six weeks.

Caird: I didn't say you were drunk.

Barran: Then what's wrong with me?

Caird: That's what I asked you to tell me.

Barran: What have I done wrong?

Caird: You know as well as I do. It's an explanation I'm looking for. You used to be a pretty good producer.

Barran: I can still give points to —

Caird: Never mind. You've been behind with three sets of *Radio Times* billing in a fortnight.[4] You've overrun four times in a month. You've been writing bad-tempered memoranda that would disgrace a spoiled schoolgirl. And now your casting, which used to be your strong point, is going to pieces.

Barran: My casting?

Caird: Or is it just an example of exquisite lack of tact and common sense?

Barran: Look here, Julian —

Caird: Is the first of this series of yours the Kovar case, or isn't it?

Barran: Of course it is.

Caird: Very well.

Barran: As Silence is introducing the series, I thought it would be sensible to start with the case in which he first made his name. Is that lack of common sense?

Caird: If I remember the case, Kovar was a man who shot his wife's lover.

Barran: Your memory is quite accurate.

Caird: Thank you. Then why on earth cast Elliott and Jennifer for Mr and Mrs Kovar, and Lanyon Kelsey for the lover?

Barran: Elliott's a bit of a ham, but he and Jennifer are good names. Kelsey is first rate.

Caird: Didn't you know that there was something of a situation between those three?

Barran: Well, I —

Caird: Didn't you?

Barran: I'd heard gossip, of course.

Caird: And chose to disregard it.

Barran: Yes, as a matter of fact.

Caird: That's not very wise when you're dealing with theatre people. They love it, and often live it as well.

Barran: I didn't think of it when I was casting. They didn't have to accept

---

[4] The BBC journal detailing all radio programmes.

the parts.

Caird: Presumably they accepted independently, without knowing.

Barran: I'm sorry. One can't think of everything.

Caird: You can try a bit harder. I don't like it, Tony. You weren't just being a bit malicious for some private fun, were you?

Barran: I don't know what you mean.

Caird: I think you do. You see, I do pay attention to gossip. And a little bird told me that you'd been running after Jennifer yourself a good bit at one time.

Barran: I don't think that's part of your official business, Julian.

Caird: Maybe not. Don't believe me, if you don't want to, and fly off the handle if you like. But I'm talking to you for your own good.

Barran (*sneering*): Thank you, auntie. You ought to transfer to the *Children's Hour.*[5]

Caird: I could do worse.

Barran: Are you afraid that Elliott Vandeleur will murder Kelsey in front of that microphone?

Caird: I like a quiet life. So does the Corporation. It doesn't need murder to make things and me very uncomfortable.

Barran: I'll bear that in mind.

Caird: Thanks.

Barran: That all?

Caird: Nearly. Have you been having trouble with Administration?

Barran: Not more than usual. Why?

Caird: Another little bird, that's all. You're sure you've not been told to pull up your socks or go?

Barran: Go on.

Caird: You wouldn't fancy a glorious row or explosion of some kind as a background to make your final exit more colourful?

Barran: Oh, don't talk rot!

Caird: I've talked it – if it is rot.

---

[5] A BBC programme broadcast between 1922 and 1964, which aimed to address children's wants and needs in a balanced and entertaining way. Highlights included the adventures of the boy detectives Norman and Henry Bones and Dorothy L. Sayers' controversial radio serial about Christ, *The Man Born to Be King* (1941), produced by Val Gielgud.

He signals for Helen to come out of the Listening Room. She does so.

Got the preliminary announcement there, Miss Searle?

Helen: Of course. 'Eight thirty to nine. Murderers' Row. The first of a new series of real-life crime stories. The Kovar Case. Dramatised for broadcasting by Paul Temple, and introduced each week by Chief Inspector Silence, who will first present the problem, and the following week explain the solution. The cast includes — '[6]

Caird: I know that bit, thank you. I wish I didn't. Tony, I want to meet Mr Silence. You don't mind if I sit in on the show, do you?

Barran: A fat lot of good it would do if I did mind.

Caird: That of course is true — if a little crude.

He takes out his pipe. Miss Searle exclaims in horror, and points to NO SMOKING notice.

Damn! Miss Searle, sometimes you're too perfect a secretary to be human.

Helen (*demurely*): I do my best, Mr Caird.

Caird: I'll go and smoke outside in peace. I might have a word with Silence at the same time.

Barran: By all means.

Caird: Where would I be likely to find him in this Chamber of Horrors?[7]

Barran: With apologies to Helen, there's a Gentlemen's Convenience at the end of this passage. He's probably putting a cold towel round his head.

Caird: Nervous?

Barran: As a basketful of kittens.

---

[6] Temple, the creation of the mystery novelist Francis Durbridge is probably the most famous of the BBC's "radio" detectives. With "Steve," his wife, Temple appeared in serial mysteries broadcast between 1938 and the late 1960s.

[7] The infamous exhibit of wax murderers at London's Madam Tussaud's. Carr used this as the setting for a radio play "Menace in Wax," first broadcast in the CBS series *Suspense* on November 17, 1942; and "The Adventure of the Wax Gamblers," a Sherlockian pastiche first published in *Collier's,* June 20, 1953.

Caird: A good time is clearly about to be had by all. Anything else I have to do tonight, Miss Searle?

Helen: Yes, Mr Caird, there's that programme —

Caird: My question, Miss Searle, was one of those expecting the answer No. There is nothing more I have to do tonight. That's flat.

Helen: Shall I come with you, or wait here?

Caird: You can hardly come with me — where I'm going. I'll be back in plenty of time, Tony.

Barran: I'm sure you will.

Caird goes out.

Barran: Helen!

Helen: Yes.

Barran: It's a hell of a time since we saw each other.

Helen: About four months.

Barran: So you remember?

Helen: It wasn't the sort of thing I was likely to forget, was it?

Barran: It was just bad luck.

Helen: I think it was bad manners.

Barran: If that's all —

Helen: It isn't. I don't want to talk about it.

Barran: But I do.

Helen: It won't do any good.

Barran: Damn it all, I'm not a criminal — even if I did kiss you in the taxi.

Helen: You tried. And I hate being mauled.

Barran: You shouldn't be so damned attractive.

Helen: I shouldn't have gone out with you.

Barran: Why not?

Helen: You were running after Mrs Vandeleur. Lots of people told me.

Barran: I didn't get very far.

Helen: Do you think I care how far you got?

Barran: To judge from your tone, I fancy you do.

Helen: Shut up! You behaved like a cad that night in — the taxi. Then you asked me to dinner pretending you wanted me to forgive you. Then you put me off with a yarn about an urgent job. And then I saw you dancing with Jennifer Sloane at the Savoy![8]

Barran:　You had no business to be at the Savoy.

Helen:　No — it was bad luck for you, wasn't it?　Let's leave it at that.

Barran:　What's at the back of Julian's hints to me?

Helen:　I don't know.

Barran:　Nor care?

Helen:　Nor care.

Barran:　What a little liar you are!　It's no use pulling the perfect secretary's discretion stuff with me!　Come on — tell me what's up.　I know I behaved stupidly when I was in London.　But I was crazy about you — and I still am.

Helen:　You must be, if you are.　I'm going to have some coffee.

Barran:　Helen — please.　If you knew what it's been like down here all these dismal weeks —

He tries to take her hands.　She draws away.

Helen:　It's no good, Tony.　Besides, I know you're still after Jennifer Sloane. She's been down here quite a lot, hasn't she?

Barran:　Who told you so?

Helen:　Lanyon Kelsey.　I saw him the other day in Broadcasting House.

Barran:　O damn Lanyon Kelsey!　One day I'll — Helen —

But Helen has gone out of the studio.　Before Barran can follow, the two Programme Engineers come out of the Listening Room, the first is a fat girl with pince-nez.　The second, Herbert Pope, is thin and pale.

Pope:　We're all set, Mr Barran.　Just going outside for a cigarette.

Barran:　All right.　But hurry.

Pope:　Coming, Edna?

Edna:　I don't smoke, you know.

Pope:　You'll learn — if you can find any fags to learn on.

Edna:　O.K.

Pope:　Coffee?

Edna:　I'd like a cup of tea.

Pope:　Engineering's on the down grade!

Pope and Edna go out.　Sloane comes in from the Listening Room.

---

[8] The Savoy Hotel in London.

Barran: The war's getting serious. Girls and programme engineers! Is little fatty there all right?

Sloane: Pope called her a bit of all right yesterday.

Barran: God help the show. Now, George.

Sloane: What's the mystery, Mr Barran?

Barran produces a .22 revolver.

Barran: See this gun?

Sloane: Yes. What about it?

Barran: It's all right, man. The thing's only loaded with blanks!

He forces the gun into Sloane's unwilling hands.

Now — when we get to the shooting sequence tonight, you just —

Sloane: Here, wait a minute!

Barran: Instead of hitting that chair with that footling cane, I want you to hold this gun up in the air, and fire five shots out of it.

Sloane: Mr Barran, you're crazy!

Barran: I don't think so.

Sloane: But you can't do that!

Barran: I know. But you can.

Sloane: I can't.

Barran: Why not ?

Sloane: We'll blow a transmitter — there'll be the hell of a row —

Barran: How do you know? Has it ever been tried?

Sloane: The engineers always said —

Barran: All progress is called impossible — until someone has the guts to try it.

Sloane: You know you can't do it, Mr Barran.

Barran (*feverishly*): I've always wondered whether they were right about that. And tonight, since I'm leaving anyway ... (*correcting himself*) ... things being what they are, I'm going to find out.

Sloane: Sorry. I can't do it.

Barran: Why not?

Sloane: Think I want to lose my job?

Barran: I tell you, I accept all responsibility!

Sloane: Yes; that's all very well. They'll only say I shouldn't have obeyed you. Besides, there's my sister.

Barran (*confused*): Your sister? What sister?

Sloane: My name's Sloane, you know. Jennifer Sloane's my sister.

Barran (*enlightened*): By God, yes! So she is! (*Laughs*)

Sloane: What's so funny?

Barran: Nothing. I saw her smile at you and give you a pinch, but I thought — never mind.

Sloane: Do you think I want her to fluff her lines and make a hash of it? That's what she'll do, if I start shooting guns in the air. She's got enough to worry her without that!

Barran: Highly strung, I suppose?

Sloane (*hotly*): Yes, she is. Always has been. Besides, I'm not risking my job.

Barran: Suppose I told you you'd lose your job if you *didn't* do it?

Sloane: Meaning what?

Barran: I was just thinking about some gramophone-equipment that disappeared from ...

They look at each other.

(*Suddenly sincere*) Now, look. I'm sorry to sound like a blackmailer; I'm not, and you know it very well. (*Fiercely*) But I've been intending to do this for a long time, and I bloody well mean to do it!

Sloane: I needed that stuff, Mr Barran.

Barran: Yes, I know all about your Polytechnic training.

Sloane: And I know all about your training as an air-gunner.

Barran (*furiously*): You say one word about that, and ... Are you going to do what I tell you?

Sloane (*coolly*): Certainly. If I see a thing's got to be done, I do it.

Barran: Good. Stand well out of the engineers' line of sight. Now, when ... s-ss-t! Put the gun in your pocket!

The staircase door opens, Jennifer hurries in, followed by Vandeleur. She throws her coat on the piano and he does the same. Sloane hastily hides the revolver.

Barran: Excuse me. Back in half a tick.

He goes out. Jennifer walks across towards the sofa. Vandeleur hesitantly follows.

Sloane (*timidly*): Jenny.

Jennifer (*distraught*): Oh, it's you. Now go away; there's a good boy. I don't want to talk about anything now.

Sloane: It was just to tell you ...

Jennifer (*coaxingly*): George, do be a good boy and leave us alone! I'm all upset. I have a headache.

Sloane: I've got some aspirin here?

His hand goes to the inside breast pocket of his coat. The audience can see, if they notice, that his right hand goes to an inside left *breast pocket.*

Jennifer (*in despair*): Please!

Sloane: Right you are.

He goes into the Listening Room.

Vandeleur: Why are you always so short with the boy? He's very fond of you.

Jennifer (*going to sofa*): Everything I do is wrong, isn't it?

Vandeleur: I don't say that.

Jennifer (*sitting down*): But it's mostly wrong, isn't it?

Vandeleur: Jenny, I will not be drawn by that old trick of yours. First you ask me if something isn't so, and then tell me I said it. After all, you must admit I'm broad-minded.

Jennifer (*not loudly*): You and your broad-mindedness.

Vandeleur: If you would only come out and say, "Yes, I've fallen for the fellow, and I admit it," it wouldn't hurt so much.

Jennifer: Would you rather I said that?

Vandeleur: Yes, if you really feel it! But if you don't feel it, as you say you don't ...

Jennifer: I know.

Vandeleur: Doesn't this (*holding up script*) embarrass you at all?

Jennifer: Horribly. There were times at rehearsal when I wanted to drop through the floor.

Vandeleur: That's more like you.

Jennifer: You mean you'd like me to live up to your dignity.

No reply.

Jennifer (*suddenly*): Well, what if I am in love with him?

Vandeleur begins to walk slowly up and down by the sofa.

Vandeleur (*quoting*): "So you've been sleeping with my wife, eh?"

Jennifer: Does that make you feel any better?

Vandeleur: I'm glad you've got it off your conscience, at least.

Jennifer (*quietly*): Elliott, I could strangle you.

Vandeleur (*politely*): So? What have I said now?

Jennifer: Your conscience. That's it. That's just it!

Vandeleur: I don't understand you.

The staircase door opens. Caird ushers in Silence, who clutches a script in his right hand and an unlighted cigarette in his left. Neither wears overcoat or hat. Caird nods and waves his hand to Jennifer and Vandeleur, who respond and begin to study their scripts.

Silence (*heavily*): Must be pretty nearly time, isn't it?

Caird: Yes, it won't be long now.

Silence: That's what I thought. (*Starts towards piano*) Water.

Caird: Don't drink that! It's got dust in it.

Silence comes back.

Now I know you'll read it like an old stager. It's perfectly simple. Here, let me show you. (*Places him at microphone*) You see those two lights?

Silence: Yes.

Caird: When the red light flashes on, that means broadcasting is in progress. The announcer will introduce you. When he says, "Chief Inspector Silence," you begin reading. That's all. Now try a few lines.

Silence (*suddenly*): I can't do it.

Caird: Nonsense! Of course you can. Now! (*Imitating announcer*) Chief Inspector Silence.

Silence (*shakily*): "In presenting to you the case of ..."

The staircase door is thrown open. Croker puts his head in and utters a loud sinister hiss.

Croker: I just wanted to tell you, an air-raid alert's been sounded. (*Ominously*) They're coming o-o-ver.

The door closes.

Silence (*exasperated*): Who is that little beam of sunshine who keeps popping in and out of here?

Caird: Never mind. Don't let it put you off. Try again.

Enter Helen Searle, in coat. She walks past Silence, sees the cigarette in his hand, taps his arm, points to the sign, and goes on to the sofa.

Helen (*before sitting down*): Do you know there's a warning on?

Silence (*in a hollow, sepulchral voice*): "In presenting to you the case of Thomas Kovar, at Brighton in nineteen twenty-three, a case which many of you doubtless followed in the Press at the time ..." (*breaking off, despairingly*) Here is the News, and this is Edgar Allan Poe reading it.

Caird: No, that's fine! Go on.

Silence: "In presenting to you the case of Thomas Kovar, at Brighton in nineteen twenty-three, a case which many of you doubtless followed in the Press at the time ..."

As Silence begins for the second time, enter Kelsey, removing overcoat. He tosses overcoat on piano, passes by Silence — who eyes him without continuing — while Kelsey sits on the arm of the sofa at the far end.

Kelsey: By the way, do you know there's a warning on?

Silence (*breathing deeply*): It's all right. I can manage. But I'd rather meet One-Eyed Ike or Louis the Lizard on a dark night in Poplar.

Caird: Perfectly natural. Try just once more.

Silence: AGAIN?

Caird: Why not? If you can get through the first paragraph without a slip, you'll be as safe as houses.

Silence: Yes. That's true. All right. (*Getting a grip*) "In presenting to you the case of Thomas Kovar, at Brighton in nineteen twenty-three, a case which many of you doubtless followed in the Press at the time, I will begin with a challenge. I will begin by asking you to spot the flaw in the murderer's plan."

Caird: Good! Excellent!

Silence (*gaining confidence*): It wasn't bad, was it?

Helen: It was admirable, Mr Silence.

Silence: It's not so very hard, you know, once you get the hang of it.

Caird: Didn't I tell you? Go on!

Silence (*almost breezily*): From Brighton to Hove, ladies and gentlemen, it is only a short distance as the cry flows.

Silence stops suddenly, aware of something wrong.

Silence: It — is — only — a — short — distance — as — the —

Kelsey (*urbanely*): No, Inspector. Not "as the cry flows." You mean "as the flow cries."

Silence (*paralysed*): Oh, God, that's done it!

Caird: Steady, now! It's all right.

Silence: I'm going to say it! I tell you, I'm going to say it!

Kelsey: You'd better make up your mind, old man. It's less than three minutes before that red light goes on.

Caird: For the love of Mike, just forget the clow fries.[9] Strike out the words and don't try to read 'em!

Silence: Are you going to stand by and lend moral support?

---

[9] A slang term of uncertain meaning.

Caird: No, I'll be in the Listening Room with Tony. Where *is* Tony, by the way?

Kelsey: He was chasing out the building, the last time *I* saw him.

Caird: Then he'd better get back in a hurry.

They look round expectantly. Enter Cheston, advancing to piano and removing coat.

Cheston: I say, you people. Do you know ...

Everybody (*together*): YES!

Caird: You haven't seen Tony Barran, have you?

Cheston: Right behind me, old chap. On his way down now.

Sloane comes out of the Listening Room and goes to the Effects-panel. Barran, followed by Pope and Edna Nasmith, enter by the door.

Barran: Places, everybody. Two minutes to go.

Silence (*galvanized*) I smell whisky!

Barran (*hurriedly*): Just a little nip I had tucked away. All set, George?

Sloane: All ready as ordered.

Pope and Edna go into the Listening Room.

Barran: That's right, Mr Silence. Stay where you are, with Basil. Wife and lover — ready.

Barran goes into the Listening Room.

Caird (*to Silence*): Don't forget, now. Once that red light is on, anything you say can be taken down and used in evidence.

Caird follows Barran. Silence and Cheston are at microphone. Jennifer and Kelsey move forward at a little distance from it. Sloane is at "Effects." Helen sits on sofa, following script. Vandeleur sits beside and beyond her. Barran and Caird can be seen through glass panel of Listening Room.

Long, deathly stillness. Silence makes noises in his throat

Silence (*suddenly and loudly*): In presenting to you —

Cheston (*fiercely*): S-ss-s-t! (*Points to red light.*)

The red light flashes on.

This is the BBC Home Service. Tonight we present "The Kovar Case," the first of a new series entitled *Murderers' Row* ...

*

All lights go out, and the theatre is blacked-out while the curtain descends. After some seconds it ascends again to denote the lapse of twenty-five minutes.

*

Silence and Cheston now sit on the settee below the piano. Vandeleur and Kelsey are at the microphone, Jennifer is on sofa, beside and beyond Helen. Others as before.

Vandeleur (*reading*): "Odd, isn't it?"

Kelsey (*laughing*): "Very odd. Quite a joke!"

Vandeleur: "I come downstairs in the middle of the night, expecting to find a burglar ..."

Kelsey: "And instead you find me, your friend."

Vandeleur: "I find you, wearing a mask — wearing clothes nobody would ever recognize as yours — burgling the back sitting-room window and getting in. What if I'd fired at you?"

Kelsey: "That would have been unfortunate."

Vandeleur: "Indeed it would."

Kelsey: "But don't you think you can put away the gun now?"

Vandeleur: "No hurry! No hurry! Why *did* you play burglar, old man?"

Kelsey: "A bad joke, I'm afraid."

Vandeleur: "A joke put up between you and my wife?"

Kelsey: "My dear fellow! What's your wife got to do with this?"

Vandeleur (*flatly*): "You damned swine. Do you think I don't know what's been going on between you two? You want her to go away with you, don't you? You know she's got jewellery worth a couple of thousand, don't you? That's why she wrote to you today."

Kelsey: "Wrote to me?"

Vandeleur: "The stuff was to go. But it was to be a perfect outside job, so I shouldn't suspect her. She was to leave the stuff openly in her dressing-room. You were to play burglar, messing up flower-beds and jemmying windows: making it a real, foolproof outside job."

Kelsey: "I wish you'd stop this raving. Your wife never wrote me any such letter."

Vandeleur: "You're quite right there."

Kelsey: "I beg your pardon?"

Vandeleur: "She didn't write the letter. *I* did."

Kelsey: "Put down that gun, you lunatic!"

After this speech, Kelsey tiptoes away from the microphone and crosses to the sofa. At the same time Jennifer gets up, and walks a little way out. Kelsey, grinning sardonically, sits on the sofa beside and beyond Helen. Jennifer moves further out as Vandeleur continues.

Vandeleur: "They'll never find that letter, my lad. All *I* know is that I heard a noise in the middle of the night. I came downstairs. A masked burglar attacked me in the dark. I fired in defence of my home, as any householder has a perfect right to do. In *both* senses you see, I am protecting my home."

While he is speaking both Sloane and Vandeleur take .22 pistols from their pockets. Vandeleur points his in front of him. Sloane holds his in the air with his left hand, his back to the audience, the gun pointing to the ceiling.

"They may suspect me. They probably will. But no court on earth will ever be able to prove it. So, you've been sleeping with my wife, eh, you swine!"

Green cue-light flashes on. Sloane fires five shots. Consternation in the Listening Room. Caird turns angrily on Barran, back to the engineers, opens the glass panel and beckons furiously to Helen.

Jennifer and Vandeleur jump, stammer, and go on with the play. Helen goes to the panel and whispers to Caird.

Cheston jumps up and looks round bewilderedly, Silence begins to stand up then realises things are going forward normally and sits still.

Vandeleur: "What a pleasure this is! What a complete pleasure!"

Jennifer (*distant*): "Tommy! Tommy!"

Vandeleur: "Yes, my dear?"

Jennifer: "What was that n— *Oh!*"

Vandeleur: "Yes, my dear?"

Jennifer: "What have you done to him?"

They look up for any emergency instructions. Helen tiptoes from the glass panel and signs to them to go right on.

Vandeleur: "I've done to him precisely what he deserved, no more and no less."

Jennifer: "That revolver —"

Helen turns back to her seat on the couch, and suddenly stops dead staring at Kelsey, whose body has slumped back.

Vandeleur: "Oh, the revolver is only a blind. You mustn't believe everything you see. Why don't you go really close and look at him? Or don't you dare look at your lover like that?"

Helen lets out a muffled shriek. General amazement and Caird emerges into the studio full of wrath, to glare at Helen and urge the actors by signs to carry on.

Jennifer: "His head's back! He doesn't move! There's blood all over his chest!"

Vandeleur: "Yes. He's not a pretty sight."

Helen drags Caird over to the couch. They bend over Kelsey.

Jennifer (*shakily*): "They'll hang you for this!"

Vandeleur: "No, I think not. As I explained to him before he left us, I have devised a way to commit murder and be perfectly safe. By all means ring up the police. But you will find, I feel sure, that no blame can possibly —"

Caird has turned from Kelsey's slumped figure looking very white. Helen has collapsed at the end of the couch. Vandeleur, sensing some disaster, dries up. Cheston whips into galvanic movement and crosses swiftly to Caird. They whisper together in obvious agitation. Jennifer clutches at Vandeleur. Silence stands up slowly. Barran leans through the glass panel, his face contorted.

Cheston crosses to the microphone.

Cheston (*hoarsely*): Ladies and Gentlemen, we regret that it is impossible for us to complete the first of this series of specially written crime programmes owing to — to —

He looks about him as if desperately searching for aid.

A slight — er — technical hitch!

He signals to the engineers to buzz out the studio. The red light goes off.

Cheston wipes his forehead. The body of Kelsey rolls off the couch and falls on the floor.

CURTAIN

ACT II

The scene, and the positions of the actors are precisely as at the end of the first act, with the attention of everyone concentrated upon the fallen body of Kelsey.

As the curtain rises, the studio door is opened, and the face of Croker peers in.

Croker: Fat Stock Prices is back again — Mr Barran!

Sloane: What the hell — ?

> *May Matheson pushes past Croker into the studio, flurried and angry, and bursts into a torrent of speech without noticing that anything odd has happened.*

May Matheson: It's really too abominable! I'd only just begun to walk to the town when the sirens went — the guns began —

Barran (*emerging from the Listening Room*): Just what the blazes does everyone think they've been doing to my programme?

May Matheson: Really, Mr Barran! I can put up with —

Caird: Miss Matheson, please!

Barran: What's up with Kelsey ? Is he drunk?

Caird: He's dead.

Barran: Nonsense!

Jennifer: No — Oh no!

Vandeleur: My God!

Cheston: I don't believe it.

Helen: He was shot. Look!

> *Jennifer screams.*

Sloane: How on earth *could* he have been shot?

Silence: That's what we want to find out.

> *Most eyes travel to the revolver in Sloane's hand.*

May Matheson: And that man in a car who picked me up on the road insisted on bringing me back here because he said it was safer! He wouldn't stop here himself.

Jennifer: George!

Sloane: Well?

Jennifer: Why did you fire those real shots?

Sloane: *Real* shots! You don't think I did it, do you?

Jennifer: I don't know! You never used a pistol in the play before — and you're a dead shot — Oh George —

Sloane: Don't be such a little fool, Jenny!

Caird: Please, everybody! We can't have all this splashing about! Pope, get on to the police, and get me a line to the Duty Officer at Broadcasting House.

Pope: Yes, Mr Caird.

He goes into the Listening Room and picks up telephone.

Caird: Now, Sloane. What the devil is all this about your pistol?

Barran: That's my funeral.

Caird: Yours?

Barran: I told him to use the gun. I wanted shots that sounded like shots for a change!

Caird: What a bloody fool you are, Tony!

Barran: You think so?

May Matheson: I must say that this language with ladies present —

The studio lights flicker wildly and go out for a second or two. May Matheson shrieks.

Vandeleur: Now what's happened?

Caird: Don't panic! It's only the lights.

The lights go up again.

There you are! Bound to happen once or twice during any raid. Is it a bad one, Miss Matheson?

May Matheson: Terrible! I thought my last hour —

Cheston (*aside*): Alas — just wishful thinking.

Jennifer: I can't stand this — I can't!

Vandeleur: Steady, my dear.

He puts a hand on her shoulder. She shrinks away.

Helen: What do you say to a glass of dusty water?

She leads Jennifer across the studio to the settee below the piano, and gives her water.

Vandeleur: Well, what do we do? We can't just stand about like this! What happens next?

Pope emerges from the Listening Room.

Pope: Sorry, Mr Caird. Can't get the police station.

Caird: What about Control Room?

Pope: Can't even get a line to Control Room. I'm afraid we're cut off altogether for the moment.

Barran: Oh blast! It would be like that!

Caird: Mr Silence!

Silence: Yes.

Caird: I think you'd better take charge of things, don't you — in the circumstances?

Silence: We've got to get in touch with the police somehow. How far is the nearest town?

Caird: Three miles.

Silence: Haven't you got a car?

Barran: The BBC car that brought us here has gone back. You know that. What about yours, Julian?

Caird: Also gone back. It looks as though we're stuck here for the night.

Jennifer (*pointing to body*): With that?

Vandeleur: You liked him well enough, my dear, when he could talk.

Jennifer (*hopelessly*): I didn't like him at all. That's what you don't understand. That's what makes it so horrible.

Caird: There's only one thing for it, Mr Silence. You've got to take charge until the police can get here.

Silence (*slowly*): Yes. I suppose I'd better. (*Warningly*) I don't like it, mind! But I suppose I'd better.

Jennifer: His eyes are open. Every time I look anywhere, I keep on seeing him. Can't you get him out of here?

Vandeleur: Unfortunately, my dear, he can't be moved or touched until the police get here. (*Bitterly*) You've surely read enough detective stories to know that.

Jennifer: Then we can get out of here. Come on, Elliott.

Pope: I shouldn't advise it, miss.

Vandeleur: Why not?

Pope: I don't want to scare you. But there's a dummy air-field only a quarter of a mile up the road. Jerry comes over and plasters it about once a fortnight.

Jennifer: But we'll all be *killed*!

The door suddenly opens and Croker appears.

Croker: I shouldn't be surprised, miss. I shouldn't be a bit surprised.

Helen (*tenderly*): Here's our sunshine again.

Croker: They're coming over in 'undreds. Ooo, it's terrible up there.

Cheston: Look here, Calamity Jane. Would you mind getting out of here and staying out?

Caird: And that goes for the rest of us.

Croker goes out.

Silence: I think that some of you are forgetting that there's a murder been committed in this room, and that the murderer's in this room now!

Jennifer: Elliott!

Caird: Sorry, Silence. We're all of us just the least bit in the world on edge.

Silence (*briskly*): Now, then. Can two of you manage to carry Mr Kelsey's body upstairs?

Vandeleur: You're not going to move him?

Silence: He's already been moved, worse luck. Didn't you move him, Miss Searle?

Helen: I — I shook him, and gave him a little push. (*Illustrating*) To see whether there was any life in him. And he rolled off the couch.

Silence: So it's too late to learn anything about the angle of fire. Which is the whole point of the rule about moving the body.

Barran (*thoughtfully*): Angle of fire.

Jennifer: Tony Barran, you gave George that revolver.

Barran: Perfectly true. But I didn't tell him to fire a real bullet.

Sloane: I didn't fire a real bullet. So help me God, there are only blank cartridges in this thing. Do you think I didn't look to see?

Barran: I hope so.

Sloane: And, anyway, I aimed at the ceiling! You told me to aim at the ceiling, and I did. I'm not going to be framed for something I didn't do.

Silence (*quietly*): Just a moment. Let me see that revolver, son.

Sloane hands it over.

As matter of fact, this young fellow's quite right. He did fire at the ceiling. I was watching him.

Sloane: Thanks.

Silence breaks open revolver, examines magazine, and shuts it up again. He hands it back to Sloane.

Vandeleur: Well ?

Silence: That gun contains five exploded blank cartridges and one unexploded blank cartridge. (*To Sloane*) Buck up, son. Nobody's going to frame you.

Helen: Then *it* didn't kill him?

Silence: It didn't kill anybody.

May Matheson: It was a silly idea anyway. George is a nice boy.

Sloane: Thanks.

May Matheson: But why do you want to be so silly in any case, firing guns all over the place? Why has Elliott Vandeleur got to stand there waving that other pistol?

They all turn to look at Vandeleur. Sloane puts his own pistol in his hip-pocket.

Vandeleur (*holding up revolver*): Is this what you're looking at?

May Matheson: Yes, it is.

Vandeleur: And can I guess what you're thinking?

Barran: Very probably.

Vandeleur: As you say, I still have the revolver. It can offer the best possible proof that *I* didn't kill my philandering friend.

Jennifer: How?

Vandeleur: Because it isn't loaded.

Barran: You know, I seem to have heard that somewhere before.

Vandeleur: Would you care to examine the revolver, Mr Silence?

Silence takes it from him. Breaks it open, and smells at barrel.

Silence: He's right. This gun is not only unloaded. It's clean.

Jennifer: Clean? Meaning what?

Silence: Meaning that the barrel's unfouled. It has never been fired. (*Hands it back to Vandeleur*) Both those guns, which weren't used, are .22's. Now let's see.

Goes to body and bends over, studying.

Hm. Looks a bit high for the heart, but that's where it got him. Angle: difficult to tell. No burning, blackening, or tattooing. Small orifice, lips of wound compressed. Might be a .22.

Cheston (*abruptly*): I say!

All turn to look at him.

Silence: Well?

Cheston: Isn't that rather odd?

Caird: So you've spotted that.

Cheston: I mean to say. Two guns, both .22's. But one was empty and the other was full of blanks. Where's the gun that did kill him, then?

Silence: That's what we're going to find out. All right. Get him upstairs, somebody.

Sloane (*coming forward*): I'll do it, sir.

Pope: And I will.

Silence: Right. Stop a bit!

Silence runs his hands down Sloane's sides and side-pockets, slapping at them as though searching him. Touching a revolver in the inside left breast-pocket, he takes it out.

I'd better take this property gun with the blanks. It's evidence. (*Slips the revolver in his side-pocket*)

Barran: Evidence of what?

Silence (*to Pope*): Now, you, son. (*Searches him*) All right, you two. Cut along.

Sloane and Pope carry out body. Door closes.

Barran (*more loudly*): I said, evidence of what?

Silence: Somebody told that young fellow to fire five blank shots in the air. While he was doing it, some other clever bloke cut loose under cover of the noise, and fired the real bullet.

Vandeleur: I hate what you say. I detest what you say. But I'm afraid you're right.

Silence: The gun that really killed Mr Kelsey is still in this room.

Barran: I see. So you want to search the rest of us as you searched George and Herbert?

Silence: Yes. Any objections?

Barran: None at all. Only you certainly don't think that anybody in the Listening Room ... myself, for instance, or Julian, or Edna Nasmith could have fired the shot?

Silence: I'm dead certain you didn't.

Barran: My humblest thanks.

Silence: I'm dead certain nobody fired through a glass panel, and round a corner — all in that little space — while three other people in the Listening Room saw nothing of it. You're out of it. But all the same, if you don't mind ...

Rapidly but thoroughly searches Barran.

Barran: Satisfied?

Silence: Yes.

Caird: You might follow with me. (*Same search*)

Barran: And still the elusive pistol is missing? Suppose you don't find it on any of us?

Silence: I tell you, it's got to be here! Now, you — (*flustered, turning to*

May Matheson) — you, Miss ... Miss Pushface.

May Matheson (*screaming*): I BEG your pardon?

Silence: Sorry, sorry; I thought I heard someone call you that!

May Matheson: And who had the effrontery to call me Miss Pushface?

Silence: Madam, I can't stop to argue the point. I'm nearly going loony already. Will you take Miss Pushface ... I mean, will you take that young lady in the Listening Room, whatever her name is, will you take her upstairs and search her.

Edna (*coming out of Listening Room*): I don't mind. I only want to go home.

May Matheson: I still demand to know who called me —

Silence furiously points to door. May Matheson and Edna go out.

Jennifer: You don't intend to do that with all of us? You don't mean to search me too?

Silence: I'm afraid it's necessary.

Jennifer: I won't be searched! I won't! I won't leave this room under any circumstances!

Silence: Then we've got to do it down here, that's all.

As he speaks, Barran slips out, closing door.

Now, Mr Vandeleur, it's your turn.

Vandeleur speaks as he is being searched.

Vandeleur: It seems to me unlikely that, with an empty revolver in one hand and a script in the other, I stood in front of the microphone and shot Kelsey. However, go on ... Have you found anything?

Silence: No.

Caird: You don't suppose the murderer got rid of the gun somehow?

Silence: How? That's what I want to know. I kept everybody in plain sight. And where was it put?

Helen: But if you don't find it ...

Silence: I'll find it. You can bet your shirt on that. I may be an old-style copper, but I know how to use my eyes. Mr Cheston, you're next.

Cheston: Carry on, by all means. Only I can assure you, on the word of an old Hartonian, I haven't got it.[10]

---

[10]Given the explicit reference earlier in the play to Cheston's old school-tie, this is a reference to another Harton House, and not that featured in Frederick Farrar's famous *Julian Home* [1859].

He speaks as Silence searches.

Helen: Has he got it, Mr Silence?

Silence (*angrily*): No.

Caird: The ruddy gun has got to be somewhere.

As he speaks, May Matheson comes back.

Silence: Don't you worry. I'll find it. I'll go over this place with a tooth-comb ...

May Matheson: You mean a fine tooth-comb.

Silence: Madam, if I say a tooth-comb I mean a tooth-comb. Did Miss What'shername have anything on her person?

May Matheson: Nothing of the kind you mean.

Silence: No revolver?

May Matheson: Nary a revolver.

Helen: I can't stand this. What beats me is that the whole thing took place slap under our eyes, and yet nobody saw what happened.

Caird: We were wrongly placed, that's why. If only there had been some people sitting on this side of the room, (*indicating audience*) they would have seen everything that happened.

Jennifer: I hate to talk about this. I don't even like to think about it. And yet ... (*hesitating*) What about you, Julian? What about the people in the Listening Room?

Cheston: That's an idea.

Caird: Not much good, I'm afraid.

Jennifer (insistently): You were looking straight at Elliott and me. Surely you'd have known if El — if either of us did anything?

Caird (*gloomily*): You'd certainly imagine so.

Vandeleur: Well?

Caird: But I can't. As soon as those shots started banging, I lost interest in everything but the sound-recording machinery. So did the engineers.

May Matheson: Tony Barran *is* a fool.

Silence: I wonder.

Caird: Naturally I know, Elliott, that neither you nor Jennifer had anything to do with this. The trouble is, I can't swear to it. Perhaps Tony could give you an alibi.

Vandeleur (*thoughtfully*): Perhaps he could.

Jennifer: Tony would swear to anything. It does seem a little too much. Just when *I'm* safe at last, my husband isn't safe.

All are startled.

Vandeleur: And what did you mean, my dear, by that curious remark?

Jennifer (*waking up*): Nothing. I'm sorry. I was only thinking.

May Matheson: Go on thinking my dear. Inspector Pushface will never
   catch up to you, if I'm any judge. (*Sweetly*) Have you got any clues,
   Inspector?

Silence: Madam, I'll be frank with you. My only clue so far (*takes gun out
   of his pocket*) is a .22 revolver loaded with blanks. (*Drops gun back in
   pocket*) I may add that your presence makes me regret more and
   more that the gun is only loaded with blanks.

Cheston (*suddenly*): Look here ....

Silence: Yes, Mr Cheston?

Cheston (*slowly*): Latest reports indicate that the situation is not clear.

Silence: Yes. You could put it like that.

Cheston: It needs clarification before a statement can be issued.

Silence: Exactly.

Cheston: All the same, I've been thinking. I read a story once ...

Helen: Please, Basil!

Cheston: No, I mean it. I've always been considered a very observant sort
   of chap. Not brilliant, you understand; but observant.

Caird: Well?

Cheston: While I was watching the play a while ago, I noticed something
   rather odd. Sets a chap thinking, to notice something rather odd. Or
   at least it does me. So I started to draw deductions from it, just like
   Lord Peter Wimsey when he was a guest of the *Brains Trust* ...[11]

Helen: Basil, please!

Cheston: Don't you want to hear what I've got to say?

All Together: NO!

---

[11]"Wimsey, Dorothy L Sayers' aristocratic detective, would have
been a perfect choice for the eclectic *Brains Trust.* In this long-running BBC
programme, members of the public were able to pose curious and sometimes
seemingly unanswerable questions to a panel of erudite and witty
personalities.

Cheston: That's what Professor Joad said too.[12] He wouldn't let anybody else get a word edgeways. So all I can say is that *I* haven't got the gun. Are you satisfied?
Silence examines the coats on top of piano. Also "Effects." Walks slowly round room and returns.
Silence: All right, Mr Cheston. Thank you.
Cheston: Thank *you.*
Caird: D'you mind if I leave you, Silence?
Silence: No.
Caird: I want to see if I can't snaffle a passing car or something. I must manage to get a report to Head Office somehow — or kittens will be had by all. I'll just cut up and see how slaphappy Hermann is making out.
Cheston: I'm with you, old boy. I'd like some fresh air.
Caird: Right you are.
Caird and Cheston go out of the studio.
Jennifer: Can't we all go somewhere — anywhere else? I want some fresh air too.
Silence (*gravely*): I'm afraid that's impossible just for the present.
Jennifer: But why?
Silence: I can't let anyone who was not in the Listening Room leave the studio without being searched.
Jennifer: I told you — I —
Silence: Miss Searle.
Helen: Yes, Mr Silence.
Silence: I fancy your head is screwed on your shoulders, pretty as it is.
Helen: Thank you.
Silence: I don't want any of you ladies upset needlessly. But this search is essential. Will you look after it for me, Miss Searle? Miss Matheson will help, I'm sure.
Helen: I'll do my best.
Silence smiles at her, and goes to the studio door.
Silence: Come along, Mr Vandeleur. We're not wanted.

---

[12] The eccentric Cyril Joad was a regular member of the *Brains Trust* between 1941 and 1948, until his summary dismissal after pleading guilty to fare evasion, which for Joad was more of a hobby than a crime.

Vandeleur: I'm not at all sure that I can leave my wife like this.

Helen: I'll take care of her, Mr Vandeleur.

Vandeleur: Thank you. Keep your chin up, Jenny.

Jennifer: I'm perfectly all right.

> *Silence and Vandeleur go out of the studio. Jennifer begins to laugh hysterically.*

May Matheson: Don't start that, dear, please.

Jennifer: I tell you, I won't be searched — I won't.

Helen: But why not? We can just run over each other. It won't take a minute.

Jennifer: I won't, I tell you!

Helen: Nobody thinks you've anything —

Jennifer: It's so — so humiliating!

May Matheson: Well, dear, you've nothing to hide if your legs are anything to go by.

Helen: Come on — I'll give you a lead. (*She slips her frock over her head.*)

May Matheson: Very nice indeed, dear, if you ask me. But just where a girl could be expected to hide anything, not to speak of pistols, with modern undies, beats me!

Helen: So I pass, do I?

May Matheson: Of course, dear. Let me give you a hand.

> *She helps Helen back into her frock.*

Helen: You see, Mrs Vandeleur. There's nothing to it.

Jennifer: I'm sorry. I was just being a hysterical little fool.

Helen: No one's going to blame you. It's not been exactly a normal evening.

Jennifer: I'd like to get it over.

> *In her turn she slips out of her frock, and reveals nothing but a charming set of underclothes and a delightful figure.*

Helen: There you are. Clean, white, and twenty-one.

Jennifer (*shakily*): Thank you.

May Matheson: I'm afraid I can't compete with you girls. Now twenty years ago —

> *She takes off her skirt and displays bright pink bloomers.*

Come along, dear, and give me the once over. Though, seeing as I was on the stairs when it happened —

> *Croker puts his head round the door.*

Croker: Cor strike me pink!

May Matheson: And what do you want?

Croker: Mr Barran — and I've got more than I bargained for! When's the balloon going up?

May Matheson: Let me tell you, when I played principal boy in the Brixton Pantomime in — well, when I played principal boy, the men were glad to pay to see my legs!

Croker (*gloomily*): Sorry, miss. Times have changed.

Helen: Mr Barran must be somewhere upstairs.

Croker: Right you are, miss.

> *He goes out.*

May Matheson: Impertinence! (*She gets back into her skirt.*)

Jennifer: I think he's rather sweet. What do we do now, Miss Searle?

Helen: Well, we can all leave the studio now at any rate. I'd better let Mr Silence know that none of us were concealing revolvers about our persons.

May Matheson: The sooner I can get out of this place, the better I shall be pleased.

Helen: What do you say to a cup of coffee anyway, to be going on with?

Jennifer: Oh yes.

> *Barran comes in.*

Barran (*grinning*): I've just met Croker. I gather I'm late for the strip-tease.

May Matheson: I'd like a word with you, Mr Barran.

Barran: Not another? Jenny, I'd like —

Helen: Mr Barran, Mrs Vandeleur is just going to have a cup of coffee in the canteen. She needs it rather.

Barran: I see.

Jennifer: Thank you.

> *Jennifer runs out.*

May Matheson: Mr Barran, have we got to stay here all night?

Barran: It looks gloomily like it.

Helen: How's the raid going?

Barran: Pretty lively, I'm afraid.

May Matheson: I'll never accept another of these engagements —

Barran (*with meaning*): No, I don't think you will.

May Matheson: And you haven't heard the last of your treatment of me, Mr Barran, I promise you.

Barran: If you'd like to doss down for the night, there are blankets and
mattresses in the little room beyond the canteen. Quite proper —
Ladies Only and everything.

May Matheson: Thank you.

Barran: I won't offer to come and kiss you goodnight.

Helen: I'll join you there, Miss Matheson. I just want to see that Mrs
Vandeleur has got her coffee. It's quite comfortable.

May Matheson goes out with a final glare at Barran.

Barran: Helen!

Helen: Well?

Barran: I'm sorry about all this —

Helen: I imagine we all are.

Barran: I mean, that you should have been in the middle of the beastly
business.

Helen: It's far worse for some of the others.

Barran: You mean — Jennifer.

Helen: I didn't mean anything. And I wish you'd stop talking to me about
Mrs Vandeleur. She's dreadfully upset.

Barran: Of course she is.

Helen: Of course?

Barran: It can't be much fun to see your boy-friend bumped off.

Helen: And I used to think you were so clever!

Barran: Meaning ?

Helen: The person Mrs Vandeleur is worrying about is her husband.

Barran: Rot!

Helen: It's true. You'd never believe it, because you don't want to.
You're still in love with her — what you call in love. But I've watched
her looking at him this evening, and I know.

Barran: I wonder.

Helen: I want my coffee.

Barran: You're rather hard on me, Helen, aren't you?

Helen: It wouldn't be necessary, if you hadn't always been so soft with
yourself.

Barran: You don't think I did it, do you?

Helen: You couldn't have done it. You heard what Mr Silence said.

Barran: Then, if Jennifer is in love with Elliott — won't you give me
another chance?

Helen: I don't make the same mistake twice, Tony. Sorry.

The lights go out. There is a little scream from Helen.

Barran: Don't worry, Helen darling. I don't make the same mistake twice either. I'm not going to try and kiss you. In fact I'm beating it — with what dignity I can muster in the dark.

The lights go up. Barran has gone into the Listening Room and is sitting there out of sight.

Jennifer and Vandeleur come in.

Jennifer: Don't you want any coffee, Miss Searle? I feel ever so much better for mine.

Helen: That's good.

Vandeleur: I wish they'd stop these tricks with the lights. It gets on one's nerves.

Helen: Mrs Vandeleur, I'm going to lie down for a little. Mr Caird'll probably want to dictate a report to me all night when he comes back. If you feel like a mattress, there's a room for us beyond the canteen.

Jennifer: Oh I couldn't sleep a wink.

Helen: Well, if you want me, I'll be there.

Helen goes out.

Vandeleur: There's a nice girl.

Jennifer: Yes.

Vandeleur: A sort of lovely certainty about her.

Jennifer: She's awfully pretty.

Vandeleur: I hadn't noticed that.

Jennifer: What nonsense, Elliott!

Vandeleur: It's not nonsense. You've been here all the time, haven't you?

Jennifer: Are you trying to pay me compliments?

Vandeleur: It's not very difficult. You see I love you.

Jennifer: Do you, Elliott?

Vandeleur: Yes.

Jennifer: You said that as if you meant it.

Vandeleur: I do mean it.

Jennifer: Do you?

Vandeleur: I love you more than anything in the world!

Jennifer: I believe you, but —

Vandeleur: But what, Jenny?

Jennifer: I wish you didn't!

Vandeleur: Jenny!

Jennifer: I'm not worth it! You know that I'm not worth it!
> *She stares at him with a sort of desperate intensity.*
>
> Elliott, how much did you really know about me — and Lanyon Kelsey?

Vandeleur: Don't you think we might leave that alone? After all, the fellow's dead.

Jennifer: Oh, don't be so damned magnanimous! He's no more dead than John Brown's Body!

Vandeleur: Jenny, what on earth are you getting at?

Jennifer: Kelsey's body is lying out there in that room under a dirty sheet. And someone killed him. I told you — about an hour ago — that I'd fallen for him —

Vandeleur: No. I said that if you'd admit that you had fallen for him instead of playing me up — Of course I knew that he was in love with you.

Jennifer: Was that all you knew?

Vandeleur: Jenny, listen to me, please! This can't do any good. Whatever there may have been between you is over now.

Jennifer: Over!

Vandeleur (*gently*): Over and done with. Kelsey's dead — and you're on the edge of hysteria. Let's go along and see what Helen Searle can find you in the shape of a bed.

Jennifer: Do you think I could sleep — with Kelsey in there?

Vandeleur (*gently*): Can't you forget Kelsey for one minute?

Jennifer: You've got to tell me, Elliott! Did you believe that Kelsey and I were lovers?

Vandeleur: I can't answer that.

Jennifer: You mean you won't! And you won't because you love me — I do believe that. You think we can pick up the pieces even now. Well, I can't do much for you, Elliott, but I can tell you one thing. I didn't love Lanyon Kelsey. I loathed him. I loathed him far more than you did.

Vandeleur: Then why on earth did you see as much of him as you did? Lunch with him? Get yourself talked about with him?

Jennifer: Did I make you very unhappy?

Vandeleur (*simply*): Damnably.

Jennifer: Why did you put up with it?

Vandeleur: If you're in love with a woman you have to put up with things.

Jennifer: Even with her lover?

Vandeleur: You must — if you can.

Jennifer: That's what I'm trying so desperately hard to find out. *Could* you?

Vandeleur: I admit I was getting towards the end of my tether —

Jennifer: Oh God!

Vandeleur: Why did you hate him, Jenny? After all, if he was in love with you —

Jennifer: He wasn't my lover, Elliott. He was my husband.

There is a pause, while they stare at each other.

Vandeleur (*quietly*): This is a nightmare. It simply isn't possible.

Jennifer: Oh yes, it is. When you're happy.

Vandeleur: Jenny!

Jennifer: I married him four years before I met you. Of course I was a fool — and that's no excuse. But I was very young, and he had charm, and I thought he loved me — he did too, in his own beastly way!

Vandeleur: Do you want to tell me all this, Jenny?

Jennifer: Yes. I'm sorry if it hurts you, but I must tell someone. What fools people are who despise the confessional! If only I'd told you before —

Vandeleur: Go on, my dear.

Jennifer: Of course it didn't work. A woman would have needed tricks and technique to hold Lanyon Kelsey, once he got tired of her body. I hadn't got either. Then he got a New York offer, and left me — It was like coming to life again! And then —

Vandeleur: You met me.

Jennifer: Yes, I met you, Elliott. I hadn't known before that it was possible for a man who was in love with you to be kind to you as well.

Vandeleur: And that made so much difference?

Jennifer: All the difference.

Vandeleur: The swine!

Jennifer: You must believe me, Elliott. I never dreamed he'd come back. He wasn't the man to do without women, and I was so sure he'd stay in America, and be as keen to keep out of my way as I was to keep out of his. He was doing so well when he went. He was dead sure that his next stop would be Hollywood at fifty pounds a minute!

Vandeleur: But it didn't work out like that.

Jennifer: No. He came to grief — two or three flops. You know what the States are like when you're not doing so well.

Vandeleur: And then he remembered that he had a wife in England, and
came back.

Jennifer: You see, I knew he was alive when I married you. One does
mad things when one's desperate, and I was desperate then. So he'd
got me. I had to pay his bills, and feed his vanity by going out with
him — and other things —

Vandeleur: Jenny — no!

Jennifer: Oh yes — that was the nature of the beast. Just as he'd have seen
me go to prison for bigamy, and had a good laugh — and we were so
happy, so unbelievably happy, Elliott, you and I, till he came back six
months ago. Weren't we?

Vandeleur: Of course we were.

Jennifer: I'm not defending myself. There's never been such a fool as
I've been! But I did try to keep it from you, to look after that
happiness of ours —

Vandeleur: Yes. You tried.

Jennifer: But I didn't succeed.

   A pause.

   Was that why you killed him, Elliott?

Vandeleur: Jenny!

Jennifer: I've told you everything. Won't you tell me, and make us quits?
Wouldn't it help?

Vandeleur: After what you've told me I could cheerfully kill him three
times over.

Jennifer: Once was enough.

Vandeleur: You don't really believe —

Jennifer: How can I help it? It was you who insisted on our taking this
job. I did all I knew to back out when I heard that Barran had
booked Kelsey. You were in on the script from the beginning, so you
knew all about the mechanics of the broadcast. You asked specially
for that revolver —

Vandeleur: Jenny, stop! Stop torturing yourself! That revolver never
fired. I hated Kelsey enough to have smashed his face, but when he
was killed I didn't know that he had to die to make you safe.

Jennifer (*hysterically*): But they'll find out, Elliott. They'll discover that I
was married to Kelsey. And then they'll never believe that you didn't
know too. Your motive will be there, cut and dried, sticking out a
mile! They'll hang you, Elliott, and it'll be all my fault — mine and

Lanyon Kelsey's — and you talk calmly about everything being over because he's dead! —

Through the glass panel of the Listening Room, Barran comes into view pressing down the loudspeaker reverse switch. His voice booms through the speaker into the studio.

Barran: I say, you two, I suggest you take that scene rather more on the soft pedal.

Vandeleur: What the devil —

Jennifer: Tony!

Barran comes into the studio, grinning like a Cheshire cat.

Barran: Definitely overplaying — both of you.

Vandeleur: What in hell were you doing?

Barran: Listening to a bedtime story.

Jennifer: Tony! You mean you heard — Oh!

She bursts into tears and runs through the Studio door.

Barran: I'm sorry, Jennifer. I didn't mean — (*He starts to follow her.*)

Vandeleur: Barran!

Barran: Well ?

Vandeleur: Leave her alone.

Barran: I'm afraid she's rather upset.

Vandeleur: And whose fault is that, you spying little cad?

Barran: Hold on. How was I to know you were going to choose this studio for your heart to heart talk?

Vandeleur: For two pins I'd break your neck!

Barran: That's better.

Vandeleur (*puzzled*): Better?

Barran: I mean it's better than calling me a "spying little cad." That's out of a script.

Vandeleur: A man who listens to a private conversation —

Barran: There it goes again. That's out of a script too.

Vandeleur (*slowly*): Look here, Barran. Do you *always* sneer? Don't you ever have any human emotions of your own?

Barran: Too damned many. So have you.

Vandeleur: Then why is it so very funny when I happen to show them?

Barran: It isn't that. It's the way you elderly fellows carry on.

Vandeleur (*furiously*): Elderly, eh?

Barran: Well! Middle-aged, anyway. You're knocked endways over this business. You're mad and hurt and ruddy near blind ...

Vandeleur (*sits down with his head in his hand*): Thanks.

Barran: It's the nearest thing to anguish you've ever known in your life. You mean it. But what do you do?

Vandeleur: I spoke of breaking your neck, if you remember.

Barran: You don't walk out of here and hide, as *I'd* want to do.

Vandeleur (*bitterly*): As *you'd* want to do!

Barran: Yes. You don't even stutter and gobble like an ordinary man. All you can do is throw up your hands and start to spout bad lines ...

Vandeleur: Lines! Lines! Lines!

Barran (*despondently*): Maybe you can't help it. Maybe none of us can help it. Everything we think and say and do comes out of a script. You're worse because you belong to an older generation. You couldn't even die except to slow music.

Vandeleur (*not loudly*): You could die, Barran. You could die.

Barran: Like Kelsey? Yes.

Vandeleur: I don't know anything about that. (*Gets up*) But I warn you —

Barran: Look, Elliott. Don't start it all over again.

Vandeleur: You ought to be ...

Barran (*pouncing*): "Horsewhipped." You very nearly said it, didn't you?
    Vandeleur sits down.
    I didn't enjoy listening to your little family row, you know.

Vandeleur: I wonder if you'll ever tell a bigger lie than that.

Barran: Don't *you* ever listen to a private conversation?

Vandeleur: Certainly not.

Barran: Who's lying now?

Vandeleur (*confused*): I mean ... !

Barran: Well, who was more embarrassed? The people you heard talking —or you? It was you, wasn't it? And, after you'd got over your first curiosity, you wanted to get away a good deal faster than they did. *I* wanted to get away. But how the hell *could* I get away, in that place. What I can't understand is why you're so upset.

Vandeleur: You see, I belong to an older generation.

Barran: Suppose you do? You ought to be relieved, instead of raging like a lunatic. At any rate, you know Kelsey wasn't Jennifer's lover.

Vandeleur: So my vanity ought to be soothed, eh? Nothing counts but vanity. Lord, how young *you* are!

Barran (*critically*): You either are a gaffer, or you're not. Make up your mind which it's to be. As I say, you know Kelsey wasn't Jennifer's lover ...

Vandeleur: And *you* know he was her husband.

Barran: Yes.

Vandeleur: You know she married me bigamously. A criminal offence.

Barran: That's right. She ... (*suddenly realizing*) Look here: you don't think I'm likely to run to the police about it?

Vandeleur: To the police. (*Thoughtfully*) No. Maybe not.

Barran: Then what are you shouting about?

Vandeleur: Not to the police. No. But you wouldn't think of telling it to all our friends, would you? You wouldn't think it made a very good story, to be whispered wherever you went under the pledge of deep secrecy?

Barran: Candidly, I think it would make a rip-roaring story. "Bigamy at the BBC or Who Done Her Wrong?"

Vandeleur jumps up.

(*quietly*) But I haven't any intention of telling it, Elliott.

Vandeleur: You mean that?

Barran: I mean it, so help me.

Pause. They look at each other.

Vandeleur: You know, Barran ...

Barran: Yes?

Vandeleur: For a second, there, I almost believed you.

Barran bows ironically.

Vandeleur: But whether I believe you or not doesn't matter. What does matter is this. If I'm an old fogey, if I haven't got much to look back on and still less to look forward to ...

Barran: Easy, now!

Vandeleur: ... that's all the *more* reason why it matters. The only thing in this world I care anything about is my wife. Say what you like about me; it's probably true. But anybody who hurts Jennifer, or slights her, or even as much as says a word against her, is going to wish he'd never been born. When I say I'd do anything in the world for her, I mean just that. I don't mean a lot of fancy speeches. I mean I'd lie for her or crawl for her or steal for her or kill for her. Jennifer may be a thousand miles away from being perfect. But, by God, Barran, she's perfect to me.

Barran: You know, Elliott.

Vandeleur: Yes?

Barran: For a second, there, I almost liked you.
    Jennifer re-enters with Helen Searle.
    Hello — I thought the girls were all in bed. I was just coming along to bring you some bread-and-milk and a goodnight kiss.
Helen: Mr Silence wants to do some sort of reconstruction of the crime, I think.
Barran: What ho! Truth *is* stranger than fiction.
Jennifer: I'm sorry, Elliott. I was behaving very stupidly just now.
Barran: My fault, Jennifer. I'd like to apologise.
Vandeleur: The best thing you can do is to keep out of our affairs from now on.
Barran: Very well, if you say so.
Vandeleur: I do say so.
Helen: I think we're all to stand or sit where we were when the shooting happened, Mr Barran.
Barran: A nod, Helen dear, is as good as a wink. I'm going.
    Barran goes into the Listening Room and sits at the Producer's desk. The others group themselves as they were during the climax of the broadcast. Meanwhile Silence has come in.
Silence: Oh you're already lined up, are you?
Helen: I told them, Mr Silence.
Silence: If I can manage to hang Mr Caird, will you come and work for me?
    Re-enter Caird and Cheston.
Caird: Did I hear my name? Anything I can do?
Silence: Yes — but you won't do it! How's the raid?
Caird: Poisonous, isn't it, Basil?
Cheston: Despite bad weather, many large fires were started; and heavy explosions were observed in the —
Caird: Not a ghost of a car. I'm afraid the marooning is complete.
Silence: I imagine the police will have their hands full with other things.
    He makes a complete tour of the studio, peering, and taking angles of sight from the point of view of positions of the different characters at the time of the shooting.
Caird: What on earth are you up to now?
Silence: Just elimination.
Caird: Just.
Silence: No one in the Listening Room there could conceivably have fired

the shot. I just want to find out how much anyone who *was* in the Listening Room could have seen of the performance in the studio at the time of the shooting. (*He beckons through the glass to Barran who comes to the door of the Listening Room.*)

Barran: Want me?

Silence: No. I want to have your chair in the Listening Room for a few moments. Come and keep me company. I may want to ask a few technical questions about your gear.

Barran: I'm honoured. Shall I give them a green cue-light when you want them to re-enact their dismal scene?

Silence: That would be fine.

Barran: On your marks, everybody.

Helen: Where's George Sloane?

Jennifer: He was drinking his coffee when we came down just now. In the canteen.

Vandeleur: I'll get him.

He goes out. Silence and Barran go into the Listening Room. Silence sits in Barran's chair. The latter stands beside him.

Jennifer (*suddenly*): I'm not sure I can stand this!

Helen: Steady does it.

Re-enter Vandeleur and George Sloane.

Sloane: I'm sorry. I didn't know I was wanted. Jenny, are you all right? You look awful.

Jennifer: I'm only tired.

Sloane: Is there any point in all this?

Silence's voice booms through the talk-back.

Silence: Yes, young man, there is. Would you mind getting set as you were at the end of that play?

Sloane: Very well. But I haven't any gun now, you know. You've got it.

Silence: I've not forgotten. Now when Mr Barran gives the green light, I want Mr Vandeleur to go right ahead.

Vandeleur: Right.

Sloane takes up his original position amidst his effects, and lifts his left hand. Vandeleur and Jennifer open their scripts. Helen, Caird and Cheston on their respective settees. Meanwhile in the Listening Room can be seen in pantomime Silence indicating that he can't see comfortably from Barran's chair — and wants to change places. The change is made, no one in the studio noticing it. Barran is now next to the Listening Room door.

Cheston (*unexpectedly*): I say!

Caird (*exasperated*): For the love of Mike, what is it NOW?

Cheston: It's my observation.

Caird: Observation?

Cheston: I tried to tell you, only you wouldn't listen.

Helen: About what?

Cheston: At the rehearsal it was one way. In the play it was another way. And now it's the same way all over again.

Vandeleur: I don't think any of us can put up with much more of this drivelling. If Barran's ready, can't we get on with this?

Barran (*through talk-back*): Light coming.

At that moment again the studio lights fail.

Vandeleur (*exasperatedly*): Oh damn, not again!

Caird: I love little Adolf, his coat is *so* warm!

Vandeleur: What do we do now?

Barran (*talk-back*): Keep your places everyone. They'll be on again in a moment.

Jennifer (*shrilly*): I can't stand it — I simply can't!

Vandeleur: Jenny!

Caird: Haven't we any candles in this dam' place?

Croker: Did you say candles, sir?

Caird: Who the devil's that?

Croker (*aggrieved*): Only me, sir — Croker.

Caird: Can't you get some candles, or lamps, or glow-worms, or some thing that illuminates?

Croker: I came down to ask you if you wanted candles, sir.

Caird: Croker, we do want candles.

Croker: Very good, sir. It'll take me about three minutes. They're in the scullery, sir.

Caird: I don't care if they're in your collar-box! Get 'em!

Croker: Very good, sir, I'm going.

Vandeleur: Going, going, gone!

Jennifer: Don't, Elliott — I shall scream.

Vandeleur: Sorry, darling.

Cheston: Hasn't anyone got a torch?

Caird: If you can find my overcoat —

Jennifer: If any of you start crawling about in the dark, I shall have screaming hysterics. I'm sorry — but I've had almost as much as I can stand.

Helen: I suggest we all sit still. The candles will be here in a minute.

Silence (*talk-back*): Miss Searle, you've more sense than any girl I ever met —
God, what's that? Barran!

Vandeleur: What's happened?

Caird: These infernal lights!

Vandeleur: But what's happened?

Croker appears in the doorway with a couple of candles. In their dim light everyone can be seen in their positions as they were when the lights went out, except that Caird and Helen are standing up. Through the panel of the Listening Room Barran is apparently leaning against Silence. The studio lights go on again full. Caird dashes to the Listening Room door and drags it wide open.

Caird: Silence — is anything wrong?

Barran pitches sideways away from Silence, rolls forward through the door of the Listening Room, and falls forward on his face.

Caird: Tony!

With a screams Jennifer collapses into her husband's arms.

General appropriate reactions.

CURTAIN

ACT III

It is now some hours later. As the Curtain rises, Silence and Caird are on the stage. The NO SMOKING notice is now hung upside down on the wall. Caird sits slumped down on the settee, against the wall right, smoking a pipe. Silence's head and shoulders are buried under the raised top of the grand piano, inside which he seems to be grubbing. There is a long, angry rattle across the piano-wires, and Silence straightens up.

Caird: Find anything?

Silence: No.

Caird: Find anything anywhere?

Silence: No.

Caird: I suppose we are still sane?

Silence: I'm beginning to doubt it. Look here.
   Takes out a packet of cigarettes, lights one, and squares himself.
   The gun that killed Kelsey has disappeared. Pfft! Just like that. Now it did exist. It couldn't have melted in the air. But where the hell is it?

Caird: You tell me.

Silence: I searched this room, if you remember, just after I searched Here-Is-The-News?

Caird: Yes

Silence (*pointing*): The coats on the piano. The Effects. Round the walls. That settee.

Caird: Granted.

Silence: You can testify, can't you, that the gun couldn't have been hidden in the Listening Room?

Caird: I can.

Silence: God knows I searched everybody before any person was allowed to leave this room. I've just finished a second search of the place. But that's not all. I saw at the time that nobody *could* have got rid of a pistol after shooting Kelsey.

Caird: That's rather steep, isn't it?

Silence: Well, look at the individual cases. Take Cheston, for instance.

Caird: Basil's hardly my idea of a murderer.

70

Silence: Never mind. Just think back. I was sitting beside Cheston, on this settee (*illustrates*) when the shot was fired. Do you think he could have pulled a gun, shot Kelsey, and got rid of it — without my seeing him?

Caird: No.

Silence: Then there's young Sloane. I was actually *looking* at him when he fired those blanks at the ceiling.

Holds up his right hand, hesitates as though thinking, and then dismisses it.

Next, there's Mr and Mrs Vandeleur. (*Walks to microphone*) Here they were, facing each other on opposite sides of the microphone. How could either of them have got rid of a gun? Where? In the middle of the bare floor, where? How, without being seen?

Caird: *I* don't know.

Silence: There's the Listening Room. (*Goes and taps on glass panel*) With four of you crowded in there, could anybody have drawn or ditched a gun without being seen?

Caird: No, that's definitely out.

Silence: And that leaves only your own secretary, Miss Searle, sitting where you are now.

Caird: I hope you don't suspect Helen?

Silence: No; because the same rule applies to her. That's the finish. Ladies and gentlemen, I thank you.

Caird: So nobody could have killed Kelsey.

Silence: That's what the evidence shows. Have you any answer to it?

Caird: Yes. The man's dead.

Silence (*irascibly*): Don't sit there and tell me that. I know he's dead. All I say is that by police regulations he oughtn't to be.

The door opens, and Helen comes in.

Helen: I came to tell you ...

She sees them smoking, turns sternly to point to NO SMOKING sign, and finds it turned upside down.

Silence and Caird: YES!

Helen: So you're breaking regulations, eh?

Caird: In more ways than one.

Helen: How do you mean?

Caird: That's what the evidence shows. I suppose you didn't kill Kelsey yourself, did you?

Helen (*quickly*): Why do you ask that?

Caird: Because, Miss Searle, the BBC has suddenly become a house of mystery. I should not be surprised to see bodies falling out of cupboards and clutching hands coming through the curtains.

Helen: Don't say that! Don't joke about it, not now! When I think of poor Tony ...

Caird (*sitting up*): 'Poor' Tony! That's a new one, isn't it?

Helen (*waking up, icily*): Is it? What happens to Mr Barran is no concern of mine. And never will be. But, when any person gets hurt, it seems to me that in common humanity ...

Silence (*unimpressed*): Nonsense! All he got was a cosh over the head.

Helen: *All* he got?

Silence (*cheerfully*): Yes. Wouldn't have so much as dented my helmet in the old days.

Helen: Really.

Silence: You're going to say I've got a harder head than he has. And so I have. But what I want to know is, WHY should anybody have done that to him? Why should somebody have slipped in there with a ... a ...

Caird: A blunt instrument?

Silence (*taking this seriously*): I don't know what kind of instrument it was. Something fairly light, anyhow.

Caird: Attempted murder?

Silence: Then why not make a good job of it? You've all been talking about attempted murder. But somehow I can't quite swallow that. It's another part of this monkey-business. Why, when the lights were out, did somebody sneak in there and slug him?

Helen: Perhaps some of his friends could tell you.

Silence: You don't like him much, do you?

Helen: I neither like nor dislike him.

Silence: Well, maybe you're right. I can't quite decide whether that fellow is three parts dirty dog and one part decent; or one part dirty dog and three parts decent. But I have felt a couple of times that a swift kick in the pants might do him a lot of good.

Helen (*with quiet fury*): Do you think you're being quite fair to Tony, Mr Silence?

Silence (*musing*): Eh?

Helen: I said, do you think you're being quite fair to Tony?

Silence: Miss, I wasn't trying to be fair or otherwise. I was only —

Helen: Of course, it's nothing to me whether you understand him or not. I dare say the parts of decent and dirty dog are so mixed up in all of us that it's hard to tell which is which. As I say, I regard Mr Barran as I should regard ... well — anything else I passed in the street, like the Albert Memorial or ... (*floundering*) ... Were you grinning at me, Mr Caird?

Caird (*politely*): No. At the Albert Memorial.

From the beginning of Helen's last speech, Silence has been moodily prowling round outside the Listening Room panel. Now he stands staring at it, a half-enlightened expression on his face.

Helen: I seem to be talking a lot of rubbish.

Silence (*explosively*): Holy suffering shades of Shickelgruber!

Caird (*jumping*): Eh?

Helen: What is it?

Caird: What's wrong?

Silence (*blankly*): Nothing. I was just remembering something.

Caird: That's rather an anti-climax, if you ask me. What was it?

Silence: I was just remembering what happened when Barran and I were in the Listening Room. And something that the rest of you didn't notice. (*Thinking*) But *that* can't be, because it would make ... (*His voice trails off.*)

Caird: This sounds like inspiration.

Helen: Or something

Silence (*worrying at it*): The impossible can't be impossible. Stands to reason.

Caird: *Vive la logique.*

Silence: Therefore ... in the old days, I could always see everything clearly if I could write it down. A. B. C. D. Like that. If I could write this down ... Has anybody got a notebook?

Helen: I — I'm sorry. I seem to have mislaid mine.

Caird: When Helen Searle mislays her notebook, that's a bad sign. I've got one, if it's any good to you.

Silence: Let me have it, will you?

Caird gets up from the settee. He stands facing the audience, opens his coat, and reaches into the inside breast pocket, holding the coat open.

I've never understood why some tailors put buttons on inside pockets. If you're fat-headed enough to button 'em, it takes twice the time to ...

Silence: Wait a minute! Stop just where you are!

Caird (*blinking*): All right. Why?

Silence: That coat of yours.

Caird: What about it?

Silence: Take it off, will you?

Helen (*sotto voce*): The old devil really is out of his head.

    Caird removes his coat, and hands it to Silence.

Caird: Policemen in general always make me feel guilty, even when I haven't done anything. What's wrong with the coat? It's an ordinary coat.

Silence (*instantly*): Yes. That's just the point.

Helen: What is?

Silence: That it's an ordinary coat. You know, I don't think I'm going to need that notebook after all.

Helen: But —

Silence (*with slow, heavy seriousness*): You've got to excuse me. I'm not a very rapid thinker. Sort of heave-ho and get-there-somehow. When I see two pieces of evidence, one after the other in a couple of seconds, it's apt to tie up my mental process, and maybe I don't make myself quite clear.

Caird: Candidly, you don't.

    Silence hands the coat back.

Silence: Let me give you an illustration. Eh?

Caird: Fire away.

Silence: Suppose you're a copper.

Caird: All right. Suppose it.

Silence: You're sent out to arrest a man who's stolen a thousand pounds' worth of bonds. Got that?

Caird: I think so.

Silence: You nab the crook. You go through his hideout. You find the bonds. You recover them, every last one of them. It's a fair cop and the swag's recovered. All right! Does it occur to you to look for any *more* bonds in the same series?

Helen: Certainly not.

Silence: No? Why not?

Helen: Because you've recovered everything you were sent to look for. You've got back everything that was stolen.

Silence (*dismally*): Yes. That's what I thought. That's the mistake *I* made.

Caird: About the bonds?

Silence: About the murder.

Helen (*meekly*): As a mere woman, I'm afraid I'm too practical-minded for all this. What's more, I'm slowly going out of my mind. Will you kindly tell us what all this talk about crooks and bonds has to do with Lanyon Kelsey's murder?

Silence (*argumentatively*): And yet it's the simplest thing in the world, if you only come to think of it. Tell me, Miss Searle. Where is Tony Barran now?

Helen (*quickly*): What about him?

Silence: I only asked, where is he?

Helen: Lying down under restraint, and using perfectly foul language.

Silence: Do you think he's steady enough on his pins to come in here? (*Grimly*) Never mind. He's *got* to come in.

Helen: What do you want with him?

Silence: Never mind. Go and get him.

Helen (*quietly*): Is that an order?

Silence: Yes.

> *Helen hesitates. Then she goes out quickly. Silence wanders about in a black study, hitting his hands together. Caird, who has put on his coat, watches him.*

Caird (*looking at his watch*): Four hours until daylight, and the raid still going like billy-o. Hoy there! Chief Inspector!

Silence (*rousing himself*): Eh?

Caird: Do you know what I think you know?

Silence: Yes.

Caird: Do you know how the disappearing revolver came to disappear?

Silence: Yes.

Caird: Do you know where it disappeared to?

Silence: Yes.

Caird: Is it in this room now?

Silence: Yes.

Caird (*wildly*): But where? For God's sake, where? And what's the meaning of all this? And who's been making a fool of us?

Silence: Me.

Caird: What's that?

Silence (*impatiently*): I. Me. Whatever the grammatical term is. I'm glad old Superintendent Mason never saw me this time.

Caird: Look here. I don't have to tell you of all people how serious this is. As it is, I'm half afraid of what's going to happen before we're many minutes older. Hadn't you better stop this mystification?

Silence: It's not mystification.

Caird: Then can't you come out straight and tell me how the murderer disposed of the gun?

Silence (*wearily*): All right. I'll tell you. The gun is ... (*breaking off*) S-ss-t!
Barran comes through the studio door, leaning heavily on Helen. He is very pale, and his head is bandaged. Caird crosses to meet them.

Caird: How are you, Tony?

Barran: Lousy, thanks.

Silence: I'm sorry to worry you with questions, but —

Barran: I've such a glorious headache already that I doubt your being able to make it worse!

Helen: Now don't talk more than you've got to. Could we have a chair, Mr Caird?

Caird: Of course.
He goes into the Listening Room and brings out a chair.

Barran: I'd far rather go on leaning on you.

Helen: That's why I asked for the chair.

Barran: 'A ministering angel, thou!'
Caird places the chair roughly left centre of stage and Barran sits in it. Helen stands behind it.

Helen (*anxiously*): Do you really think you're up to it?

Barran: Just. It would help me if I could hold your hand.
She pulls it out of reach.

Barran: Well, Mr Silence, where do we go from here? Have you worked it out?

Silence (*gloomily*): No.

Barran: Not a sausage?

Silence: Not even a Canadian egg.[13] That's why I'm worrying you.

Barran: I can take it. Worry away.

Silence: Can you think of any reason why you should have been slugged?

Barran: With the famous blunt instrument of fiction — I can't. Unless of course —

---

[13] "Canadian egg" is a slang term with various definitions.

Caird: What?

Barran: Was May Matheson around? I don't remember.

Helen: Don't be silly!

Barran: I'm not being silly. I've injured her vanity, cut her part, insulted her appearance, and generally walked on her with hob-nail boots! And hell hath no fury —

Caird: Shut up, Tony. This is serious.

Barran: You're telling me! Swap your head for mine, and you'll know just how serious things are.

Caird: Well, we're not bothering about May Matheson as a possible suspect.

Barran: You should. How about the least likely person? It always works in fiction.

Helen: Oh do stop talking nonsense, Tony. You're only tiring yourself.

Barran: I repeat, if you'll let me hold your hand —

She drops a hand over his right shoulder, and he puts up his right hand to hold it.

Thank you, Helen. Now I will be good.

Silence: Miss Searle, your help remains invaluable.

Caird (*humorously*): You might remember sometime, Miss Searle, that you're my secretary. However —

Silence: Leaving Miss — er Pushface out of it, is there anyone else you know of who has a grudge against you?

Barran: To the point of murder? Hardly. There's a tailor and a wine-merchant — but one's in Sackville Street, and the other at Oxford. I guess you can include them out!

Silence: Is that the best you can do?

Barran: No. Do you really want the truth?

Silence: Of course.

Caird: Certainly.

Barran: No matter who it is.

Caird: Don't be a fool, Tony!

Barran: Very well. You say that you can't find out how the thing was done, so it's hardly surprising that I don't know either. I can't help it, if it still looks impossible. But I do know who did it.

Helen: Who?

Barran: Elliott Vandeleur.

Caird: Nonsense!

Barran: What's the good of asking me footling questions then?

Silence: Mr Vandeleur had an empty revolver in one hand and a script in
the other. Miss Searle was practically facing him as she sat on that
settee there. How could he have fired — ?

Barran: The fatal shot! Quite. How could he? It's your job to find out
how, I only know he did it.

Caird: What makes you so sure?

Barran: Vandeleur's the only person with adequate motive for both
crimes.

Helen: Do you mean — ? (*She pulls her hand away.*)

Barran (*brutally*): No I don't. Vandeleur didn't shoot Kelsey because
Kelsey was having an affair with Jennifer, and he didn't slug me
because I'd once wanted to have an affair with Jennifer. Is that straight
enough for you?

Caird: We're not interested in reasons that weren't operative. Can't we
leave the gossip-column angle out?

Silence: Mr Barran — leaving the Kelsey murder out of it for the moment
— why should Mr Vandeleur have attacked you?

Barran: Because he knew that I knew his motive for murdering Kelsey.

Silence: Go on.

Caird: Get on with it, Tony! What did you know?

Barran: I happened to be in that Listening Room when Vandeleur and his
wife were having a private conversation in here. The circuit had been
left live after the broadcast. I'm sorry to say that I was so interested in
what they were saying that I forgot to be a gentleman.

Silence: What was it that interested you so much?

Helen (*quietly*): It isn't too late to remember, Tony.

Barran: Helen!

He looks round and up at her. She gives him back her hand.

Caird: Come along, Tony.

Barran (*slowly*): I'm sorry, Julian. That crack on the head seems to have
fogged my memory for the time being.

Caird: Now don't be a damned fool!

Barran: Sorry — not a thing.

Helen (*smiling*): Yes, one thing.

Caird: What do you mean, Miss Searle?

Helen: He's remembered how to be a gentleman, Mr Caird.

Silence: Maybe, Miss Searle. But you've let me down. I thought I could rely on you.

Helen: I'm sorry.

Caird: I'm amazed. The girl's human after all!

Helen: Thank you, Mr Caird.

Silence: Which is all very nice and very pretty, but it's my business to solve this case. And I'm going to do it, however many gentlemen turn up unexpectedly in the course of it —

He breaks off, for Jennifer and Vandeleur have entered the studio.

Vandeleur: Quite a party! How do you feel, Barran?

Barran: Lots better, thanks.

Jennifer: I'm so glad.

Barran: Thank you.

Vandeleur: I suppose you've been questioning Barran, Mr Silence?

Silence: Yes.

Vandeleur: Has he told you anything interesting?

Silence: Something.

Vandeleur: Well, you needn't bother — nor need be! Jenny and I have made up our minds to come clean and get it over —

Barran: Don't be a fool, Elliott! I've told him nothing.

Vandeleur: What?

Barran: Not a thing. I've forgotten anything I might have been able to tell him. This crack on the head you know — rotten for the memory!

Jennifer: Oh Tony!

Barran: So why not go to bed?

Vandeleur: It's good of you, Tony. But it won't do.

Silence: I think you're wise, Mr Vandeleur.

Vandeleur: So do I. You see I happen to be innocent. You know that I couldn't have shot Kelsey. It was a physical impossibility. And I didn't slug Barran. Those being the facts, you may as well know that I had every reason to kill Kelsey, and a pretty good one to want to kill Barran.

Caird: Elliott!

Silence: Go on, Mr Vandeleur.

Jennifer: It's really my story, Mr Silence. You see I married Lanyon Kelsey in America. I left him, and married Elliott bigamously. Lanyon was blackmailing me.

Caird: My God!

Jennifer: Everyone thought we were having an affair. But that was the truth. And I only told Elliott tonight after — the shooting.

Vandeleur: That was the conversation Barran overheard. That was why I
    might have been justified in wanting his blood.
Jennifer: But he didn't do it, Mr Silence. I swear he didn't do it.
Vandeleur: No, oddly enough, I didn't do it.
Silence: I know.
Caird: What?
Silence: I know Mr Vandeleur didn't shoot Kelsey.
Caird: How do you know?
Silence (*slowly*): Well, it's like this. The person who shot Kelsey was the
    same person who slugged Mr Barran. Right?
Caird: I suppose so.
Silence: We've got to believe that or retire to a madhouse. Now, Mr
    Vandeleur there had a motive to shut Barran's mouth. So if he had
    tried to cosh Barran, that would have been reasonable enough.
Barran: *Tried* to cosh me? Is there any doubt about that?
Silence: Oh, no. You got hit, right enough.
Barran: Thanks.
Silence: But, you see, there's something I forgot up to a minute ago.
Vandeleur: Well?
Silence: You remember our reconstruction of the case? Mr Barran was
    sitting on that chair in the Listening Room, and I was standing by the
    door.
Vandeleur: Quite right.
Silence: Yes. *But* just before the lights went out, Mr Barran and I
    changed places. *I* sat down in the chair. *He* went over to the door.
    And none of the rest of you noticed it.
Helen (*suddenly*): I think I begin to see.
Silence: The lights went out. Somebody slipped across and took a wallop
    at the man standing by the door, but why?
Helen (*excitedly*): Then the murderer wasn't trying to hit Tony at all! He
    wasa trying to hit ...
Silence: Got it, miss. He was trying to hit me.
Caird: But why?
Silence: Ah! That's the whole point. Why?
Barran: And you've known that all the time you were making my head
    ache with questions about *my* enemies?
Silence: Oh, yes.
Barran: Then why bother to let me talk a lot of rot?

Silence: For one thing, son, I hoped you might confess.

Helen (*crying out*): No!

Barran (*quietly*): That depends on what you mean.　Confess what? Murder?

Silence: Oh, no.

Barran: Then what in Satan's name *do* you mean?

Silence: You might tell us, for instance, why you played that fool trick with the blanks.

Barran (*flatly*): Helen my dear, he's done me.

Jennifer: He's doing something, anyway.　I feel as though any minute something might fall on us from the ceiling, or ...

Silence: Any confession, son?

Barran (*bitterly*): You're determined to pry it out of me, aren't you?

Silence (*placidly*): Yes.

Barran: All right.　You may as well know now as later.　And in a way, mind you, I'm rather glad to get it off my chest.

Helen: Tony, do go on!

Barran: I *am* leaving the Corporation, as Julian seems to have guessed. So I gave George that gun, and told him to make the welkin ring.　I've been wanting to do it for years.

Helen: But *why* are you leaving?

Barran: Spot of trouble with the administrative boys.　You've gathered that much.　But the fact is ... (*hesitates*) ...

Helen: Yes?

Barran (*defiantly*): The fact is, I've volunteered for an air-gunner.　I go on Tuesday.

Caird: So!

Barran: Now, wait! (*Fiercely*) Anybody who gets slushy about this, or attributes patriotic motives to me, will promptly be assaulted.

Helen: Including me, Tony?

Barran: Yes, including you. (*Violently*) *I am not patriotic.* I hate all that slush and slosh.　I mean, I hate it when people talk about it.　If I can't go through life with my thumb at my nose, I won't walk at all.　But I'm a damn good gunner, if you'll pardon my modesty.　And if I can only make things as uncomfortable for Jerry as I seem to have made 'em for my friends ...

Helen: If you go on, Tony, you may be saying some pleasant things you'll regret.

Barran: That's all there is to it.

Helen: All?

Barran: Yes. George Sloane knew my guilty secret about the training. He even told me he thought I might have a go at trying a real gun on the recording machinery. (*Glowering*) But you people aren't so bad ... most of you.

Vandeleur: Miss Searle's right. He'll be practically handing out compliments, in a minute or two.

Barran: I'm sorry I played the fool. Is that apology enough?

Jennifer: You don't need to make any apology, Tony.

Barran: No? If I hadn't bullied George into firing that gun, we might all have had a decent night's sleep. And ...

Jennifer: And ...?

Barran: We should all have waked up in the morning. Including Lanyon Kelsey.

Jennifer: Tony Barran, I never knew you were so sentimental. I'm glad you helped kill him. (*Fiercely*) I'm *glad*!

Vandeleur: Jennifer! No! Easy!

Silence (*sharply*): Just a moment.

Vandeleur: I knew it. It's started again.

Silence: Miss Searle. You did search Mrs Vandeleur, didn't you?

Helen: Of course I did!

Vandeleur: Can't we leave my wife out of it by this time? Her back was turned to Kelsey, and she had no weapon.

Caird: Neither had anybody else. That's the whole trouble.

Silence (*dubiously*): Well ... no. That's a bit too strong. I shouldn't go so far as to say *that*.

Caird: As to say what?

Silence: That nobody had a weapon.

Barran: Vandeleur's right. Here we go again.

Helen: Mr Silence, *please* let me ask you one straight question. Was Lanyon Kelsey shot with a .22 revolver held in the hand of somebody in this studio?

Silence: Yes. He was.

Caird: Then what are we waiting for?

Silence: Well, maybe it's the slowness of my wits. Maybe I'd like you to see it for yourselves. Maybe I don't see it too clearly myself ...

Helen: Or maybe not?

Silence (*unheeding*): The thing to do, as old Superintendent Mason used to say, is to see what's under your nose. Now when I joined the Force in nineteen-o-two ...

Barran: Isn't this going to take rather a long time, if you fill up all the gaps in between?

Silence: No. It would take a very short time if you could answer me just one question.

Vandeleur: What's that?

Silence (*doggedly*): Why anyone should want to slug *me*. — Apart from the reason you're thinking of, that is.

Helen: I'm glad you mentioned that.

Silence: Somebody ran a terrific risk to slip in and cosh me ... why?

Caird: You tell *us*. If you've got some proof against the murderer ...

Silence (*explosively*): Proof? Did you say proof?

Vandeleur: That was the word.

Silence: Then I ask you, man to man. What possible proof *can* I have?

Jennifer: Don't look at *me*, please.

Silence: You know everything I know. You've seen and even handled everything I've seen. And by every law or sanity there isn't anything at all. I won't say any more. Silence is my name, and Silence is my nature. Just answer that one question: why should anybody want to slug *me*?

Barran: I wish they hadn't, believe me! (*He caresses his head.*)

Caird: We can't leave things like this.

Jennifer: I'm beginning to feel as if I must have done it with a split personality or something horrid like that.

Helen: The whole thing's a nightmare.

Barran: Personally I'm content not to wake up.

Silence: It won't do. I feel — personally affronted. I'm afraid there's only one thing for it.

Caird: What's that?

Silence: We never finished that reconstruction, you know.

Vandeleur: Must we go through all that again?

Silence: I'm sorry, but we must.

Caird: Very well. Whom do you want?

Silence: Let me see. Most of us are here. I can do without your programme engineers in the Listening Room.

Caird: You'll want Sloane.

Silence: Of course.

Caird: And Cheston.

Silence: We can't do without the News.

Barran: They're both in the canteen — snoring.

Caird: Collect 'em, Miss Searle, will you?

Helen: Very well. What about Miss Matheson?

Silence: We'll spare Mr Barran that, as he's an invalid. No, she was definitely outside the studio at the time of the shooting.

Helen goes out.

Vandeleur: Buck up, darling. We'll soon be out of the wood.

Jennifer: I don't mind really. I feel you and I are out of it already.

Vandeleur: You really feel that?

Jennifer: Really and truly.

Vandeleur: Then they can reconstruct all night for all I care!

Silence: We haven't seen Sunshine lately. I wonder how the war's getting on.

Caird: It looked like hell down in the town the last time I had a look-see.

Silence: I'm not sure I wouldn't exchange all the same. I don't mind crimes. But I hate a crime that doesn't make sense! And this doesn't.

Helen comes back with Sloane and Cheston. Cheston is as im- maculate as usual. Both look gummy-eyed and sulky.

Cheston: Who wouldn't sell his little farm and go to the BBC?

Sloane: What's up now?

Silence: I'm sorry to wake you up. But I must have my reconstruction.

Sloane: Oh hell!

Jennifer: Now be a good boy, George!

Sloane: You sound very cheerful all of a sudden.

Jennifer: I am.

She slips her hand into Vandeleur's. Sloane stares.

Sloane: Well — that's something.

Cheston: What's the betting those infernal lights go out again at the critical moment?

Caird: No takers.

Silence: By the way, air-raids apart, where are the studio light-switches?

Barran: Just there — beside the Listening Room door.

Silence: Well, to avoid any — er — mistake, suppose you lean up against that door and keep an eye on them, Mr Barran.

Barran: Right you are.

Silence: Now group yourselves, will you?

They do so, as in Act I except that Barran now stands against the Listening Room door, instead of inside it, and Caird sits in Kelsey's place.

Oh, Sloane — I was forgetting — here's your gun.

He takes it from his pocket and hands it to Sloane. Sloane holds it in his right hand.

Sloane: You don't want me to use it, do you? You didn't when we were reconstructing last time.

Silence: Last time, if you remember, I was just looking at positions.

Jennifer: Must we have any more bangs?

Helen: Yes, must we?

Silence: There's only one blank left. It won't do you any harm.

Sloane: Is it all right, Mr Caird?

Caird: Get on with it, you idiot! We're not transmitting now.

Jennifer: But you don't want us to go through a whole rehearsal, do you?

Vandeleur: My God, no!

Silence: No, that won't be necessary. I just want the line leading up to the shooting.

Vandeleur (*grimly*): I think I know that one.

Barran: You surprise me!

Jennifer: Well, shall we start?

Silence (*significantly*): But just before you start —

They all turn to look at him.

I ought to warn you that I haven't been quite frank with you.

Helen (*under her breath*): Here it goes!

Vandeleur: Not frank? How?

Silence: I know who killed Kelsey. I know how he was killed. I know what happened to the gun.

Jennifer cries out.

Vandeleur: Then what the hell are we doing, playing charades? If you know, why don't you tell us?

Silence: If I did tell you, you wouldn't believe me. I want you to see it with your own eyes. Go on, Mr Vandeleur. Deliver your line.

Vandeleur: But I —

Silence: Deliver, your line, man!

Vandeleur: 'So you've been sleeping with my wife, eh, you swine?'

Barran: Now the shots. No green light.

Silence: Just a second!

Sloane: What is it?

Silence: Haven't you got that gun in the wrong hand?

Sloane: I don't think so.

Caird: Searle, what about it?

Helen: Sorry, Mr Caird; I was following the script.

Cheston: Hold on! *I* can tell you!

Silence: You?

Cheston (*aggrieved*): Dash it all, I've been trying to tell you all night. Sloane had the gun in his left hand. But at the rehearsal — when he was using the little stick to hit the cushion — he held the stick in his right hand. I kept wondering why he changed over for the play. I say: you aren't left-handed, are you?

Sloane: No. Sorry; I never thought about it. (*He changes the gun to his left hand.*)

Caird: Come on! Let's get on with it.

Silence: Line again, Mr Vandeleur.

Vandeleur: 'So you've been sleeping with my wife, eh, you swine?'

Silence (*quietly*): Shots, please.

Long pause

Barran: Something wrong with the gun?

Silence: Well? Why don't you shoot?

Sloane suddenly turns round and throws the revolver on the floor. He is trembling.

Sloane: I'm sick of this nonsense, do you hear? I won't have anything more to do with it!

Silence: Listen, all of you. (*He picks up the revolver.*) You want to know why he didn't fire. I'll tell you. If he had fired, he'd have blown a hole in the ceiling. This gun is loaded with live cartridges. It's the gun that killed Lanyon Kelsey.

Jennifer: George!

Silence: It's the gun we've been looking for. It's the gun that I like a chump have been carrying about in my pocket all evening.

Caird: But you took that gun from ...

Silence: From George Sloane's *breast* pocket, yes. Look here!

He goes over and throws open the left hand side of Sloane's coat, twisting him so that he faces the audience.

Sloane: Get away from me!

Silence (*holding him*): Keep still! (*To the others*) Did you ever see a

man's coat with the inside pocket on the *left* hand side?
The men automatically feel at the right hand pockets of their coats.
Of course not. Let me show you how it was done.
With his back to the audience, he raises his left hand in the air.
Note where I'm standing. No one in the Listening Room can see me. Miss Searle is watching her script. Mr Cheston, or anybody on that side, is looking at my left hand — which holds a gun loaded with blanks.

Caird: But that gun ...

Silence: Wait! Where's my right hand? (*He turns round.*) My right hand, holding a second gun loaded with real bullets, is in a specially sewn pocket on the left hand side of my coat.

Vandeleur: But Sloane fired at the ceiling!

Silence: With the blanks, yes. With his left hand, yes. But with his right band, under cover of the blank shots and under cover of his left arm — *Silence turns round with his back to the audience.*
He fired the shot that killed Kelsey. (*He turns round again.*)

Barran: I'm beginning to see this. After the shots, you examined the gun with the blanks.

Silence: Exactly. It was obviously harmless. I gave it back to Sloane, and he put it ...

Helen: In his *hip*-pocket! I remember seeing him do it.

Sloane (*fiercely*): Yes. You would notice, wouldn't you?

Silence (*taking hold of Sloane*): I should keep quiet, if I were you. The deadly gun was in his inside breast pocket ... here. Now do you see?

Caird: Yes!

Silence: I searched him, before he could object. I found the real gun *here* if you remember, and I thought it was the harmless gun I'd given him back. That was my big mistake. Detectives make 'em as well as criminals, you know.

Barran: In fact, the gun that the detective has been looking for has been in the detective's pocket all the time.

Vandeleur: But what about the harmless gun, with the blanks?

Silence: Once Sloane had been searched, he was free like the rest of you to go in and out of the studio as he liked. When you've searched a person and found one gun, you don't go on looking to find a second. *I* didn't. Sloane had a dozen opportunities to dispose of that second gun later. Perhaps he'll tell us where it is?

Jennifer: George, don't say anything! Don't let them trap you into saying anything! I know you didn't do it! So do you; don't you, Elliott?

Vandeleur (*rallying*): It's ... it's just a bit too ingenious, if you ask me.

Silence: Ingenious? It's the oldest trick in the world.

Caird: What do you mean?

Silence: Ever see a conjuror? He draws your attention to one hand, and does his really dirty work with the other. In this case, it was the harmless pistol in the left hand that got all the attention.

Barran (*honestly horrified*): My God, and I gave him the opportunity!

Helen: You couldn't possibly have known.

Jennifer: He didn't do it, I tell you! He didn't do it!

Sloane (*flatly*): It's no good, Jenny.

Vandeleur (*hurriedly*): If you're wise, you'll admit nothing.

Sloane: I'm not ashamed of it. I'd do it again. I told Mr Barran that if I see a thing's got to be done, I do it. Well, this had to be done. I'd been waiting for an opportunity to do it for weeks.

Jennifer: Then you knew about ...?

Sloane (*almost sneering*): Do you think anybody in your family didn't know about it? Lanyon Kelsey wasn't fit to live. He was a brute and, a blackmailer, and he was ruining your life. If I hadn't stopped him, who would have? Tell me that!

Barran: Steady on, George. What I want to know is, why did you have to cosh me on the back of the head?

Sloane (*whirling round*): I wasn't after you. I was after that gun in Silence's pocket.

Silence: That's it. If he could have got rid of that gun while I still thought it was loaded with blanks, he'd have been safe.

Sloane: Well, Mr Barran, you owe me one, at any rate, for that cosh on the head.

Barran (*thoughtfully*): I think I owe you more than that.

Helen: Tony! Wait!

Jennifer: You're not going to turn him over to the police?

Caird: I don't like it any better than you. But what else can we do?

Jennifer: You might at any rate give him a sporting chance. George, get out of here! Run for it! They can't stop you!

Silence: Here, wait a minute!

Jennifer: You've got no authority to stop him, and you know it.

Silence: I'm between him and the door at this moment. It's up to you,

Mr Caird. It's your responsibility.

Caird: God knows I don't want to hand him over.

The studio lights go out.

Cheston: Hullo! Here we are again.

Helen: You mean, here they are again.

Jennifer (*screaming*): Run, George! For God's sake get out!

Barran: Jerry's done the decent thing for once.

Caird: What are you talking about? Silence! Can you see him?

Jennifer: Mr Silence, please!

Silence (*deliberately*): I can't see a thing. I can't even see the door. (*Long pause*) And now, if everybody's agreeable, I'd like a cigarette. Mr Barran! Would you mind putting those lights on again?

The lights go up. Barran has his hand on the light-switch. Sloane has disappeared.

Jennifer: He's gone. Thank God!

Helen (*under her breath*): Well done, Tony.

Barran (*drawing his hand back innocently*): Me?

Caird: Come on, Tony. We're not all born fools. Why did you put out those lights?

Barran: Didn't you tell me to?

Silence: Who told you to?

Barran (*hesitantly*): I know you told me to do something with 'em.

Silence: I told you to keep an eye on 'em.

Barran: You get so confused after a knock on the head. Still, he's got away, hasn't he? Too bad! I said I owed him one for that cosh on the head.

Helen: I think you've paid him, Tony.

Barran: I hope so.

Jennifer: Do you think he's got any chance to get clear away, Elliott?

Vandeleur: With any luck, my dear, in times like these, I think he might.

Jennifer: What do you think, Mr Silence?

Silence: I have no opinion, madam. I only hope you realize that we're all accessories after the fact. In all my professional career, I never met a bigger bunch of crooks.

Jennifer: What does that matter, so long as he really gets clear?

Cheston: I'm not sure, I sincerely hope this won't be on my conscience when I read the eight o'clock news.

Croker opens the door, puts his head in, and gives a long, sinister hiss.

Helen: What is it?
Barran: You haven't seen —
Vandeleur: You haven't stopped —
Croker: I just came down to tell you as it's All Clear.
    He turns back to the door.
    A-a-all Clear

CURTAIN

AFTERWORD

With its central problem of a seemingly impossible shooting, *Inspector Silence Takes the Air* recalls Carr's *The Third Bullet* (1937), although the details of the mystery are entirely different. The Kovar Case, the "real-life crime" that formed the basis of the episode of *Murderers' Row* that Silence was to have presented has some similarities with Carr's short story "A Guest in the House" (1940) as well as the novel *The Gilded Man* (1942), as by "Carter Dickson."

The licensing authority required two cuts[1]: the word "bloody," uttered by Antony Barran while speaking to George Sloane towards the end of Act I, which had to be replaced by "damn"; and the word "body," uttered by Jennifer Sloane in her conversation with Elliott Vandeleur in the middle of Act II. We have used the original text and hope we have not given offence.

---

[1] "Reader's Report", 6 April 1942. British Library: *Lord Chamberlain's Plays, Manuscripts Collection, Folder No. 4318.*

Thirteen to the Gallows

A Play in Three Acts

by

John Dickson Carr
and
Val Gielgud

Thirteen to the Gallows

The Characters

Dorothy West	Programme Engineer
Jill Whitehead	Junior Programme Engineer
Carol Mayne	Who carries a notebook and scripts
Jonas Whitehead	Who plays a flute
Penelope Squire	Who recites poetry
Sandoz	Who has sea-lions
Major John Burnside, MC[1]	BBC Station Director
Wallace Hatfield	Tried for murder 4 years ago
Paul Phillimore	A teacher
Judith Phillimore	His wife
Tony Barran	BBC Producer
Leila Ponsonby	BBC Announcer
Colonel Sir Henry Bryce	Former head of the Indian Police

ACT I

The scene is laid in the basement of a school building on the outskirts of a provincial town in the Midlands which has been adapted for use by the BBC as a war-time emergency studio. It is the morning of a winter day in 1944.[2]

---

[1]The Military Cross, a British military decoration awarded to recognise acts of bravery during combat operations on land.

[2] The date given in two places in the original script is 1942 but, as Roland Lacourbe has noted in his enjoyable and handsomely illustrated overview of Carr's work *John Dickson Carr: Scribe du Miracle* (Amiens:

It is a large bare room with stone walls and a vaulted ceiling. Set at an angle and taking up perhaps a quarter of the right-hand side of the stage is a studio Listening Room, fitted with gramophone bank, loudspeaker and mixing unit. The main door to the studio with its red, green and white lights above it, is backstage left. To the right of the door, set against the wall, is the usual studio couch and there is a second one downstage left.

When the curtain rises, two girls wearing zip-fastened trousers, pullovers and harassed expressions are battling with a stop-ladder and the final hanging of the last section of grey drapes which swathe the stone walls. The couch down left has been pushed away from the wall and the ladder is set up where the couch is usually situated. Right in the middle of the studio is a stand microphone (movable) and there is a loudspeaker set against the glass front of the Listening Room, above the mixing unit. Jill Whitehead, the Junior Programme Engineer — a girl about sixteen, in all respects rather like the nicer kind of Skye-terrier puppy — is balanced precariously on top of the ladder hammering nails. Holding the ladder is Programme Engineer Dorothy West, a plump and rather consequential young woman who knows her job and has no sense of humour. Between the ladder and the microphone is standing Carol Mayne, an attractive girl of about twenty-seven carrying a stenographer's notebook and a bunch of scripts.

Sitting on the couch, back, as far away from each other as possible, are Jonas Whitehead, an old gentleman of seventy-three with a long white beard and shiny black trousers, fingering a flute nervously, and Penelope Squire, an extremely pretty and unbelievably dumb blonde of twenty-two wearing a fur coat. She is clasping a script to her bosom and mouthing words soundlessly as she gazes blankly before her.

Encrage Editions, 1995) that date would undermine the chronology of the events of the play because it is stated that the first death took place in 1940. The date of "1942" is therefore assumed to have been a typing error, in both places.

Whenever the hammering stops, Jonas Whitehead produces a few notes from his flute. At intervals from outside come the distant machine-gun like effect of a couple of pneumatic drills in full blast.

Jill hammers her thumb and drops the hammer, narrowly missing Dorothy's head.

Jill: Ow!

Dorothy: Mind what you're doing!

Whitehead plays several notes of "My Bonnie Lies Over the Ocean."

Carol (*turning to Whitehead*): Mr Whitehead, please — we aren't re-hearsing yet! (*To the girls*) Haven't you two nearly finished? The Major'll be here in a minute.

Jill: The Station Director in person. Wooh-hooh! Give me that damned hammer.

Dorothy (*primly*): You're too young to use that sort of language, Jill.

Jill: The Major would make me use that sort of language at any age!

She comes down the ladder to pick up the hammer, but Carol picks it up first.

Carol: Let *me* do it. (*Pause*) The atmosphere in here is shocking! Can't you engineers do something about it?

Dorothy (*rather primly*): In November 1939 this studio was passed by the Senior Superintendent (Engineering Division) as fit for emergency broadcasting. That covers gear *and* ventilation.

Carol: Oh God!

Dorothy: I've got the memo if you want to see it.

Carol: I'm sure you have. Skip it!

She goes gloomily up the ladder. As she grapples with the draping, Penelope Squire rises from the couch, advances towards the microphone and recites:

Penelope: Last night, ah, yesternight, betwixt her lips and mine.

There fell thy shadow, Cynara,

And I was desolate and sick of an old passion ...

Carol drops the hammer. There is a burst of firing from the two pneumatic drills. Carol waves at Penelope furiously and she goes back to the couch, mouthing soundlessly. Whitehead plays four notes on his flute.

Carol (*screaming*): Please — one thing at a time. (*To the girls*) Now!

All the incidental noises burst out in a cheerful symphony. Enter Major John Burnside, M.C., BBC Local Station Director. He has a brisk military manner, wears a short black coat, striped trousers and soft black hat. He carries an umbrella. He stops just behind the ladder and stands looking up at Miss Mayne's legs with what he imagines to be a genial expression.

Burnside (*shouting*): Well, Miss Mayne, everything all right?

Carol gesticulates madly with her hands. The noise subsides.

Carol: I beg your pardon, Major Burnside?

Burnside (*still shouting*): I asked you if everything — (*normal*) Oh, I beg your pardon. I asked if everything was all right. You don't seem to be quite ready.

Dorothy: The memorandum requesting that this studio be made available for use specified eleven o'clock. It is now (*looking at her watch*) ten fifty.

Burnside: I'm quite aware of that, Miss West. I'm glad you are. Miss Mayne, I should like a few words with you in private.

Penelope rises.

Penelope: Oh, Major Burnside!

Burnside: Hello, Penelope. I didn't think you'd be here as soon as this. I'll talk to you later. Your father all right?

Burnside enters Listening Room, followed by Carol. Listening Room door closes.

Jill: Wooh-hooh!

Dorothy: That'll do, Jill. Go down to Control Room and tell them to give me a white light when they're ready for a mike test.

Jill: Right you are.

Exit Jill.

In the Listening Room, Burnside sits in one of the chairs at the mixing unit. Carol stands beside him.

Burnside: Miss Mayne, I'm not sure that I approve of this habit of wearing no stockings when you are on duty.

Carol: I'm sorry, Major Burnside. I'm afraid I don't know any American Bomber pilots.

Burnside: I'm quite aware of the difficulties, Miss Mayne.

Carol: Quite, Major Burnside.

Burnside: Good. Sit down. I understand we're to expect Mr Barran from London to handle this programme.

Carol: Yes, Major Burnside.

Burnside: And a London announcer into the bargain. I must confess I hardly see the necessity. After all, *I* handled programmes from this station in 1926. Very good programmes they were, too!

Carol: Mr Barran has handled over a hundred *In Town Tonight* programmes. I suppose they thought he'd be the right person to handle the first *Out of Town* programme.

Burnside: I suppose Barran's a clever fellow in his way. I find it difficult to be sympathetic with these theatrical young men. All long hair and pullovers! I wonder what my old C.O., Colonel Bryce, would have said about 'em!

Carol (*indignantly*): He hasn't got long hair and I've never seen him in a pullover.

Burnside: What I mean by long hair, Miss Mayne, is what Barran would prefer no doubt to call temperament. We didn't bother with temperament in the Army — not when the Army was the Army!

Carol: I'm afraid he'll have some excuse for temperament when he gets here this morning.

Burnside: What d'you mean by that?

Carol: Major Burnside, Barchester's contribution to the *Out of Town Tonight* programme is three turns.

Burnside: I know that. Well?

Carol: First, an interview with Mr Jonas Whitehead, the only school bell-ringer in the Midlands who plays the flute.

Burnside: Quite so. One of the finest old chaps in this town.

Carol: Second, Miss Penelope Squire. Elected last week as beauty queen of the Barchester Small Arms munition-factory.

Burnside: I hope Barran realises she's a trained elocutionist and that her father's an old friend of mine. I hope he doesn't propose to confine her turn just to an interview.

Carol: Oh, no, Major Burnside. She'll finish her interview by reciting 'Cynara.'

Burnside: Yes, yes, of course. Swinburne.

Carol: Dowson, I think.[3]

---

[3] "Dowson, I think" — The poet Ernest Dowson, whose best-known poem is "Non Sum Qualis Eram Bonae sub Regno Cynarae" with its refrain,

Burnside: Of course — Dowson. And the third?

Carol: That's the trouble.

Burnside: Trouble? Miss Vera Lynn's the best known sentimental singer in England.[4] Miss Lynn was the reason why Barchester got this important place in the *Out of Town* programme. You're not going to tell me ...?

Carol: I'm afraid I am. Vera Lynn's got laryngitis. Her mother rang up half-an-hour ago.

Burnside: Good Gad!

Carol (*looking at her watch*): And Mr Barran's train should be in by now.

Burnside: Do you realize what this means, Miss Mayne? (*Spluttering*) Something will have to be done!

Carol: Don't worry, Major Burnside. Mr Barran will fix up something. He always does.

Burnside: I sincerely hope he will. Oh — before he arrives, there's something personal I want to talk to you about.

Carol: Oh?

Burnside: I believe you know Mr Hatfield, Mr Wallace Hatfield?

Carol: Mr Hatfield?

Burnside (*impatiently*): Yes. The fellow who built this school and rigged up this studio.

Carol: Well?

Burnside: You do know him?

Carol (*defiantly*): I know him rather well.

Burnside: Miss Mayne, speaking not as your chief, but in the friendliest possible spirit; do you think it's quite wise for you to associate with Mr Hatfield?

Carol: *Quite* wise.

A white light flashes over the door. Dorothy West, who has been

---

"I have been faithful to thee, Cynara, in my fashion." The other poems quoted in the play are Byron's "Childe Harold's Pilgrimage" (1812-1818) and Wilde's "The Ballad of Reading Gaol" (1898).

[4] Known as "the forces' sweetheart" for her wartime broadcasts and visits to troops at the front line, Dame Vera Lynn was, in her day, the most popular female entertainer in Britain.

standing by the microphone, springs to life.

Dorothy: 1, 2, 3, 4. 1, 2, 3, 4. Stand microphone, Emergency Studio B.X. O.K?

The white light flashes in reply.

Burnside: You're not a native of Barchester, Miss Mayne. Do you know who Mr Hatfield is?

Carol: Please go on.

Burnside: Don't make this embarrassing for me, Miss Mayne. I believe in fair play —

Dorothy West walks briskly into the Listening Room, goes to the gramophone bank and puts on a record of "The Teddy Bears' Picnic," switching on the loudspeaker in the Listening Room so that this can be heard. After a few bars of the record, she leans across Burnside to the microphone on the mixing unit, presses down the switch and speaks into it:

Dorothy: Gram. Bank, turntable number one, Listening Room, Emergency Studio B.X. Teddy Bears' Picnic. Teddy Bears' Picnic. O.K?

White light flashes in reply.

(*To Burnside*) Sorry to disturb you, Major Burnside.

She goes back into the studio, leaving the talk-back on.

Burnside (*slowly and with emphasis*): Wallace Hatfield was tried four years ago for the murder of his wife.

Talk-back has been left on, so people in the studio can hear this line. They react appropriately. Hatfield appears in the doorway and hears it through the loudspeaker. Carol sees him through the glass wall of the Listening Room.

Carol (*hard*): And acquitted of that charge, Major Burnside.

Jonas Whitehead shakes hands with Hatfield. Penelope Squire walks to the couch against wall left and sits at its furthest end.

Burnside: So you do know the whole story?

Carol: Certainly. He's told me all about it.

Burnside: That's to his credit, Miss Mayne. The thing is not only to avoid evil, but the appearance of evil. It does you no good to associate publicly with a man like Hatfield. I'm speaking entirely in your own interests — and as a man old enough to be your father.

Carol: Then what do you advise me to do?

Burnside: I advise you to stop seeing him. That's straight enough, isn't it?

Carol: Even if he happens to be innocent?

Burnside: Even if he happens to be innocent.

Carol: What you're saying is exactly what the whole town's saying and has said for the last four years! Do you think that's fair?.

Burnside: It's the way of a wicked world, Miss Mayne. I can't help it and neither can you. I only wish my old C.O., Colonel Bryce, had been here. He'd have solved the problem in jig-time.

Carol (*stubbornly*): I like Mr Hatfield and I'm sorry for him.

Burnside: Miss Mayne, listen to me. Another woman was sorry for Hatfield, the wife of the principal of this school. Her name was associated with his at the time of the trial. You've seen how people treat her since. Just think that over.

In the studio, Penelope Squire and Hatfield have exchanged glances of obvious mutual embarrassment.

Carol: Major Burnside, I'm afraid this conversation hasn't been as private as we wanted it to be. (*She leans forward and clicks back the talk-back.*) And by the way, Mr Hatfield is also in the studio if you would like to say anything to him about it. I think *I've* had enough!

Carol goes out of the Listening Room and straight up to Hatfield, who stands staring at her with a sort of bewildered pathos.

Carol (*shakily*): Good morning, Mr Hatfield. I wasn't expecting you.

Hatfield: Good morning. I wanted to see Major Burnside — on business.

Carol: He's just here.

Hatfield: I know.

There is an awkward pause. Burnside emerges from the Listening Room.

Carol (*hurriedly*): Miss Squire, Mr Whitehead. Mr Barran hasn't arrived yet. There are one or two things about the scripts I'd like to go over with you — if you'll come with me ...

She shepherds them hastily out of the studio, leaving Hatfield and Burnside facing one another.

Burnside: Look here, Hatfield, I'm sorry about this!

Hatfield (*looking after Carol*): You notice she didn't shake hands with me?

Burnside: That's what comes of having half-trained girls as engineers! Left the switch turned over! (*To Hatfield*) What do you mean? Why *should* she shake hands with you?

Hatfield (*quietly*): You notice it when people don't, that's all.

Burnside: Anyway, I'm sorry. Can we leave it at that?

Hatfield: Yes, I'd like to leave it at that.

Burnside: Good. I'm sorry to have dragged you down here this morning, but they only let me know yesterday afternoon from London that they wanted the studio reopened for a broadcast tonight, and I couldn't get you on the phone.

Hatfield: To tell you the truth, Major Burnside, I was glad to be dragged down here.

Burnside: Really?

Hatfield: Seeing human beings again, talking to human beings — it's very pleasant. Never mind that. What do you want?

Burnside: Merely business, I'm afraid.

Hatfield: I'm grateful for business, these days, Major Burnside. Tell me, what can I do for you?

Burnside: You remember we gave you the contract to make this place suitable for an emergency studio in the first month of this war when the school children were evacuated?

Hatfield: Didn't I do a good job?

Burnside: We haven't had to use the studio before this. We made certain tests last night and there are two things ...

Hatfield: I suppose you were *glad* not to use the studio.

Burnside: Why?

Hatfield: Well, considering what happened ...

Burnside: I thought you wanted us to leave that?

Hatfield: I *can't* leave it. How can I? You *were* glad not to use the studio, weren't you?

Burnside: Quite frankly, I don't think I thought about it very much. Can we stick to the business point at issue?

Hatfield: Yes, of course. I forgot. The complaint you were making ...?

Burnside: It's not a complaint, Hatfield. I want to be perfectly fair. The work had to be done in a great hurry and under great difficulties.

Hatfield: Major Burnside, it was while I was working on this studio here that somebody killed my wife.

Burnside: You mean, Hatfield, that the tragedy of your wife's death occurred?

Hatfield: Yes. No, that's *not* what I mean! That's not what I mean at all!

Burnside: I was speaking of our tests.

Hatfield: Yes, yes, of course.

Burnside: We're not happy about the ventilation. Of course, I'm used to an open-air life. Did a lot of shooting in my younger days, polo and so forth — But I'm sure, Hatfield, you'll agree that it's rather uncomfortably stuffy.

Hatfield (*nervously*): If you want anything done, I'll be very happy to do it myself. I haven't the staff that I had. They've all been called up. They've left me. Yes, they've left me. So you understand that any work I do, if you can give me any work, I shall have to do with my own hands. What else was it you said you wanted?

Burnside: When I arrived this morning, I couldn't help hearing the appalling noise that those pneumatic drills ...

Hatfield (*bursting out*): For God's sake, don't take my last job from me!

Burnside (*staggered*): I beg your pardon?

Hatfield: I shouldn't have said that! I didn't mean it! The Town Council have given me an order for four new air-raid shelters. They supplied the men. They chose the location for the shelters. I can't help the pneumatic drills. You must apply to the Council.

Burnside: I understand that, of course. But after all, the studio *was* handed over to us as a sound-proof concern. Damn it, Hatfield, when I came here this morning they sounded as if they were in the next room, not in the next street!

Hatfield: There can be no sound-proofing against a pneumatic drill that goes through steel with eighty pounds pressure to the square inch. Those drills won't be working when any broadcast is being done.

Burnside: Well, perhaps you'd have a word with the Town Clerk?

Hatfield: If you like, Major Burnside.

Burnside: And now, my dear Hatfield, may I speak to you for a moment as man to man?

Hatfield: By all means.

Burnside: I don't feel happy about your having overheard my unfortunately frank remarks when I was in the Listening Room.

Hatfield: I wonder if you can guess, Major, how pleasant it is to have it said in front of you, rather than behind your back?

Burnside: Anyway, I should like to give you a piece of advice.

Hatfield: Yes?

Burnside: Either reconcile yourself to the situation.

Hatfield: How?

Burnside: Ignore the rather natural prejudices of conventionally minded people ...

Hatfield: Or?

Burnside: Leave this place and go away. Make a new life for yourself, somewhere else.

Hatfield: What new life? Where? How? Why? Where is a man to go — except to the devil!

Burnside: There are other places besides Barchester. There are other professions besides building.

Hatfield: Nowadays — in wartime — without money ... Oh, let's not talk about money! When you're haunted ... when you've got a thing hanging round your — better not mention hanging! No, I don't want to seem too upset about the things! Just stand in the dock for murder! *You* won't forget it, Major!

Burnside (*stubbornly*): And that's not all. I think you should leave Miss Mayne alone.

Hatfield: When you say "leave her alone" what do you mean?

Burnside: Exactly what I say. I'm making no insinuations.

Hatfield: I'm glad.

Burnside: Miss Mayne is a young and comparatively inexperienced girl. She has an affectionate nature. I think you're exploiting it.

Hatfield: Exploiting an affectionate nature by taking sympathy — one person's sympathy! Or doesn't the almost-murderer dare take sympathy from anybody? May I ask you a question, Major Burnside?

Burnside: Certainly.

Hatfield: Before God, do you believe I killed my wife? I ask you again; before God, do you believe I killed my wife?

Burnside (*uncomfortably*): I can't answer that question. You were legally acquitted by the judgment of your peers. I accept that verdict. As a citizen, I'm bound to do so. But you must realise, Hatfield, that certain appearances were against you and remain against you.

Hatfield: Can you talk of appearances when the jury acquitted me?

Burnside: It's not a question of talking! It's a question of feeling. And I feel it's intolerable that Miss Mayne should be put in a false position.

Hatfield: Listen, Major Burnside, I was acquitted of that charge because an admirable lawyer challenged the prosecution to prove that any crime had been committed. Do you remember what happened?

Burnside: Very well. The prosecution couldn't prove it.

Hatfield: They found my wife's body outside this building. Her head was crushed. She had fallen from the belfry — seventy or eighty feet.

Burnside (*uneasily*): Does this really do any good?

Hatfield: She was lying on the flagstones outside there when I found her. I was in the building — the only other person in the building.

Burnside: I know.

Hatfield: So they said I threw her out of the belfry. Pushed her out! My lawyer — he was very clever. He said to them, "Show us that any crime has been committed. Show us that it was not an accident. The ledge up there — the railing round the belfry — it's very low. Show us that any crime has been committed." And he got away with it. The jury said it was an accident.

Burnside: What are you getting at?

Hatfield: It was not an accident. She didn't fall. Somebody threw her. It was murder. It was murder! But I didn't do it, Major Burnside! Sooner or later I'm going to *show* I didn't do it! That's all I wanted to say.

Re-enter Carol.

Burnside: Yes, Miss Mayne?

Carol: You're wanted on the telephone in your office, Major Burnside. London. The deputy Director-General would like to speak to you as soon as possible.

Burnside: Thank you.

He looks uneasily at Carol and Hatfield and exits.

Carol: Has he been beastly to you?

Hatfield: Not at all. No, not at all. We were just talking.

Carol: Advising you to give up the pleasure of my society — trying a little gentlemanly blackmail?

Hatfield: Just advising me not to brood.

Carol: That was good advice. *I've* done that.

Hatfield: Yes, but you didn't talk like Major Burnside.

Carol: I can't. I was never in the Army when it *was* the Army.

Hatfield (*laughs*): Yes, yes! It does me good to laugh, Miss Mayne. I haven't had that pleasure for a long time.

Carol: Now don't be pompous! "Miss Mayne," indeed!

Hatfield: All right. I suppose I am allowed to call you by your Christian name?

Carol (*laughing*): If you do anything else, I'm liable to spit in your eye! What brought you down this morning, anyway?

Hatfield (*simply*): I wanted to see you. Now that I'm here, I've got a job of work to do.

Carol: What?

Hatfield: The ventilation's wrong. Apparently my work wasn't right —

Carol: I've got to spend the rest of the day in here with Tony Barran. A little fresh air *would* be a help.

Hatfield: Tony Barran? Isn't that the man you worked for in London?

Carol: Yes.

Hatfield: But he produces *In Town Tonight.* What's he doing down here?

Carol: He's coming down here to produce *Out of Town Tonight.* It's *In Town Tonight* split up between three separate towns in Great Britain — Edinburgh, Birmingham, and Barchester. We've got three items from here and Tony Barran's looking after them.

Hatfield: I've imagined from just a few things you've let drop that you're rather interested in this fellow Barran.

Carol: You don't know much about women, do you? What you should have said was "Barran's rather interested in you" — it would have been more polite.

Hatfield: All right, I will say it. Is he?

Carol: He *was.*

Hatfield: Not any longer?

Carol: I don't much want to talk about it.

Hatfield: He's a *young* man, isn't he?

Carol: *Too* young! He's so young that he thinks it's paying a girl a compliment to imagine that if she goes out with him to dinner she expects him to kiss her in a taxi — and I hate being mauled.

Hatfield: I guessed that. Had you noticed?

Carol: No.

Hatfield: When's Barran getting here?

Carol: He ought to be here any minute.

Hatfield: I — I met him once, you know.

Carol: Oh? Where?

Hatfield: In London. Do you know what he said to me?

Carol: No idea.

> *Studio door is flung open and Tony Barran bursts in. He is a tall, lean young man, vital, and with a good deal of charm. He is wearing an overcoat of rather loud checks, no hat, a tweed jacket and grey flannel trousers. He stares hard at Carol and Hatfield, who are*

standing rather close together.

Barran: Hello, Hatfield, come to re-visit the scene of the crime?

Embarrassing silence.

Good morning, Carol. The bad penny is once more in circulation. I hope you've been doing all the essential preliminaries for me, as a good secretary should?

Carol (*coldly*): You're late.

Barran: You don't sound as sorry as you should. Well, I don't want to interrupt what appears to be a very agreeable social occasion, but I'm afraid, Hatfield, old man, that we've got some work to do.

Hatfield: I was just going. You won't mind if I come down later on to see to something for Major Burnside?

Barran: For Burnside?

Hatfield: Yes. Carol will explain.

Barran (*coldly*): Carol?

Hatfield: Er — Miss Mayne will explain. I must get along now. I've some work to do on those air-raid shelters. I'll try to keep in mind what you were saying C ... Miss Mayne, and don't worry. I don't think I shall be brooding so much, now.

Exit Hatfield.

Barran takes off his overcoat and heaves it on to the nearest sofa. He goes up to Carol.

Barran (*aggressively*): Look here, Carol, what are you playing at?

Carol: I thought you said we had *work* to do.

Barran: We have. I'm already half-an-hour late. I propose to *be* thirty-six and a half minutes late! I've wanted a little talk with you for quite a time. Why didn't you answer my letters?

Carol: Why did you write the letters?

Barran: Because I'm fool enough to be in love with you. (*Gently*) I *am* in love with you, you know.

Carol: Then that's good enough excuse for not answering them.

Barran: It doesn't make sense to me.

Carol: It probably wouldn't. It *does* make sense to me. It did and it does.

Barran: All right, pass that up! What's going on between you and this fellow Hatfield?

Carol: Wallace Hatfield is an unhappy man. He's the unhappiest man I've ever met.

Barran: "A ministering angel, thou!" My God!

Carol: He's been hurt more than anyone has a right to be hurt.

Barran: My dear Carol! Wallace Hatfield is the luckiest man in England.

Carol: Why?

Barran: If he wasn't, he would have been hanged by the neck four years ago!

Carol: Why do you dislike him?

Barran: I have an old-fashioned prejudice against murder.

Carol: It seems almost asking too much of you to ask whether you have heard that he was acquitted.

Barran: I know he was acquitted. You're being very sorry for Wallace Hatfield. Well, I'm being very sorry for someone else.

Carol: Who?

Barran: His wife. She was a nice woman and Wallace Hatfield is not a nice man.

Carol: Have you ever asked yourself — suppose he didn't kill her? Suppose ...

Barran: Let it go! Four years is a long time. The case is finished. *You* see Hatfield walking about brooding, to use his own word, looking rather like the Wandering Jew! Just get rid of the sentimental froth, will you? Wallace Hatfield treated his wife badly.

Carol: That's not true.

Barran: I think it is true. What about the school-master's wife?

Carol: You mean that silly scandal about poor Mrs Phillimore?

Barran: Just that.

Carol: I asked Wallace Hatfield whether he knew anything about women. Apparently you know even less.

Barran: Perhaps that's why I'm in love with you. And perhaps that's why I really dislike Wallace Hatfield.

Carol: So you've guessed it finally, Tony Barran. Suppose he proved to you that he isn't guilty! Suppose he proved it to everybody in the world!

Barran (*casually*): I couldn't care less, but it *would* make a rather good broadcast. And talking of broadcasting, we've had our six minutes. Come on, my girl, work!

Carol: Where do we begin?

Barran: Is the studio tested?

Carol: More or less.

Barran: The usual feminine substitutes for engineers?

Carol: Yes

Barran: Our darling little fat friend who knows all the answers, Dorothy West?

Carol: She's here, giving information as usual.

Barran: I feared as much. Tell me more.

Carol: Major Burnside ...

Barran: No, don't tell me. I know. Burnside has been here talking about his old C.O. Colonel Sir Henry Bryce.

Carol: Perfectly right.

Barran: I wish I could meet his old C.O., Colonel Sir Henry Bryce. I'd like to tell him precisely what I think about him and his favourite subaltern Lieut. Burnside and his exploit when he rounded up the jewel thieves in Seringapatam in the Dark Ages.

Carol: It's all very well to be funny about him Tony, but Sir Henry Bryce had the biggest sort of reputation when he was head of the Indian Police.

Barran: We're not in India tonight — we're Out of Town Tonight — let's get back to it.

Carol: I've got some bad news for you, Mr Barran. I'm rather pleased to give it to you.

Barran: I'll be pleased to hear it, Miss Mayne.

Carol: We have two turns tonight.

Barran: We have three turns tonight, Miss Mayne, unless you or your beloved Major have gone stark, staring mad! Three turns from Barchester in the *Out of Town Tonight* programme.

Carol: *Two* turns from Barchester in the *Out of Town Tonight* programme. That's the bad news.

Barran (*coldly*): Continue.

Carol: We have Penelope Squire.

Barran: I know, and she's not so hot. Still, the youngest munition factory beauty queen in England reciting a poem of passion ought to please some of our more sophisticated listeners! Don't say that Jonas Whitehead has broke his neck, or his flute?

Carol: No. Vera Lynn's got laryngitis

Barran: What?

Carol: Vera Lynn's got laryngitis. She can't sing tonight.

Barran (*dangerously*): And what have *you* done about that?

Carol: I haven't done anything about it, Tony. What could I do? We've got two possible substitutes.

Barran: Let me know the worst.

Carol: It's a choice between a sea-lion imitator and a detective-inspector.

Barran: Between *what?*

Carol: A sea-lion imitator and a detective-inspector.

Barran: My dear girl! When you were last in London and we went out together, I discovered that Barchester had made you provincial; but I didn't know that living in Barchester had affected your mind!

Carol: Don't you worry about my mind! You must have seen Sandoz?

Barran: Sandoz?

Carol (*patiently*): Sandoz of Sandoz and his Sea-Lions. The music-hall turn.

Barran: Are you proposing to let a lot of sea-lions loose in the studio? Do you forget there's a war on? What do they eat — sardines or spam?

Carol: But we don't have to give them a meal here.

Barran: We don't have to have them here and we're not *going* to have them here! What's the other bright idea?

Carol: The other idea, bright or not, is ex-Detective-Inspector Harvey, formerly of the C.I.D.

Barran: The man who took the Surbiton murderer? But he was quite a big noise. D'you mean to say he lives here?

Carol: Well, he moved here six months ago. Retired or something.

Barran (*slowly*): That sounds more hopeful.

Carol: I suppose he must have had some experiences at Scotland Yard he could talk about.

Barran: I believe you may have hit something, at that. Have you spoken to him?

Carol: I haven't met him. But I can get in touch with him.

Barran: Well get! And get quick!

Carol: What shall I ask him to do?

Barran: I'll see about that. But get him here.

Carol (*sharply*): Tony ...

Barran: Well?

Carol: What were you thinking about just a moment ago?

Barran: Just an idea.

Carol: But what do you want this ex-detective-inspector to do?

Barran: It just crossed my mind that when most people read the name

Barchester they think of a famous unsolved crime.

Carol: Tony Barran, that crime was solved.

Barran: In law, yes. But it might be quite interesting to hear the opinion of a famous ex-detective-inspector on various aspects of the case, don't you think?

Carol: He wouldn't be allowed to talk about it.

Barran: Why not?

Carol: The case is closed.

Barran: I am not asking him to reopen it.

Carol: Do you hate a certain person as much as that?

Barran: *He* doesn't seem to mind talking about it.

Carol: He might mind a good deal if he heard it discussed over that microphone.

Barran: Of course I'd ask him first.

Carol: And you think he'd give permission?

Barran (*gloomily*): I don't suppose so. Gosh! If only I thought he would! (*with growing excitement*) If only he'd agree to be interviewed! Wallace Hatfield interviewed by ex-Detective-Inspector Harvey of Scotland Yard about the Barchester case. Scoop! The Drama boys will be green with envy. I wonder what linking music would be suitable?

Carol: Are you absolutely out of your mind?

Barran: I wonder what records Fatty's got on tap — Danse Macabre, Valse Triste — couldn't use Wagner in war-time ...

Carol: This isn't a show, Tony. This man's alive! What are you thinking of?

Barran: This *is* a show, Carol, and in case you're forgetting it's due on the air precisely eight hours from now! We need a turn and we need a good turn.

Carol: If this weren't so impossible, I'd think you meant it.

Barran: I mean every word of it. You go and get Harvey on the phone. Ask him to lunch with me.

Carol: I won't do it.

Barran: Now don't be an ass!

Carol: I'm sorry. I'll get him on the phone. But you aren't to mention the case! Wallace Hatfield's been humiliated enough without suggesting this!

Barran: I don't want to become tiresome and official, my pet, but I am in

charge of this show, in case you're forgetting it. You go and phone
Harvey and ask him to lunch. The rest is my business.

Carol (*flatly*): Very well.

Barran: And tell Dorothy West to come and see me here right now — and
tell her to bring her list of gramophone records with her.

Carol (*angrily*): If I thought you had a chance of getting Wallace Hatfield
to agree to this ...

Barran: I'm not going to think. When you've invited Harvey to lunch,
ring up your damned sea-lion merchant and ask him to have a drink
with me — no, tell him to come here at 2.30 this afternoon, but
without his sea-lions! Now get cracking!

Carol: Do you want Jonas Whitehead and Penelope Squire to rehearse?
They're in the waiting room.

Barran: Yes, I'll see them. Have them in — Penelope Squire first.

Exit Carol.

*Barran goes into the Listening Room and picks up the telephone,
which is on the mixing unit desk.*

Hello, Control Room. Mr Barran here. I want you to get me a call to
London and it's urgent. Get it through for me, will you? I want to
speak to the Variety Director. Variety Director — ever heard of him?
I shall be here for the next half-hour rehearsing.

*He rings off with a slam. He goes out of the Listening Room and
meets Dorothy West and Penelope Squire coming in.*

Oh, good morning Miss Squire. I shall be ready for you in two
minutes. Sit down, won't you.

She does so.

Now, Dorothy — got your list of records?

Dorothy: Of course, Mr Barran. (*Produces typewritten list*) "L'Apres-
midi d'un faun," "In a Monastery Garden," "Selection of British Sea
Shanties," "Waltz Medley — Strauss," "Selection of Regimental
Marches," "Yeomen of the Guard Overture," "Teddy Bears' Picnic" ...

Barran (*snatching list*): A perfect reservoir of originality! I was looking for
something faintly sinister — something with gooseflesh in it!

Dorothy (*seriously*): I think there's a "Mother Goose Suite."

Barran: What about the "Pavane for a Dead Infanta?" I want to make
flesh creep and hair stand on end!

*He suits his actions to his words. Penelope Squire looks on
nervously.*

Dorothy: It isn't on my list. We've got the "Danse Macabre" — but it's cracked.

Barran: It would be. Well, let it go! You know what I want. Dig me out anything you think might be suitable, will you?

Dorothy: Mr Barran ...

Barran: Well?

Dorothy: Has Major Burnside told you about the pneumatic drills?

Barran: Pneumatic drills?

Dorothy: They're putting up four air-raid shelters in the next street and they're using pneumatic drills.

Barran: Well, what do you expect me to do about it?

Dorothy: They make a certain amount of difference to the studio, Mr Barran.

Barran: Why?

Dorothy (*quoting*): A pneumatic drill of average size can be relied upon to drill in a mild steel plate one inch in diameter holes at the rate of one inch to one and one-half inches deep per minute, and larger or smaller holes in proportion, the air consumption varying from thirty cubic feet in the average drills to fifty or sixty in the larger tools. Usual air pressure: eighty pounds per square inch. The jet of compressed air is forced with great violence through a pipe ...

Barran: For God's sake why should I care?

Drills starts outside.

For love of Abraham, Isaac and Jacob, what's that?

Dorothy: That, Mr Barran, is one pneumatic drill in operation.

Exit Dorothy.

Barran (*recovering himself with difficulty*): Well, well; what a day we're having! Now, Miss Squire, go up to the microphone, will you? I see you have a script. Dowson's "Cynara" isn't it?

Penelope (*rather nervously*): Yes, Mr Barran.

She goes towards him, displaying considerable agitation.

Is it going to be very awful?

Barran: Well, it isn't as bad as going to the dentist, if you know what I mean.

Penelope: If you're going to give me gooseflesh, I'd rather not.

Barran: My dear Miss Squire just forget that I'm a BBC producer. It's difficult, I know, but try and think of me as a human being. You've probably heard funny stories about BBC producers. People think we're either mad or bad — principally mad. As a matter of fact, we're perfectly ordinary people. You hear a lot about producers' temperaments. Well, just look at me. I know I'm not good looking, but just look at me for one minute. Now I'm completely without temperament. Completely! Let's get that perfectly clear. I'm more like, shall we say, a doctor with a bedside manner. I'm just here to be helpful, just to tell you where to stand and how to speak. That's all there is to it.

Penelope: Yes, Mr Barran. But why do you want to give me gooseflesh?

Barran: Gooseflesh?

Penelope: You said gooseflesh.

Barran: That's another part of the script, Miss Squire. Don't bother your head about gooseflesh. Keep your mind on Dowson.

Penelope (*bewildered*): Who's he?

Barran (*patiently*): He's the author of "Cynara"; the man who wrote the poem you're going to recite. Now you talk into this microphone here; I'll just go into the Listening Room.

Penelope squares up to the microphone rattling her script with shaking fingers. Barran goes into the Listening Room.

(*over talk-back*) Miss Squire, in the old days of Savoy Hill,[5] we used to have a notice in the studio: "If you cough or rattle your script you will deafen thousands of people." At the moment, you're deafening *me*. You're rattling your script, Miss Squire! Hold it still!

Penelope: Yes, Mr Barran. Is this right?

Barran: Now don't shout. Think of one person.

Penelope: Ernest Dowson?

Barran: Not Ernest Dowson. Think of your aged mother sitting by the fireside. Recite it to *her*!

Penelope: But I thought I was broadcasting to thousands and thousands of people.

Barran: You are. Forget it. Think of your aged mother with her silver hair.

Penelope: My mother was only forty-six last birthday.

Barran: Forget it. Think of her aged seventy-six, sitting by her fireside

---

[5] The BBC occupied the Savoy Hill studios between 1923 and 1932, when it moved to what is now its international headquarters building, Broadcasting House.

with a cat on her knee.

Penelope: My mother doesn't like cats.

Barran: All right. A boa constrictor on her knee! Her puppy, her boy friend — let's get started!

Penelope (*wretchedly*): All right, Mr Barran. Am I in the proper position?

Barran: Yes, so long as you don't breathe heavily. Now take it easy.

Penelope (*raising the roof*): Last night, ah, yesternight, betwixt her lips ...

Barran: Oi!

Penelope: That's what it says in the poem, Mr Barran.

Barran: I'm aware of what it says in the poem, Miss Squire. Gently! Quiet! A microphone exaggerates, Miss Squire! Will you kindly forget that you were ever taught elocution, Miss Squire?

Penelope: You don't want me to say it at all?

Barran (*as if to a child*): I want you to say it gently and with feeling. Try again.

Penelope (*whispering*): Last night, ah yesternight, twixt her lips and mine ...

Barran emerges like a tornado from the Listening Room.

Barran: Miss Squire, listen — I've practically got no time in which to rehearse you! Between now and the broadcast I've got to find a completely new turn — and probably train a couple of sea-lions! All I want you to do is to stand up in front of this microphone and recite Ernest Dowson's "Cynara" in a perfectly straightforward, simple and unexaggerated manner. Now, can you do it or can't you.

Penelope: I can, if you don't give me gooseflesh.

Barran: Miss Squire, I told you I was the least temperamental producer that ever lived: I may be giving you gooseflesh, but you're rapidly giving me temperament! Now stand a foot further away — here! Don't speak directly into that infernal machine and think of your ... no, don't think of anything! Just say it — and remember, don't speak directly into the microphone!

He goes back into the Listening Room. Penelope stands with her back to the microphone.

Go ahead.

Penelope: Last night, ah yesternight ...

Barran: For the love of St Michael and all angels, will you address the microphone!

Penelope: You said I wasn't to!

Barran: Not directly, you damned little fool! Speak across it!

He re-emerges from the Listening Room, grabs her by the shoulders and pushes her into roughly the right position.

(*recovering himself a little*) Miss Squire, I'm sorry. Let's start again from the beginning. Do you really like the works of Ernest Dowson?

Penelope: No. He's a favourite of my mother's.

Barran: Let's leave your mother out of it! You know, Miss Squire, Dowson's a very difficult poet to read aloud. Suppose we try something else?

He roams round the studio. On an occasional table are three or four books. He picks up a couple and glances at them.

The Life and Death of Socrates — too morbid. *How to Write Broadcast Plays* [6] — no-one knows! Try this!

He hands her a third volume.

Penelope: Do you want me to read this?

Barran: Yes, go ahead.

Penelope: Starting where?

Barran: There. (*He goes back into the Listening Room.*)

Penelope (*reciting*): He did not wear his scarlet coat, for blood and wine are red.

And blood and wine were on his hands when they found him with the dead.

The poor dead woman whom he loved and murdered ... I can't read that, Mr Barran.

Barran: All right, turn over a couple of pages.

Penelope (*reciting*): We waited for the stroke of eight;

Each tongue was thick with thirst;

For the stroke of eight is the stroke of Fate

That makes a man accursed,

And Fate will use a running noose

For the best man and the worst.

Barran (*quietly*): That's better. That's coming. Go on ...

Penelope: With sudden shock the prison-clock

Smote on the shivering air,

And from all the gaol rose up a wail

---

[6] *How to Write Broadcast Plays* by Val Gielgud. London: Hurst & Blackett, 1932.

Of impotent despair,
Like the sound the frightened marches hear
From some leper in his lair.

Barran: Now you're getting it. Keep it up ...

Re-enter Hatfield. With him is Leila Ponsonby, BBC announcer. She is a smart, sophisticated and self-possessed young woman, in a well-cut suit, with a button-hole, an amusing hat, and a languid expression. She goes to join Barran in the Listening Room. Hatfield stands in the doorway. As she begins the next verse of the poem, Penelope catches sight of him.

Penelope: And as one sees most fearful things
in the crystal of a dream,
We saw the greasy hempen rope
Hooked to the blackened beam.
And heard the prayer the hangman's snare
Strangled into a scream ...

As she gets to the end of the verse she slows down, expresses extreme agitation and bursts into hysterical tears.

Barran: Oh, for God's sake!

He tears out of the Listening Room.

Now, now, pull yourself together! You were doing it very nicely. You got real feeling into it. You were really painting a picture one could see. It was exactly what I wanted.

Penelope twists away from his hands and bolts out of the studio.

Now what have I done? Tell me, someone, what have I done? Could anyone be more reasonable, more helpful, more sympathetic? Hello, Hatfield. You back again?

Hatfield: You haven't done anything, Mr Barran. I'm responsible, as usual.

Barran: I see.

Leila Ponsonby comes out of the Listening Room.

Leila: Tony, I lost my way between here and the hotel. This gentleman was good enough to bring me to the studio.

Barran (*meaningly*): I know. Perhaps I should introduce you. Mr Hatfield here is the News and this is Leila Ponsonby.

Leila: That might be funny if they *let* women announcers read the news.[7]

Barran: And this, Leila, is Mr Hatfield. (*Slowly*) Mr Wallace Hatfield. You will remember Mr Hatfield. He's quite a well-known figure in Barchester.

Leila (*realising*): O-oh! (*She withdraws a step.*)

Hatfield: Was that quite necessary, Mr Barran?

Barran: Perhaps not. I'm sorry.

There is a little pause while they look at each other. Enter Paul Phillimore, the Principal of the school. A thin, cadaverous person with a hearty manner.

Phillimore: May I come in?

Barran (*wearily*): I suppose so.

Phillimore: I fancy I left one of my books in here. You wouldn't happen to have seen it? *The Ballad of Reading Gaol and Other Poems* by Oscar Wilde?

Barran: Would it be this, by any chance?

He picks it off the floor by the microphone where Penelope has dropped it.

Phillimore: I thought I put it down on that table.

Barran: You did.

Phillimore: Do you mean to say that someone ...

Barran: I'm very much afraid I do.

Phillimore: I — er — I rather wanted to speak to Major Burnside.

Barran: You'll find him in his office. He's telephoning to London.

Phillimore: Oh, thank you. Then I'll go down to see him. I have my bicycle.

Exit Phillimore jauntily.

Leila: And who might that odd type be?

Hatfield: That's Mr Paul Phillimore. When this school *was* a school as Major Burnside would say, he was its principal.

Leila: Why isn't it still a school?

Hatfield: The children went away under the evacuation scheme of 1940.

Barran (*impatiently*): That's extremely interesting but what about my rehearsal? What the Hell am I going to do now? Vera Lynn goes

---

[7] Gielgud's knowledge of the BBC let him down as the news was first read by a woman, Sheila Borrett, in 1933.

down with laryngitis! Penelope Squire goes into hysterics!

Hatfield: I'm sorry, Mr Barran. I'll make myself scarce.

Barran: You'll do nothing of the kind. There's something I want to talk to you about. Leila, be a pet and find that Squire girl and give her a cup of tea, or an aspirin, or a bromide, or something, and persuade her I'm not Boris Karloff![8] Get her back here decently and in order before lunch.

Leila: An announcer's lot is not a happy one. Anything for a quiet life.

Exit Leila.

Barran: Now, Mr Hatfield, let's sit down and be comfortable.

They sit down on the couch against the wall down left.

Hatfield: Isn't this a change of attitude for you, Mr Barran?

Barran: I'm speaking strictly in my professional capacity, Mr Hatfield.

Hatfield: Professional capacity?

Barran: Yes. I've had an idea.

Hatfield: About me?

Barran: Indirectly, yes.

Hatfield: I'm never quite sure whether you're joking or whether you're serious.

Barran: I'm extremely serious. You've heard of Detective-Inspector Harvey?

Hatfield: What about him?

Barran: I understand that on his retirement he came to live in Barchester.

Hatfield: Yes, that's true. He lives in Meadow Vale Road.

Barran: You know we're short of one item for our programme tonight.

Hatfield: Oh, I see. And you want Inspector Harvey?

Barran: Exactly. I want Inspector Harvey to come and give his opinion on the most famous unsolved murder mystery of recent years.

Hatfield (*slowly and with meaning*): The murder of Lucy Hatfield. Is that it?

Barran: Yes.

Hatfield: I never thought that help would come from you.

Barran: Help?

Hatfield: The jury, you know, said it was *not* murder. They said it was an

---

[8] Karloff was best known for his performances in some of the most famous horror films of the 1930s. He also appeared as Perceval March in *Colonel March of Scotland Yard* (1952-1955), a television series based on Carr's Colonel March stories.

accident.

Barran: Just a moment, Mr Hatfield. All I want from you is a letter which you will sign, giving your agreement to the inclusion of this item in our programme.

Hatfield: Do you really mean that you need my permission to discuss my case?

Barran: The BBC's policy is to be as considerate and as careful of people's feelings as possible. If you object to the whole idea, I must chuck it up. I've an alternative idea — a Mr Sandoz (*with sarcasm*) who, I believe, imitates sea-lions too marvellously!

Hatfield: I've no objection to make if you'll let me know what Harvey's going to say.

Barran: You can help him say it, if you like.

Hatfield: I can help him write what he's going to say?

Barran: I'll tell you what! We'll do this thing in the form of an interview.

Hatfield: You don't mean have me talk?

Barran: Inspector Harvey shall ask you questions, which you'll answer in front of the microphone.

Hatfield: With everybody listening to me?

Barran: I can't guarantee everybody, Mr Hatfield. You'll probably have an audience of about three million.

Hatfield: Would you let me say what I liked?

Barran: With the usual qualifications, yes.

Hatfield (*wavering*): I don't see —

Barran: Now listen! Harvey's lunching with me. I can talk it over with him. We'll be back here shortly after 2.30. *Be* here at 2.30! Harvey, you and I will work out a script.

Hatfield: Let me understand this. I can say what I like?

Barran: Yes.

Hatfield: Nobody will stop me?

Barran (*amused*): The item is limited to five minutes.

Hatfield: I can say what I like within five minutes?

Barran: Yes, provided you give Harvey his cues and so forth.

Hatfield: If by any chance I catch the real murderer, would you admit you were wrong about me?

Barran: Now, Hatfield ...

Hatfield: That's a fair question. Would you?

Barran: This programme is *Out of Town Tonight,* not *The Armchair*

Detective.[9]

Hatfield: I thought you wanted my story.

Barran: I want your personality over that microphone. I'm not interested in wildcat theories. Let's get that straight.

Hatfield (*thinking aloud*): To speak to three million people. To express what a man feels when he's innocent and can't prove it —

Barran (*interrupting*): Right! Bring me the covering letter when you come back after lunch, will you?

Hatfield (*sarcastically*): The letter clearing you of responsibility for whatever I say?

Barran: You can't clear me of all responsibility. I just want a formal note to the effect that you're quite happy about the general notion of the programme item.

Hatfield: Happy, Mr Barran, is too mild a word. You shall have your letter.

Barran: Many thanks. I'll see you at half past two.

Exit Hatfield.

Barran: By God, what a scoop!

Enter Dorothy West.

Dorothy: Mr Barran ...

Barran: Yes?

Dorothy: I've got precisely the record you want.

Barran: Well? What is it?

Dorothy: H.M.V. record DX 5781 — "The Funeral March of a Marionette."

CURTAIN

---

[9] Properly *For the Armchair Detective*, this popular programme was first broadcast on the BBC in 1942. Introduced by Ernest Dudley, it was an unusual and possibly unique amalgam of reviews and dramatised excerpts. Dudley played himself in the film *The Armchair Detective* (1951), inspired by the series.

ACT II

The scene is the same nearly two hours later. Jonas Whitehead is standing before the microphone making melancholy noises upon his flute. Dorothy West stands not far away with an expression of prim disapproval upon her pouting face. Carol is listening to him over the loudspeaker in the Listening Room. Leila Ponsonby is facing Whitehead across the microphone. Both Leila and Jonas Whitehead have scripts." Jonas has his on a music stand beside him. After some efforts he succeeds in achieving a rather shaky version of "My Bonnie Lies Over the Ocean" and finishes it.

Carol (*over talk-back*): Mr Whitehead!

Whitehead: Eh?

Carol: Mr Whitehead!

Whitehead: Eh?

Carol: Dorothy, would you ask Mr Whitehead if he can play anything else?

Dorothy (*shouting*): Mr Whitehead, can you play anything else?

Whitehead: Yes.

Dorothy (*shouting*): Play it, please, Mr Whitehead.
    Whitehead repeats, with much feeling "My Bonnie Lies Over the Ocean."

Carol: I think that's enough, thank you.

Dorothy: How about balance?

Carol: Good enough.

Leila: And now we'll finish the interview.

Carol: Yes.

Leila (*from script*): And so, Mr Whitehead, you've been bellringer in this school for fifty-three years?
    She gestures towards Whitehead's script. He picks it up and reads without expression.

Whitehead: Yes, I wish to say I have been bellringer in this school for fifty-three years, six months.

Leila: That must be almost unique, Mr Whitehead. You must have met a great many interesting people during those fifty-three years, six

123

months.

Whitehead: During those fifty-three years, six months I have met interesting people, including many of our most distinguished notabilities, seen at a distance.

Carol: Not quite so loud!

Whitehead (*shouting*): For fifty-three years, six ...

Carol: I said not quite so loud.

Dorothy: Not quite so loud, Mr Whitehead.

Whitehead: Thank you, I'm not deaf ... I feel I have had a hand in shaping the youth of this town. I am proud to have rung bells for the youth of this town.

Leila: Is there anything else you would like to say?

Whitehead (*dropping his script*): I wish to say here and now that Mr Wallace Hatfield never done that murder. He never done that murder at all. That's what I wish to say.

Carol: Oi, oi! That's not in your script!

Whitehead: I've known Mr Hatfield twenty-six years, and a pleasanter gentleman I never wished to meet.

Dorothy (*shouting*): Mr Whitehead, you must stick to your script.

Whitehead: No offence meant, ma'am, but you asked me if I wished to say something else and that's all I wished to say, thank you. I'll play my flute again, if you like.

Leila (*hurriedly*): Perhaps you'd better.

Carol (*emerging from Listening Room*): Now it's quite clearly understood, Mr Whitehead, isn't it, that you say nothing whatsoever that isn't in your script?

Whitehead: But, Miss, it makes me mad. They go on against Mr Hatfield though he never done that murder.

Carol: I quite understand your feelings, Mr Whitehead, but you must stick to your script.

Whitehead: What would they do to me if I didn't?

Dorothy (*primly*): Cut you off the air.

Whitehead: Eh?

Leila: I'm afraid it would just spoil the whole broadcast programme, Mr Whitehead.

Whitehead: Then I mustn't do it. No offence intended, I'm sure.

Carol: Then that's all right. We needn't bother you again until the final run-through, Mr Whitehead, say in an hour's time.

Whitehead: Do I go now, Miss?

Carol: Yes.

Whitehead: Thank you very much, I'm sure. (*Exit*)

Leila: Do you think he's reliable? I feel as if I might have kittens any moment.

Carol: You must just smother him if he talks out of turn. One of your cleaner stories might be used at a pinch.

Leila: Thanks for the compliment!

Dorothy (*looking at her watch*): Mr Barran's sixteen and a half minutes late.

Carol: If you ever get married, Dorothy, I shall advise your husband to break every clock in the house or he'll never get any sleep.

Dorothy: Well, I like producers to be punctual.

Leila: You, my girl, are much too good for an imperfect world. Here he is now.

The door opens, but it is Major Burnside beaming all over his face.

Burnside: Ah, Miss Mayne. Mr Barran here?

Carol: We're expecting him any moment.

Burnside: I thought his rehearsal was called for 2.30. It's now ... (*Looks at his watch.*)

Dorothy (*interrupting*): Thirteen minutes to three.

Burnside: I can tell the time, Miss West, thank you very much. Aren't London producers habitually punctual, Miss Mayne?

Carol: I expect Mr Barran has been kept over lunch by Inspector Harvey.

Burnside: Inspector Harvey? Well, he needn't worry about Inspector Harvey. I've solved his little bit of trouble for him.

Carol: Solved it? What do you mean, Major Burnside?

Burnside: Remarkable piece of luck. Who should I run into on my doorstep ... (*Noise of a sea-lion.*) Who should I run into on my doorstep ... (*Noise of a sea-lion.*) For heaven's sake, what's that?

Dorothy: It sounded like a sea-lion, Major Burnside.

Burnside: Don't be flippant, Miss West. I detest flippancy. What do you imagine a sea-lion would be doing in one of my studios?

Noise of sea-lion, nearer.

Carol: My God, Sandoz!

Burnside: I beg your pardon, Miss Mayne?

The door is flung open and Sandoz, of Sandoz and his Sea-lions, appears at the entrance. He is a bald little man with long waxed moustaches, wearing a morning coat and striped trousers and carrying a bowler hat. The morning coat is about six inches too long. His eyes sparkle with vitality. He displays all the gesticulating vigour of a denizen of Central Europe. He is about fifty.

Sandoz: The BBC, yes? Sandoz is here. *Me voila!*

Burnside: Was it you, sir, who was responsible for those extraordinary noises outside?

Sandoz: Extraordinary noises? I understand I am to encourage my sea-lions before the microphone. You have just heard my imitation of the sea-lion how she call when she mate. We make mate, yes? Your troubles would be over.

Burnside: Do I understand that you will bring mating sea-lions before this microphone?

Sandoz: I understand your Mr Barran wish to see me about my art. I am here. You are Mr Barran. Shake hands.

Burnside (*recoiling*): I am not Mr Barran.

Sandoz: No?

Burnside: Definitely, no.

Dorothy: Shall I ...

Burnside: Go away, Miss West, and leave me to deal with this. This is no matter for women.

Sandoz: My art is very popular with women.

Burnside: Go away, Miss West. Now, sir. Do I understand you are here at Mr Barran's invitation?

Dorothy West goes out; Sandoz flings himself on to the couch.

Sandoz (*offended*): I am here at Mr Barran's invitation. I stay here until I see Mr Barran. I say no more.

Burnside: Miss Mayne, I shall have something to say to Mr Barran when he comes back from lunch — if he ever comes back from lunch. I must say this gives me a very poor opinion of the manners and methods of head-office producers.

Carol: I am sure Mr Barran will be as distressed as you are, Major Burnside.

Burnside (*to Sandoz*): Have you brought any of your menagerie with you?

Sandoz (*still offended*): I say nothing.

Burnside: Miss Mayne, kindly see if there are any animals in the hall. We can't have ...

Sandoz rushes to the door and plants himself in front of it.

Sandoz: No one leaves this studio until Mr Barran arrives. I say — I, Sandoz.

Burnside: Are you ordering me?

Sandoz: I am Sandoz. I am universal. I was known as an artist all over Europe.

Burnside: Do you mean to say you have always gone about with troops of sea-lions?

Sandoz: My art is appreciated everywhere until here.

Carol: I'm sure of that, Mr Sandoz. But tell me, what gave you the idea? Were you born in a circus?

Sandoz: I was born in Vienna. I was of the Vienna State Police.

Burnside: And people have reproached me for calling foreigners "crazy"!

Sandoz: I was responsible to the Emperor for the prevention of crime in the Zoological Gardens in Vienna. Every day, my duties took me past the cage of the sea-lions.

Carol: So that's how ...

Sandoz: I appreciated the sea-lions and every day they would bark when they see me coming. They appreciated me. The understanding was mutual. I learned their language. We exchanged conversation. You heard me just now. That is how a sea-lion would say, "Here I am — take me" in the mating season.

Carol: You know, Major Burnside, I think perhaps I ought to go out into the hall and see what's happening.

Burnside (*to Sandoz*): Are there any sea-lions outside?

Sandoz: If they were outside I could bring them in.

Burnside: For God's sake, don't do that!

Sandoz: But there are none.

Carol: Thank God for that!

Burnside: Miss Mayne, please!

Carol: I'm sorry, Major Burnside.

Sandoz: So I cease to inspect in police and I train sea-lions. I have trained sea-lions ever since. I am Sandoz. (*Sits down again.*)
From outside the door comes a stifled shriek.

Burnside: If that's one of your infernal animals savaging one of my staff, I'll —I'll ...
The door bursts open and Tony Barran rushes in, obviously in a flaming temper.

Barran: What the hell's happening to everybody?

Burnside: I'd like to ask you that question, Barran. You're eighteen minutes late for your rehearsal and at your invitation an apparently dangerous lunatic has established himself there. (*Pointing to Sandoz*)

Barran (*disregarding him. To Carol*): What happened to Inspector Harvey? I thought you arranged for us to have lunch together?

Carol: I did.

Barran: Well, he didn't turn up. Why not?

Carol: I made the arrangements for him to meet you at the Barchester Arms for lunch.

Barran: I've been waiting to give him lunch at the Barchester Arms for the last hour and a half but he didn't show up. Why not?

Carol: How should I know?

Burnside: My dear Barran, I think I can answer your question and give you a most pleasant surprise into the bargain.

Barran: What?

Burnside : I may say a very pleasant surprise! Your problem is solved.

Barran: What on earth are you talking about?

Burnside: Inspector Harvey will not be here.

Barran: You're telling me! Why not?

Burnside: Because I instructed the Inspector not to come.

Barran: *You* instructed ...?

Burnside: Prepare yourself, my dear Barran, for the surprise. You will not entertain Inspector Harvey. You will entertain none other than Colonel Sir Henry Bryce — my old C.O. — late of the Indian Police.

Sandoz: You are seeking a policeman, yes? I am here — I, Sandoz of the Austrian Imperial Police.

Barran: Are you Sandoz?

Carol: He *is* Sandoz and we don't know whether his sea-lions are or are not in the passage outside. We heard a scream. Was one of them eating Dorothy West?

Barran: No such luck. I'm afraid I bumped into her coming down the staircase.

Burnside: Let's leave Mr Sandoz for a moment while I explain about my old C.O.

Barran: Oh, damn your old C.O.!

Burnside (*very much on his dignity*): Are you aware, young man, that under Internal Instruction 5427 paragraph "C" visiting producers to a region come under the direct authority of the Regional Director so long as they are drawing subsistence allowance in that Region. I must first of all ask you to show proper respect! Secondly, I might point out that I was trying to do you a good turn.

Barran: I don't want any damned amateurs trying to do me a good turn when I'm on a job!

Burnside: Amateurs! Do you refer to my old C.O., Sir Henry Bryce, late of the Indian Police, as an amateur?

Barran: I wasn't referring to your bloody C.O.! I was referring to you, Major Burnside.

Burnside: Inspector Harvey may be all very well in his own but he is not Colonel Bryce and if you want a competent authority to interview Wallace Hatfield ...

Barran: Now, look here, Burnside. You may be a hell of an authority on India and even on sea-lions for all I know but ...

Sandoz: No one else is an authority on sea-lions. I am *the* authority on sea-lions.

Barran: Shut up!

Burnside: Speaking of sea-lions — no, I wasn't speaking of sea-lions.

Barran: I wish you wouldn't speak at all. Do you realise I've got a programme to do in four hours from now?

Burnside: And I offer you what I consider one of the best programme items we could ever use. Wallace Hatfield interviewed by Colonel Sir Henry Bryce of the Indian Police. Could you ask for anything more interesting?

Barran: I know what I should like to ask for, Burnside, but I suppose that would be insubordination, too. However, as you seem to have committed us to this aged curry merchant from Poona I suppose I have got to put up with him. But when I have a little more time I shall have great pleasure in discussing with you at any length you like the respective spheres of authority of a producer and a Regional Director, who is clearly not fit to choose the items for a penny reading!

Burnside: I think that will do, Barran.

Barran: It certainly will. Where is your superannuated police friend? We want a policeman — let's hear what he has to say.

Sandoz: I could say much of my experience in the Vienna Police. Vienna night-life — very interesting.

Barran: You're telling me! Carol, put something in your ears.

Carol: I'm feeling a little *de trop* all round. Don't you think we'd better stop screaming at each other and get down to work?

Burnside: That's the first sensible thing I've heard in this studio for some time.

Sandoz: Are you Mr Barran?

Barran: Yes, I'm Barran. What about it?

Sandoz: Mr Barran, I have been asked to come here and bring my sea-lions.

Barran: That would be the last straw!

Sandoz: You don't want me to bring my sea-lions here?

Barran: Definitely; no. No sea-lions.

Sandoz: Well, what do you want me to do?

Barran: Go away.

Sandoz: I was invited by a lady to come here for an engagement by Mr Barran. You are Mr Barran. What is the engagement? When? How much? What do I do?

Barran: It appears, Mr Sandoz, that the situation has changed. Personally I should have been delighted if you would have imitated one or even two sea-lions for us.

Sandoz: I can imitate twenty-three different sea-lions.

Barran: But it appears that Major Burnside has different ideas. He prefers curry and chota-pegs.[10]

Sandoz: What a digestion! How I admire the English!

Burnside: Miss Mayne, were you the lady who invited Mr Sandoz here?

Carol: Yes, I'm afraid I was.

Sandoz: Why be afraid? I am harmless.

Burnside (*ignoring him*): In that case, Miss Mayne, would you be good enough to make Mr Sandoz your personal apology and take him away.

Carrol: I don't see how I can do that.

Barran: Look here, I've had enough of this. Your friend the policeman, whether you invited him or not, isn't here. I'm thinking about my programme. Mr Sandoz *is* here and I want to hear what he can do.

Sandoz: You ask what I can do? I tell you — in Vienna, in Berlin, in Warsaw, in Blackpool — in every glamorous city of Europe I and my sea-lions have been applauded. You want sea-lions, I give you sea-

---

[10] "Chota-pegs" — Anglo-Indian slang for a tot of whiskey or other spirit.

lions. You want a policeman, I am a policeman. What more do you want?

Barran: We must try your voice in front of the microphone, you know.

Sandoz: So I do my imitation now, yes?

Barran (*gloomily*): Go on.

Burnside: This is entirely contrary to my better judgment. I tell you at any moment Sir Henry Bryce ...

Barran: Listen, Burnside. I've had just about enough — just about all I can stand. I know you can probably have me thrown out of the Corporation on my ear when I get back to Town, but if you say one more word about this doddering, fat-headed, bleary-eyed, bat-eared, bucktoothed son of a cock-eyed half-caste Indian constable, I'll — I'll ...

During this tirade, the door of the studio has opened in time for the incoming person to hear the greater part of these delightful adjectives. He stands there unnoticed by the small party in the studio. A large, fat man with white hair and shrewd eyes, he wears loose-fitting country tweed and carries a heavy walking stick. He is smoking a cheroot.

And who in hell are you?

Bryce: I don't think you should ask me that, young man, considering the fluency of your description.

Burnside: My God, Barran, don't you realize that's Sir Henry Bryce?

Barran: It would be!

Bryce (*to Burnside*): My dear Tadpole! How are you?

Barran (*wildly*): Don't tell me *you* imitate *tadpoles?*

Bryce: Certainly not. My best imitation is that of a policeman.

Sandoz: You are a policeman? Shake hands. (*Sir Henry shakes hands with him cordially.*) We must each other get to know much better.

Burnside: I really must apologise. Mr Barran has been a little upset by various things.

Barran: Of course, I'm sorry, Sir Henry, but not only have I been upset — I remain entirely upset.

Bryce: I understood there was some question of preparing a script. Wouldn't it soothe all our nerves to get down to it?

Barran: Get down to it? Under down it? Under the eyes of this sea-lion merchant here, and Tadpole?

Carol (*sweetly*): Why does he call you Tadpole, Major Burnside?

Bryce: I always tell the truth to a lady. Burnside looked rather like a tadpole when he joined the regiment. I'm afraid he never quite lived it down — eh, Burnside?

Burnside (*laughs*): I did my best.

Bryce: We policemen understand each other. Mr Sandoz, Major Burnside will make you comfortable in his office, and I shall look forward to a chat with you later, when we can be alone.

Sandoz: I understand you have appealed to me, Sandoz. No one appeals to Sandoz in vain.

He goes out, and is followed by Burnside.

Barran: Ye gods and little fishes!

Carol: Perhaps I should introduce myself, Sir Henry. I'm Carol Mayne, Mr Barran's secretary.

Bryce: Lucky fellow. In the days when I had a secretary he was Indian, six-foot two and an ex-thug. And yet they deny progress! Well, where do we go from here? Apparently my presence is not altogether welcome.

Barran: Let me put it ... your arrival was unexpected.

Bryce: There's no harm done. I must confess I was interested in what Tadpole told me.

Barran: About the Hatfield case?

Bryce: Yes, about the Hatfield case.

Barran: You've studied it?

Bryce: Say, rather, that I've read about it.

Barran: Formed an opinion?

Bryce: No. Keeping an open mind.

Barran: Tadpole told you the idea of the broadcast?

Bryce: Yes, I think I understand that.

Barran: You ask Hatfield questions in front of that microphone. He answers them.

Bryce: Yes.

Barran: Five minutes.

Bryce: Mr Barran — just how leading are these questions to be?

Carol: Do you think this is fair, Sir Henry?

Bryce: If I were a man like Barran, I should answer that all's fair in love, war and the entertainment industry. As an older man, I should say that I was glad when Tadpole told me his idea.

Barran: That's hardly unfair, is it?

Carol: Even if it is fair, I think it's horrible.

Barran: Carol, will you shut up?

Carol: Very well. But I still hate it, you know.

Bryce: You seem to show a great interest in Hatfield, Miss Mayne.

Carol: I'm sorry for him. I'm not ashamed of being sorry for him. I think people have been foul to him.

Bryce: Then if he can prove his innocence, shouldn't you be glad?

Carol: I don't know. I just hate the whole thing.

Barran: Sir Henry, the responsibility for this is mine and I have taken it. If you don't want to play I can still get Inspector Harvey.

Bryce: I very much want to "play" as you put it. The one fact that intrigued me most ...

Barran: Well?

Bryce: Why should a body found at the foot of a tower be surrounded by flowers?

Studio door opens. Hatfield comes in quietly.

By the way, what were the flowers, Mr Barran?

Hatfield: The flowers were Arum lilies.

Bryce: What?

Hatfield: I should know. I found them. Wallace Hatfield.

Barran: Oh, this is Sir Henry Bryce, who's going to interview you.

Hatfield: But I thought Inspector Harvey ...

Barran: So did I. Major Burnside thought differently. Does it matter who interviews you?

Hatfield: Not at all. But what's Sir Henry Bryce's connection —

Bryce: With the police? It's been severed for some years. I'm just an old dodderer on the shelf. Ask Mr Barran. He knows.

Hatfield: This is going to be a little more awkward than I thought. Does Miss Mayne stay here while we write the script?

Barran: The procedure is quite simple. Sir Henry frames the questions, you answer them. Miss Mayne takes them down in shorthand and has the script typed when you're through. I just vet for length and content. Suppose we sit down and start?

Bryce: I should like to understand something clearly at the start, Mr Hatfield. May I ask you any question that occurs to me?

Barran: Take that down, Carol. Go on.

Hatfield: Yes, any question. (*Aside*) Take that down, too, Miss Mayne.

Barran and Carol sit down, the latter with notebook. Bryce and Hatfield remain standing.

Bryce: Before I ask any definite question ... you needn't take this down,

Miss Mayne ... let me see if I have the facts straight. (*To Hatfield*) Your wife was — ?

Hatfield: She was formerly a teacher in this school. Phillimore got her the position.

Bryce: You had been married — how long?

Hatfield: Six years.

Bryce (*hesitantly*): On the afternoon of the ...

Hatfield (*fiercely*): Say it! It *was* murder!

Bryce: On the afternoon of the murder, as I understand it, you were in this schoolhouse.

Hatfield: Yes. And in this basement.

Barran: Why? What were you doing here?

Carol: It isn't *your* interview, Tony.

Barran: Sorry.

Hatfield: I was fitting up the studio for the BBC. I expected Phillimore to come down here and join me — he said he was coming — but he never turned up. So I was alone.

Bryce: Did your wife come here with you?

Hatfield: No. I hadn't seen Lucy since lunch.

Bryce: Was anybody else in the building at the time?

Hatfield: Not to my knowledge. The school had been evacuated weeks before.

Barran (*under his breath*): Better take this down, Carol.

Bryce: Go on, Mr Hatfield.

Hatfield: About half past four I got tired waiting for Phillimore. My — my work was done.

Barran: And well done.

Hatfield: Must you interrupt me, Mr Barran?

Bryce: Go on, please.

Hatfield: I went upstairs, and out of the front door. Then I saw Lucy's body lying in the stone-paved yard. She had fallen head first from the tower. It — wasn't pleasant. Scattered round her body lay an armful of Arum lilies. I noticed that first, after the blood.
    Carol drops her pencil.

Barran: Don't lose your nerve, Carol!

Carol: I'm all right.

Bryce: What did you do then, Mr Hatfield?

Hatfield: I didn't do anything. I just stood there stupidly. Then I shouted for help.

Bryce: Did anyone answer?

Hatfield: Yes. Old Jonas Whitehead. He happened to be passing at the time.

Bryce: And then?

Hatfield: It seemed pretty clear that Lucy had fallen from the belfry-tower. We — went up there.

Bryce: There's no doubt, I suppose, that your wife *had* fallen from the tower?

Hatfield: None at all. The police found her footprints in the dust up there.

Bryce (*quickly*): Anyone else's footprints?

Hatfield: No.

Bryce: No other footprints at all?

Hatfield: A few smudges; nothing more. They also found two more of the Arum lilies ...

Bryce: Where?

Hatfield: Lying on the low stone balustrade round the bell-platform.

Bryce: As though Mrs Hatfield had been carrying an armful of the lilies when she was attacked?

Hatfield: Yes.

Bryce: Where did she get the lilies? Had she brought them from home?

Hatfield: No. And the police couldn't trace anyone who gave them to her. Those flowers appeared out of nowhere. They were just — meaningless.

Bryce: Which shows, of course, that they mean something.

Carol: But what?

Bryce (*thoughtfully*): This death, I suppose, *could* have been an accident?

Hatfield: Yes. That's what saved my neck at the trial. Lucy's footprints — and nobody else's. Very well, said my counsel, how did the murderer get at her?

Bryce: And how *did* he get at her?

Hatfield: I don't know.

Barran (*suddenly*): Look here, Hatfield, you've got a better case than I ever thought.

Hatfield (*drily*): Thank you.

Barran: *I* never heard that point about the footprints before.

Hatfield: Few people *will* take the trouble to read evidence. They skim a newspaper report, and say, "That's the murderer." Just like the good people of Barchester. Do you understand now why I've nearly gone mad?

Carol: But if the whole thing was an accident after all — ?

Hatfield: It wasn't an accident. All this fine talk can't account for the bruise.

Bryce (*sharply*): What bruise?

Hatfield: A bruise on the right-hand side of Lucy's back, just below the shoulder-blade. As though —

Bryce: As though what?

Hatfield: As though someone had struck her with the end of a heavy walking-stick. The main point in all this ...

Bryce: I think you miss the main point, Mr Hatfield.

Hatfield: Which is?

Bryce: What was your wife *doing* in the bell-tower? Why did she go up there in the first place?

Hatfield (*despairingly*): I don't know. Over and over they asked me that at the trial; and I don't know. I didn't even know she was in the building.

Bryce: But presumably she *had* a reason?

Hatfield: I imagine so. Lucy was the most sensible woman I ever knew.

Bryce: Did anyone see her enter the schoolhouse that afternoon?

Hatfield: No. We were alone in the building together. That's why they said I killed her. That, and — Mrs Phillimore.

Barran (*alarmed*): Wait a minute! None of that kind of talk on the air!

Hatfield: What kind of talk?

Barran: Scandal. It's o-u-t.

Bryce (*suavely*): Still, for my private information ... *Were* you interested in Mrs Phillimore?

Hatfield: *No!* Not in that way, anyhow. (*To Carol*) I want you to believe that, if you don't believe another word I say. I want you to believe that the devil isn't so black as he's painted, and that a middle-aged man accused of murder is only a bewildered human being after all.

Barran: Fine. Very nice curtain line. That will see us out very nicely. Now, Sir Henry, there will have to be some sort of summing up of your view just before. A good, authoritative sort of exposition.

Bryce: Good God! You won't expect me to make up like Joad?

Barran: No, we'll spare you that.

Bryce: But seriously, Mr Barran, you can't expect me to turn you out a considered opinion as if I was opening a tin of Spam. I've got a lot more questions to ask, and I think (*looking from Barran to Carol*) I had better put them to Mr Hatfield in private. He's entitled to privacy as well as publicity.

Carol: Thank you, Sir Henry.

Barran: Remember, I have to see anything that goes down in this script.

Bryce: Good God, young man, do you think I don't know about this infernal tin-can factory of yours? I had a private transmitter of my own in India — and a damned good one. It talked several languages, several of them unknown to modern science. I know all about broadcasting requiremenst and regulations. We know more about regulations in the Army than you'll ever learn. Is there somewhere I can go with Mr Hatfield where we can be safe from mutton-headed interferers? You can't do your best detective work in the atmosphere of a tube station.

Hatfield: You sound as if you've got an idea about this thing. Where can we go?

Barran: Try the Listening Room. We must have a final rehearsal for Jonas Whitehead and set-up, and run through of your interview within the next half-hour, and no one will bother you in the Listening Room — unless Dorothy West wants to play "Teddy Bears' Picnic" to us.

Bryce: We shall be ready in less than half an hour. Will you go ahead, Mr Hatfield?

Carol: I shall have to have your script typed, you know.

Bryce: I do know, young woman. Are you all in a conspiracy to pretend that I'm a congenital imbecile? I may tell you that I invented my own shorthand and it's a damned sight better than Pitman's.

Hatfield and Sir Henry go into the Listening Room and sit down. During the ensuing scene they can be seen but, of course, not heard, carrying on question and answer.

Carol: Feeling pleased with yourself, Tony?

Barran: Very.

Carol: So you like Major Burnside's idea, after all?

Barran: Since I've heard him called Tadpole, I could forgive him any-thing. As for Hatfield — I — I'm not quite sure. Did you hear that point about there being no footprints in the belfry except Mrs Hatfield's?

Carol: No.

Barran: It certainly makes a lot of difference. But let's stop talking about Hatfield just for a minute.

Carol: You want to stop talking about him just when you're beginning to think he's innocent?

Barran: Oh, damn his innocence or his guilt; I'm thinking about something else.

Carol: Thinking about what?

Barran: Us.

Carol: Must we always go back to that subject when we've got anything else to talk about?

Barran: Is it such a bad idea?

Carol: At any other time, it mightn't be.

Barran (*cheerfully*): We progress.

Carol: But now, just this minute, I'm afraid ...

Barran: Afraid?

Carol: Don't you see it might be dangerous to open a grave?

Barran: Come off it, Carol. Cut out the melodramatic trimmings. I want you to tell me one thing, quite truthfully.

Carol: What's that?

Barran: I'll promise to behave the gentleman if you do tell me.

Carol: Very well. What is it?

Barran: Are you in love with Hatfield? I may as well know, you know.

Carol: I told you once before I was very sorry for him.

Barran: Don't hedge. Are you in love with him?

Carol: I don't think I am — and yet ...

Barran: Well, think again and make up your mind, because if you are I'll call the whole thing off. It'll annoy Tadpole, anyway.

Carol: Just now I'm not sure I want you to call it off.

Barran: You still haven't answered my question. It's a lot to me, you know. I don't compete with anyone.

Carol: Isn't that rather arrogant?

Barran: I'm rather an arrogant chap.

Carol: I know. Maybe that's why I don't answer you.

Barran: Carol darling, if you're the sort of person I think you are — the person I'm in love with — you couldn't possibly be in love with Wallace Hatfield. But if you are in love with him, for the sake of the idea of the you I'm in love with I'll scrap that interview. (*Lightly*) And if that's not a helluva good gesture, I don't know what is! "Exit Sydney Carton through gap in hedge."[11]

Carol: I'll tell you this, Tony. I'll call Sydney Carton back and tell him what I really think of him if ...

Barran: Well?

Carol: If we succeed in clearing Wallace Hatfield.

Barran: You're certainly a woman, every inch of you. That gets me on your side, doesn't it? Well, that's O.K. by me. Listen. You'd better tell old Jonas and our dumb blonde friend that we shall need them for links and general set-up rehearsal in about twenty minutes. One other thing.

Carol: Yes, Mr Barran?

Barran: Just one other thing, Miss Mayne. I believe there is no regulation allowing for mutual embraces on Corporation premises, so kindly consider yourself kissed.

Carol: Would you like me to ask Dorothy West about that?

Barran: No, no! Now run along.

Exit Carol.

Barran goes up to the glass panel of the Listening Room and raps on it, making interrogative gestures. Hatfield starts violently. Sir Henry turns round and makes various faces.

O.K., O.K.! I only wanted to know if you were ready.

Bryce (*pushing down switch of talk-back*): Oh you do, do you? Kindly remember that I know all about this set-up. Why can't you take your love-scene somewhere else?

Barran: I wouldn't mind continuing my love-scene, Sir Henry, in Trafalgar Square. Switch off the loudspeaker in there. You don't seem to know everything about it.

Bryce (*flicking back switch of talk-back*): Bah!

Bryce turns off loudspeaker in Listening Room. He and Hatfield continue their interview in dumb show. Barran raises his voice disgruntedly in "My Bonnie Lies Over the Ocean." Enter Mrs Phillimore, a middle-aged woman of forty-five or so, the relics of her good looks now marred by a drawn and haggard expression. She

---

[11] Sydney Carton is the self-sacrificing hero of Dickens' *A Tale of Two Cities* (1859).

wears a coat and skirt and a rather shabby fur stole.

Barran (*cheerfully*): I beg your pardon — looking for someone?

Judith: I wish to see the person who is in charge of this studio.

Barran: Oh, you mean old Tad — er — Major Burnside. I expect he's in his office.

Judith: I know Major Burnside, thank you. I don't wish to see him. Who's in charge of this programme tonight?

Barran: I can't think why, but I am. It's a way they have in the BBC. My name's Tony Barran.

Judith: My name's Judith Phillimore.

Barran (*suddenly serious*): Mrs Phillimore?

Judith: Yes. Does that convey anything to you?

Barran: I know that your husband was the principal of this school when it was a school.

Judith: You know nothing more than that, Mr Barran?

Barran (*awkwardly*): If you're thinking about rumour, Mrs Phillimore, I spread it, but I never listen to it.

Judith: You talk of gossip? Has it occurred to you what you will be doing tonight?

Barran: You haven't been talking to Miss Carol Mayne by any chance, have you, Mrs Phillimore?

Judith: No. I've been talking to my husband.

Barran: I see. And I suppose Major Burnside has been talking to him too.

Judith: I lived this down once, or almost lived it down. Why must you start it all over again?

Barran: My dear Mrs Phillimore, I can assure you that we are confining ourselves strictly to the facts of the most interesting unsolved murder. You needn't worry. The script has to be passed by me and the BBC doesn't stand for intimate revelations of people's private lives. To be perfectly frank, very few private lives would stand it.

Judith: Are you trying to console me merely by saying that my name won't be mentioned?

Barran: I should have thought that was the important thing.

Judith: Has it occurred to you that everyone in Barchester who hears this broadcast will be waiting for a mention of Judith Phillimore's name and that if they don't hear it they'll be asking each other why?

Barran: Hang it all, you know, the original idea of this wasn't mine.

Judith: Then whose was it?

Barran: Mr Wallace Hatfield.

Judith (*astounded*): Wallace wanted this to be done?

Barran: Emphatically

Judith: May I ask why?

Barran: He seems convinced of his ability to convince the world that he was hardly done by.

Judith: Didn't he think of me, and what I might feel about it?

Barran (*gently*): Mrs Phillimore, having denied any association with you, why should he worry?

Judith: Don't people always deny associations with each other, guilty or innocent? Does that mean anything? What do you think my husband will say? Four years ago I had to deny that I was Wallace Hatfield's mistress. He didn't believe me then. But he's just about beginning to forget it. Do you think he's going to believe me now?

Enter Phillimore.

Phillimore: What are you doing here?

Judith: I only came to see Mr Barran.

Phillimore: That's curious. So did I.

Barran: What can I do for you?

Phillimore: I was just wondering if I had left any more of my books here. I value all my possessions.

Barran: Quite.

Phillimore: I don't care about finding my books on the floor of your studio and I think my wife could find a better use for her time.

Judith: I only ...

Phillimore: I know quite well what you came for. It's very foolish of you. It might easily cause talk. If I'd felt it desirable to interfere with this broadcast, I would have said so to Major Burnside when he first told me about it.

Judith: You're quite content for everything to be brought up again?

Phillimore: Perfectly. We've nothing to hide, have we?

Judith: I know you haven't, but ...

Phillimore: You mean to say you have?

Judith: Of course not. But it you're afraid of talk ...

Phillimore: You ought to know I'm afraid of nothing and of no one. Haven't I got proof of that?

During this last speech, Bryce can be seen in the Listening Room getting out of his chair and opening the Listening Room door.

Bryce (as he emerges): I think that's got it. You've convinced me of one thing, Mr Hatfield. I'm keeping an open mind still as to who murdered your wife. But somebody killed her.

Bryce comes into the studio, followed by Hatfield. Hatfield and Judith Phillimore stare at each other, regardless of everybody else. Phillimore watches them, frowning. Appropriate reactions all round.

Bryce: Would somebody have the goodness to effect some introductions, like a reasonable person? Or is an ex-policeman outside the social ...?

Barran: I beg your pardon, Sir Henry. Mr and Mrs Phillimore, Sir Henry Bryce.

Phillimore: How do you do? May I ask if Sir Henry forms part of your pro-gramme this evening?

Bryce: Yes, I do.

Phillimore (*to Judith*): You see, my dear, the thing will not only be in good but in distinguished hands.

Judith: Yes.

Phillimore: Then don't you think we might go and have a cup of tea?

Hatfield: Look here, Phillimore, I'd like a word with you.

Phillimore: I'm sorry, Hatfield. I'm a creature of habit. Each act in its appointed place. I prefer to have my meals at regular intervals. Come along, Judith.

With a final miserable look at Hatfield, Judith goes out and her husband follows her.

Hatfield: There you are. That's the sort of thing ... Now you can see with your own eyes what I've had to put up with.

Bryce: My dear Hatfield, as a man of experience, I can tell you that life consists of putting up with things. It's not my business to say so, but you're too damned sorry for yourself altogether. (*Thoughtfully*) Would you call Mr Phillimore a representative citizen here?

Hatfield: My God, I hope not. Even Barchester can't be that awful.

Bryce: A capable man, I should judge, at whatever he undertook.

Hatfield: He's capable all right. How a man like that ever became principal of a school in Barchester is beyond me.

Barran: Have you sorted out your ideas, Sir Henry? Miss Maine wants that script.

Bryce: They're fairly well sorted out, young fellow, but there's just one more thing I should rather like to know.

Hatfield: What's that?

Bryce: What was old Jonas Whitehead doing near the school when Mrs Hatfield died?

Hatfield: I can't possibly answer that. Why not ask him?

Bryce: I think I will.

Barran: He'll be here in a minute. You can ask him then. I'm having a run-through of the skeleton of the whole programme in a few minutes.

Bryce: The skeleton of the programme, young man? Is that basic English?

Barran: I suppose you had no technical terms of your own in the India Service?

Bryce: I'll ignore that. Who are the vertebrae of this skeleton, if I may ask?

Barran: Besides yourself and Mr Hatfield, Sir Henry ...

Bryce: My God, young man, do I look like any part of a skeleton?

Barran: I think I'd better ignore that, Sir Henry. The other people concerned are old Jonas Whitehead, Miss Penelope Squire — a sight for sore eyes, Sir Henry, but you'd better not talk to her. My God, I'm forgetting my sea-lion merchant. Now, do I need him or don't I?

Sandoz enters, closely followed by Carol.

Sandoz: You need Sandoz? Sandoz is here!

Barran: So I see.

Sandoz: You have decided about me? Yes?

Barran: Yes. No! Carol, take Sir Henry and Mr Hatfield and get that script cleaned up and hurry. We'll have the run-through as soon as you're ready. Bring Jonas Whitehead and Penelope with you when you come.

Sandoz: But what about Sandoz?

Barran: You and I, Mr Sandoz, are going to have a little chat.

Sandoz: I tell you the story of my life?

Barran: I said a little chat, Mr Sandoz.

Sandoz: Then I tell you part of the story of my life.

Barran: Well, perhaps a very small part.

Sandoz: I was born in Vienna.

Barran: I'm sure you're dying to listen to this, Sir Henry, but we must get along and do some work. You too, Mr Hatfield.

Carol shepherds them out.

Sandoz: I was born in Vienna.

Barran: A beautiful city, Mr Sandoz.

Sandoz: You know Vienna?

Barran: The BBC sent me to Vienna to have a look at Austrian broad-casting in the days when there was an Austria.

Sandoz: But you didn't see me, Sandoz?

Barran: Unfortunately, no. Why should I? Didn't you tell me you were a policeman there as well?

Sandoz: I made noises for broadcasting.

Barran: Noises? Didn't you miss your sea-lions?

Sandoz: It was before I am an imitator of sea-lions. I am trains, I am steamers, I am avalanches, I am the battle of Waterloo. I am the battle of Austerlitz. I am Sandoz.

Barran: Now, at least, I know the meaning of a one-man band.

Sandoz: Do you know how I am an avalanche?

Barran: Frankly, no.

Sandoz: I show you. (*He rushes into the corner, upstage right, where a certain amount of Effects gear is lying about, rushes back to the mike with a small drum on which he proceeds to roll four potatoes with a vigorous circular movement of his arms.*) You see? Avalanche in the Carpathians. Smaller potatoes — avalanche in the Alps. (*He pulls a match-box from his pocket and crushes it in front of the mike with a vicious gesture.*) I am ship-wreck. By an iceberg. The tragedy of the sea.

Barran: I am sure you must have been horses in your time?

Sandoz: Horses? You have a gramophone record of hand-clapping?

Barran: I expect so. Dorothy West will know.

Sandoz: Run it at quarter-speed. It is horses. I tell you. I Sandoz.

Barran: I'm much obliged to you.

Sandoz: You wish me to be horses in front of your microphone tonight?

Barran: Quite frankly, Mr Sandoz, now that Sir Henry Bryce has put in an appearance, I don't think that I can find room for you after all.

Sandoz: Not find room? Then I waste my time. You give me cheque, yes?

Barran: Perhaps a nominal fee, Mr Sandoz.

Sandoz: How much?

Barran: Oh, I think we could manage a couple of guineas.

Sandoz: Two guineas? I have six sea-lions to support. Do you know what they eat? Do you know what they cost? Do you ...

Barran: I don't know a damned thing about sea-lions, and I couldn't care less!

Sandoz: I murder you for those words. My sea-lions are my children. *Door opens. Carol enters.*

Carol: You were talking about sea-lions, Mr Sandoz?

Sandoz: I always talk about my sea-lions.

Carol: I think you'd better do something more than that. I understand that two of them have got loose in the High Street. The Chief Constable is practically calling out the Home Guard.[12] One of them got the Clerk to the Council by the trousers.

Sandoz: Trousers? His digestion will be ruined. (*He rushes out.*)

Barran: Now you've done it!

Carol: Didn't you want it done?

Barran: Want what done?

Carol: Sandoz removed by hook or by crook? This time, crook!

Barran: Do you mean to say the sea-lions haven't got the Clerk to the Council by the trousers?

Carol: I'm afraid not.

Barran: That's a pity. The picture was a pleasant one. However, you're a good secretary, Miss Mayne. You know your job, I give you that. You may consider yourself kissed again. That script ready?

Carol: It's being typed now, but Mr Hatfield's got a new idea which he wants to ask you about.

Barran: Oh God! Are Jonas and Penelope Squire waiting?

Carol: Yes.

Barran: In that case, we must take the run-through now. We can talk about changes after that.

Carol: Yes. Just as you say.
She goes out just as Leila Ponsonby, followed by the two Programme Engineers, comes in.

Leila: Ready for us, Carol?

---

[12] On May 14, 1940, the British Government asked "men of all ages who wish to do something for the defence of their country" to establish themselves as Local Defence Volunteers to protect the country in the event of a German invasion. The Volunteers were later renamed the Home Guard and disbanded on December 31, 1945.

Carol: In a few minutes. (*She goes out.*)
   Dorothy West goes into Listening Room and sits at the mixing unit.
   Jill follows her and can be seen sorting records out into a rack above
   the turntables.
Leila: All set, Tony?
Barran: Practically.   I just want a skeleton run-through, with cue for
   linking music.
Leila: Well, what's the order?
Barran: Jonas and his flute, Penelope and "Cyrana" and finally Sir Henry
   and Wallace Hatfield. You've got your script for the interviews with
   Jonas and Penelope. The last script's being typed.
Leila: Quite a party! (*She goes over to the sofa and sits down to look at*
   her script.)
   Enter Hatfield.
Barran: Hello, Hatfield. What's all this about a last-minute change?
Hatfield: I think I know how my wife was killed.
Barran: The deuce you do!
Hatfield: If I did know; if I did happen to be right, would you let me tell it
   over that (*pointing to microphone*)?
Barran: If you've an interesting theory that holds water, that's fine.
Hatfield: It was something Sir Henry said. All of a sudden it came to me.
   I may be wrong — I may be right.
Barran: Just a minute. You mustn't try to pin it on to anyone else.
Hatfield: But that's the only way to bring it ...
Barran: I can't help that. We're not re-trying the case. We are discussing
   it as an interesting unsolved crime.
Hatfield: I shouldn't want to mention names. I promise not to mention
   names.
Barran: Well, we can't alter the script at this stage. We'll talk about it
   after the run-through.
Hatfield: Whatever you say. When do we begin?
Barran: Now.
   Carol comes back, followed by Sir Henry, Jonas Whitehead and
   Penelope Squire. The two latter sit on the sofa looking at their scripts.
   Carol distributes further scripts to Barran, Leila, Hatfield, and Sir
   Henry. Then she goes into the Listening Room, followed by Barran.
   Barran sits next to Dorothy at the mixer. Carol stands behind him
   with her notebook. Sir Henry is making explosive noises.

Leila: Feeling nervous, Sir Henry?

Bryce: Nervous be damned! This studio's giving me claustrophobia. I'm used to wide open spaces. Don't think much of your ventilation, Miss Ponsonby, if you want my honest opinion.

Leila: I think you should discuss that with Mr Hatfield. He turned this place into a studio, you know.

Bryce: Really? Pity you didn't make a better job of it.

Hatfield: I made an excellent job of it. As a studio, it does exactly what it was designed to do and I paid special attention to the ventilation, if you're interested. Jonas!

Jonas looks up from his script.

Whitehead: You were saying, Mr Hatfield?

Hatfield: That handle for the emergency ventilation. It's just over your head. Give it a turn, would you? Half-down. I think you'll notice a difference in a minute or two, Sir Henry.

Bryce: I hope so.

Barran (*over loudspeaker*): Can we get on? Take a green light each time, Leila, will you, and let the artists take the cues from you. I just want the finish of Jonas Whitehead's final flute piece, and your opening with Penelope Squire, the end of her recitation and your announcing of Sir Henry and Wallace Hatfield.

Leila: All right, Tony. Go ahead.

Barran: Flute forward, Mr Whithead!

Jonas comes to the microphone, beside which a music stand has been placed, on which he puts his script.

Jonas: I have been bellringer in this school for fifty-three years ...

Barran (*over talk-back*): No, no, no! Just your final flute passage, Mr Whitehead. Keep him in hand, Leila, for God's sake.

Leila hands Jonas his flute. He plays "My Bonnie Lies Over the Ocean." *At the close of it, a green light goes on.*

Leila: Our second visitor from *Out of Town Tonight* is Penelope Squire.

She beckons Penelope — obviously shaking in every limb — from the couch.

Penelope, I need hardly say, is an extremely pretty girl. As you would expect from one who has been chosen Beauty Queen of Barchester Small Arms factory.

Penelope giggles self-consciously.

Penelope's one of our young girl war-workers, of whom we're all so proud. But life is not all work, is it Penelope? Penelope is one of the leading lights of the Barchester Poetry Society, and whenever there's a party, Penelope is always asked to recite. So tonight, for our big party all over England, our big party that is *Out of Town Tonight*, I'm going to ask Penelope Squire to recite Oscar Wilde's poem "The Ballad of Reading Gaol."

Penelope opens her mouth, but no words issue forth.

Barran (*over talk-back*): Get on, for God's sake!

Leila jabs Penelope in the ribs and she begins in a high voice.

Penelope: He did not wear his scarlet coat ...

Barran: That will do. Go to the end, will you?

Penelope: The coward does it with a kiss,

    The brave man with a sword.

Barran makes a gesture to Jill, who puts on a record. After a pause, the light goes on again.

Leila: Finally, from Barchester in *Out of Town Tonight*, we are broadcasting a discussion on the subject of the most famous crime that ever stirred this old-world provincial city. Four years ago Mrs Wallace Hatfield died in Barchester under mysterious circumstances. Her body was found outside this very building from which I am speaking at the moment. Tonight Mr Wallace Hatfield and Colonel Sir Henry Bryce, the distinguished ex-Chief of the Indian Police Service, will discuss various aspects of this fascinating unsolved mystery. Mr Wallace Hatfield and Sir Henry Bryce. Now, Mr Hatfield, will you lead off?

Hatfield: I'll lead off all right. I've been waiting for this chance and I'm making the most of it. I'll answer your questions, Sir Henry, but before I answer them I'm going to tell you how I believe my wife was killed.

Barran: Oi, oi! That's not it. What's happened to your script?

Hatfield: Damn your script! This is the way I'm proposing to change the script. You can tell me if you don't like it.

Barran: I'm trying this run-through for a timing, blast you!

Hatfield: I won't over-run my five minutes. Let me go on, and Miss Mayne can take it down.

Barran: All right, have it your own way.

Hatfield: That's it. Now I'll tell you. When I was talking to Sir Henry Bryce just now, he told me a story of India; of a case in which he was concerned. A woman was murdered and the body was smothered with flowers. Who was the murderer? A man whose wife had been having an affair with the husband of the murdered woman. But it was the murdered woman's husband who was accused of the crime. The flowers were the flowers he was known to give her on every anniversary of their wedding. He was hanged for it. I believe this murder was a deliberate plot. A plot against me. A plot to get me hanged. Designed by a man who had a grudge against me. A man who knew every foot of this building. A man who could walk about with a school blackboard pointer and no one think anything of it. A man ...

Barran (*emerging from Listening Room*): Now look here, Hatfield, this isn't cricket. You're doing just precisely what I told you you couldn't do. You can't say things like that.

Hatfield: I've said them. I stick to them.

Barran: You're as good as calling Phillimore a murderer.

Hatfield: I've mentioned no names.

Barran: You're leaving no doubt in anyone's mind who knows anything of the case.

Bryce: Young fellow — I'm not a difficult man, but if this interview is going to be changed to a soliloquy by Mr Hatfield I think I'm wasting my time.

Barran: I couldn't agree with you more, Sir Henry.

Hatfield: Don't any of you want to know the real truth?

Bryce (*grimly*): Go on!

Hatfield: There's Jonas Whitehead. Ask him your question.

Bryce: Could I trouble you to come here, Mr Whitehead?

As he comes up, Hatfield, tugging at his collar and wiping his forehead, walks over to the ventilation handle, and gives it another turn, then comes back. This should be an unobtrusive movement.

Bryce: I want to ask you a question, Mr Whitehead.

Whitehead: Eh?

Bryce: I want to ask you a question.

Whitehead: I'm listening.

Bryce: What brought you into the schoolhouse on the day when Mrs Hatfield was killed?

Whitehead: Eh?

Bryce: What brought you ...

Whitehead: I'm not deaf. I came into the schoolhouse because I heard the bell ringing.

Bryce: Damn it, why shouldn't the bell ring?

Hatfield: You're forgetting something, Sir Henry. At the time of this tragedy, the ringing of school bells and church bells was prohibited, except in case of invasion.

Whitehead: I came in to see who was playing tricks with my bell. Clerk to the Council instructed me that the bell wasn't to ring. None could ring it now.

Bryce: Eh, what's that?

Whitehead: No one can ring it now. Door to the belfry's locked and I've got the key. (*Pulls it out of his pocket.*) No one's going to ring that bell again.

From some distance overhead sounds distinctly the striking of a bell, beginning slowly and increasing in tempo.

Hatfield: My God! What's that?

Bryce: Sounds to me like a bell.

Whitehead: That's my bell. That's my bell! Who's ringing my bell? (*He hurries out through the door.*)

As the others leave to follow him, Penelope slides off the couch in a dead faint.

Barran: For God's sake, everybody, pull yourselves together! This programme's going to hell and Jericho. Damn it, haven't any of you ever heard a bell ring before?

Hatfield: Yes, that's the trouble.

Leila and Sir Henry have lifted Penelope on to the couch.

Leila: She'll be all right in a minute.

Barran: This programme's not going to be ready if we're not careful. Where're you going, Sir Henry?

Bryce: Like Jonas Whitehead, I want to see who's ringing that bell — in a locked belfry. (*He goes out.*)

Hatfield (*following him*): And so do I, by God! (*Exit*)

Barran: Oh, hell, flames and Judas Iscariot!

Carol: Tony!

Barran: Well?

Carol: I'm scared — horribly!

Barran: What on earth is there to be scared about?

Carol: I don't know — that's why I'm scared.

Barran: Did you get down Hatfield's theory?

Carol: Yes.

Barran: Then you can just scratch it all out. We're not using it. I'm not risking a libel notion from our Mr Phillimore. He looks like being a difficult customer.

Carol: It might be the truth, all the same.

Barran: I wonder. (*Hatfield, followed by Sir Henry, re-enters, carrying an armful of Arum lilies.*) My God, what on earth are you doing with those?

Carol: I think I know.

Bryce: Old Whitehead will never ring that bell again.

Hatfield: Jonas Whitehead is lying dead at the foot of the tower. We found him where I found my wife. His skull was crushed, like hers. These flowers were scattered round his body. (*He drops the lilies on the floor.*)

CURTAIN

ACT III

*The scene is the same about two hours later. When the curtain rises,
Carol is sitting on the couch down left, with an expression of distress
and exhaustion. Dorothy West comes into the studio, carrying a
number of gramophone records.*

Dorothy: I've got all the records lined up. Where's Mr Barran?

Carol (*wearily*): In conference. And for once it's true.

Dorothy: Well, we haven't too much time. Isn't Jill here?

Carol: She's not.

Dorothy: Why not?

Carol (*patiently*): Jill's uncle ... died about two hours ago, my dear
Dorothy.

Dorothy: What's that got to do with it? She's on duty ...

Carol: ... and the show must go on! You needn't tell me. Well, I don't
know whether the show's going on, just yet. But Jill Whitehead's gone
home. I sent her.

Dorothy: You had no business to do that. Jill's my assistant.

Carol: Did you ever study anatomy at school?

Dorothy: What *are* you talking about?

Carol: Somewhere on the left side of the body there's an organ called the
heart. Ever hear of it?

Dorothy: Of course. Don't be silly.

Carol: Then have one. Jill's only a kid, and she was very fond of the old
boy. Besides ...

Dorothy: I'm not supposed to handle a show without a Junior Programme
Engineer.

Carol: That's just too bad. For once you have to ... if there is a show.

Dorothy: Haven't they made up their minds about it yet?

Carol: Major Burnside was getting on to London, I believe.

Dorothy: Of course I'm very sorry, and all that! But I still think it's most
extraordinary and irregular. I shall be in the control-room if and when
the decision's been made. I must see the engineer in charge.

*Dorothy takes the records into the Listening Room and puts them on
a chair. Enter Hatfield.*

152

Hatfield (*quietly sympathetic*): Hello, Carol. All alone?

Carol (*pointing to Listening Room*): Our engineers are always with us.

> *Dorothy overhears this as she comes out of the Listening Room.*

Dorothy (*acidly*): Seen but not heard. Please don't mind me! (*She goes out.*)

Hatfield: She seems upset.

Carol: I expect we're all rather upset.

Hatfield: Very naturally. It's a horrible business.

Carol: Ghastly!

Hatfield: Perhaps now you can realise how I ... No! I oughtn't to have said that.

Carol: I think I always realised it.

Hatfield: I know; and I'm grateful. More grateful than I've ever been able to tell you.

Carol: I didn't want you to tell me. I just thought people were being unfair. And now I *know* they were.

Hatfield: You *know*?

Carol: Of course. However Jonas Whitehead died, *you* couldn't have killed him.

Hatfield (*slowly*): No, I couldn't. Could I? (*Pause*) My God, no! I was with Sir Henry Bryce when it happened! He can prove it! I wasn't anywhere near the belfry! Do you know, I'd only just thought of that? (*Quickly*) But I mustn't start thinking about myself now.

Carol: Who else should you be thinking about? It's too late to think about poor old Jonas.

Hatfield: I'm not thinking about Jonas. I'm thinking about somebody else.

Carol: Who?

Hatfield: Can't you guess?

Carol: No. Who?

Hatfield: You.

Carol: Me?

Hatfield: The one person who's always believed in me. The only person who's been kind to me.

Carol: Please! You mustn't exaggerate you know.

Hatfield: I don't want to exaggerate. I only wanted to ask you something.

Carol: Yes?

Hatfield (*awkwardly*): Well, I'm assuming the broadcast will be cancelled.

That's the only decent thing.

Carol: That's not settled yet. I agree it would seem the obvious thing to do.

Hatfield: Exactly. So I thought perhaps you'd let me give you some dinner. It's a quarter past six now. What about the Barchester Arms at half past seven?

Carol: That's very kind of you; but I really don't think ...

Hatfield: Please! You wouldn't begrudge me my own little private celebration?

Carol (*startled*): Celebration?

Hatfield: Well ... I *have* established my innocence, haven't I?

Carol: Yes.

Hatfield: And there are a lot of things I should like to say to you, where engineers are not always with us.

Carol (*lightly*): I'm afraid you wouldn't find the dining room of the Barchester Arms as quiet as all that. It's the only place hereabouts with prices high enough for American Army privates.

Hatfield (*seriously*): No. We don't want to be in a crowd, do we?

Carol (*uneasily*): No. Of course not.

Hatfield: Don't misunderstand me. They have one or two very comfortable private rooms. I could get one.

Carol (*lightly*): I'd never have thought you were that sort of man, Mr Hatfield. Major Burnside wouldn't approve at all.

Hatfield: Please don't joke with me! ... It would mean a very great deal to me if you could come.

Carol: I'm afraid I can't possibly accept until I know what's been decided about broadcast.

Hatfield: All right. But, if the broadcast is on, I'm in it too. And we'll dine together afterwards. I've just got time to nip down to the Barchester Arms and arrange about that room. Yes! I'll do that, and come straight back for you.

He moves towards her. Dorothy West comes in.

Dorothy: Sorry to butt in; but the engineer in charge wants to know what's happening.

Hatfield (*with meaning*): I'll see you later, Miss Mayne. Tell Mr Barran I'll be back in a quarter of an hour if I'm wanted.

Carol: You won't be later than that, will you? Or you'll be cutting it fine.

Hatfield: I never do that, Miss Mayne. I'm a careful man. (*He goes out.*)

Dorothy (*looking after him*): Cold-blooded fish, isn't he?

Carol (*sharply*): That comes well from *you*, doesn't it?

Dorothy: I'm not cold-blooded. It's not my fault if I'm the only person here who attends to business in an emergency.

Carol: That's one way of looking at it. But my business is with Tony Barran. And where *is* he?

Barran (*heard off*): I don't know yet, Mr Hatfield. I'll tell you when you come back!

Enter Barran and Bryce.

(*continuing, to Carol*) No, don't ask me! The Major has rung Head Office twice, and now seems inclined to cover himself with the Ministry of Information and Number 10 Downing Street. Meanwhile, we have five minutes left of a quarter of a show, nothing to fill in with, and three quarters of an hour before we go on the air?

Bryce (*with interest*): Tell me, young fellow. Does everybody at the BBC get as excited as you do?

Barran: I'm not excited! I never get excited!

Bryce: Why not look at the problem calmly and practically? When I ran the broadcasting station at Jubbulpore ...

Barran: I wish I was producing in Jubbulpore and not in Barchester.

Bryce: Imagine for the moment that you are.

Barran: For God's sake, why? Do you want to give me *more* headache?

Barran: My boy, I can assure you that in Jubbulpore we never knew from one half hour to another what we were going to put on the air. Now, what's your problem?

Barran: Jonas Whitehead is dead, so he can't play his flute. Penelope Squire has collapsed, and can't recite "The Ballad of Reading Gaol."

Bryce: What about your sea-lion merchant?

Carol: I'm afraid he's in gaol.

Barran (*to Bryce*): *In gaol!* Do you hear that?

Bryce: I must say I'm sorry to hear it.

Carol: He hit the Town Clerk in the eye for abducting one of his sea-lions. Anyway, he's not available.

Bryce: Would you be willing to leave this to me?

Barran: What do you mean?

Bryce: Just an idea, young fellow. It struck me that five minutes was rather short commons for a slap-bang, first-class murder mystery feature. Suppose you let me extend it to fifteen?

Barran: My God, I think you've got something!

Bryce: I know I have. That's one of the advantages of being elderly and
.fat.

Barran: But can you do it in the time?

Bryce: Time, young fellow, is relative. Read Einstein.

Dorothy (*patiently*): Can I tell the engineer in charge that the programme's going ahead?

Barran: We've got to wait for Major Burnside. Go on, Sir Henry.
What's your idea?

Enter Burnside, looking important.

Bryce: Ah, Tadpole! You were always on the spot when wanted, weren't
you?

Burnside: I hope so. By the way, must you keep on calling me Tadpole?

Bryce: Of course. You've grown into a big fish now. I must remember.

Carol and Barran gleefully shake hands.

Dorothy: What shall I tell the engineer in charge, Major Burnside?

Burnside (*with an air of finality*): The business is cancelled.

Barran: Oh, my God!

Burnside: That's a direct order from Head Office, Barran, and I don't
want any argument.

Barran: Argument? I'd as soon try and argue with the Albert Memorial.

Burnside: A man we all knew has just died here. Kindly don't forget it.

Bryce (*quietly*): He may even have been murdered by someone we all
know.

Burnside: My dear Colonel, that aspect of it had better be left to the
police. You can have every confidence in the Chief Constable. He's a
personal friend of mine.

Barran: Let's face it. We all know there's been another murder.

Carol (*pointedly*): And that the murderer, incidentally, *isn't* Wallace
Hatfield.

Barran (*viciously*): Yes, damn him! He's innocent.

Bryce: Damn him?

Burnside: Really, Barran!

Barran: I'm sorry. But isn't it reasonable for me to be a little worked up?

Burnside: You're always getting worked up, Barran. (*Uneasily*) As for
this whole question of murder, we don't *know* there was a murder ...

Barran (*satirically*): Don't we?

Burnside: Officially, no! The whole thing is *sub judice* until the police have finished their investigations.

Barran (*furiously*): Officially! *Sub judice*! Investigations! Two people have fallen from a belfry, with some maniac throwing flowers around them when they fall! And you —

Bryce (*suddenly dominating*): Maniac, young fellow? Don't jump to conclusions. I can sympathise with you. I hate being deprived of the opportunity of making my English debut at the microphone. I wanted to try out my idea. But there's still the problem of those two deaths, and I confess I don't see light ... yet.

Carol: You mean you think you will?

Bryce: I might.

Burnside: Get along, Miss West! Get along!

Dorothy: Yes, Major Burnside. I was just going. (*She goes out.*)

Barran (*to Burnside*): If my programme's gone, it's gone. Did you find out how Head Office propose to fill up the space?

Burnside: Naturally.

Barran: Well?

Burnside: They propose to revive *Monday Night at Eight* ...

Barran (*delicately*): On Saturday night at seven?

Burnside: Certainly. (*Barran groans.*) You may like it, Barran, or you may not. But there's nothing here to argue about. The programme has been cancelled. There's nothing more for us to do here, and the sooner we all get home the better.

Barran: Yes. It's past six o'clock, isn't it?

Burnside (*unheeding*): Miss West is informing the engineers. Miss Mayne! Please see to it that the studio is left in clean and orderly condition. Perhaps you will ring up Miss Squire and find out how *she* is. And if you, Barran, will inform Mr Hatfield we no longer require him tonight ...

Bryce (*sharply*): Just a minute, Burnside. We *do* require Hatfield. We *do* require the use of this building tonight.

Burnside (*flustered*): I don't understand you!

Bryce (*seriously*): Look here, Tadpole. You used to have a lot of respect for me in the old days. Do you still have it?

Burnside (*spluttering*): Well ... !

Bryce: Do you?

Burnside (*with dignity*): Naturally!

Bryce: Very well. You spoke of the Chief Constable just now. This is a time for plain speaking on *my* part. I know him too; and he's God's gift to criminals. Someone is going to get away with a double murder unless we ... all of us ... do something about it.

Burnside: But what can *we* do?

Bryce: You can do what I suggest. In a case of murder ...

Enter Phillimore.

Phillimore: Did I hear someone mention the word murder, gentlemen?

Carol: Mr Phillimore!

Burnside: What can I do for *you*, Phillimore?

Phillimore: Nothing, thank you. It's something I can do for you. *Did* someone mention the word murder?

Bryce: Certainly. I did.

Phillimore: I've just come from the police, gentlemen. I told them they could set their minds at rest; and now I've come to tell you too. There was no murder.

Carol: No murder?

Burnside (*angrily*): Oh, I've had about enough of this! I'm going home! (*He stalks across angrily to pour himself a glass of water at the table.*)

Phillimore: Old Jonas Whitehead was not murdered. Don't you want to hear the truth, Major Burnside?

Bryce: I'm very anxious to hear the truth, Mr Phillimore. Why are you so certain Jonas Whitehead wasn't murdered?

Phillimore: Because I was there. I saw the whole thing happen.

Pneumatic drill starts outside, violently. Burnside, who has started to pour out a glass of water, drops the glass on the floor.

Carol: Major Burnside! What on earth is the matter?

Burnside: Nothing at all! It's these damned pneumatic drills. They remind me of a machine-gun. Eh, Colonel?

Bryce (*startled; then slowly*): They do, rather. They make *me* think of ... (*stops*) Well, Mr Phillimore? Go ahead.

Phillimore: I was in the belfry when it happened.

Burnside: In the belfry? That's impossible!

Phillimore: Why?

Burnside: Old Jonas was the bell-ringer. No. He had the only key to the belfry-door.

Phillimore: I beg your pardon. No. I am, or was, the principal of this school. I also ... (*suavely takes key from waistcoat pocket*) ... I also have a key to that door.

Bryce: What took you up into the belfry?

Phillimore (*agreeably*): I was following a trail. Of flowers. A trail that led up into the belfry.

Barran (*under his breath*): For the love of Mike, is this man out of his head?

Phillimore: Out of my head? Not at all.

Bryce: Then what *do* you mean?

Phillimore: A little more than two hours ago ...

Bryce (*quickly*): You mean *before* Jonas Whitehead died?

Phillimore: Yes.

Carol: Did you see who killed him?

Phillimore: Wait!

Bryce: Go on, man!

Phillimore: I was passing this school on the way to my dentist's. You can confirm the appointment which I did not keep. On the paving-stones of the yard, just under one of the arches of the belfry, I saw a flower. Do I need to tell you that the flower was an Arum lily?

Bryce: Go on!

Phillimore: A windy day, gentlemen. Do I need to remind you? While I stood there, thinking of flowers and blood, another of those flowers drifted down as though from the gold bar of heaven. (*Changing his tone*) Actually, from the belfry.

Bryce: You seem to be enjoying your story, Mr Phillimore.

Phillimore: I have always been susceptible to the literary aspect of crime, Colonel Bryce. Pen, pencil, and poison. Shall I continue?

Bryce: What did you *do*?

Phillimore: I took this key. (*Holds it up*) I opened the belfry door, and I went up the winding staircase.

Bryce: Expecting to find a murderer waiting for you? You're a brave man.

Phillimore: *I* can take care of myself.

Barran (*intently*): But if you had the only other key ... you could be certain there'd be nobody there.

Burnside: Quite true. (*Suddenly*) Barran! What are you suggesting?

Phillimore (*unheeding*): I went up those winding stairs, past the little windows that let light into the tower. And I heard what you all must have heard. I heard the bell begin to ring. But there was a very odd thing about that. I could see the whole length of the bell-rope, which hung down into the tower. And there was no hand pulling at that rope.

Barran (*under his breath*): Look here, this fellow's off his chump!

Carol: Quiet, Tony!

Phillimore: It was a ghostly business, I assure you. The moving rope. The clanging bell. But nobody there. (*Slight pause*) Then I heard footsteps ... slow footsteps ... coming up the stairs behind me.

Burnside: Jonas Whitehead?

Phillimore: Yes. Old Jonas. I drew back into the embrasure of a window, and he went past without seeing me. I followed him.

Barran: By the way, you're wearing rubber-soled shoes.

Phillimore: He wouldn't have heard me anyway. The bell was making too much noise.

Carol: And then?

Phillimore: I followed Jonas into the belfry. (*To Bryce*) It's a small belfry, Colonel, with only one ledge you can walk round. A perilous place, where the soul may drop if the body doesn't. That was where I saw the bunch of lilies.

Bryce (*sharply*): Where?

Phillimore: On the edge of the little stone parapet. Not far from the door. I could see them past the bell. Jonas saw them too. He went towards them. He put out his hand ...

Burnside: But who attacked him?

Phillimore: Nobody attacked him. He stumbled.

Bryce: Stumbled?

Phillimore: As he stretched out his hand to touch those flowers he screamed and fell forward. Then I heard his body strike the paving-stones below. It was as though an invisible hand had ...

Burnside (*drily grim*): The same invisible hand, I suppose, that rang the bell?

Phillimore: Perhaps. I don't know.

Burnside (*explosively*): I've had *more* than I can stand of this!

Bryce: Take it easy, Tadpole!

Burnside: Invisible hands ringing bells! Invisible hands throwing people out of towers ... !

Phillimore: Excuse me. I said merely that he stumbled, and that nobody attacked him.

Burnside (*pulling himself up*): Of course, you know, if it (*with relief*) *was* an accident after all ...

Carol: It wasn't an accident. We all know that!

Burnside: Then how, I ask you, did poor Whitehead die? You can't kill a man with thin air.

Bryce (*thoughtfully*): No. Of course not. Have you told this story to the police?

Phillimore: Yes.

Bryce: And do they believe you?

Phillimore (*agreeably*): Oh, no. In fact, they asked me to tell it to them all over again so that they can catch me out. In the meantime, I wanted to tell the story to independent witnesses. Good-bye. (*He turns towards the door.*)

Bryce: One moment, Mr Phillimore. When must you go back for this interview with the police?

Phillimore: At half past eight. I thought of getting myself a little dinner before my arrest. The condemned, as they say, always eats a hearty meal.

Bryce: Would it upset your arrangements to come back here for half an hour at seven o'clock?

Phillimore: Why at seven o'clock?

Bryce: I am ... "compèring," I believe is the word ... a short broadcast feature about the Barchester murders.

Burnside: Colonel Bryce, I thought you understood ...

Bryce (*meaningly*): I understand perfectly, Tadpole. So, I hope, do you. I am compèring this short feature at seven o'clock, and in its altered form it would be an enormous help if I could include a few questions to Mr Phillimore. I can't believe Mr Phillimore will object.

Phillimore: Certainly not. Do I have to rehearse?

Bryce: Barran and I are trying an experiment. Impromptu interview without rehearsal.

Barran (*dazed*): Will someone kindly wake me up?

Carol: If this is a dream, Tony, we're both dreaming it.

Bryce (*impatiently*): Can I count on you, Mr Phillimore?

Phillimore: Certainly ... if I'm not arrested in the interval. Would you like my wife as well?

Bryce: Could you persuade her to come?

Phillimore: I fancy I can. (*To Burnside*) It's not my business, Major Burnside, but aren't you taking rather a risk with this programme?

Burnside: Mr Barran is responsible for the production of this programme. Not I.

Barran (*spluttering*): *Responisble?* I?

Bryce: I shall look forward to seeing you and your wife, Mr Phillimore, in
about twenty minutes. I'm very grateful.

Exit Phillimore.

Everyone stares bewildered at Bryce.

Barran (*to Bryce*): Look here, sir! What's the joke?

Bryce: There's no joke. I've never been more serious in my life.

Burnside: Serious?

Bryce: It's the duty of every good citizen, Tadpole, to assist the law.
That's all I'm asking you to do. I give you my word that I can solve
this mystery if you'll help me.

Burnside: How?

Bryce: Very simply. Carry on with your programme.

Barran (*explosively*): But this programme is o-u-t. We've been forbidden
to go on the air!

Bryce: But we're going on the air.

Carol: What's at the back of your mind, Sir Henry?

Bryce: Wait and see.

Burnside: This is the most irregular thing yet! I ... I can't allow it!

Bryce (*intently*): Listen, Tadpole. Did you say you trusted me, or not?

Burnside (*at a loss*): Well! ...

Bryce: What risk are you running, if I give you my word to cover you with
your Head Office?

Burnside: No risk, I suppose. But — can you do it?

Bryce: Let's call it settled. I especially want you to be present, Tadpole.
Come with me while I telephone to London.

Burnside (*resignedly*): All right. But I wash my hands of it! And if you're
adding Mr and Mrs Phillimore to this programme ...

Carol (*awkwardly*): Mr Hatfield should be back any minute now.

Barran: Why?

Carol: Mr Hatfield wants to take me out to dinner.

Barran: Oh, he does, does he?

Burnside: Very well. You'd better wait here and explain that the broadcast is on after all.

Barran: But what about scripts, Sir Henry?

Bryce: I've a notion, young fellow, ssh! (*He puts a finger to his lips.*)

Exeunt Bryce and Burnside.

Barran: Carol.   Kindly put some ice on my head and play me the "Knightsbridge March."[13]

Carol: I could crown you with pleasure.

Barran: What have I done now?

Carol: You're not usually so dumb, Tony.

Barran: You mean to say you understand what's happening?

Carol: Of course.

Barran: Then would you mind explaining to your idiot boy?

Carol: There isn't time; and Wallace Hatfield will be here any minute

Barran: Yes. He will, won't he? What's this about your having dinner with him?

Carol: He asked me to dine with him at the Barchester Arms.

Barran: He did, did he?

Carol: He suggested a private room, Tony.

Barran: Well, I'll be damned! He's got a nerve! You're not going?

Carol: I was thinking about it.

Barran: Stop. And stop now!

Carol: Don't order me about, Tony Barran! I'll dine with anyone I like wherever I like.

Barran: Do you know, I think you're leading me on.

Carol: *What?*

Barran: Of course you are. Dumb-bell I certainly am! You never meant to dine with Hatfield in a private room. Your whole tone about him is quite different, suddenly. What's happened?

Carol: It sounds silly. But I suppose I was only sorry for him because you all thought he was guilty. When you all know he's innocent, and he knows you know it, I ...

Barran: Well? You begin to think of him as a person; is that it?

Carol (*reluctantly*): I suppose so.

Barran: And not even as a particularly nice person.

Carol: I suppose it's natural enough for him to want to gloat a bit.

Barran: Gloat?

---

[13]"Knightsbridge March" was a movement from Eric Coates' *London Suite* used to introduce *In Town Tonight*, the programme on which *Out of Town Tonight* was based.

Carol: Yes, Tony. That's what it came to. He was really gloating over poor old Jonas' death, because it proved his innocence. I didn't like it, and I didn't like *him!*

Barran: And so perhaps you take a rather better view of me!

Carol: I don't know. I'm scared, Tony.

Barran: There's nothing to be frightened of. I think old Bryce has got a bee in his bonnet; but I swear he's as safe as houses! Give me your hand.

Carol: My pulse is perfectly regular, thank you.

Barran: Give me your hand! Always hold hands when you're scared.

Carol: Tony!

Barran: And I've been told that a kiss can be a comforting thing.

Carol: Do you want your face smacked?

Barran: By all means, in a good cause. (*He kisses her.*) Weren't you going to smack my face?

Carol: Yes. I still am. (*She kisses him.*)

Barran: That was a very pleasant slap in the face. You must make a practice of knocking me about. Somehow, I don't think you'll be dining in a private room with Mr Wallace Hatfield this evening.

Carol: Nor do I.

Barran: It seems a pity to waste the room. Shall I ring up the Barchester Arms? (*She smacks his face.*) So you've begun kissing me now, have you?

Carol: Tony, this isn't a time for fooling about. What do you think's at the back of Colonel Bryce's mind?

Barran: He suspects somebody. What I'm wondering is ... who?

Carol: Do you think he believed Phillimore's story?

Barran: I know *I* didn't. The things's an absurdity; and it's all too slick.

Carol: You mean you think Phillimore himself ...

Barran: No.

Carol: He's not guilty?

Barran: He's not guilty, Carol; but he's shielding somebody. Otherwise, why tell that story?

Carol: But who would he be shielding?

Barran (*slowly*): There's Mrs Phillimore.

Carol: Stop, Tony! If we go on like this, we'll end by suspecting each other. Or Jill Whitehead! Or Dorothy West! Or Major Burnside!

Barran (*amused*): Come off it, darling! You can go as far as you like, in general, but that's going too far. Major Burnside as a murderer is something to dream about!

Carol: I know that, of course. I suppose it's because he's just as edgy as the rest of us. Did you notice him drop that glass?

Barran (*impatiently*): It was the damn pneumatic drill, that's all. He was shell-shocked in the last war.

Carol (*remembering*): Yes! He complained about those drills this morning. That was when he was warning me so strongly against Wallace Hatfield.

Barran: The point is, Carol, that Phillimore's story is impossible! Then why did he tell it?

Enter Hatfield.

Hatfield: Well, Miss Mayne, are you ready?

Barran: Carol, you're not going to ... ?

Carol: You'd better see Sir Henry, and find out what he's up to, Tony. I'll just explain to Mr Hatfield.

Barran: I think I'd rather ...

Carol: Please, Tony!

Barran looks uncertainly from her to Hatfield, and then goes out.

Hatfield: What about his new "arrangement?" Does that mean ... ?

Carol: It means the broadcast stands, but in a slightly different form.

Hatfield: I'm surprised to hear that. I'm ... sorry to hear that. It means we can't dine before eight o'clock.

Carol: I'm afraid I can't dine with you at all.

Hatfield: Not ... I see. (*He moves away from her; then back again.*) Perhaps I was asking too much, all of a sudden. You mustn't blame me for having dreams about you; impossible and lovely dreams. I felt free suddenly; and I lost my head.

Carol: I understand.

Hatfield: I'm sure you do. You've always understood me. I ought to have remembered that I'm a middle-aged failure of fifty, and that you're very young and very beautiful. You're in love with Tony Barran, aren't you?

Carol: Yes.

Hatfield: You'll let me wish you happiness, won't you? I know he doesn't like me; but perhaps you'd both give me the pleasure of dining with me after the show?

Carol (*touched*): Mr Hatfield! That's awfully ...

Hatfield (*stifling emotion*): Let's not talk any more about it. (*Quickly*) Er
— what are the new arrangements for the show?

Carol: Sir Henry Bryce is going to fill the time. Impromptu questioning, I
expect of you ... and Mr and Mrs Phillimore.

Hatfield (*amazed*): Phillimore?

Carol: Yes. Have you heard this extraordinary story he's told the police?

Hatfield: Yes. I met him, and he told me. But I didn't know he'd told
the police. I thought he was pulling my leg. I'm sorry he's told the
police.

Carol: Why?

Hatfield: Because it's incredible!

Carol: Do you think he's guilty?

Hatfield: No! You heard what I said just before old Jonas was killed —

Carol: Well?

Hatfield: I was thinking of motive. (*Fiercely*) Thinking his idea was to kill
Lucy and get me hanged for it.

Carol: Then why kill Jonas Whitehead?

Hatfield: Exactly! That's the snag! Why kill poor old Jonas, and tell this
incredible story on top of it? You *admit* it's an incredible story?

Carol: Of course! Everybody does!

Hatfield: Maybe Sir Henry will be able to tell us. Has Phillimore agreed
to take part in this broadcast?

Carol: Yes. He's just gone to fetch his wife.

Hatfield: I envy him, his nerve.

Carol: Then you do think he's guilty?

Hatfield: I don't know what I think now. I just feel bewildered and rather
stupid. I think I'll sit down and try to pull myself together.

Carol: You're not feeling ill?

Hatfield: No, no!

He goes to one of the settees, and sits down as Barran, Bryce,
Burnside, and Leila Ponsonby come in, followed by Dorothy West.

Barran: Aren't the Phillimores here yet, Carol?

Carol: Not yet.

Barran (*to Bryce*): I think I've got the whole thing straight, sir, but if they
don't turn up —

Bryce: They'll turn up, all right.

Barran: Well, it's your production. How do you want people arranged?

Burnside: I presume you can find room for me in the Listening Room,

Barran?

Bryce: If you don't mind, Burnside, I prefer you in the studio. I may have one or two questions for you.

Hatfield: But what about scripts and the censorship you were making so much fuss about this morning?

Burnside: I have communicated specially with Head Office, Mr Hatfield. The acceptance of responsibility by Sir Henry Bryce naturally makes all the difference.

Bryce: Naturally.

Hatfield: I see.

Barran: Very well; let's get lined up. (*Looks at his watch*) Eight minutes to go! Where the hell are the Phillimores? Carol, you go into the Listening Room with Dorothy. By the way, Dorothy, which channel is the microphone in the belfry on?

Dorothy: Number three, Mr Barran. (*She goes into the Listening Room, followed by Carol.*)

Hatfield: Microphone in the belfry?

Bryce: Just an idea of mine, Mr Hatfield. Local atmosphere, and all that. I think I'll be on the side of the microphone looking towards the Listening Room. Then Barran can make faces at me if he wants to. Eh, young fellow?

Barran: I've warned you I've a censorship-switch. One indiscretion, and you're out. Cut.

Leila: Six and a half minutes, Tony!

Barran: I know! (*Enter Mr and Mrs Phillimore.*) Ah, here's the rest of the cast! Just in time!

Phillimore: You didn't think I was going to disappoint you, surely?

Barran: Show them their positions, Leila, will you? I must just take a test. (*He goes into the Listening Room.*)
  Leila places the Phillimores and Hatfield on one side of the microphone; Bryce and Burnside on the other. Mrs Phillimore edges away from Hatfield.

Leila: You'll have to let me in for my announcement, Colonel Bryce. No, Mrs Phillimore: between your husband and Mr Hatfield, please.

Judith: But I ...

Leila: Please, for balance! Each of you men can speak over her shoulder.

Barran (*over speaker*): Just a few lines for voice-test.

Bryce: "Now is the time for all good men to come to the aid of the party."

Barran (*over talk-back*): You're booming.

Bryce: Of course I am, young fellow. I like to boom.

Barran: Yes, sir. But it frightens the microphone. About six inches back, please.

Bryce grunts explosively, and moves unwillingly.

Barran: Now, you others! Mrs Phillimore.

Judith: I don't know what to say. I wish I hadn't come. But when Colonel Bryce told me ...

Phillimore: That'll do, Judith! Personally, I'm more than glad of the opportunity to tell my story to the world.

Hatfield: And so am I, by God!

Barran: Oi! Oi! No blasphemy, please! That balances all right. Now don't move about; don't cough; keep your heads and watch Colonel Bryce. He'll pull you through. Have you and Hatfield got your scripts, Colonel?

Leila hands them over.

Leila: Ninety seconds to go, Tony!

In the Listening Room, Barran picks up the control-room telephone. The red lights over the studio door and the Listening Room window begin to flicker. They steady. Dorothy West can be seen starting a gramophone record. Barran gives a green-light cue for the announcer.

Leila: *Out of Town Tonight!* Once again we stop the current of busy life in towns and villages throughout the British Isles, and bring to listeners some of the interesting people who are "out of town tonight."

Barran is seen gesticulating to Dorothy to bring up her gramophone-record to full. There is a pause, and again the green light.

Tonight, the first of our items in this programme comes from Barchester, that old-world Midland town well-known for its picturesque countryside, its quiet river, and its superb industrial achievement. In Barchester tonight, in the basement of the old schoolhouse, is Colonel Sir Henry Bryce, K.C.S.I.,[14] once a famous head of the Indian Police Service. He is going to discuss a famous

---

[14]"K.C.S.I." — Knight Commander in the Most Exalted Order of the Star of India, an order of Knighthood in the British Honours system, created in 1861, moribund since India was proclaimed independent and partitioned into India and Pakistan in 1947.

Barchester mystery, an unsolved murder mystery which took place in this very building four years ago, when Mrs Wallace Hatfield was found dead at the base of the school's belfry. With Colonel Bryce tonight are Mr Wallace Hatfield, husband of the victim; Mr Paul Phillimore, principal of the school, with his wife — and Major Burnside, our own Regional Director. Here is Colonel Sir Henry Bryce.

Bryce (*thunderously*): Haa, h'mm! (*Barran gesticulates furiously at him.*) Ladies and gentlemen, you'll realise that we are confined to question and answer. We have no time for a long explanation of circumstances. I must assume you are familiar with the background of the tragedy. Now, Mr Phillimore, you'll agree with me that the question of motive is paramount.

Phillimore: Certainly.

Bryce: Is it a fact that you had the strongest possible reason for a personal dislike of Mr Hatfield?

Phillimore: Yes.

Bryce: You agree, Mrs Phillimore?

Judith: Have I got to answer that? Major Burnside — ?

Burnside: Not if you don't want to.

Bryce: Conclusions can be drawn from refusal to answer, you know. What have you to say, Mr Hatfield?

Hatfield: I deny it absolutely. May I ask a question, Sir Henry?

Bryce: Mr Hatfield, I am the question master and my next question is, was Mr Phillimore carrying a blackboard pointer in his hand when he visited these premises on the day of Mrs Hatfield's murder?

Hatfield: The very question, Sir Henry.

Bryce: Quite. You mentioned it this morning. Well, Mr Phillimore?

Phillimore (*puzzled*): No, of course I wasn't carrying a blackboard pointer.

Bryce: But there would be such a thing on these premises?

Phillimore: Yes. But I don't see ...

Hatfield: I do.

Bryce: At least it would not look very unusual for you to be seen carrying such a thing.

Phillimore: I suppose not.

Bryce: Now, Major Burnside ...

Burnside (*nervously*): What can I tell you?

Bryce: A very simple thing. Could the bruise found on Mrs Hatfield's body — a small bruise about the size of a sixpence — have been made by a violent jab from a blackboard pointer?

Mrs Phillimore screams.

Phillimore: Quiet, Judith!

Judith: But he's practically accusing you ...

Bryce: I'm accusing nobody. I'm asking questions.

Hatfield: And most interesting questions, too.

Bryce: Is it true, Burnside, there were no footprints found in the belfry except Mrs Hatfield's?

Burnside: Quite true.

Bryce: Mr Hatfield, it was your idea about the pointer that started me on this line. Have you any theory about the footprints that weren't there?

Hatfield: Yes. The ledge round the belfry is exposed to wind and weather. Suppose the murderer, carrying his pointer, walked round that exposed parapet.

Bryce: Most ingenious. Shall we go up and look at this parapet?

Judith: Look at it?

Bryce: Ladies and gentlemen, in broadcasting jargon, we are now taking you over to the scene of the crime.

Hatfield: The scene of the crime?

Bryce: Major Burnside and his engineers have been good enough to fix a microphone in the belfry itself. There will be a delay of perhaps half a minute while we are climbing — just how many steps, Burnside?

Burnside: Good God, how should I know? Er — ladies and gentlemen, I beg your pardon.

Bryce: Granted, I'm sure. There are, I believe, fifty-nine steps.

Hatfield: You're a keen observer, Sir Henry.

Bryce: So I've been told. Shall we go?

Judith: You mean you believe this fantastic story about my husband and the blackboard pointer? Even if there had been something between me and Wallace Hatfield ...

Phillimore: That's enough, Judith.

Hatfield: Quite enough.

Bryce: Perhaps I may as well say, so that you can think it over while we're on our way up, that the theory, though ingenious, is not the true explanation. By the way, Major Burnside, one more question.

Burnside: Well?

Bryce: Isn't it getting very stuffy again in this studio?

Burnside: Perhaps it is a little oppressive.

Bryce: Then would you mind pushing down that emergency ventilation handle. By the door, there.

Burnside: You really want me to?

Bryce: Definitely.

Burnside: Very well.

Phillimore: Isn't this rather a waste of time?

Bryce: I don't think so.

Burnside crosses to the door and pulls down the handle.

Right down, please, a full turn. Now, Mr Hatfield, will you lead the way to the belfry?

Hatfield: I?

Bryce: You have a key, I believe?

Hatfield: Nothing of the kind.

Bryce: Have you lost it?

Hatfield: What do you mean?

Bryce: I just want you to lead the way up fifty-nine steps to a belfry where there is no one to ring a bell that we shall all hear in about thirty seconds from now.

Hatfield: I tell you I haven't got a key. Phillimore has one. Let him go ahead.

Phillimore: Certainly.

Bryce: No thank you, Mr Phillimore.

Phillimore: Why not?

Bryce: Well, Mr Hatfield?

Hatfield: Well?

Bryce: I'm merely asking you to lead the way up to the belfry and stand precisely on the spot where Mrs Hatfield stood when she entered the belfry and saw a bunch of Arum lilies lying so inexplicably upon the parapet on its further side. Where she was standing, Mr Hatfield, when that bell began to ring?

From overhead comes the clanging of the bell.

Hatfield: I won't go. The murderer must be up there. Can't you hear the bell?

Bryce: My last question — shall I tell you why you won't go?

Hatfield: If you think you can.

Bryce: I know I can.

He moves swiftly to the ventilating handle and pushes it up. During
the next few lines the bell gradually dies down and stops.
Do you still refuse to go up to the belfry, Mr Hatfield?

Hatfield: It's damned foolery, but have it your own way.

Bryce: I've had it. If you'd entered that belfry when I invited you to,
you'd have died as your wife died and as Jonas Whitehead died.

Burnside: My God, Bryce, what do you mean?

Bryce: Just this. Mr Hatfield's a builder. Mr Hatfield built this schoolhouse. Mr Hatfield turned this basement into a broadcasting studio.
Mr Hatfield could make a key of any door in the place. Mr Hatfield
is an owner of pneumatic drills, two of them are working on those air-
raid shelters outside. You've heard them.

Phillimore: Go on, man, go on!

Bryce: You needn't hurry me. There's plenty of time, now. Do you
know what pneumatic drills are run by?

Phillimore: You mean compressed air?

Bryce: Compressed air — the thin air which Major Burnside said today
couldn't kill a man. Compressed air generating eighty pounds
pressure per square inch. Compressed air governed by the turning of
that handle on the wall there, forced out from a pipe set in that belfry
by its builder Mr Hatfield at an angle which struck anyone crossing its
floor like the kick of a mule. Or the jab of a blackboard pointer.

Hatfield: All right, damn you. Anything else you want to know?

Bryce: I don't think so. You were tired of your wife and you killed her.
The alibi you'd arranged for Phillimore here came to grief because he
was late. You had killed your wife, but you couldn't prove you hadn't.

Hatfield: You can't prove anything now.

Bryce: Not even when I show the police the jet that carried the compressed air?

Hatfield: Compressed air can drive a rivet. It *could* knock a victim out of
that belfry. But how does anyone make the victim cross the line of the
compressed air?

Bryce: Have you forgotten the aAum lilies?

Phillimore: They were the bait.

Bryce: Of course. There was one narrow path leading round the edge of
the belfry. Whoever walked it, died.

Burnside: And the ringing of the bell?

Bryce: If the compressed air was driven in bursts like the working of a pneumatic drill, the bell would ring. The bell hung in the path of that jet, until someone came between.

Hatfield: Are you forgetting that I was acquitted of the murder of my wife and that I can't be tried again for the same crime?

Bryce: Are you forgetting that Jonas Whitehead died by the same method this afternoon? Died while you were surrounded by witnesses to your alibi to show how genuinely innocent you were.

Hatfield: Prove it.

Bryce: When I was in India, I had a considerable reputation as a picker of pockets. This comes from your overcoat pocket, Mr Hatfield. (*He holds out a piece of paper.*)

Burnside (*snatching it*): Hemple & Dawes, Florists; Two dozen Arum lilies.

Hatfield: Aren't you forgetting that this performance has been broadcast to the world. It'll need a good deal of explanation in a Court of Justice!

The red lights go off. Barran comes out of the Listening Room followed by Carol.

Barran: I'm afraid *not*, Mr Hatfield. Experiment on a closed circuit only. Thanks for putting me on to the most interesting feature I have *not* broadcast in years!

Carol puts her hand into Barran's.

Hatfield: Well, I've had four years ... four years to watch a man I hated break his heart, eh, Phillimore? Four years in which to watch a town of fools I despised shuddering every time they looked at me. Four years of supreme satisfaction. All I regret is that they weren't forty-four. I think I deserved them. Yes, you're an observant man, Sir Henry Bryce.

Bryce: That is my reputation. I've observed one other thing.

Hatfield: What is it this time?

Bryce: Wallace Hatfield, there are fifty-nine steps to that belfry. There are only thirteen to the gallows!

CURTAIN

AFTERWORD

Carr first used the central device of *Thirteen to the Gallows* in the radio play "The Man Without a Body" broadcast on CBS in the series *Suspense* on June 22, 1943. Unlike the majority of his scripts for *Suspense*, Carr did not adapt the script of "The Man Without a Body" for the BBC's *Appointment with Fear.* There is, of course, also a similarity with the Carter Dickson novel *He Wouldn't Kill Patience* (1944). Both that novel and "The Man Without a Body" appear to have been inspired by the secret of "Psycho," an illusion first presented by John Nevil Maskelyne, one of the magicians whose career was described in Carr's BBC radio documentary, "Magicians' Progress," broadcast on July 21, 1944. A portable version of the means of murder features prominently in the Oscar-winning film *No Country for Old Men* (2007).

Intruding Shadow

A Play

by

John Dickson Carr

Intruding Shadow

The Characters

Story-teller	The Man in Black
Richard Marlowe	A writer
George Parsons	Marlowe's uncle
Ellen Parsons	His wife
Stephen Sowerby	Divisional Inspector
Bruce Renfield	West End blackmailer
Anne Corbin	Who is being blackmailed
Flint	Marlowe's manservant

The scene is the study of Richard Marlowe's house in Regent's Park.

Out of a dark theatre we hear the musical introduction, and then the voice of the Narrator.

Story-teller: Appointment with Fear! (*Musical theme*) This is your Story-teller, the Man in Black, here to bring you the living shapes and scenes from our nursery tales, *Appointment with Fear.* As usual, good friends, I myself shall remain invisible; and yet, before the end of the evening ... (*chuckles*) ... I trust I shall be very close to you. There are many amusing stories in this notebook of mine. Let me tell you first as we sit here cosily together, of a man who thought of a good joke. A good joke: yes. This man dealt much with crime, as I do; I knew Richard Marlowe well. And so, one summer night ... take care, now! For things are not quite what they seem ... one night at half-past eleven o'clock, upstairs in the study of his house in Regent's Park ...

177

Faint music is heard under as voice fades. The lights go up to show Richard Marlowe's study.

It is a richly furnished, book-lined room, of a sombre description with a hint of the macabre. As we look at it from the front, we have, facing us back centre, heavy double-doors now closed. In the right hand wall, up, is a door leading presumably to a bedroom. In the left hand wall, down, is another door presumably to a cupboard. In this same wall is a fireplace, with built in book shelves on either side. On the mantelpiece is a clock, with a large picture of a macabre quality hanging on the wall above. A little way out from the screened fireplace is a library table, with a typewriter pushed to one side of it ... the surface of the table being scattered with books and papers. The room is lighted by electric wall-candles and by a lamp standing on the library table: all being controlled, apparently, by a wall-switch beside the double-doors to the right. There are overstuffed easy chairs, with divan standing slanted on the right so that anyone sitting on it will be almost full-face to us. We have, in any case, an uninterrupted view of the double-doors at the back.

As the lights slowly go up, we see George Parsons standing facing us behind the library table. In appearance he is a meek, mild, absent-minded man in his fifties: a minor civil-servant in type. He wears spectacles and his hair is scanty. His clothes, though neat and well-brushed, are rather shabby.

He picks up, one after the other, the books lying scattered on the table, and dubiously reads the title of each aloud before putting the book down.

Parsons: *On Murder, Considered as One of the Fine Arts* ... Hans Gross: *Criminal Investigations* ... *Poisons and their Detection* ... *The Trial of* — *(Shaking his head, he puts down the book and absent-mindedly picks up the first one he has consulted.)* Nothing to read in this house but — !
The double-doors at the back are opened, giving us a glimpse of a dimly lighted hall with the suggestion of a staircase going down. Ellen Parsons, his wife and Richard Marlowe's aunt, puts her head in. She is a rather large woman in her late forties; she might have once been handsome. You would call her kindly, if somewhat futile and with a

tendency to be flustered. Just now she is agitated.

Ellen (*calling softly*): George!

Parsons (*jumping*): Yes, my dear?

Ellen (*voice rising*): George! What on earth — ?

Parsons (*points nervously to door to right*): Sh-h! Richard's in the bedroom!

Ellen: Then what are you *doing* here, George Parsons? You *know* Richard doesn't like people in his study!

Parsons: It's all right, my dear, I won't disturb him.

Ellen: You *will* disturb him, if he sees you! Don't you think you might have a little consideration for *me*?

Parsons: All I want, Ellen, is something to read in bed.

He wanders to one side of the table, well down left, near the cupboard door, to peer at the bookshelves there. He is still holding a book in his hand.

Ellen (*desperately*): George, come away from there! Considering we practically live off Richard ... !

Parsons (*wistfully*): A nice Western now. Or something funny.

Muffled voices are heard off, behind the closed door to the bedroom. We can faintly distinguish the words, "where the devil's my coat?" and the reply, "Here, sir."

Ellen (*crying out*): George!

Parsons, now alarmed, looks round quickly; sees he hasn't time to reach the double-doors to the hall; and bolts like a rabbit into the cupboard, nearly closing the door after him. Ellen retires, closing the double-doors. Richard Marlowe hurries in. He is a tall, personable man in his late thirties, with an engaging charm of manner, just now struggling to repress some emotion. He wears a silk dressing-gown, with a silk scarf tied at the throat, over ordinary clothes. He is smoking a cigarette, and speaking half over his shoulder as though completing a tirade.

Flint, his manservant, is a cold-eyed, watchful man of forty-odd. He is well-spoken, and nobody's fool. He follows Marlowe, carrying the jacket of a dark lounge-suit..

Richard: In any case, Flint, I can't stand there arguing all night. I tell you ...! (*He stops short, looking across at the clock on the mantelpiece.*) Twenty-five minutes to twelve! Is that clock right?

Flint: Yes, sir. Just right.

Richard goes to the library table and stubs out the cigarette in an ashtray.

Richard: Twenty-five minutes to twelve! She should have been here nearly half an hour ago!

Flint: Maybe the young lady's not coming, sir.

Richard: She'll be here, Flint. She's got to be here. Anyway, she doesn't know.

Flint: Doesn't know she's going to watch a murder?

Richard (*uneasily*): Sh-h!

Flint: Is anything wrong, sir?

Richard: I tell you, Flint, it's only a joke! Don't make it sound as though I were really going to kill the man!

Flint: No, sir. But — may I speak frankly?

Richard: Naturally.

Flint: I don't like it, sir.

Richard (*with heavy patience*): Listen, Flint. I keep writing and writing on the subject of murder. What do I actually know about murder?

Flint: Quite as much as you need to know, sir.

Richard, unheeding, goes upstage, back, and indicates books in a shelf.

Richard: *Death in the Summer-House*, by Richard Marlowe. *The Nine Black Clues*, by Richard Marlowe. *Murder at Whispering Lodge*, by Richard Marlowe. A whole line of cheap detective novels with no more relation to real life than a child's story-book. (*He comes back again.*) Think of it, Flint! Murder! The most serious crime in the world!

Flint: Yes, sir. But ... !

Richard: The temptation that won't let you go. The urge to kill somebody you hate. The impulse that blinds you, and destroys your judgment, and turns a normal person into a raving lunatic. You don't think of the consequences. You don't think of anything! Just so long as a sneering face, a hated face, can be ... (*He breaks off.*) and I treat it as though it were a parlour-game to pass away a dull evening! (*Annoyed*)

Flint: Don't you think that's — well, the best way to treat it?

Richard: No, Flint. Not for the book I'm *going* to write. (*He goes to the table, and swings round again.*) Let's take, for instance, the sort of thing that does happen. A certain girl, let's say, has been badly treated by a man who deserves to die ...

Flint (*startled*): Excuse me, sir. You don't mean that Miss Corbin and Mr

Renfield ... ?

Richard (*amused*): No, Flint. Not at all in the way *you* mean.

Flint: Sorry, sir.

Richard: Another man — myself, let's imagine — decides to kill him.

He goes to the fireplace, where he picks up a heavy iron poker. He returns to the table and stands behind it, weighing the poker in his hand.

What are that girl's reactions, when she really thinks she's going to see Renfield's head battered in? What does she say? What does she feel? What does she think? And the oh-so-bored Mr Renfield? What does he feel, what does he think, when he believes it's his last second on earth? When I approach him, very slowly, in this room? When ... (*Slowly he brings the poker up and over, as though hitting with it.*)

Flint: Do you think it's quite fair to the young lady, sir?

Richard: She'll enjoy it, Flint. Deep down in her heart she wants to see that fellow dead.

Flint: She'll never let you go through with it.

Richard: I think she will, Flint. Ever hear of the rabbit fascinated by the snake?

Flint (*woodenly*): Yes, sir.

Richard throws the poker on the table.

Richard: As for Mr Bruce Renfield, he deserves to be scared within an inch of his life. And that's exactly what he's going to get. The great thing is for me to convince both of 'em, convince 'em absolutely, that I've turned into a murderer. I've got to put on an act that will ...

The buzzer of the front-doorbell, apparently in the hall just outside the double-doors, sounds insistently.

Richard: There she is, Flint. That's Anne now.

Flint (*bursting out*): I don't like it, sir! I wish you wouldn't touch it!

Richard: Confound it, man, nobody's going to get hurt! You know me!

Flint (*slowly*): Sometimes, sir, I wonder whether I do know you.

Richard: Meaning what?

Flint: Nothing, sir.

Richard (*mildly exasperated*): My good Flint. If I really meant to kill Bruce Renfield, do you think I'd be standing here telling you about it?

Flint: No, sir. But — accidents will happen. And ...

The buzzer sounds again, insistently.

Richard: Don't you hear that doorbell, man? Go downstairs and answer it!

Flint (*starting to turn away*): Very good, sir.

Richard: You're sure you've got your instructions right?

Flint: Yes, sir.

Richard: When you've let Miss Corbin in, leave the front door unlocked. Then go to your room and don't stir out of it afterwards. (*Hesitates*) Wait a minute! My aunt's gone to bed, hasn't she?

Flint: I believe so, sir.

Richard: And Uncle George is never up after eleven. What's delaying you, Flint? Go on!

Flint (*waking up*): Excuse me, sir. (*Holding up the jacket*) Your coat!

Richard: Give it to me. I'll change for myself.

He takes the coat from Flint, who goes out through the double-doors and closes them. Richard stands looking round the room for the moment; then he goes into the bedroom, right, and closes the door.

The clock chimes the three-quarter-hour. George Parsons emerges from the cupboard, left His manner is one of doubt and indecision. He goes to the table, and looks at the poker there. Then he looks at the title on the back of the book he still carries.

Parsons: *On Murder, Considered as One of the Fine Arts.* (*Shaking his head*) Dear, dear!

He throws the book on the table, and starts hurriedly to the double-doors as they are thrown open.

Anne Corbin is a slender, pretty, fashionably dressed girl in her late twenties: imaginative, emotional, very feminine. Just now she is nervous and excited.

Anne (*beginning in a rush*): Richard ... (*She checks herself.*) Oh!

Parsons: Good evening, my dear.

Anne: Good evening, Mr Parsons. (*Hesitates*) My — I know it's awfully late to be calling. But Richard said it was very important. I couldn't find a taxi, and ...

Parsons (*fussed*): That's all right, my dear. Only — don't speak so loudly, will you?

Anne: Why not?

Parsons: Richard doesn't like anyone in the study when he's (*slight pause*) concocting one of his plots. You won't give me away, will you?

Anne (*half-smiling*): No, of course not!
Parsons hurries to the double-doors; but hesitantly turns round again.
Parsons: I don't like thrillers myself. No. I like a Wild West story, or
something funny. My wife is different about that. My wife ...
(*breaking off*) Oh, lord, why is everything so complicated! Good
night!
(*He hurries out, closing the doors. Anne gives a puzzled glance aftr
him, and then comes to the middle of the room.*)
Anne (*calling*): Richard! Richard!
*Richard comes out of the bedroom. They look at each other. He is
now wearing a dark lounge-suit.*
Richard: Hello, Anne.
*They hurry to each other, and he kisses her violently. After a moment
she draws away.*
Anne: Richard, what is it? Over the phone you sounded as though ... I
don't know what! Is anything wrong?
Richard: On the contrary, Anne. Everything's right. Sit down. Let me
take your coat. (*He takes her coat and throws it over the back of a
chair, she sits down on the right of the sofa.*) I want to ask you just
one question, and a lot depends on it.
Anne: Well?
Richard: Does anybody else — anybody in the world — know what Bruce
Renfield knows?
Anne (*in despair*): Must we go through all that again?
Richard: Yes. I'm afraid we must. Answer me! Does ... ?
Anne (*bitterly*): How could Bruce get money out of me, if anyone else
knew? I ... (*breaking off*) When you rang, Richard, I was afraid it
might be something like that. Is it — Bruce again?
Richard: In a way, yes.
Anne: I can't stand much more of this, Richard. It's got to a point where
I feel physically sick every time the phone rings or the letter box
rattles. I tell you I can't stand it much longer!
Richard: You won't have to stand it much longer. I'm going to kill him.
Pause as Anne slowly lifts her head and looks at him.
Anne (*incredulously*): What did you say?
Richard: I'm going to kill him, Anne. Here. Tonight. In this room.
Anne: Are you out of your mind?
Richard: No. (*She gets up quickly from the sofa; he walks behind the*

table.) Let's admit it, Anne. He's got you in a corner. Look at it from the newspapers' standpoint!

Anne: Please!

Richard: You're out driving at night. You knock down a woman and seriously injure her. (*Raising his hand*) Admittedly, you didn't know it at the time. But who would believe that now?

Anne: Nobody, I suppose.

Richard: Our good friend Renfield waits a few weeks; then produces the evidence and puts the pressure on. By your silence ... and you can't prove it was *innocent* silence ... you've turned the whole thing into a criminal offence. On top of that, you're fool enough to write him some letters virtually admitting it ...

Anne (*helplessly*): I'm sorry, Richard.

Richard (*pulling up*): I'm sorry, too. I shouldn't have spoken like that.

Anne: It doesn't matter.

Richard: But I happen to be in love with you. I'm not going to see you wind up in prison or a lunatic asylum. Bruce Renfield, our dear West End blackmailer, will be here just before midnight. (*Suddenly*) I hate that man, Anne, as I've never hated ... ! (*Checks himself*) And I want to tell you exactly what you're to do.

Anne (*staring at him*): Richard! Listen! You don't ... really *mean* this?

Richard: Mean what?

Anne: About ... ?

Richard: Killing Renfield? Oh! Yes I do! (*He picks up poker.*) Tell me, my dear. Haven't you ever thought of it?

Anne: No! Of course not. (*Hestitates*) That is ...

Richard: Hasn't it crossed your mind ... Not even once? ... What if he were dead? The other evening, when you first told me about this. You were ill and hopeless and nearly frantic. You said, if only something would stop him! If only something would stop him! How else can you stop a blackmailer from going on and on and on?

Anne (*desperately*): Darling! Listen to me!

Richard: Well?

Anne: People say a lot of things they don't mean. Crazy notions come to you, and you can't keep them out. But I didn't *really* mean it. I didn't really *think* it!

Richard: That's where we differ. I do.

Anne: Richard, you can't do it!

Richard: Why not?

Anne: They'd hang you! They'd hang both of us!

Richard: Not if you do exactly what I tell you.

Anne (*staring at him*): You don't expect me to ... ?

Richard: Lend a hand? Oh, no. Just be a spectator.

Anne: Of ... what?

Richard: Renfield, I repeat, will be here in a very few minutes ...

Anne: You told him to come?

Richard: Yes. I told him to bring your letters. I said I'd give him ... well, more money than I'm ever likely to have. Now follow what's going to happen! (*He goes quickly up near the double-doors, still carrying the poker.*) The front door is unlocked. Renfield, to show he's here, is to give three long rings on the doorbell. Then he's to come straight up. It will take him maybe twelve or fifteen seconds to cross the downstairs hall, come up the stairs facing these doors, and in here. He'll find this room in darkness.

Anne: In darkness?

Richard: He suspects funny business, and he'll probably be armed. I've got to grab him, in the dark, before he can draw a gun or shout for help ...

Anne: Your aunt and uncle ... !

Richard: They've gone to bed. Flint's in his room. Then, my dear ... (*He takes from his pocket a short, folded length of clothes-line, and a silk scarf; he shows these to Anne, and throws them on the sofa.*) I gag him and tie him up. I sit him down on this sofa. I tell him exactly what I'm going to do, I watch that swine's nerve crumble to pieces, before I ... (*He raises the poker and brings it down.*) It's perfectly soundless, and there'll be very little blood.

Anne: Kill him *here*? In your own house? Where anybody may come in at any moment?

Richard: Will you trust me, Anne, when I tell you I've got a fool-proof way of disposing of him afterwards?

Anne: What way? Answer me! What way?

Richard (*slowly*): It's my best plot. It's the perfect alibi for both of us.

Anne: Richard. Please believe this. I won't let you do it!

Richard: Can you deny you'd like to see him dead? Can you?

Anne: I won't have it on my conscience! I couldn't stand it! I'd break down and tell the police! I'd ...

Richard: Anne. Go over and stand by that fireplace.

Anne: What for?

Richard: It's close on midnight. At any minute ...

Anne: I won't let you go through with it. I'll warn him! I'll scream for help ...

Richard: Oh, no, you won't. You can always back out.

Anne: Back out?

Richard: Wait till he gets in here, Anne. Watch me tie him up. Watch me take the letters out of his pocket. Then if you still feel you can't go through with it ...

Anne: You *promise* that?

Richard: I promise to do nothing that isn't your wish. Go over and stand by the fireplace! (*She backs away until she is standing by the empty fireplace.*) There's just one thing I want to impress on you. Whatever you do, don't move or speak after you've heard those three buzzes on the doorbell. Do you understand?

Anne: Richard, wait! I ...

A long buzz from the doorbell. Slight pause, then another. Slight pause, then a third..

Richard goes quickly to the sofa. He puts down poker, and picks up clothesl-ine and gag, which he stuffs into his side pocket. He goes to the double-doors and stands on the right of them; putting his hands on the light switch.

Richard: "Will you walk into my parlour?" said the spider to the ...

The lights are switched off. The room is in pitch darkness except for a faint yellow line of light under the double-doors.

Anne (*crying out*): Richard!

Richard: Quiet, now!

Pause. Slowly and clearly, the clock is heard to chime through the three-quarters to the hour. It strikes twelve, while we listen to every stroke.

Anne: Richard, for God's sake, turn on those lights!

Richard: Quiet, I tell you!

Anne (*almost whimpering*): I know you don't really mean it. I know you won't hurt him. But don't frighten me. Don't ...

Richard: What the devil's delaying him?

Anne: Delaying him?

Richard: It shouldn't have taken all this time to walk up a few flights of stairs.

Anne: Maybe he knows it's a trick! Maybe he's turned back!

Richard: Listen! Outside the door!

There is a scratching noise, as of hands at wood. The double-doors are suddenly flung wide open. Silhouetted against the dim yellow light, which falls into the room from the hall outside, we see the figure of a man.

He faces the audience. One hand is partly raised in air, the fingers crooked, the shoulders humped; the whole posture suggests intense agony. He sways there, trying to keep his balance. He takes three or four swaying steps forward, as though groping, then he pitches forward on his face.

Richard moves partly into the light from the door. Anne across right; so that Richard and Anne stand at each side of the tunnel of light, looking at the fallen figure ahead of them.

Richard: Get up, you fool! What kind of tomfoolery is this? (*Even more alarmed*) Get up!

Anne is so frenzied that she speaks almost quietly, but with a dangerous tensity.

Anne: Richard!

Richard: Well?

Anne: The back of his skull ... there's blood coming through.

Richard: But *I* didn't ... (*He checks himself.*)

Anne: What happened?

Richard: I don't know!

Richard touches the light switch, and the lights go up. Anne lets out a cry, which he shushes. Before we can see much more than that the man on the floor is young and well dressed, Richard hurries to cover the man's head with the silk scarf: hiding whatever injury we like to imagine.

Richard: Close the doors! Quick!

Anne closes them.

Anne: Is he ... ?

Richard (*bending over Renfield*): I don't know. I can't feel any pulse.

Anne: Richard, what *happened*?

Richard (*as though slowly realising*): I can tell you what happened. As he came up those stairs ...

Anne: Go on!

Richard: Somebody did attack him, that's all. With a weapon very much like this ... (*He goes to the sofa and picks up the poker, his nervousness is increasing.*) The front door was unlocked. Renfield must have a lot of enemies. Anybody could have followed him in. But if I were to be found here now, with *this* ...

Anne: Put it down! Put it down!

He drops the poker, as though finding it red hot.

Richard: My God, what have I got myself into?

Anne: A few minutes ago you were very sure of yourself. You were going to kill Bruce and (*nearing hysteria*) g-get my letters back. You had a great scheme for an alibi after you'd killed him ...

Richard: There isn't any great scheme, Anne.

Anne (*staring at him*): What do you mean?

Richard: I wasn't going to kill him. I told Flint I wanted to watch your reactions, and *his*, when you really thought ...

Anne: You'd do that to me, Richard Marlowe? Frighten me half to death just because ... !

Richard: No! That was only what I told Flint! *Will* you listen to me!

Anne: Well?

Richard: I wanted to scare Renfield into giving up those letters. And I couldn't do that unless you believed I was serious. Panic is catching! It sweeps people away. If I got the whole thing sufficiently worked up, I thought I could make him believe it too, and now ...

Anne: Now they'll hang you! Who's going to believe that? They'll hang you!

Richard: Oh no, they won't!

Anne: How can you *explain* this?

Richard: I don't know. But I'll think of a way.

Anne (*bitterly*): Out of books?

Richard: Yes! Why not?

Anne (*helplessly*): I know you mean well, my dear! But ...

Richard has begun to stride up and down.

Richard: We've got to keep you out of this. That's the first consideration. I can't go back on my story about a "joke" to get literary material; because Flint already knows it ...

Anne: You say you told Flint?

Richard: Damn it, Anne, I couldn't tell there was going to be a real murder. But there's nobody in the world who can connect you in any way with Bruce Renfield. He was a casual acquaintance of yours, just as he was of mine. If those letters ... (*He stops short*) Letters!

Anne: My letters? What about them?

Richard: Renfield must be carrying them. (*He goes to Renfield and kneels down beside him.*)

Anne: Don't touch him!

Richard: I've *got* to touch him. If those letters were destroyed, you're absolutely safe. But if by any chance the police were to find them ... (*Sharp, heavy knocking on the outside of the double-doors; Richard jerks back, Anne stands frozen.*) Did you lock those doors?

Anne: No! No! I ... (*The knocking is repeated.*)

Richard (*raising his voice*): Who's — there? (*A heavy voice is heard from the other side of the door.*)

The Voice: I'm a police-officer, sir. Mind if I come in?

The doors slowly open. Divisional-Inspector Sowerby, in uniform, is a tall heavily built man in his late forties. Ordinarily he has a pleasant, reserved, non-committal air; his voice is not entirely uneducated.

Sowerby: Sorry to trouble you at this time of the night, sir. But — (*He sees Renfield, and stops short.*)

Richard: Aren't you Inspector Sowerby? From Albany Street police-station?

Sowerby: That's right, Mr Marlowe. And it seems I got a straight tip after all.

Richard: How do you mean, straight tip? What are you doing here?

Sowerby (*curtly*): Information received, sir. Excuse me.

He goes to Renfield, bending down between the body and the audience, hiding Renfield's head. He takes the scarf off; feels underneath the chest for a heart-beat; then takes out watch and holds glass to Renfield's lips. As he does so, Flint appears and stands motionless just inside the double-doors.

Anne (*bursting out*): *We* don't know anything about it, Inspector! *We* didn't kill him!

Sowerby (*stolidly*): Nobody's killed him, miss ... not yet. I'm pretty sure he's dying, but he's still just alive. (*To Richard*) Got any place we can carry him?

Richard (*pointing*): My bedroom. In there. But ...

Sowerby: Get his feet, will you?

Flint (*moving forward*): Allow *me*, sir.

Sowerby takes Renfield's head and shoulders; Flint his feet; they turn him over and carry him through the door to the bedroom. Richard, with a fierce shushing gesture to Anne, follows them.

Anne, now nearly hysterical, mechanically picks up the silk scarf on the floor. As though finding blood on it, she drops it quickly and rubs her hands together. She hurries to the sofa, picks up the poker, and starts to run towards the fireplace ... to hang it among the fire-irons there ... when Ellen Parsons, in nightgown and dressing-gown, puts her head in at the doors and hesitates. Anne stops short.

Ellen: Excuse me, my dear. Aren't you ... aren't you Miss Anne Corbin?

Anne: Yes. That's right.

Ellen: I *thought* I recognized you! I'm Richard's aunt, you know. I won't come in, my dear, because Richard doesn't like people to be in here. But ... have you seen my husband?

Anne: Mr Parsons? Isn't he with you?

Ellen: No! He hasn't come up to bed at all. And I never noticed, you see ... not until a few minutes ago ... because I was reading *such* a lovely book. All about murder.

Anne (*throwing poker on sofa*): Were you?

Ellen: I never used to care for those books, you know, any more than George did. But that's how it goes, isn't it? Richard's practically converted me to liking murders.

Anne (*bursting out*): Mrs Parsons! Please! Go away!

Ellen (*startled*): Is anything wrong, my dear?

Anne: There's been ... a bad accident.

Ellen (*staring at her*): To George? (*Slight pause*) Is that why he didn't ... ? Is he hurt? (*Crying out*) George!

Anne: Sh-h! Please! It's not Mr Parsons.

Ellen: Then who is it?

Anne: — a friend of Richard's named Bruce Renfield. He ... fell and hurt his head.

Ellen (*anxiously*): You won't fool me, my dear? You *are* telling me the truth? Where is *George?*

Again calling the name, she goes out and swings the door to behind her, just as Inspector Sowerby strides out of the bedroom, followed by Richard and Flint. Anne goes over to the table.

Sowerby: Where's your telephone, Mr Marlowe?

Richard: Downstairs, Inspector. (*Brushing this aside*) But I've been trying to tell you ...

Sowerby (*to Flint*): Mind showing me where it is?

Flint: Not at all, sir.

Sowerby and Flint start for the double-doors.

Richard: Inspector. *Will you listen to me!* (*Sowerby turns round.*) Every word I've been telling you is true. The whole thing was a hoax, put up to test these people's reactions. And Flint can confirm it! Can't you, Flint?

Flint (*surprised*): I, sir?

Richard: Just before Miss Corbin got here, I told you all about it! I told you everything I was going to do. Didn't I?

Flint: I can't recall your saying anything like that, sir.

Long pause..

Richard: Look here, Flint. What kind of dirty work is this?

Flint (*not looking at him*): You said you expected Mr Renfield. You said he would get exactly what was coming to him.

Sowerby (*sharply*): Did you say that, sir?

Richard: Yes! (*Pause*) But that was only part of it! I said ...

Flint (*raising his voice*): If you must know, Inspector, I believe Mr Marlowe was in a dangerous state of mind. That's why I phoned the police-station and asked you to come over here.

Richard (*dazed*): You ... *phoned* ...

Flint: And if you want my guess, Inspector — I think Mr Renfield was ... some kind of blackmailer.

Richard: Don't be a fool, man! Renfield was only a casual acquaintance of mine. What would he be blackmailing me about?

Flint: Perhaps — not you, sir.

Sowerby: Then what are you suggesting?

Flint: Nothing at all, Inspector. But if you searched Mr Renfield's pockets ... searched his pockets here and now ... you mind find —

Sowerby (*thoughtfully*): Search his pockets, eh?

Richard has retreated, down, past the front of the sofa. Sowerby starts slowly towards the bedroom door.

Flint: There may be nothing in it. (*Suddenly*) I ... I'm sure I don't want to make trouble! But Mr Marlowe certainly never told me anything about a "joke."

Flint stops, turning towards the bedroom door. George Parsons is standing there.

Parsons (*exasperated*): In the name of sense, Flint, why do you want to tell such infernal lies? (*In a kind of mild dudgeon, muttering and shaking his head, he stumps across to the table, a little down from Anne, and turns around.*) Lies, lies, lies!

Sowerby (*sharply*): Who are you? And how did you get ... (*Points to bedroom door*) ... in there?

Parsons: It's all right, Inspector. I didn't touch anything.

Sowerby: I asked you how you got *in* there!

Parsons: There's another door from the landing outside. (*Nods towards the double-doors.*) I wander about, you know. Yes. I was in that cupboard ... where is it? Yes ... (*He blinks round at the cupboard and back again.*) ... When Richard told Flint about this psychological experiment. That's one reason why I know Richard's telling the truth. The other reason ...

Sowerby: Go on!

Parsons: Well! I saw the real murderer.

Pause. The clock rings out the quarter-hour chime after midnight.

Anne: You ... saw the real murderer?

Parsons: Yes, my dear.

Flint (*quickly*): Who was it?

Richard (*just as quickly*): Why do *you* care, Flint?

Parsons (*troubled*): This young man whose skull was crushed ... what was his name?

Anne: Renfield! Bruce Renfield!

Parsons: Thank you, my dear. (*Ruminating*) I used to know a Renfield in South Africa. Don't suppose it can be the same man. Anyway, the Renfield I knew was much older.

Sowerby strides forward.

Sowerby: Let's get this straight! You say ...

Parsons: Renfield was killed on the stairs. Not in here. Just as Richard's been trying to tell you.

Sowerby: You *saw* this?

Parsons (*apologetically*): I'm afraid I did.

Sowerby: Where were you?

Parsons: In the drawing-room, downstairs, looking for something to read. I felt restless tonight.

Sowerby: Well? What happened?

Parsons: I heard the front doorbell ring, you see. Then the door opened and closed. I thought that was odd, you know; rather odd. So I went to look. That young man ... Renfield ... was going upstairs. I saw somebody following him.

Sowerby; Following him?

Parsons: Deep carpet on the stairs. Dim lights. That part was *easy*.

Sowerby: Who did you see following him?

Parsons: Some man. Dark hat and gloves. I couldn't see his face. Just as Renfield got to the top of the stairs, this man swung up something like an iron spanner, and ... (*Parsons lifts his hand slowly, and brings it down as though striking. Exhaling his breath*) Easy! Just like that. (*During the progress of this recital, Inspector Sowerby has been looking more and more satisfied.*)

Sowerby: I see, Mr ... ?

Parsons: Parsons, my name is. George Parsons.

Sowerby: Very useful bit of confirmation, Mr Parsons. (*More sharply*) What did you do then?

Parsons: I ran back into the drawing-room and stayed there. I'm not what you'd call a brave man. No. All I can tell you, young What's-his-name was killed on the stair and ...

Anne (*desperately*): Inspector, that's absolutely true! He *must* have been killed out there. Richard and I were in this room. If you don't believe we're telling you the truth ...

Sowerby (*blandly*): As a matter of fact, miss, I know you're telling me the truth.

Anne: You know? How can you know?

Sowerby: I'll be very glad to show you, miss, just as soon as I've put through a phone-call. Where's —
He has turned toward the double-doors, beckoning Flint to follow him, when he stops. Ellen Parsons comes in. Terrified, she holds between the tips of her two fingerd — keeping it well away from her — a long, heavy motor-car spanner.

Ellen: George! Thank the lord you're safe! You weren't upstairs, you weren't downstairs, you weren't ... (*Suddenly she seems to catch the others' emotional temperature; she looks from one to the other of them; she holds out the spanner.*) I found this on the stairs. There's blood on it. (*She throws the spanner on the floor.*)

Richard: Take it easy, Aunt Ellen!

Sowerby (*grimly*): There's blood on it ma'am, because somebody's been murdered. Or as good as murdered. Will you tell me why you had to mess about with the evidence?

Ellen (*bewildered*): Evidence?

Richard: Aunt Ellen didn't mean any harm, Inspector! (*He come closer and points to the floor.*) Is that — ?

Sowerby: Yes, sir. That's the spanner. I saw it on the stairs when I came up. *And* two blood-spots on the landing. Mr Renfield was attacked on the stairs, right enough. He had just strength enough to stagger in here before ...

Ellen: Richard! What *is* all this? Miss Corbin said there'd been an accident!

Sowerby: Not exactly an accident, ma'am. (*Looking very hard at her*) By the way. Haven't I seen you somewhere before?

Ellen: I daresay. My husband and I have been living here for nearly a year.

Sowerby (*puzzled*): No. I didn't mean that. I meant ...

Parsons: My wife, Inspector, was once a very famous person. Yes. *Very* famous.

Richard (*proud of her*): Ellen Fairgrove, Inspector. Otherwise Ellen Parsons. Songs, monologues, and male impersonations! Stage-door favourite! Admirers galore!

Ellen (*bitterly*): And yet I married ... oh, what difference does it make? Won't *anybody* tell me what happened?

Sowerby: *I'll* tell you what happened, with great pleasure. Somebody coshed that young man in there, and tried to put the blame on Mr Marlowe.

Anne: That's exactly what Richard thinks! Somebody followed Bruce in from the street ...

Sowerby: Oh, no, miss! I wouldn't mind betting nobody followed him in from the street.

Richard (*staring*): What do you mean?

Sowerby: Is it likely any outsider would have heard of this hoax of yours? Known just when to step in and kill with a spanner, so that you'd be caught? Oh, no! Somebody had this thing taped. Somebody.
Flint clears his throat and hurries forward.

Flint: A minute ago, Inspector, you were going to have a look at the contents of Mr Renfield's pockets. Have you forgotten that?

Sowerby: Look here. Why are you so interested?

Flint: I'm — making a guess, that's all.

Sowerby: What kind of a guess?

Flint (*desperately*): *Will* you do it, sir?

Sowerby (*slowly*): All right, my lad. Just to see what the game is, I'll have a look now. Please stay where you are, everybody! (*He strides towards the bedroom door.*)

Anne: No! Wait!

Sowerby stops and turns around.

Richard: Steady, Anne! It's all right!

Flint (*stonily*): Is it all right? I wonder!

Sowerby gives them a slow look, and then goes out. Richard goes to Anne, up beyond table, and takes her arm. Parsons and Ellen go to sofa and sit down. Flint remains roughly in the middle.

Ellen (*helplessly*): I declare, George Parsons, this whole place seems to be turned into a madhouse! What on earth is that police-inspector *after*?

Parsons (*mildly*): I'm afraid, my dear, he thinks somebody in this house committed a very unpleasant murder. Odd. Very odd. And a bit frightening. (*Starts to laugh faintly*) I ... er ... I didn't do it myself, of course ...

Ellen: And *I* certainly didn't!

Flint: Well I didn't! Why should I?

Ellen: I've never set eyes on the man, even yet!

Flint: And I only knew him because — well! I was in his employ a few years ago.

Parsons: As for me — dear, dear! *I* hardly had anything to gain by getting Richard arrested. But it's very disturbing. Very! (*To Richard*) What do *you* think, my boy?

Richard: To tell you the truth, Uncle George, *I'm* beginning to think ...

Parsons: Well?

Richard: That somebody in this room is a remarkably fine liar. But for the life of me I can't tell which.

Parsons (*distressed*): Surely, my boy ... well! *You* don't believe in Flint's suggestion?

Richard: Flint's made a lot of suggestions, Uncle George. Which one do you mean?

Parsons: About young Renfield being a blackmailer.

Ellen: After all, George, I must say *you* took it pretty coolly.

Parsons: Eh, my dear? Took what pretty coolly?

Ellen: You see this mysterious man on the stairs. You actually see him hit the poor man with the spanner. And yet you don't even turn a hair. You treat it as though ...

Suddenly Ellen sees she has made a slip, and stops dead. Parsons gets up from the sofa and backs away. Flint comes very slowly forward.

Flint: Excuse me, madam.

Ellen (*very lordly*): Yes, Flint?

Flint: How do *you* know what Mr Parsons saw? You weren't here when he told us.

Ellen (*to Parsons, trying to turn it off*): Really, George ...

Parsons: I think you'd better answer, my dear.

Ellen: My dear George! I was listening at the door, of course.

Parsons: You were ... ?

Ellen (*naively*): My dear George, all women listen at doors. It's a part of women's rights, like going through your husband's pockets or reading his letters.

Parsons: That's not the point, Ellen!

Ellen (*offhandedly*): Isn't it?

Parsons: When you came in here with that spanner, why did you pretend you didn't know anything about this?

Ellen: Because something dreadful had happened, that's why!

Parsons: Well?

Ellen: And I'd picked up that wretched spanner before I knew anything about it. Then I heard you say — what did you say. Well! Wasn't it better to pretend I didn't know anything? If you look flighty enough, dear, men will always believe you.

Flint: Not always, madam.

Parsons (*sharply*): What do you mean?

Flint (*realising*): Ellen Fairgrove! Of course!

Ellen (*placidly*): As you say. Of course.

Flint: "Songs, monologues, and *male impersonations.*" That figure on the stairs.

Long pause.

Ellen (*suddenly realising, almost screaming*): George! Did you hear what that man said?

Richard: Look here, Flint. I wish you'd make up your mind what you do mean. First of all you accuse me ...

Flint: I'm not accusing anybody, sir. I'm talking like this just because I
don't know!

Ellen: It's the silliest thing I ever heard of. *Me!* (*Searching for a wild
illustration.*) Why, they might just as well accuse George!

Parsons: Exactly, my dear. So they might.

Ellen: George, the most harmless and inoffensive person in the world.
(*Considering*) Though he did have a wonderful record in the last war.
Two decorations or was it three? I think that was why I married him.
He killed and killed and killed and ... (*Breaking off*) ... Oh dear! I
mean —

Parsons: That's all right, Ellen. You needn't help me out any further.

Flint (*fiercely, to Richard*): Who did it, sir? *Who did it?*

Richard: I wish I knew!

Anne (*despairingly*): Oh, Richard, what does it matter? Whoever tried to
kill Bruce, it won't prevent the scandal now! That policeman is
searching Bruce's pockets. He's bound to find ...

Sowerby appears in the doorway and takes a step forward.

Sowerby: Find what, Miss?

Anne: Didn't you ... (*She checks herself suddenly.*)

Sowerby: There's nothing in the gentleman's pockets but an identity card,
a watch, and keys, and some money, and (*slight pause*) a loaded
revolver. What did you expect me to find?

Anne (*faltering*): I ...

Richard: Inspector, can't you see Miss Corbin's hysterical? She doesn't
know what she's saying!

*Parsons begins to laugh again, a little louder. They look at him in
amazement. He checks himself.*

Parsons (*distressed*): I beg your pardon! I really do beg your pardon!
But I was just thinking. If I hadn't seen that man in the hall ...

Ellen: What man, George?

Richard: Uncle George saw the murderer! A man in hat and gloves!

Ellen: A man in hat and gloves? Then it couldn't have been one of us!

Parsons: I seem to remember reading, you know, that head wounds are
very odd injuries. A man can manage to walk long distances even after

he's fatally hurt.[1] That Mr What's-his-name might have been struck before he even got to this house. In that case the murderer could have been Miss Anne Corbin herself ...

Richard: *What's that?*

Parsons: Because I seem to remember she was late in getting here. Or anybody from outside. But that won't do, of course, because I did see the man. Forgive me.

Sowerby (*drily*): Thanks, Mr Parsons. I'm glad you can see you're talking rubbish.

Ellen (*bridling up*): And why is it rubbish, may I ask?

Sowerby: Well ma'am, he must have been reading a very funny kind of medical jurisprudence, rubbish indeed. You don't walk "long distances" with a crack in your head like that. The young man in there couldn't have. (*Sowerby partly turns round to indicate the open door of the bedroom; he looks into it, and his gaze becomes fixed.*) *Good God almighty!*

Still staring, he starts to back away from the door towards the middle of the room. All follow the direction of the Inspector's glance instinctively moving back.

Bruce Renfield stands in the doorway, swaying and clinging to the edge of it. He is now seen to be a handsome man, but pale as a corpse, glazed of eye, wild of expression, kept on his feet by sheer vindictiveness.

Renfield (*hoarsely*): Ever talk to a dead man, copper? You're talking to one now.

Anne: Bruce!

He tries to move forward, but has to clutch at the overstuffed chair beside the door.

Renfield (*struggling*): People know when they're done for. You can feel it. Something says, "this is death." And you're more surprised than anything else. That's it, copper. Surprised.

Sowerby: Mr Renfield! Listen to me! Did you see the person who attacked you?

Renfield's face lights up vindictively.

---

[1] Notwithstanding Sowerby's later remark, Carr made excellent use of this fact in one of his most famous detective novels.

Renfield: Yes!
Sowerby: Is that person here now?
Renfield: Yes!
Sowerby: Who was it, Mr Renfield?
Renfield: It was ...

As he lifts his finger to point, every light in the theatre goes out to pitch-blackness, and there is a sharp knife-chord. After a moment, music is heard, and the narrator speaks through.

Story-teller: A very curious case. And, as I see when I turn over the pages of my notebook, a still more curious ending. (*Chuckles*) I am still tempted, good friends, to leave the matter there and let you decide this problem for yourselves. And yet, it may be, there are some who feel a certain curiosity. If there are any such who listen to me now, come with me to watch another scene. Look once more into the study of that house in Regent's Park, at a drugged hour of the morning when ...

Out of darkness we hear the chime of the clock. As it runs through to the hour, the lights slowly go up. The clock strikes four.
Only one light — the big lamp on the table — is now burning in the study. An easy chair has been drawn up to the right of the table, facing the audience. George Parsons sits in this chair, an open book in his hands. As the clock finishes striking, Parsons begins to read aloud.

Parsons: "People begin to see" ... h'm ... "that something more goes to the composition of a fine murder than two block-heads to kill and be killed ... design, gentlemen, grouping, light and shade, poetry, sentiment, are now deemed indispensable to attempts of this nature. The finest work of the ..."[2]

The double-doors open and close. Richard comes in. He walks slowly towards the sofa. Parsons puts the book on the table beside

---

[2]Quote from De Quincey's "On Murder Considered as One of the Fine Arts," *Blackwood's Magazine*, February 1827. De Quincey believed that the strange death of Sir Edmund Godfrey in 1678 was "the finest work." Carr presented a solution in *The Murder of Sir Edmund Godfrey* (1936).

him, and looks round.
Have they all gone, Richard?
Richard: Yes, all gone.
Parsons: Tired, my boy?
Richard: Very tired. (*He sits down on the sofa.*)
Parsons (*musing*): A pity, wasn't it? That Renfield tumbled over and died before he could name the murderer?
Richard: In a way, I suppose it was. (*Glancing across at him*) That person is a murderer now.
Parsons: Yes. He ... (*Suddenly waking up*) Why are you looking at me like that?
Richard: Just wondering.
Parsons: Wondering what?
Richard: Oh, various things. What the future would be like, for instance.
Parsons: This murderer, Richard. The police, you know, will never rest till they do find him.
Richard: They won't find him, Uncle George.
Parsons: Why not?
Richard: They haven't any evidence. They may guess and guess and guess. Just as we were all guessing tonight. But that's a very different thing from taking a man out in the cold light one morning, and binding his hands with leather straps, and putting a rope round his neck, and ...
Parsons: Don't talk like that!
Richard: Why not?
Parsons picks up the book from the table.
Parsons: I — I don't like these books of yours. But they get into the mind, somehow. They stick there. This business tonight, Richard! It might have been one of your own plots.
Richard (*deliberately*): As a matter of fact, Uncle George ...
Parsons: Yes, my boy?
Richard: It *was* one of my own plots. I committed the murder.
Long pause. Parsons stares at Richard in slowly growing horror, as he realises Richard is serious. Richard is smiling. Parsons suddenly gets up from the chair, dropping the book on the floor, and begins to back away.
Parsons (*shrilly*): You *did* do it after all! You were ...
Richard: I was the man in hat and gloves. *Yes.*

He gets up from the sofa. He crosses towards Parsons, who has backed towards the cupboard down. On his way Richard picks up the fallen book with his left hand. He puts his right hand on the shoulder of Parsons, who cries out, and gently leads him back to the chair.

Richard (*blandly*): Sit down, Uncle George. You'll keep my secret. (*He pushes Parsons into the chair.*)

Parsons (*crying out*): But. You had ...

Richard: I had an alibi, you were about to say?

Parsons: Yes!

Richard: Didn't you ever hear, Uncle George, of the double-bluff? (*Holding the book, Richard moves away from him towards the middle of the room.*) The first part of the bluff was to convince Flint that I meant only a "joke." So that he could confirm it afterwards. Unfortunately, I didn't convince him. He suspected me all along ...

Parsons: And rightly?

Richard: And rightly ... But don't you see now why I *had* to get Anne Corbin here?

Parsons: No!

Richard: As a witness, my dear uncle.

Parsons: A witness?

Richard: A witness to testify that I never once left this room. It was no good taking Anne into the secret. She would only have broken down and confessed. She had to believe, absolutely believe, that I never left her side. Even in darkness.

Parsons: But you did leave her?

Richard: Oh, yes. Do you remember when the front doorbell rang? And Bruce Renfield came in?

Parsons: Yes!

Richard: I was standing by the only light-switch. *This* light-switch. (*He goes to it.*) I warned Anne not to speak. I . . .

He turns on the switch. The stage, which has been almost in darkness, is lighted up. We see Anne standing in the doorway to the bedroom, staring at him. Richard jumps back.

Anne! Did you hear . . . ?

Anne: Yes. (*In horror, as he makes a move towards her*) Don't touch me!

Parsons: He did it for you, my dear! After all, he . . .

Anne: He committed murder.

Richard: Yes! And I'd do it again!

Anne (hypnotized): I want to know *what* you did, that's all. You warned me not to speak. You turned out the lights. And then — ?

Richard: There were forty seconds of absolute silence and darkness while the clock was striking. That was when I acted.

Parsons: You mean you — ?

As Richard speaks, Anne goes past him to the table at the other side of the room.

Richard: Observe my dark suit, Uncle George, Anne couldn't see me. I slipped into the bedroom there. The spanner and the hat and gloves were ready. In the bedroom there's a door ... you mentioned it yourself ... that leads ... where?

Parsons: Out on the landing!

Richard: That's right. As Renfield got to the top of the stairs I stepped out behind him and struck. You never actually saw me going upstairs. You only assumed that because you saw me at the top of them.

Parsons: Stop a bit! The landing was the only place where that inspector found blood-stains!

Richard: Right again.

Parsons: And in that forty seconds ... ?

Richard: I struck Renfield to his knees, got a certain bundle of letters out of his pocket. These letters.

He takes from his inside pocket three or four letters tied with a white ribbon. After holding them up, he puts them down conspicuously on the arm of the sofa.

I threw the spanner downstairs. I was back in here before the clock finished striking. (*He turns round to both of them.*) The human mind, my dear uncle, my dear fiancee, is very gullible. I *admitted,* you see, that I meant to bring Renfield in here, tie him up with ropes, threaten him, and possibly kill him with a poker. Therefore nobody dreamed I would upset my own scheme by killing Renfield with a spanner before he even got here. That's the double-bluff, my dear uncle. I was blackening my character in order to whitewash it. And nobody suspected me.

Anne: Flint suspected you! Probably he still does.

Richard: Yes. Flint very nearly dished me. He was supposed to see the intruding shadow ...

Parsons: Intruding shadow?

Richard: The sinister figure in the hat and gloves, which couldn't have been me. I counted on his curiosity for that. But you served just as well.

Parsons (*hollowly*): I testified ...

Richard: You did it in good faith, Uncle George. Don't worry.

Parsons: Don't *worry*? (*Querulously*) Why are you telling me all this?

Richard: Because you must be very sure, when you tell your story next time, that the intruding shadow came from outside. Otherwise ...

Parsons: Otherwise — what?

Richard: Some member of this family might be arrested for murder, and we don't want that. (*As though testing Anne*) Or do we?
Parsons moves slowly forward and points to the letters conspicuously lying on the arm of the sofa.

Parsons: Listen, my boy. Are those ...?

Richard: Yes. Anne's letters.

Anne: The letters that prove *I'm* a criminal too?
Richard swings round to her.

Richard: That's what I did, Anne. I didn't want you to overhear ...

Anne (*bitterly*): No. I imagine you didn't.

Richard: But you did hear; and that's that. I killed him, and I still say I'd do it again. Can you find it in your heart to blame me?

Anne: I don't blame you. I only hate you.

Richard: Hate me?

Anne: Hate you for putting me in a position like this. (*As he starts to protest*) Oh, I suppose I ought to say I'm grateful! I suppose I ought to say it makes me love you more than ever. And, in a way, I do care more than ever. But all I can think of is ...

Richard: Is what?

Anne: That police-officer.

Richard: What about him?

Anne: When he left here tonight, he said they'd be back tomorrow. And the next day, and the day after that. They'll never give up.

Parsons: That's what *I* told Richard!

Anne: If the case were ended, if I never saw them again ... well! That might be different. But I hate you, and I hate myself, because sooner or later I'm going to confess and give you away. Oh, yes, I am! I can't help myself.

Richard (*fiercely*): Anne! *Will* you trust me?

Anne (*flatly*): You asked me *that* once before. Didn't you?

Richard: All we've got to do is keep our heads. I'll take care of any difficulties that arise. If that policeman were to come back here at this moment ...

There is a sharp knocking on the door. Pause. Richard hesitates before calling out.

Who's there?

Sowerby opens the doors and stands there looking at them. All make an instinctive movement towards the packet of letters, but check themselves.

Sowerby (*not unpleasantly*): Yes, Mr Marlowe? What *would* you do if he came back at this moment?

Richard (*suave and amused again*): First of all, Inspector, I'd say he was very conscientious ...

Sowerby: Thank you, Mr Marlowe! Thank you.

Richard: And then I'd invite him downstairs for a much-needed drink. Can I tempt you?

Sowerby: Sorry, Mr Marlowe, but we don't drink while we're on duty. Didn't you know that?

Parsons: From my experience of policemen, Inspector, I didn't know it.

Sowerby: Er — mind if I come in?

Richard: Not at all, Inspector.

Sowerby: And — may I sit down?

Richard: By all means. Make yourself comfortable.

Sowerby strolls to the sofa. Again they make an instinctive move-ment, and check themselves as he sits down on the sofa, almost against the arm on which the letters are resting.

Sowerby (*comfortably*): Maybe I'd better explain, Mr Marlowe. The real reason I came back here, at this hour of the morning ...

Anne: Well?

Sowerby: I want to apologize to that manservant of yours. Flint.

Richard: Apologize to Flint? Why should you?

Sowerby: Because he was right, you know. He was dead right after all. Bruce Renfield *was* a blackmailer.

He rests his arm comfortably on the arm of the sofa. Once he even taps his fingers thoughtfully on the letters, not even seeming to see them.

Anne: How can you tell that?

Sowerby: We sent his fingerprints to the Criminal Records Office. They identified 'em in ten minutes. Renfield specialized in blackmailing women. Indiscreet letters: that sort of thing.

Richard: Suppose he was a blackmailer! Does that prove ... ?

Sowerby: Prove somebody in this house killed him?

Richard: Yes!

Sowerby (*leisurely*): Let *me* do a bit of supposing, sir. Mind! − it's only supposition.

Richard: Well?

Sowerby: Suppose I was wrong about the whole thing. Suppose you killed this fellow after all.

Anne comes quickly downstage, so that she is facing him from the other side, some distance away.

Anne (*quickly*): You can't think that, Inspector!

Sowerby (*quickly*): Why not?

Anne: Richard was with me the whole time. Don't you believe that?

Sowerby: I think *you* believe it, miss. Or did believe it.

Anne: What do you mean?

Sowerby gets up. Turning his back on them, he goes over in the same leisurely way to the bookcase, right, and stands looking into it.

Sowerby: These are Mr Marlowe's books, aren't they? Oh, ah. I thought I noticed 'em.

Anne: You notice a lot of things, don't you?

As she speaks, Parsons begins to move forward very slowly, his hand stretched out to take the letters.

Sowerby: *Death in the Summer-House.* I read that one. All about a perfect alibi that fooled the police ... (*Sharply*) Don't do it, Mr Parsons!

Parsons: Don't do what?

Sowerby: Don't touch those letters. It won't help now. (*Sowerby turns round.*) By the way. Speaking of letters ...

Parsons (*bursting out*): Can't you stop these cat-and-mouse tactics?

Sowerby: Your nephew used the same kind of tactics. Didn't he?

Richard: Yes! But I used them on a blackmailing swine who ...

Anne: Richard! Careful!

Sowerby: Suppose I found a packet of letters from Miss Anne Corbin to Mr. Bruce Renfield. Just suppose that!

He walks forward slowly, picks up the letters absent-mindedly; and, as

they all watch him, he goes behind the desk and stands facing out.
That would be motive, sir! M-o-t-i-v-e, motive. The one thing we
lacked. You've got an alibi, yes. Depending on Miss Corbin's word.

Richard: Well? Suppose it does?

Sowerby: But Miss Corbin herself is involved now. Will a jury believe
what *she* says?

Parsons: They'll think Anne was in it too, Richard! They'll think she lied
on your behalf ...

Sowerby: And they'll hang both of you as sure as the sun will rise
tomorrow.

Anne (*dazed*): But I didn't do it, I tell you! I didn't have *anything* to do
with it!

Sowerby: *We* know that, yes. But the jury won't. (*Pause*) Cleverness, Mr.
Marlowe, can cut both ways.

The double-doors open.

Ellen: I declare, George Parsons, I ...

She sees the tense group, and stops.

Parsons (*on edge*): Ellen, get out of here! For the love of heaven get out
of here!

Ellen (*brightly*): Well, really now! Is *that* any way to speak to your wife?

Parsons (*harassed*): I'm sorry, my dear. But ...

Ellen: When all I've done this whole night — and it's four o'clock in the
morning now — is slave away getting coffee for a lot of stupid policemen who ...

*She catches sight of Sowerby, who has taken the ribbon off the letters
and is holding them thoughtfully in his hand.*

(*Wearily*) Oh, dear, are *you* back again?

Sowerby (*woodenly*): That's right, ma'am.

Ellen: And I daresay you've come to lecture me again? Is that it?

Sowerby (*still without turning round*): Lecture you, ma'am?

Ellen: If I live to be a hundred, I swear I'll never hear the end of that
wretched spanner I picked up off the staircase. Never tamper with
evidence! Never tamper with evidence! Never tamper with evidence!

Sowerby: That's right, ma'am. Never tamper with evidence.

*Still looking straight ahead of him, he slowly tears the packet of letters
in half. Violent reaction from everyone except Ellen.*

You may think, for instance, a rather decent young fellow was only
trying to protect his girl. You may think a swine of a blackmailer got

just what was coming to him.

He tears the letters again.

You may think, for once, the police might turn a blind eye.

He tears the letters again, and drops the pieces on the desk. He turns round, walks to Ellen, and in passing puts his hand on her shoulder.

But never tamper with evidence, ma'am. It's against the law. Good night.

He goes slowly towards the door.

Richard (*staring*): Inspector Sowerby! Do you mean ... ?

Sowerby turns round.

Sowerby (*casually*): Good night, Mr. Marlowe.

He goes out, closing the double-doors. There is a long silence. Richard, now in the centre of the stage, tries to speak and can't manage it. Finally he thinks of a way of expressing emotion.

Richard: Uncle George!

Parsons: Yes, my boy.

Richard goes to the desk. He picks up the book Parsons has been reading, and looks at the title.

Richard (*bitterly*): *On Murder, Considered As One of the Fine Arts.*

With a gesture almost of loathing, he flings the book down on the desk. Parsons turns away. Anne sobs, leading to:

SLOW CURTAIN

AFTERWORD

In his biography of Carr, *The Man Who Explained Miracles* (1995), Doug Greene noted similarities between *Intruding Shadow* and two of Carr's novels, *The Emperor's Snuff-box* (1942), and the Carter Dickson novel *The Peacock Feather Murders* (1937). Close similarities can also be identified between the play and the atmospheric but otherwise unsatisfactory *Death-Watch* (1935). In *Intruding Shadow*, Carr boldly shows precisely what he only described in Death-Watch — and then somewhat misleadingly — namely the moment when murder is committed. And to quote from Carr's brilliant novella *The Third Bullet* (1937), Richard Marlowe — like the murderer in *Death-Watch* — recognised that "deliberate walking into the hangman's noose was the only sure way of making certain it never tightened round his neck." It was also a neat means of misdirecting the reader.

Richard Marlowe has much in common with Carr. In particular the titles of two of Marlowe's detective stories — *Death in the Summer-house* and *The Nine Black Clues* — are similar to the titles of two of Carr's radio plays: "The Devil in the Summer-House," broadcast in its original form on the BBC on October 15, 1940; and "The Nine Black Reasons," broadcast in the *Cabin B13* series on CBS on August 9, 1948. The third of Marlowe's books, *Mystery at Whispering Lodge*, does not have any obvious connection with Carr's work.

Carr would go on to reuse the principle of the deception in *Intruding Shadow* one final time, and then less convincingly than in *Intruding Shadow*. The radio play "A Razor in Fleet Street" was broadcast in America on July 5, 1948, as the opening episode of the CBS radio series *Cabin B13*.

Carr's characteristic decision to allow Marlowe to evade arrest at the end of *Intruding Shadow* reflects his questionable views on the means of justice and might. It is interesting to note that, in an unpublished biographical note, written in 1954, Carr recalled his childhood ambition to become a barrister, in which capacity he should have "prefer[red] to defend guilty men."

She Slept Lightly

A Play

by

John Dickson Carr

She Slept Lightly

The Characters

Story-teller	The Man in Black
Pierre	The miller
Lady Stanhope	A noble lady
Captain Thomas Thorpe	A British cavalry officer
The Girl	A Mystery
Major von Steinau	A Prussian Hussar

Out of a dark theatre we hear the musical introduction, and the voice of the story-teller.

Story-teller: Appointment with Fear! (*Musical theme*) This is your Story-teller, the Man in Black, here to bring you another tale in our nursery series: a fitting tale for the end of an evening. Close your eyes for a moment, now, and dream. Let me lead you back into the past, far back, for more than a hundred years. To another time when death walked in `the land. To another time, when the world was menaced by one man: Napoleon Bonaparte.

Faint roll of gunfire. Then the slow, measured tapping of a drum, which is at first heard faintly under the narration, but grows louder and quicker.

"Boney," in his famous grey overcoat and cocked hat. "Boney," fabled and terrible. For sixteen years his war-eagles flew from the Pyrenees to the Baltic. All Europe shook to the tread of the Grand Army. Yet it happened, during those hot summer days in Belgium, that rumour flew fast. The Allied Armies — England, Prussia, Belgium — had moved out of Brussels for battle. "Boney" would at last come to death-grips with the English. (*Slight pause*) Lonely in the Forest of Soigne, some league out of Brussels, there used to stand an ancient windmill: gaunt stone, its sails tattered. At the very top of it

211

lived old Pierre the miller. Far away, you would have said, from the singing of the bugles and the rumble of gun-carriages. And yet ... from dawn on that June day, until now when twilight begins to come down, there has been in the distance only one sound ...

The lights slowly come up as the voice fades.

We are looking at a semi-circle of dark, rough stone blocks: half the room at the top of the circular windmill. It has two windows, narrow oblongs on the stone, at the back: one set high up, the other lower down so that a man could just get his chin above the sill to look out. Outside can be seen part of the motionless windmill sails. We are in the room above the shaft and cogs which drive the mechanism of the mill, so that none of this can be seen.

It is a squalid, dingy place. Back, left ... seen from the audience ... is a doorway covered by a coarse burlap curtain; this presumably leads to a winding stair. There is another door, down left; a practical door leading to a tiny store-room. Longways under the windows is a rough board camp-bed. A battered wooden wardrobe stands against the wall, right, opposite the store-room door. Nearly in the middle of the room, pushed a little down right, is a kitchen table bearing a tin pitcher of water, a dusty wine bottle, a glass, a plate, and rough cutlery. There are two wooden chairs, both beside the table.

Pierre the miller, a stooped gnomelike man, thin but hard and wiry from heavy work, is heard outside the doorway with the burlap curtain. He backs in as though escorting someone; with one hand he opens the curtain, and with the other he holds a box-lantern with a candle burning inside, while he calls to someone outside.

Pierre: *Par, ici, madame ... Prenez garde a l'escalier! ... (More slowly)* mind ... the ... step!
He backs away holding up the lantern. The curtain is pushed aside by Harriet, Lady Stanhope. She is a heavy, sombre, autocratic woman in her sixties: her enemies might call her a little mad. She wears a bonnet, and a dust-cloak over a traveling costume of the year 1815. Lady Stanhope, breathing hard, looks slowly round the room.

Lady Stanhope: God's body, what a way you've led me! Stairs and stairs and stairs and ... (*Suddenly realising*) You speak English?
Pierre bows. He is strung up with suppressed excitement and nervousness. His look is very ugly, though he tries to conceal this under deference.
Probably I didn't make myself understood in French. I want transportation, do you understand? Transportation!
Pierre: I ... hear you, madame.
Lady Stanhope (*still breathing hard*): That cannonade frightened the horses. My carriage over-turned ...
Pierre: Yes, madame. (*Softly*) And ... the young lady?
Lady Stanhope (*sharply*): What young lady?
Pierre: But, madame! The young lady who was with you in the carriage.
Lady Stanhope: There was no one with me.
Pierre (*suspicions growing*): But, madame! I thought I saw ...
Lady Stanhope (*fiercely*): There was no one with me, do you hear? (*Slowly*) Not a living soul.
Rumble of cannon.
Pierre: *Bien*, madame. Will it please you to sit down?
Lady Stanhope: Yes! For a moment.
She goes across to a chair beside the table, on the left of it, facing the audience. Pierre softly puts the lantern on the table. Then he draws back to watch her, well back and to her right. His face is not pleasant. She does not look round.
(*coughing*) Powder-smoke in the air, even here! How far away is the fighting?
Pierre: Two or three kilometres. You hear for yourself.
His eyes are fixed on her. He takes a bright bladed knife out of his sleeve, puts the fingers of his right hand firmly round it, and hides the hand behind his back.
Lady Stanhope: And ... how does the fighting go?
Pierre: Who can say, madame? All I can see from my window is black smoke.
Lady Stanhope: Powder-smoke in the air! Powder-smoke in the lungs! Powder-smoke in the blood!
Pierre is rapt in a dream of his own.
Pierre: Sometimes, madame, I feel the ground shake. Yes! Even here I feel it shake. And I know that is cavalry charge. I think what it would

be like if I ... poor Pierre the miller ... were there to see it. To see, just once, the Cuirassiers of the Guard. Come charging out of the smoke. Great men on great horses, crying, "*Vive l'Empereur*"!

Carried away, he has instinctively raised the knife in his right hand. She turns her head sharply, just in time to see him conceal the knife.

Lady Stanhope: *What's that?*

Pierre (*wooden again*): Nothing, madame.

Lady Stanhope: You're a Belgian, aren't you?

Pierre: Yes, madame.

He begins to creep round, down stage, so that he is now partly facing her. Her eyes follow him.

Lady Stanhope: And therefore, presumably a friend of the English and Prussians. Very odd! To hear you talk, good Pierre, one might almost imagine ...

Pierre: Imagine ... what?

Lady Stanhope: That you favoured the Emperor Napoleon.

Pierre (*moving forward*): Let me take your cloak, madame!

Lady Stanhope: Stay where you are!

Pierre (*softly*): Yes, madame?

Lady Stanhope: This encounter, my friend, may be a very fortunate chance. (*From under her cloak she takes a lard reticule, holds it up and puts it on table.*) There's a thousand francs in gold in that bag. I want a carriage, a cart, anything with wheels; and a guide to take me through to the French lines.

Pierre (*taken aback*): The *French* lines?

Lady Stanhope: You heard it.

Pierre: But ... you are English!

Lady Stanhope: Yes. Just as you are Belgian. Does that matter?

Pierre: You *mean* this, madame? It is not ... what you call ... a trap?

Lady Stanhope: I am old; you can see it. I am eccentric; you can guess it. I am rich; you can prove it. A thousand francs. What do you say?

She gets up. He hesitates, his hand with the knife falling to his side.

Pierre (*struggling*): But, madame ... it is not possible!

Lady Stanhope: Why not?

Rumble of cannon.

Pierre: You hear that?

Lady Stanhope: I hear it.

Pierre: Can you cross through the British lines? Can you cross a battle field?

Lady Stanhope: There are other roads, surely?

Pierre (*anguished*): Madame, why not wait? The Emperor will eat them up; I say it! He will be in Brussels by morning ...

Lady Stanhope: That's too late.

Pierre: Too late, madame?

Lady Stanhope: Have you wondered, good Pierre, why I drove out from Brussels in the very direction of the fighting? (*Breaking off*) And a mighty pleasant time I had in Brussels, too! (*Mimicking*) "How do you *do*, Lady Stanhope?" they said to me. "So delightful to see you, Lady Stanhope!" "One understood, Lady Stanhope, you were under a physician's care for (*coughs delicately*) vagaries of the mind." (*Changing her tone*) Vagaries of the mind! God's truth! *I!*

Pierre (*helplessly*): Madame, I do not understand.

Lady Stanhope (*waking up*): I drove out from Brussels, good Pierre. If the Prussians over-take me now ...

Pierre: The Prussians? (*Spits, making a gesture of hatred*) They follow you?

Lady Stanhope: One particular Prussian at least. He may well see a wrecked carriage with my coat-of-arms on the panels. If he does see it, Pierre; if he does follow me ...

Heavy knocking on thick door which seems to come from below.

(*sharply*) Pierre!

Pierre: Yes, madame?

Lady Stanhope: Was that ...? (*She points to the floor.*)

Pierre: Yes, madame. The outer door.

He runs to the rough board bed under the lower window, stands on the bed, and cranes his neck outwards to look. Lady Stanhope does not move; she stares straight ahead.

Lady Stanhope: A Prussian Officer?

Pierre (*turning round*): No, madame, a British Officer.

Lady Stanhope (*quickly*): British! What uniform does he wear?

Pierre (*in agony*): Madame, I cannot tell! I think ... he is of the cavalry. But I see no horses.

Lady Stanhope: That man must not come in here, Pierre.

Pierre: Pardon, madame. He *must* come in. (*Significantly*) But he need not go out. (*Pierre jumps down from the bed and hurries towards the curtained door.*)

Lady Stanhope: Pierre! One moment!

Pierre: Yes, madame?

Lady Stanhope: You will not use your knife, my friend.

Pierre (*drily*): It would be on Madame's conscience?

Lady Stanhope: I have no conscience, Pierre. I can't afford the luxury. But you will not use that knife ... *understand?* ... unless I give you the word.

Pierre (*softly*): *Entendu, madame.*

He goes out. There is a low growl of gun-fire. Lady Stanhope stares after him, and then moves out to the middle of the room. She seems now possessed of devilish vitality. She is again surrounded, in her own mind, by a circle of friends whom she mimics and mocks with words and gestures.

Lady Stanhope: "*Dear,* Lady Stanhope!" "*Kind* Lady Stanhope!" "So delightful to see you in Brussels, Lady Stanhope!" "Such a pleasure to see you at Her Grace of Richmond's Ball, Lady Stanhope ... (*under her breath*) ... I wonder you got an invitation." "Is it true, Lady Stanhope, you're keeping some poor girl imprisoned in that ogre's house of yours, and not letting her see the light of day?" (*Becoming herself again, bitterly*) Thank you, good friends. I was always an old she-devil, wasn't I? I ...

Off, a voice says, "Get out of my way!" Lady Stanhope turns. Captain Thomas Thorpe, without using either hand, pushes through the curtained door. He is about thirty, of likeable bearing and voice. A long black cloak, torn and mud-stained, is held together at the throat by his left hand; we can see very little of his uniform. He is white faced and not too steady; he wears no helmet.

Pierre slips in after him, and hurries across to stand at the far end of the table.

Thorpe: So it *was* your carriage!

Lady Stanhope (*without looking at him*): Was it?

Thorpe: Where's the girl who was with you not ten minutes ago? I saw her. *Where is she?*

Lady Stanhope (*with evil emphasis*): Listen to me, Captain Thorpe. Three nights ago I warned you ...

Thorpe: Then you *do* know who I am!

Lady Stanhope: Curiosity, young man, is the one vice permitted to old women. Oh, yes: I asked your name and regiment! Life Guards, I believe?

Thorpe (*dully insistent*): *Where is she?*

Lady Stanhope: The Life Guards, I should have imagined, were well engaged in today's fighting.

Thorpe: They are. But ...

Lady Stanhope: But you're not with them. Is that it?

Thorpe (*desperately*): That doesn't matter! What I want to know is ...

Lady Stanhope: It doesn't matter, he says! Here's a fine noble officer to trust while the guns are going! He deserts his company ... he runs from the battle ...

Thorpe (*wretchedly*): I couldn't help it.

Lady Stanhope: Why not?

Thorpe: If you must know, they sent me back in the hospital wagon. My sword arm's gone.

Lady Stanhope (*really taken aback*): You mean ... ?

Thorpe: It's all right! The surgeon patched me up with a hot iron and bandages. You won't see any mess.

Lady Stanhope: You young fool! How did you get here?

Thorpe: Saw that wrecked carriage. Saw *her.* So I rolled off the wagon when the surgeon wasn't looking. *Had* to make sure ... I wasn't dreaming.

Lady Stanhope: ˙ Dreaming?

Thorpe: Heat. Head swimmy. Trail of blood in the dust from all the hospital-wagons. Followed that trail like a fowl with its beak to a chalk line. I ... (*He sways on his feet.*)

Lady Stanhope: Easy! Do you want to jog that amputation and bleed to death?

Thorpe: Why not? Everybody else is dying. Good fellows, too. Where is she?

Pierre takes the knife from behind his back and drives it sharply into the table, point down, so that it stands upright. He picks up a chair and carries it to Thorpe.

Pierre (*sincerely*): Sit down, *monsieur.* You are a brave man.

He gently pushes Thorpe down into the chair.

Thorpe (*dazedly insistent*): Where is she?

Lady Stanhope: For the last time, Captain Thorpe! If you won't take warning, if you won't be threatened ... well! May I *plead* with you?

Thorpe: About ... what?

Lady Stanhope: Don't meddle with powers you don't understand. Go away from here! Forget this girl you think you saw ...

Thorpe: "Think" I saw?

Lady Stanhope: Yes.

Thorpe: Do you remember three nights ago? That Ball at the Duke of Richmond's house in Brussels?

Lady Stanhope: I remember.

Thorpe: Did I dream I saw here then? Lady Stanhope? Oh, no! Did I dream the lights? Did I dream the crowd? Did I dream that hall of windows beside the garden, with only the moonlight coming in.

Faintly, music comes in behind his voice as he speaks, the lights go slowly down to pitch darkness. As the music rises the voice of the narrator is heard through.

Story-teller: "There was a sound of revelry by night
And Belgium's capital had gathered then.
Her beauty and her chivalry, and bright
The lamps shone o'er fair women and brave men;
A thousand hearts beat happily, and when
Music arose with its voluptuous swell,
Soft eyes looked love to eyes which spake again,
And all went merry as a marriage bell;
But ..."[1]

The lights slowly come up as the music dies away. We see the black silhouette of a wall pierced by four full length windows. These are not practical windows; only oblong arches, with brilliant moonlight streaming in for the only illumination. Between the two middle windows is a small gild sofa. On this ... almost invisible ... sits a fair-haired girl in a white gown.

Thorpe, in full uniform without hat or cloak, appears from outside the second window from the left. He hesitates, and comes in.

Thorpe: Is anyone here? Is any ... (*He bumps into the edge of the sofa; the Girl gives a faint cry.*) I beg your pardon! I didn't see you there,

---

[1] Quote from Byron's "Childe Harold's Pilgrimage."

in the dark.

The Girl: Please don't apologise.

Thorpe: I knocked something out of your hand, didn't I?

The Girl: Only an ivory miniature. Don't trouble please.

Thorpe: It's here on the floor somewhere. I'll ring for the lights.

The Girl: Please don't. The moonlight is pleasanter.

Thorpe: It's not necessary. I've found it.

He is scanning the floor. He bends down and picks up the miniature. He glances at it, glances at it again quickly; and then to get a better light, he moves back into the full moonlight of the window, where he scans it.

Forgive me. The face in this miniature ... isn't it a painting of you?

Slight pause.

The Girl (*quickly*): How do you know that? You can't see me.

Thorpe: I saw you a minute ago in the garden. I followed you in.

The Girl gets up. She comes to the window, where they stand facing each other against the moonlight.

The Girl: Why did you follow me?

Thorpe: Because nothing seems quite real tonight.

The Girl: Is that an answer?

Thorpe: I thought you were very beautiful. I wanted to meet you. And formal introductions don't seem to matter now.

The Girl: No. I suppose not.

Thorpe: Boney and the Grand Army somewhere ahead of us! But nobody knows where. Nobody knows anything. Eat, drink, and be merry, for tomorrow ...

The Girl: We die?

Thorpe: Some of us.

The Girl (*slowly*): How do you know what it is to die?

She goes quickly back to the sofa in shadows. He stares at her.

Thorpe: I — beg your pardon?

The Girl (*crying out*): Forgive me! I shouldn't have said that! Are there — rumours of Bonaparte?

Thorpe: Yes. But don't be alarmed. There can't be anything imminent.

The Girl: Why not?

Thorpe: Because the Duke's here tonight. I saw him myself. Looking as though he hadn't a care in the world. He —

The Girl: Sh-h! Please!

Thorpe: Is anything wrong?

She hurries to him again in the window, turning round to gesture towards the right.

The Girl: That's the door to the study. *He's* in there.

Thorpe: You mean Lord Wellington?

The Girl: Yes. With the Prussian Intelligence Officer from Baron von Mufling. I heard him call for a large scale map.

Thorpe: A large scale map! Then that means ...

The Girl (*sharply*): Listen!

Thorpe: What is it?

The Girl: Didn't you hear a bugle?

Thorpe: No. I heard nothing.

The Girl: Anyway, it doesn't matter now. (*Bursting out*) It's too late!

Thorpe: Too late for what?

The Girl: Too late to get back again. Ever!

Thorpe: Are you unhappy about something?

The Girl: I *was* in great trouble. A long, long time ago.

Thorpe: Tell me about it.

The Girl: You wouldn't understand!

Thorpe: Maybe not. There are a lot of things that puzzle me in this world. But I swear I'd understand anything that concerned you.

The Girl (*wonderingly*): I believe you mean that!

Thorpe (*fiercely*): Mean it? Words can't convey much if I don't mean it. What trouble were you in?

The Girl: They said I did — something dreadful. They put a rope round my neck. They ...

Off, in the dark, a voice speaks indistinct words which sound like: "I will see to it, Excellency! At once!"

The Girl (*terrified*): Listen! That sounded like Major von Steinau's voice!

Thorpe (*bewildered*): I think it was von Steinau. But ...

The Girl: Let me go! For god's sake let me go!

She has backed out of the window. Then he makes a motion as though to restrain her; she runs past him and off left. Thorpe stares after her, holding out the miniature.

Thorpe (*calling*): Don't go! Wait! You forgot ...

As he takes a step to follow her, Major von Steinau comes out of the shadows from the right. He wears a Prussian Hussars' uniform. He is some half a dozen years older than Thorpe: lean, blond, stiff-backed,

with a surface of joviality which is more often on the edge of a sneer.
His English is fluent, having only a trace of accent.

Steinau: You! My friend! One moment!

Thorpe (*desperately*): I'm sorry, sir! Another time! I can't stop! I ...

Steinau: You will obey a military order, Captain Thorpe. You are Captain Thorpe?

Thorpe: Yes, sir! But ...

Steinau (*pleasantly*): It pains me much to keep you from a lady, Captain Thorpe. It was a lady, no doubt?

Thorpe: Yes, sir.

Steinau (*changing his tone*): Yet you will perhaps admit, like your great Duke himself, that there is a thing or two more important? — Bonaparte has crossed the Sambre.

Off a distant bugle sounds.

Thorpe: What's that?

Steinau: You will pass the word, please, among all junior officers now in the ballroom. Each is to leave, quietly, and join his company. There must be haste; but no outward hurry. Do you understand?

Thorpe: Yes, sir. Where is Boney?

Steinau (*bitterly*): He drives back my countrymen ... *mein* countrymen! ... and takes Charleroi. He is almost in sight before your great Duke knows it. Now his left wing moves up ... so! ... to cut you off. That is all. Go.

Again the distant bugle can be heard. Steinau swings round and goes out right. A very faint sound begins to register: a rumbling of gun-carriages on stone. Thorpe hurries down from the window, as though following Steinau.

Thorpe (*calling after him*): Major von Steinau! Listen! I ...

He breaks off. Then he turns round again to find Lady Stanhope standing in the extreme left-hand window.

Lady Stanhope: Good evening, young man.

Thorpe (*taken aback*): Your servant, madam. (*Hesitating*) Have — ?

Lady Stanhope: No. You need not trouble to ask whether we've met before. You don't know me. But I should like a word with you.

Thorpe: I'm sorry; but I must ask leave to go! I'm looking ...

Lady Stanhope: You are looking, I think, for a certain person who recently left you.

Thorpe: Yes. (*Prompting*) Her name is — ?

Lady Stanhope: Her name, young man, would convey nothing to you. And you need not trouble to search any further for her. She has gone.

Thorpe: Gone?

Lady Stanhope: Gone for good. You will not see her again.

Thorpe: May I ask why not?

Lady Stanhope: Because I wish it. And I am her guardian. (*She lifts her head sharply as Thorpe starts to protest.*) One word more. You hear the noises out there?

Thorpe: I hear them.

Lady Stanhope: Gun-carriages, and still more gun-carriages. The shouts of men who go up against Napoleon. It is probable that within a few hours you will be dead.

Thorpe: I thank you humbly for your encouragement.

Lady Stanhope: But if you do survive — if you *do* survive — you will forget you have ever seen this girl. Above all, you will never mention her to Major von Steinau. (*Bursting out, almost pleading*) Don't let the Prussian hear of it, young man! Don't let the Pr—

She stops dead. Steinau has come out from the shadows to the right. He stands looking from Thorpe to her.

Steinau: It was in my mind, Captain, that I gave an order from the Duke.

Thorpe: Yes, sir. I was just ...

Lady Stanhope: Just going, he was about to say. As for me, Herr Major, I interfere with no man in (*slight pause*) carrying out his duty. Give you good-night.

Steinau: You are gracious as always, Lady Stanhope. Good-night.

The rumble of gun-carriages rises. Lady Stanhope looks steadily at Thorpe, and then goes out through the window as the rumble dies.

Thorpe: Sir, who is she? (*Cutting him off*) I know what you are going to say about disobedience ... and I deserve it. Just answer that question! Who is this Lady Stanhope?

Steinau hesitates. There is clearly something on his mind.

Steinau: A crazy old woman who drives about Europe in a red carriage with a silver hammercloth. (*Quickly*) Why?

Thorpe: She's the guardian of some girl who ... Anyway, here's the girl's face on a miniature. Look at it, Sir! Then court-martial me or any damn thing you like. But look at it!

He holds out the miniature. Steinau hesitates, takes it, and walks to the window to get a better light. After a pause he speaks in a very odd tone.

Steinau: Where did you get this miniature?

Thorpe: From the lady herself!

Steinau: Lady Stanhope, you mean?

Thorpe: No! The girl! She was sitting on that sofa, and ...

Steinau: *Lieber Gott!*

Thorpe: What's the matter with you?

Steinau (*not loudly*): Is this a British joke, Captain Thorpe? Let me warn you that I do not like jokes.

Thorpe: What do you mean, joke? Do you know her?

Steinau: Very well I know her.

With a gesture of contempt, or perhaps something else, he flips the miniature to Thorpe. Thorpe catches it.

Thorpe: Who is she?

Steinau: A spy of Bonaparte.

Thorpe (*staggered*): A spy of ...

Steinau: Yet you saw her here, you say? (*Enticingly*) You even talked to her, perhaps?

Thorpe: Yes.

Steinau: You saw her. You talked to her. Yes! How very funny! Were you perhaps in Paris with the Army of Occupation a year ago?

Thorpe: No.

Steinau: No? That is a pity. (*Tone changing*) For you come to me with a story about this pretty slut. You ask me ... (*Here he glances past Thorpe out of the window, stops dead, and stands rigid.*) Captain Thorpe!

Thorpe: Yes, sir?

Steinau: Look out of the window. There, where I am pointing.

Thorpe: Is anything wrong, sir?

Steinau: Do as I order you! Look out of the window!

Thorpe obeys.

Thorpe: Well, sir?

Steinau: What do you see?

Thorpe (*half catching his mood*): I see a moonlit garden. And the singing fountains. Yes: and the heavy guns going by.

Steinau: Nothing else?

Thorpe: Nothing else.

Steinau (*a little hysterical*): My friend ... and you *are* my friend ... you will look again. By the rose-arbor, where the moonlight strikes the spray of the fountain. There is a face, and a white gown. Is it ... ?

Thorpe: Yes! I hadn't noticed before! It's ...

Steinau: Don't touch that window! Don't go out there!

Thorpe: Why not?

Steinau: Because I forbid it.

He walks away from Thorpe to the centre window and stands silhouetted there; his back to Thorpe, his hands half raised. When he speaks, his voice is raised as though he addresses some law or god in his own mind.

I, Karl Heinrich von Steinau, ordained of God in the Koenigsberg Hussars, take oath that I have no fear. No living man has heard the cry of the undead, or seen the eyes of demons in pine-forests. These things are fables, these things are snares to affright unwary souls. Besides ... (*He swings round towards Thorpe.*) Besides, what can they accuse me of?

Thorpe, bewildered, nevertheless catches his mood and is almost shouting back.

Thorpe: Nobody's accused you of anything, sir!

Steinau (*controlling himself*): True! Very true. (*He goes across to Thorpe.*) A moment ago, Captain, you looked out of the window here. What did you see?

Thorpe: I saw the girl I've been telling you about!

Steinau (*suavely*): You are mistaken, my friend.

Thorpe: But you saw her yourself!

Steinau: I saw a shadow. The glitter of a fountain. Some mirror-trick of the mind.

Thorpe: Look here, sir. I'll *prove* ... (*He turns to the window again, but stops. Flatly*) She's gone.

Steinau: Of course she has gone. For let me repeat, Captain Thorpe: you come to me with some tale of this pretty slut. You ask me who she is, and perhaps even where she is ...

Thorpe: Yes! Where is she?

Steinau: In her grave and eaten by worms. We hanged her more than a year ago.

There is an off-stage bugle-call as the lights fade. Music comes up softly behind the narrator's voice as he speaks in darkness.

Story-teller: "Did ye not hear it? — No; 'twas but the wind,
    Or the car rattling o'er the stony street;
    On with the dance! Let joy be unconfined;
    No sleep till morn, when Youth and Pleasure meet
    To chase the glowing Hours with flying feet —
    But hark! — that heavy sound breaks in once more,
    As if the clouds its echo would repeat;
    And nearer, clearer, deadlier than before!
    Slight pause.
    ... It is — it is — the cannon's opening roar."[2]

A heavy, distant roll of gun-fire as the lights slowly come up again, to show the inside of the windmill as before. Thorpe sits in the chair, dazed and sick-looking, the cloak drawn about him. Pierre stands behind him. Lady Stanhope regards him fixedly.

Lady Stanhope: Pierre!

Pierre: Yes, madame?

Lady Stanhope: Doesn't that firing sound closer?

Pierre: Yes, madame. The Emperor is coming.

Lady Stanhope: *Vive l'Empereur*! Don't we all cry it?

Pierre: The we are together, Madama? And this poor insane young man ...

Thorpe: Insane? I tell you that was what von Steinau said! (*Intently*) Was it true? Did they ... hang her?

Lady Stanhope: Why should I tell you?

Thorpe: For God's sake have a little pity! (*He tries to get up, but sways and sits down again.*)

Lady Stanhope (*grimly*): The arm begins to hurt now, doesn't it? The shock wears off, and the pain comes in. Pierre!

Pierre: At your service, madame.

Lady Stanhope: There's tincture of opium in my bag. A little brown vial. Give him ...

Thorpe: No! Don't want drugs. Head feels light enough as it is. I ... got any wine?

Pierre hurries to the table. He pours wine from the bottle into the

---

[2] Ibid.

glass, and returns with it.

Pierre: Drink this, *mon capitaine.* (*He tilts back Thorpe's head and holds the glass as to pour the wine down his throat.*)

Thorpe: Thanks. That's better.

Lady Stanhope (*implacably*): You ask me to have pity, Captain Thorpe. Did you have pity?

Thorpe (*bewildered*): I don't understand!

Lady Stanhope: That girl was no more guilty of spying than you are.

Thorpe: But they hanged her?

Lady Stanhope: Yes. They hanged her.

> *Lady Stanhope turns away. She walks a little way towards the curtained door, and then turns round again.*

(*unemotionally*) They hanged her in the Tuileries Gardens, inside a hollow square forced by a Prussian regiment. They marched her out in the rain, while the drums tapped. They put a black bag over her head, and bound her hands, and threw her off the ladder to strangle. And all the while she hung there — twenty minutes, it was — one drum kept up a slow tap, tap, tap — like that! — until the body was quiet at last. (*Pause — tone changes to a groan.*) That girl was English. She was poor. I suppose you imagined her as noble born?

Thorpe: I don't know what I imagined; but I saw her three nights ago. I saw her as plainly as though ...

Pierre: Perhaps she sleeps lightly. They say the dead sleep lightly.

Thorpe (*frightened*): God help us all!

Lady Stanhope: Think of *her* for a moment, Captain Thorpe. Born in squalor. Brought up among mountebanks in a travelling fair. And yet ... *gentle.* What chance has she against the Prussians?

Thorpe: Against — the Prussians?

Lady Stanhope: A certain officer took a fancy to her.

Thorpe: Well?

Lady Stanhope: She hated him. She feared him. She ran from him. So this fine Prussian gentleman lodged a charge of spying against her, and swore her life away. (*Fiercely*) Can't you guess who the officer was?

Thorpe (*suddenly realising*): You don't mean ... ?

Lady Stanhope: Yes. It was your friend Major von Steinau.

> *Thorpe unsteadily gets to his feet. He fumbles inside the cloak with his left hand, and brings out the miniature. Pierre, who sees it past his shoulder, starts back.*

Pierre: Madame. This girl ... !

Lady Stanhope (*unheeding*): I heard the lying testimony in court. I watched Steinau's face — the pleasure of it! — while he tortured a frightened girl who couldn't strike back. When I heard that girl sentenced to be hanged by the neck, I made a great vow. Never mind, for the moment, what that vow was. But I worked, I schemed. I used what poor wits heaven gave me. And you, Captain Thorpe ... you wrecked it all.

Thorpe: I wrecked it?

Lady Stanhope: Yes.

Thorpe: Why are you looking at me like that? What have I done?

Lady Stanhope: I begged you not to mention this girl to Steinau. Didn't I?

Thorpe: Yes! But ...

Lady Stanhope: But you would do it. You even showed him the miniature, so that he couldn't have any doubt.

Thorpe (*wildly*): But what difference does it make? If the girl is dead ...

Lady Stanhope: Did I say she was dead?

The miniature drops out of Thorpe's hands and falls to the floor. He bends to pick it up, and dazedly puts it inside his cloak again.

Thorpe: But you said — they hanged her!

Lady Stanhope: They did hang her. In full sight of a thousand witnesses.

Thorpe: You mean ... she was revived afterwards?

Lady Stanhope: Oh, no.

Thorpe: And yet — she's alive? It was a living woman I talked to three nights ago?

Lady Stanhope: A living woman — for the time being.

Thorpe (*in horror*): What do you mean?

Lady Stanhope: I saved her life by a trick. And then *you* betrayed her to the Prussians.

Thorpe: I ... ?

Lady Stanhope: Major von Steinau, believe me, is not a fool. He wouldn't believe in a ghost; *he* guesses she's alive. That's why the Prussians are after us. For over a year, Captain Thorpe, I've kept that girl hidden away. She *was* safe, perfectly safe where nobody could touch her. But you've thoroughly well managed to hang her now!

Thorpe goes slowly to the chair. He sinks into it.

Thorpe (*bursting out*): I meant it for the best! I tell you I, I tell you ... !

Lady Stanhope: Does that help us now?

Thorpe: What are you going to do?

Lady Stanhope: Our only chance is to get away before the Prussians arrive. If we can reach the French lines ...

Thorpe (*starting*): Go over to Boney?

Lady Stanhope (*bitterly*): Why not? Will our own Allies do anything for us? Steinau may be here at any moment ...

Pierre (*sharply*): Listen!

   Pause.

Lady Stanhope: Did you hear horses?

Pierre: No, madame. I heard — silence.

Lady Stanhope: Silence?

Pierre: All day there been heard gun-fire. Like a noise of the sea. Now there is — nothing.

Lady Stanhope: The fighting may be all over?

Pierre: Yes, madame.

   Pierre quickly puts the empty glass on the table. He hurries to the bedstead, gets up on it, and peers out of the window. It is now almost dark.

Pierre: Even the powder-smoke begins to lift. A wind comes up, and soon it will turn the sails of my mill. But — I see nothing.

Lady Stanhope: Where *is* the fighting, Captain Thorpe?

Thorpe (*lifting his head dazedly*): Eh?

Lady Stanhope: You were there in the midst of it! Where is the fighting?

Thorpe: Just south of a little village called Waterloo.

Lady Stanhope: Waterloo. I don't know it.

Pierre: Soon, madame, the whole world will know it.

Lady Stanhope: Why?

Pierre (*jumping down from the bed*): Because, madame, the Emperor will be here. He has won his greatest victory.

Lady Stanhope (*flatly*): I wonder!

Pierre: You and the young lady are safe now. You have nothing to fear from the Prussians. You are enemies, yes —

Thorpe (*startled*): Enemies?

Pierre: Of the Emperor Napoleon. But that does not matter. The Emperor will know how to treat you. May I, then, let the young lady out now?

Thorpe: Let her out? Where is she?

Pierre: In this room. (*Chuckling, he addresses Lady Stanhope*) Do you think, madame, that poor old Pierre is blind? I see her ... the same face which is in that miniature, yes! ... I see her run into the mill ahead of us. She is now downstairs, no. Eh, *bien*, I ask myself, where is she? And where, madame ... (*He crosses to the door that is downstage, left, and raps on it with his knuckles.*) ... where, madame, but in my store-cupboard here? Shall I open the door?

Thorpe (*sharply*): Wait!

Pierre (*jumping*): *Monsieur*

Thorpe (*to Lady Stanhope*): Are you sure Steinau's followed you from Brussels? Are you sure of it?

Lady Stanhope: Steinau himself was watching my house this morning. What else can it mean?

Thorpe: But you don't *know* he's followed you?

Lady Stanhope: I haven't actually seen him, no.

Thorpe: Please listen. If you've got that girl in a safe place, keep her there. (*Slight pause*) Boney hasn't won. He's lost.

Lady Stanhope: What makes you think that?

Thorpe: Our orders. If Boney's cavalry broke the squares, we're to retreat on Brussels from the Forest of Soignes.

Lady Stanhope: Well?

Thorpe: We're *in* the Forest of Soignes. And there hasn't been a sound: not a sound! It's all going in the other direction. That means ...

Pierre (*crying out*): This is impossible! I don't believe it!

Thorpe: He's beaten. (*Almost incredulously*) Boney's beaten.

Lady Stanhope: If that is so, Captain Thorpe ...

Thorpe: It is so, I tell you!

Lady Stanhope: As an Englishwoman I rejoice, (*tone changing*) but as a hater of Prussians and all they stand for ...

Pierre: You need not be alarmed, madame. The Emperor will soon be here. This young lady, so well hidden, has nothing to fear now. She ... (*Instead of going towards the store-cupboard, he has again gone to the left-hand window to look out, he utters an exclamation.*) *Mon capitaine!*

Thorpe: What is it *now?*

Pierre: Madame's carriage! Down there!

Thorpe: I saw it. It was overturned.

Pierre: It has been righted again, and the horses are in harness!

Lady Stanhope: Righted? By whom?

Pierre: Looters, madame. They swarm along the roads like ...

Lady Stanhope (*grimly*): Vultures over the battlefield. Already!

Pierre: Madame, that is war! (*Insistently*) You carry gold, yes?

Lady Stanhope: Yes, but — !

Pierre: You must go down at once and buy them off. I, Pierre, will bargain for you. Then, if you wish to drive to the Emperor's lines ...

Thorpe: Don't do it, Lady Stanhope! You'll drive straight into the Prussians!

Pierre: Madame, you must make haste!

Lady Stanhope picks up her reticule from the table.

Thorpe: Lady Stanhope!

Lady Stanhope: Whoever has won the battle, Captain Thorpe, we must have transportation to go away. *You* are not an outcast.

He makes half a gesture as though to restrain her, but checks himself. She crosses past him to the door, beside which Pierre is standing. At the door she hesitates, and turns around. Her expression, for the first time, is kindly and pitying.

Lady Stanhope: This girl you seek, Captain Thorpe ...

Thorpe: *Yes?*

Lady Stanhope: You will find her. Or ... (*raising her voice*) ... she will find you. Speak quickly. You have not much time.

She goes out. Pierre bows and follows her. There is a single, distant volley of musketry. Thorpe, indecisive, turns to look slowly round the room. The door of the store-cupboard slowly opens, and the girl comes out. They stand looking at each other for a second. Thorpe starts towards her, and she stretches out her hand. But he checks himself, turns round abruptly, and sits down facing the audience. She stands behind him.

The Girl (*startled*): What is it? Why do you turn away?

Thorpe (*flatly*): No reason.

The Girl: I've been hiding in the miller's store-cupboard. Is it ... because I didn't come out before?

Thorpe: No. Of course not.

The Girl: Then why? Tell me!

Thorpe: I was going to put my arms round you. I ... (*nodding towards his right shoulder*) ... forgot. (Slight pause, the Girl comes forward a little; suddenly she begins to laugh.) Is that funny? Have I made a fool of myself again?

The Girl: No! But ... because you've lost an arm? Is that why you draw back from me?

Thorpe: Isn't it a good enough reason?

She stands behind him and puts her hands on his shoulders.

The Girl: Give me your hand ... please! Give me your hand.

He hesitates. His left hand moves up and takes her right.

Thorpe: In that store-cupboard. Could you ... hear what I was saying?

The Girl: Yes.

Thorpe: Since that night in Brussels, have you ... mind, I don't see how you could have ... but — have you ever thought of me at all?

The Girl: Every day. Every hour. Every minute.

Thorpe: You mean that?

The Girl: "Words can't convey much if I don't mean it." You said that too.

Thorpe: Yes. I said it. (*Slight pause*) I was going to have so much to tell you, when I saw you again. And now —

The Girl: Words don't seem to matter?

Thorpe: They matter. But I can't find them. Except that I love you.

The Girl: I want you to say that. I want you to say it over and over. I have been — very lonely.

Thorpe: Yes. Lady Stanhope told me the story.

The Girl: The hanging that wasn't a hanging. The humiliation of ...

Thorpe gets up from his chair, angrily, and faces her.

Thorpe: Don't think about it!

The Girl: No. I mustn't think about it. (*She turns away, and back again.*) We've seen each other only once before. I suppose people would say we're mad. You don't even know my name. And yet I want you to tell me you love me, over and over. I want to have that much to remember before ...

Thorpe: Before — what?

The Girl: Before the Prussians arrive. And they take me again.

Thorpe: They're not going to arrest you! Do you hear?

The Girl: Let's be honest, my dear. Napoleon *has* lost, hasn't he?

Thorpe: I don't know. I think so, but I don't know. Even so, why should you feel so hopeless? There is such a thing as justice. Can't we bring this before a British Military Commission?

The Girl: We *could* have. A few days ago.

Thorpe: What do you mean?

The Girl: That's why Lady Stanhope and I were in Brussels that night. To see Lord Wellington. Then the messenger arrived with news of Bonaparte, and ... (*breaking off, pleading*) Oh, I know I don't matter! I understand that! One small silly person among thousands in agony. But I ask so very little!

Thorpe: This appeal to the Duke. Can't we still ... ?

The Girl: Not while Steinau lives.

Thorpe (*with intense loathing*): Steinau!

The Girl: Please! Don't you see? Even yet? (*She stares at her*) Steinau won't let me appear before an honest court. He daren't. He *must* overtake me. He *must* hold ... what do they call it? .... A drum-head court-martial.[3] He ...

Thorpe: Listen!

The Girl: What is it?

Thorpe: There's somebody coming up those stairs now.

The Girl: Not — ?

Thorpe: I don't think so. It's probably all right. But — better get back into the store-cupboard. Hurry! Get back into the store-cupboard!

The Girl goes quickly to the store-cupboard door, and closes it behind her. Thorpe stands near the door to the stairs, staring at it. Pierre comes in, staring straight ahead of him. He does not speak. Walking very slowly, and as though blindly, he crosses towards the nearer chair beside the table.

Thorpe: Pierre! (*Pierre pays no attention; he stops beside the nearer chair, and blindly sinks down into it, staring ahead of him.*) Pierre! What is it?

He is answered. Very faintly in the distance, but gathering volume, we hear a military band: the band of soldiers on the march. The tune is "The British Grenadiers." Both Thorpe and Pierre remain motionless until this music dies away.

It is — all over?

Pierre: Yes, *mon capitaine*. All over.

---

[3] "drum-head court-martial" — summary trial for an offence committed during military operations.

Thorpe: How did you hear?

Pierre: From a courier on his way back to Brussels. The red infantry rose up from the fields of corn, and the Old Guard turned and fled. I, Pierre Duroc, have lived to see the Old Guard turn and flee.

Thorpe (*hesitantly*): Pierre! Look here! I ...

Pierre (*fiercely satirical*): You are embarrassed, eh? You do not know what to say. (*Even more satirically*) Your country breaks the power of the Emperor as I crack a walnut between these fingers, and you do not know what to say.

Thorpe: Fortunes of war, Pierre.

Pierre: Fortunes of war? Fortunes of the devil! (*He jumps up from the chair.*) Do you not wish to kill me?

Thorpe: No! Why should I want to kill you?

Pierre: Yet you guess what I am? Eh?

Thorpe: I know you're not a Belgian, anyway. I don't want to hear anything else!

Pierre (*insistently, inviting trouble*): I am a French spy, monsieur.

Thorpe: Well? Suppose you are?

Pierre (*goading him*): A dangerous spy, *monsieur.* The chief of a group stretching from here to Namur, to Mons, to the very French border. Don't you wish to kill me *now?*

Thorpe: The battle's finished. Why should I be your enemy?

Pierre: I am glad you speak so, *monsieur.* Because this young lady ... you have seen her?

Thorpe: Yes.

Pierre: I am the only person in all Belgium who can help her now.

Thorpe: You can help her? How?

Pierre: Because I can hide her, monsieur. (He crosses to the big arched window on the right as we face the stage, and nods outwards.) There is a chateau not many kilometres from here. At a word from me — yes, me — their doors will fly open. Carrier-pigeons from this loft shall tell them to make ready. A guide, one of my own men, shall drive the carriage ...

Lady Stanhope is heard calling outside, "Pierre! Pierre!" Lady Stanhope appears in the doorway to the stairs.

All is ready, madame?

Lady Stanhope: Thanks to you, Pierre, all is ready.

Thorpe sits down in the chair.

Thorpe: He's just been telling me, Lady Stanhope. Does this mean you'll be safe? Both of you?

Lady Stanhope: As safe as though we were a thousand miles away. As safe as though Major von Steinau had never existed.

Pierre: In a week, perhaps two, when the tumult has died down, this young lady's cause may be brought before the Duke at Brussels ...

Lady Stanhope: I'll set her free, Pierre, I swear it!

Thorpe: Free!

Lady Stanhope (*tentatively*): Pierre.

Pierre: Yes, madame?

Lady Stanhope crosses to the other side of the table, beyond which Pierre is standing. She begins to open her reticule.

Lady Stanhope: If there is any recompense I can ...

Pierre (*almost snarling*): Put it by, madame. Would you insult a beaten enemy?

Lady Stanhope throws the reticule on the table.

Lady Stanhope: Then why are you doing this for us?

Pierre: Madame, the good God knows.

He walks away from her, behind the pillar, and crosses to the other side so that he is now standing near the door to the stairs. There he turns.

Perhaps because this day I have seen the Emperor beaten. And my eyes sting, and I am inclined to be a fool. Perhaps because I hate the Prussians even more than you do. What does it matter?

Shrugging his shoulders, he goes to the store-cupboard. There he raises his voice.

Come out, *mademoiselle!* Come out, and have no fear! Even if the Prussian Major knows she is not a ghost ... (*He breaks off, turning round.*)

Major von Steinau, in full uniform and cavalry-sabre at his side, stands in the curtained doorway, keeping the curtain back with one hand. In his right hand he holds a cavalry pistol: in his left hand a lighted lantern. The lantern shows that his face wears an old, ugly expression, though he is trying to smile.

Steinau: Thank you, my friend. He knows *now* she is not a ghost.

Thorpe (*crying out*): Steinau!

Steinau comes in slowly, circling behind Thorpe and Lady Stanhope. He puts down the lantern on the window ledge of the right hand window, above the bed. He moves on, watching them, and comes round so that he is now down stage, right, watching them.

Steinau (*agreeably*): Your servant, Captain Thorpe. Yours, dear lady. I bring you good news of a victory.

Lady Stanhope: Bonaparte — is defeated?

Steinau (*laughs*): They ran, dear lady. They ran like rabbits when they saw the Prussian Standards in the woods beyond Ohain.

Lady Stanhope (*satirically*): You were *with* the Prussians, of course?

Steinau: Oh, no. My post is in Brussels. I deal with traitors.

Lady Stanhope: Such as?

Steinau: Yourself, for instance.

Lady Stanhope: Was it a great pleasure, Major von Steinau, to follow us here?

Steinau: Follow *you*, dear lady? You flatter yourself. I was not following you.

Thorpe (*starting to get up*): Not ... following ... (*Thorpe sits.*)

Steinau: Oh, no! It comes to our ears that a certain so-called Belgian, who likes to be known as a "poor miller," is in fact one of Bonaparte's foremost spies. (*Suddenly to Pierre*) What do you say to that?

Pierre (*fanatically*): I say ... Long live the Emperor!

Steinau (*critically*): He will not have long to live, my friend. Not much longer than you. (*To Lady Stanhope*) I came here for one Pierre Duroc. Of course, if on the way I pick up other spies who consort with him ...

Lady Stanhope: Other spies?

Steinau: You and the actress-slut. I will hang both of you.

Lady Stanhope: I see.

Steinau: It was thirsty work, that ride from Brussels. Both for me, and (*significantly*) for the men who now surround this mill. Permit me.
He shifts the pistol with his left hand. With great leisureliness he picks up the wine bottle from the table, and pours a glassful. He drinks appreciatively and drinks again, while the others watch him in suspense.

Thorpe (*bursting out*): What are you going to do?

Steinau (*with decision*): You will see.
He sets down the glass half empty. He walks across to Pierre, who still stands in front of the store-cupboard door.

Steinau: Open the door, please.

Pause

(*with sudden ferocity*) Did you hear me? Open the door!

Pierre hesitates, and then throws the door wide open.

(*cool and persuasive again*) Come out, *junge dame.* Come out!

The Girl, in a hooded cape with its hood thrown back, comes out slowly. She is in a bad states of nerves. Steinau stands back; as she turns to back away from him, he also turns and faces her.

And this, I think, is the young lady who was hanged.

With no change of expression, he strikes her across the face with his right hand. The girl cries out. Thorpe lurches up from the chair and starts falling.

That would not be wise, Captain Thorpe.

He backs upstage a little, so that he can cover them all with the cavalry pistol. His cold harshness covers a remnant of superstitious terror, though only a discerning eye would see.

(*to the Girl*) How did you do it?

The Girl: Please! Why are you looking at me like that?

Steinau: I saw you hanged. I saw the rope choke out your life. And yet ...

Lady Stanhope has been watching him closely, as though guessing at something.

Lady Stanhope: And yet, she's alive!

Steinau: Yes.

Lady Stanhope (*pouncing*): That worries you, doesn't it?

Steinau (*controlling himself*): It will be better, dear lady, for you to remain silent. (*To the gGrl*) How did you do it?

Lady Stanhope: Don't tell him, my dear!

Steinau (*thoughtfully*): After all, that is a question Lady Stanhope can perhaps answer better. In the meantime ...

He draws his cavalry-sabre.

(*to Pierre*) In the meantime, Pierre Duroc, get into your own store-cupboard. (*Slight pause*) Are you still deaf, my friend? Get into your own store-cupboard.

Pierre (*drawn up*): As you wish, monsieur.

Pierre backs slowly through the door. Steinau, sabre in right hand, follows facing him. We cannot now see either of them. But we hear Pierre's voice.

(*crying out*) Long live the —

The words end in an intense, muffled cry of agony. There is a thud, as of a body tumbling against a wall and then sliding to the floor. Half a dozen loose apples, as though disturbed from a shelf, roll out across the floor. Steinau comes back, returning the sabre to its sheath, and closing the door.

The girl has run to Thorpe. Lady Stanhope has moved to the table, where she picks up her reticule. She now stands before the table with her back to the audience.

Steinau: You will take the young lady downstairs, Captain Thorpe.

Thorpe: I won't do it! You can't give her away! I ...

Steinau: You will take the young lady downstairs. (*Fiercely*) Or must I summon my men and have her carried down?

Lady Stanhope (*turning round*): Do as he tells you, Captain Thorpe.

Thorpe: But ...!

Lady Stanhope: Do as he tells you!

She moves away from the table; a close observer could see that the knife is no longer stuck in it. Lady Stanhope goes back to the right hand window, where she takes the lantern from the edge of the sill. She hands this to the girl, speaking with careful significance.

Captain Thorpe, my dear, is badly wounded and perhaps a little light-headed. Don't let him speak to the guard. And don't you speak either.

Steinau (*sharply*): Why not?

Lady Stanhope (*satirically*): What's the matter, Major von Steinau? Are you afraid she'll escape you even yet? (*To the others*) Go! Go! Go!

Thorpe (*to the girl, heavily*): *I* gave you away.

The Girl: It doesn't matter. I told you it was too late.

She turns her head away and runs to the curtained doorway. Thorpe follows her, walking slowly and uncertainly. As he goes, we become conscious of a new noise: A heavy, slow, uneasy creaking as of wood, always in the background. Outside the window, the sails of the windmill begin slowly to revolve.

Lady Stanhope: Dark in here, isn't it? Growing very dark.

Steinau crosses to the table. He picks up wine bottle, fills the half empty glass, gulps down its contents, and suddenly stops short as he looks at the table.

Steinau (*turning round*): Lady Stanhope!

She is in the middle of the room, holding the reticule in both hands.

Lady Stanhope: Yes, dear Major?

Steinau: A little while ago there was a knife on this table. A knife stuck in the wood.

Lady Stanhope: Was there?

Steinau: It is not here now. Where is it?

Lady Stanhope: (*laughs*)

Steinau: Where is it, Lady Stanhope?

Lady Stanhope: Do you think I took it?

Steinau: That is not improbable.

Lady Stanhope: Are you afraid of me, then?

Steinau: That, dear lady, is not unlikely. I merely take all precautions. (*Amused*) Keep the knife, please, if you think it will be of use to you.

Lady Stanhope: And yet you *are* afraid of me. (*Suddenly*) Why did you send those two away? Why did you want to speak to me alone?

Steinau: Because I wished to — ask you a question.

Lady Stanhope: Well?

Steinau drags out the chair which stands to the left of the table. He sits down in front of the table, facing her, his profile towards us. The lantern light shines on his face. He puts the pistol on the table.

Steinau: The girl was dead. I saw her die. How did you bring her to life again?

Lady Stanhope: Ah! Now I *know* you are afraid of me!

Steinau: Why should I be? (*She stares at him in silence.*) Answer me!

Lady Stanhope (*slowly realising*): I gave you credit for too much intelligence, Major von Steinau. I over-rated you.

Steinau: Over-rated me? How?

Lady Stanhope: You knew about the girl three nights ago. Yet you made no arrest. Why not?

Steinau: *I* ask the questions, dear lady.

Lady Stanhope: Even today you were hounding the poor devil Pierre and not us. Why? Shall I tell you?

Steinau: If you can.

Lady Stanhope: Because you thought her ghost had come back for you.

Steinau: That is a damned lie!

Lady Stanhope: Is it?

Steinau: I forbid you to speak so! A Prussian officer ...

Lady Stanhope: A Prussian officer swore her life away. The Prussian officer was afraid she's come back for him. Conscience making cowards of us all. It works even with you.

Steinau: I have nothing on my conscience!

Lady Stanhope: Perjury? Murder?

Steinau: The girl is alive. *You* managed it. She is not so clever as that. How did you do it?

Lady Stanhope: Shall I tell you?

Steinau (*suddenly*): Listen! What's that noise?

Lady Stanhope: It might be Pierre's ghost, mightn't it? Creaking and tapping, trying to get in. As a matter of strict fact, it's only the sails of the windmill. Going round and round, round and round, like the fear in your stomach now. But it *might* be Pierre's ghost. And you're afraid of ghosts.

Steinau: Answer my question! This girl ...

Lady Stanhope: The girl, you may remember, was brought up amongst mountebanks at a travelling fair.

Steinau: Well?

Lady Stanhope: I couldn't prevent the execution, dear Major. But I could bribe both the hangman and the surgeon. They put a black bag over her head and face: Remember?

Steinau: That is the rule of executions! But ...

Lady Stanhope: Inside the hood was — a mountebank's device. The hangman fastened it to the ropes with metal grips through the cloth of the bag. Have you never seen those people who hang from wires *by their teeth?*

Steinau: And that was how ... ?

Lady Stanhope: Yes. Until the bribed surgeon pronounced her dead.

Steinau: A mummer's trick! That is all! A mummer's trick!

Lady Stanhope: As you say. A mummer's trick.

Steinau starts to get up, but sinks back again.

Steinau (*violently*): I was a fool not to have thought of it! *Ja!* I was a fool for one moment to have been afraid of ghosts!

Lady Stanhope: On the contrary, Major von Steinau. You have every reason to be afraid of ghosts. Look here!

Steinau: Don't move! Stay where you are!

Lady Stanhope goes softly and quietly to the store cupboard door. Standing to one side, she opens it. Pierre's body pitches out face forward, crumpling on the floor.

Lady Stanhope: Dead, you notice. Run through the body with your sabre.

Steinau: Well?

Lady Stanhope: Has it occurred to you that *his* ghost might come back for you?

Steinau: What devil's nonsense do you talk?

Lady Stanhope: Is it nonsense?

Steinau: Yes!

She moves upstage, left, so that she is facing Steinau diagonally from some distance away.

Lady Stanhope: Suppose, Major von Steinau, you were to be found dead beside him. Your throat cut open, let's say, with a certain knife. Pierre's knife. *This* knife.

Deliberately she opens the reticule and takes out the knife. Slinging the carrying-loop of the reticule over her wrist, she displays the knife.

Your men downstairs will assume that you attacked Pierre, and he struck back at you before he died. Nobody would question it. Nobody *will* question it, when I tell them so. (*She takes a step forward.*)

Steinau (*hoarsely*): Do you think you can ... ?

He starts to get up again, but there is something wrong with him. He sinks back heavily.

Lady Stanhope: Yes, I think I can.

Steinau (*desperately*): There's something wrong with me! What ... is ... ?

Lady Stanhope: What is dimming your eyesight? Making your head swim? Turning your muscles to water?

Steinau: Yes!

Lady Stanhope: Tincture of opium. Twenty grains. I poured it into your wine glass while you were disposing of Pierre.

Steinau cries out. He lunges forward with his right hand for the pistol on the table, but only succeeds in sending the weapon flying off the table. The pistol lands on the floor between him and Lady Stanhope.

(*Unemotionally*) That will have jarred the powder out of the firing-pan. It's quite useless now.

Steinau (*gasping*): My men are downstairs. I can ...

Lady Stanhope: You can call out to them, of course. I shall tell them later it was your death-agony when Pierre struck you. Or don't you want thirty seconds more of life?

Steinau: Lady Stanhope, for the love of God!

Lady Stanhope: Yes. For the love of God. (*She takes another step forward.*) A year ago, in Paris, I made a vow. Truth meant nothing to you. Agony meant nothing to you. Shame, humiliation meant nothing to you. I swore on the cross that I would prove this girl's innocence; or else I would kill you. I tried to bring her to Lord Wellington's attention. I wanted to enlist *his* sympathy. But Bonaparte stopped all that. Only one thing remains.[4]

Steinau: *No!*

Lady Stanhope: Listen to the windmill, Major von Steinau. Cringe and tremble and call it a ghost. Listen to the windmill, Major von Steinau: the last sound you will ever hear.

Steinau (*weakened*): You cannot do this! (*Suddenly*) You spoke of conscience ...

Lady Stanhope: Did I?

Steinau: And that is good! That is good, that is good! Your own conscience ...

Lady Stanhope: Didn't I tell you? I have no conscience.

She smiles, her thumb touches the blade of the knife. Still smiling, she begins to walk very slowly towards him ...

AS THE CURTAIN FALLS

---

[4] This exchange echoes the climax of Poe's "The Cask of Amontillado," with which Carr would have been very familiar.

AFTERWORD

The plot of *She Slept Lightly* owes a good deal to *Speak of the Devil*, a BBC radio serial written by Carr and broadcast in eight episodes between February 10 and March 31, 1941.[1] In *Speak of the Devil*, which is set in 1816 a year after the battle of Waterloo, Captain Hugh Austen is haunted by memories of a girl who, it transpires, cheated the hangman by the same means as her counterpart in *She Slept Lightly*. *Speak of the Devil* is also memorable for it marked Carr's creation of "The Man in Black," later to be immortalised by Joseph Kearns in the US radio series *Suspense* but portrayed in *Speak of the Devil* by Valentine Dyall who went on to play the character in all of the series of *Appointment with Fear*, which Carr created in 1943.

In 1988, the actress June Whitfield, who portrayed the unnamed girl in *She Slept Lightly*, recalled "how charming Irene Vanbrugh was — she personified the "dignity" of the theatre to me. The other memory is that I had to have my face slapped by Frederick Horrey when he discovered me hiding in a cupboard and I eventually developed a rash - so we cut it down to a good slap on Mondays and Saturdays and faked it the rest of the week. I believe I did meet J. Dickson Carr once when he attended a rehearsal but, being a very junior member of the cast, I didn't have the opportunity to talk to him a great deal!"[2]

After *Prize Onions* was omitted, Carr expanded the text of *She Slept Lightly* by adding two large sections of dialogue: the first between Steinau's remark beginning "No? That is a pity" and his remark beginning "In her grade"; and the second between Pierre's remark beginning "You need not be alaramed, Madame" and his remark "Even if the Prussian Major knows she is not a ghost."

---

[1] *Speak of the Devil* by John Dickson Carr; introduction and notes by Tony Medawar. Norfolk, Crippen & Landru, 1994; reprinted 2008.

APPENDIX 1

John Dickson Carr's Original Ending to "Intruding Shadow"

As noted already, when the comic interlude *Prize Onions* was dropped from the *Appointment with Fear* programme, Carr revised *Intruding Shadow*, changing the ending and adding a large section of dialogue in the middle of the play, specifically the dialogue beginning with Marlowe's speech "That somebody in this room is a remarkably fine liar" and ending with Marlowe's puzzled "I wish I knew," in response to a question from Flint. Undoubtedly, Carr's revised ending better reflects his mischievous view of how law officers ought to behave when investigating the murder of a blackmailer and, for that reason, it is the version used in the main body of this collection. The original, tighter but some-how less satisfactory, ending is set out below.

Richard: It *was* one of my own plots. I committed the murder.
Long pause. Parsons stares at Richard in slowly growing horror, as he realises Richard is serious. Richard is smiling. Parsons suddenly gets up from the chair, dropping the book on the floor, and begins to back away.
Parsons (*shrilly*): You *did* do it after all! You were ...
Richard: I was the man in hat and gloves. *Yes.*
He gets up from the sofa. He crosses towards Parsons, who has backed towards the cupboard down. On his way Richard picks up the fallen book with his left hand. He puts his right hand on the shoulder of Parsons, who cries out, and gently leads him back to the chair.
Richard (*blandly*): Sit down, Uncle George. You'll keep my secret. (*He pushes Parsons into the chair.*)
Parsons (*crying out*): But. You had ...
Richard: I had an alibi, you were about to say?
Parsons: Yes!

243

Richard: Didn't you ever hear, Uncle George, of the double-bluff? (*Holding the book, Richard moves away from him towards the middle of the room.*) The first part of the bluff was to convince Flint that I meant only a "joke." So that he could confirm it afterwards. Unfortunately, I didn't convince him. He suspected me all along ...

Parsons: And rightly?

Richard: And rightly ... But don't you see now why I *had* to get Anne Corbin here?

Parsons: No!

Richard: As a witness, my dear uncle.

Parsons: A witness?

Richard: A witness to testify that I never once left this room. It was no good taking her into the secret. Anne would only have broken down and confessed. She had to believe, absolutely believe, that I never left her side. Even in darkness.

Parsons: But you did leave her?

Richard: Oh, yes. Do you remember when the front doorbell rang? And Bruce Renfield came in?

Parsons: Yes!

Richard: I was standing by the only light-switch. *This* light-switch. (*He goes to it.*) I warned Anne not to speak. There were forty seconds of absolute silence and darkness while the clock was striking. That was when I acted.

Parsons has got up from his chair, following this.

Parsons: You mean you ... ?

Richard: Observe my dark suit, Uncle George; Anne couldn't see me. I slipped into the bedroom there. The spanner and the hat and gloves were ready. In the bedroom there's a door ... you mentioned it yourself ... that leads ... where?

Parsons: Out on the landing!

Richard: That's right. As Renfield got to the top of the stairs I stepped out behind him and struck. You never actually saw me going upstairs. You only assumed that because you saw me at the top of them.

Parsons: Stop a bit! The landing was the only place where that inspector found blood-stains!

Richard: Right again.

Parsons: And in that forty seconds ... ?

Richard: I struck Renfield to his knees, got a certain bundle of letters out of his pocket, and threw the spanner downstairs. I was back in here in time to answer Anne when she spoke. *Now* do you understand? (*He comes downstage again; Parsons backs away.*) The human mind, my dear uncle, is very gullible. I admitted, you see, that I meant to bring Renfield in here, tie him up with ropes, threaten him, and possibly kill him with a poker. Therefore nobody dreamed I would upset my own scheme by killing Renfield with a spanner before he even got here. That's the double-bluff, my dear uncle. I was blackening my character in order to whitewash it. And nobody suspected me.

Parsons goes rather shakily to the easy chair, and sits down.

Parsons (*suddenly*): Aren't you ... *scared?*

Richard: No. I can't say I am.

Parsons: But Flint suspected you! Probably he still does!

Richard: Yes. Flint nearly dished me. *He* was supposed to see the intruding shadow ...

Parsons: Intruding shadow?

Richard: The sinister figure in the hat and gloves, which couldn't have been me. I counted on his curiosity for that. But you served just as well.

Parsons (*hollowly*): I testified ...

Richard: You did it in good faith, Uncle George. Don't worry.

Parsons: Don't *worry?* (*Querulously*) Why are you telling me all this?

Richard: Because you must be very sure, when you tell your story next time, that the intruding shadow came from outside. Otherwise ...

Parsons: Otherwise ... ?

Richard: Some member of this family might be arrested for murder, and we don't want that. I'll take care of any other difficulties. If the police were to come back at this moment, I'll have a complete story ready for them.

The double-doors open..

Ellen: George Parsons!

Parsons shakes violently, even though he swings round to see who it is.

Richard: What's the matter, Uncle George? Not jumpy?

Ellen: I declare, Richard Marlowe, it's enough to make anybody jumpy! Past four o'clock in the morning, and nobody had a wink of sleep yet! And you, Richard! Reading at a time like this.

Richard (*surprised*): Reading?

Ellen: That book in your hand! I'm sure it must be very interesting, my dear, if you can find time to bother with it after all that's happened tonight! Well?

Richard: Oh, yes. The book. (*A pleasant smile crosses his face as he reads the title in a clear, thoughtful, far away voice:*) *On Murder, Considered As One of the Fine Arts.*

CURTAIN

APPENDIX 2

Notes for the Curious

Inspector Silence Takes the Air

"A Comedy Thriller of Broadcasting"

First produced at the Pier Pavilion, Llandudno, on April 20, 1942, with the following cast of characters:

Chief Inspector Silence	Leon M. Lion
Antony Barran, a BBC Producer	Carl Bernard
Elliott Vandeleur, an actor	Ivan Samson
Jennifer Sloane, his wife, an actress	Lesley Brook
Lanyon Kelsey, an actor	Eric Maturin
May Matheson, an elderly actress	Elaine Inescort
Julian Caird, Dramatic Director BBC	Ronald Simpson
Helen Searle, his secretary	Lydia Sherwood
Herbert Pope, Programme Engineer	Paget Hunter
George Sloane, Junior Programme Engineer	Keith Rawlings
Edna Nasmith, Junior Programme Engineer	Ara Thurlbeck
Basil Cheston, a BBC Announcer	Patrick Ludlow
Croker, a Studio Attendant	Bruce Winston

NB, Leon M. Lion played Inspector Silence in Carr's radio play, "Inspector Silence Takes the Underground," and he also starred in Carr and Gielgud's second play, *Thirteen to the Gallows*. Lion is best known as the star of *Number 17* (1932), directed by Alfred Hitchcock and based on the play by J. Jefferson Farjeon in which he had also appeared. Bruce Winston appeared in the whodunit curiosity, *The Arsenal Stadium Mystery* (1939) and Lesley Brook led the cast of *The Nursemaid Who Disappeared* (1939), adapted from Philip Macdonald's novel. Ronald Simpson appeared in Carr's BBC radio serial *Speak of the Devil* (1941) and, with Lydia Sherwood and Carl Bernard, he also appeared in Carr's

BBC radio play "The Man in the Iron Mask" (1942).

The full run of *Inspector Silence Takes the Air* was as follows:

April 20, 1942	Pier Pavilion, Llandudno
April 27, 1942	Grand Theatre, Blackpool
May 4, 1942	Royal Theatre, Newcastle
May 11, 1942	Royal Theatre, Glasgow
May 18, 1942	Pavilion Theatre, Bournemouth
May 25, 1942	Grand Theatre, Leeds

The play was an "E. G. Norman presentation", and produced by Leon M. Lion. The intention was that the play should transfer to London but this did not happen.

Reviews were almost wholly positive:

"Things happen fast and haphazardly but nevertheless mysteriously ... this is undoubtedly the best play of its kind we have had during the war." (*North Wales Pioneer*, April 23, 1942)

"A thriller well spiced with comedy. The secret of who killed Lanyon Kelsey, an actor, is cleverly concealed, and everybody is surprised when Inspector Silence discloses the murderer. Leon M. Lion in the part of the inspector is finely supported by the other members of the cast." (*North Wales Weekly News*, April 23, 1942)

"The play is described as a comedy thriller and if the comedy is not pronounced there is no doubt about the excitement. The out-standing feature is its absorbing interest. Possibly on account of the authors' personal experience of broadcasting procedure the incidents are recorded with a fidelity which at times make one forget that it is a play ... the plot is not particularly original [but] the treatment of it is natural and the identity of the murderer is well concealed. The remarkable fine acting of Carl Bernard ... contributes greatly to the realism of the play. It is difficult to imagine the role being played more convincingly ... [Leon M. Lion] takes the centre of the stage with the ease of a veteran actor [and] Bruce Winston contributes a perfect character study. In the other roles not a great deal of scope is provided for special acting but Lydia Sherwood and Lesley Brook take attractive parts and Elaine Inescort introduces some comedy ... Frederic Curzon deserves a compliment for his organ rendering of The Knightsbridge March." (*Llandudno Advertiser*, April 25, 1942)

" 'Who killed Lanyon Kelsey?' This was the question I put to several people at the end of the second act ... the fact that nobody guessed the criminal is a tribute to the skill of those experienced masters of detective fiction, John Dickson-Carr [sic] and Val Gielgud ... when the first act has been knit a little more closely and last night's 'technical hitches' overcome, the play should be a first class example of the modern comedy-thriller — particularly welcome because the comedy is not allowed to kill the thrills ... [Leon M. Lion's] convincing characterisation is ably supported by a clever band of artists familiar to wireless listeners." (*Blackpool Evening Gazette*, April 28, 1942)

"The story is endowed with the necessary interest, and due suspense is maintained until the fall of the curtain. Not until Inspector Silence puts all doubts at rest in an exciting last act is the mystery solved for the audience. Amongst some excellent portrayals honours must be accorded to Mr Lion not only for his excellent work in the title role, but also for the effective standard of the production. Carl Bernard, as a BBC producer, is also largely responsible for keeping the realism of the piece at a high pitch ... Elaine Inescort gets plenty of comedy out of the part of May Matheson ... and Bruce Winston gives a clever character study of Croker. [The others in the cast] all help to make a capital evening's entertainment." (*The Stage*, April 30, 1942)

"Comedy interspersed with thrills; [the play] provided tip-top entertainment." (*Newcastle Evening Chronicle*, May 5, 1942)

"Thrilling entertainment, with an abundance of sparkling humour ... the performance is particularly interesting for the introduction of several actors and actresses whose voices are well-known in broadcast plays; while an insight is given into what happens the other side of the microphone with revelations of some of the sound effects. Leon M. Lion gives a faithful portrait of the 'mike-shy' inspector ... with delightful comedy studies by Elaine Inescort and Bruce Winston." (*Bournemouth Daily Echo*, May 20, 1942)

"There is a good deal of comedy and not a few thrills. Leon M. Lion and Bruce Winston, the studio attendant, providing most of the former, with Elaine Inescort as an elderly actress doing her share ... Carl Bernard as producer manages to convey effectively the exasperation which at times must beset all producers, and not least those at the BBC. There is humour and mystery ..." (*Leeds Mercury*, May 26, 1942)

Thirteen to the Gallows

First produced at the Theatre Royal, Leicester, on April 17, 1944, with the following cast:

Wallace Hatfield	James de la Mere (*Leicester*)
	Russell Thorndike
Anthony Barran	Donald Ross (*Leicester*)
	Jack Vyvyan (*Brighton and Southsea*)
	John Lothar (*Bradford and Glasgow*)
Major John Burnside	Walter Chapman (*Leicester)*
	Eric Conley
Carol Mayne	Pearl Dadswell (*Leicester*)
	Faith Bennett
Judith Phillimore	Actor Unknown (*Leicester*)
	Helena Pickard
Paul Phillimore	Actor Unknown (*Leicester*)
	Macarthur Gordon
Jonas Whitehead	Actor Unknown (*Leicester, Bradford and Glasgow*)
	John Lothar
Penelope Squire	Actor Unknown (*Leicester*)
	Eileen Dawson
Colonel Sir Henry Bryce	Robert Hollyman (*Leicester*)

	Leon M. Lion (*Brighton and Southsea*)
	Lawrence Hanray (*Bradford and Glasgow*)
Leila Ponsonby	Actor Unknown (*Leicester*)
	Moira Stephenson
Dorothy West	Actor Unknown (*Leicester*)
	Sheila Hudson
Jill Whitehead	Actor Unknown (*Leicester*)
	Yvonne Coquelle
Sandoz	Actor Unknown (*Leicester*)
	David Bird

Among the cast for the Leicester performances were Helen Beal and Helene Sproule, described in one review as "staff" but it is unclear which parts they played. It also seems likely that the play was revised after these initial performances and that some of the minor characters only appeared in the version of the script presented in 1945. Notwithstanding the difference in spelling, the "Anthony Barran" in "Thirteen to the Gallows" and the "Antony Barran" in "Inspector Silence Takes the Air" appear to be one and the same.

NB, As well as acting, Russell Thorndike created "'Dr Syn" who appeared in six novels, and he wrote a number of other novels including, interestingly, *The Devil in the Belfry* (1932). Jack Vyvyan appeared in various thrillers, including *Old Mother Riley, Detective* (1943) and *Meet Sexton Blake* (1944). Lawrence Hanray appeared in many films, including *Murder at Monte Carlo* (1934) and Edgar Wallace's *The Missing People* (1940). John Lothar appeared in *Smoky Cell* (1939), another film based on the work of Edgar Wallace.

The full run of "Thirteen to the Gallows" was as follows:

April 17, 1944	Theatre Royal, Leicester
September 20, 1945	Theatre Royal, Brighton
October 1, 1945	Kings Theatre, Southsea
October 15, 1945	Princes Theatre, Bradford

October 22, 1945   Alhambra Theatre, Glasgow

There were no performances during the week beginning October 8.

Reviews were mixed:

"An attraction that will give plenty of scope for those scientifically inclined
to use their knowledge. Val Gielgud and his co-author have constructed
the play on sound entertainment lines with plenty of humour ... Excellent
work is done by Robert Hollyman as the old Chief of Police, and Pearl
Dadswell holds her own with a charming study of the secretary. As the
harassed BBC producer ... Donald Ross captures the spirit of his part
[and] James de la Mere successfully carries an air of innocence till the final
exposure. A special word of praise is due to Peter Purdy who was
responsible for the stage setting and effects." (*The Stage*, April 17, 1944)

"[The play is] amusing enough, and some of the digs at broadcasting
studios, much nearer to Oxford Circus than the Barchester of the play, are
cunningly wrought ... 'red herrings' [are] artfully put forward by the
authors, and there is a plentiful array of other false trails to put the unwary
in the audience off the right scent ... It is cleverly and adroitly contrived ...
the play is very well written and it is superbly cast. Leon M. Lion, whose
farewell performance this is said to be, is ideal [and] he is excellently
supported by Jack Vyvyan [while] Russell Thorndike ... gives one of the
most consistent bits of acting in the whole play. There is also a fine
performance from John Lothar as the exuberant – perhaps a trifle too
exuberant – producer of the BBC programme and Helena Pickard is
attractively convincing ... Eileen Dawson, Moira Stephenson, Sheila
Hudson and Yvonne Coquelle are good in minor parts, and a special
tribute must be paid to Eric Conley, who insisted on appearing as the
station director in spite of indisposition." (*The Stage*, September 20, 1945)

"Pantomime and drama are mixed not too well in *Thirteen to the Gallows*
... Progress is painfully slow in the first act, but warms gradually with the
introduction of a Viennese sea-lion trainer in the second. This is a delightful cameo by David Bird. Making up for a very boring introduction, the
third act is full of thrills ... the plot is cleverly contrived and original, but

far-fetched. Lawrence Hanray makes a good retired policeman, and John Lothar loses his temper effectively as the producer [and] Helena Pickard is a sympathetic secretary." (*Bradford Telegraph & Argus*, October 16, 1945)

"Lawrence Hanray is convincing as the man who solves the mystery. John Lothar is amusing as the excitable producer. Helena Pickard is an attractive secretary, and David Bird has another trade on his hands as an imitator of sea-lions." (*Yorkshire Observer*, October 16, 1945)

Appointment with Fear

"A GREAT AND UNUSUAL ATTRACTION"

"You have HEARD it on 'THE AIR' — Now SEE it on the STAGE! An Evening of Suspense and Thrills (but with nothing "horrific"). Specially written for the stage by JOHN DICKSON CARR, Author of the Famous Radio Plays ... TWO ABSORBING PLAYS - BOTH IN ONE EVENING . . . YOU <u>WILL</u> BE THRILLED! YOU <u>WILL</u> BE HELD IN SUSPENSE! YOU WILL <u>NOT</u> BE HORRIFIED!"

Intruding Shadow

"The Author Challenges You to Solve the Mystery!"

First produced, with "She Slept Lightly" and "Prize Onions" by E. Eynon Evans, under the title *Appointment with Fear* at the Palace Theatre, Westcliff-on-Sea, on April 2, 1945, with the following cast of:

George Parsons	Keith Shepherd
Ellen Parsons (his wife)	Peggy Rush
	Namara Michael (*Croydon performances and after*)
Richard Marlowe	Lewis Stringer

Flint	Robert Hey
Anne Corbin	Barbara Douglas
Stephen Sowerby	Frederick Horrey
Bruce Renfield	Ian Howard
Storyteller,"The Man in Black"	(Voice of Valentine Dyall)

NB, Lewis Stringer appeared in many plays in the *Appointment with Fear* radio series. Valentine Dyall, as well as portraying The Man in Black in almost all episodes of the *Appointment with Fear* series, appeared as the victim in Carr's first radio play for the BBC, "Who Killed Matthew Corbin?" (1939-1940). In later years, he appeared on *Doctor Who* and *The Hitchhiker's Guide to the Galaxy.*

She Slept Lightly

"A Drama of 100 years ago!"

First produced as part of a triple bill under the title *Appointment with Fear,* with "Intruding Shadow" and "Prize Onions," a play by E. Eynon Evans, at the Palace Theatre, Westcliff-on-Sea, on April 2, 1945, with the following cast:

Pierre	Keith Shepherd
Lady Stanhope	Dame Irene Vanbrugh
	Ethel Warwick
	(*Scarborough performances and after*)
Captain Thorpe	Lewis Stringer
The Girl	June Whitfield
Steinau	Frederick Horrey
Your Storyteller, "The Man in Black"	(The Voice of Valentine Dyall)

NB, Dame Irene Vanbrugh was a major figure in British theatre, having been personally cast by Oscar Wilde in the first production of *The Importance of Being Earnest* (1895), in which she appeared with Valentine Dyall's father, Franklin Dyall, who on a few occasions portrayed

Carr's Man in Black in the *Appointment with Fear* radio series. June Whitfield is better known as the mother of the monstrous Edina Monsoon in *Absolutely Fabulous* (BBC Television, 1992-2004) and for her portrayal of Agatha Christie's Miss Marple in twelve radio plays for the BBC based on the novels (1993-2001).

The full run of the *Appointment with Fear* was as follows:

April 2, 1945	Palace Theatre, Westcliff-on-Sea
April 9, 1945	Arts Theatre, Cambridge
April 16, 1945	Winter Gardens, Morecambe
April 23, 1945	Grand Theatre, Croydon
April 30, 1945	Theatre Royal, Worcester
May 7, 1945	Hippodrome, Preston
May 14, 1945	Hippodrome, Dudley
May 21, 1945	Theatre Royal, Bath
May 28, 1945	Theatre Royal, Exeter
June 4, 1945	New Theatre, Hull
June 11, 1945	Theatre Royal, Norwich
June 18, 1945	Opera House, Cheltenham
June 25, 1945	Opera House, Scarborough
July 2, 1945	Grand Theatre, Blackburn
July 9, 1945	Theatre Royal, Hanley
July 16, 1945	Hippodrome, Margate
July 23, 1945	Theatre Royal, Bolton
July 30, 1945	Princes Theatre, Bradford

"Prize Onions," which won first prize in the comedy section of a competition run by the British Drama League, began life as a radio play; the plot concerns the rivalries involved in a competition between people growing vegetables. The play was cut from Bournemouth and Carr expanded both of his plays to ensure a full programme.

The plays were a "William Watt presentation," and both were staged and directed by Martyn C. Webster "as on the radio." Webster produced and directed much of Carr's radio work and the early *Appointment with Fear* radio series. A copy of the programme for *Appointment with Fear,* autographed by Dame Irene Vanbrugh and Lewis Stringer, is owned by Croydon Local Studies Library. For some performances, all profits from the performance were donated to charities such as the Channel Islands Hospitals' Relief Fund and the Young Women's Christian Association.

While contemporary reviews of "She Slept Lightly" were uniformly very favourable, commentators were a little more reserved in their praise for "Intruding Shadow ."

"Dame Irene Vanbrugh holds the show together and her brilliant acting unfortunately is to be seen only in the last of three one-act plays. There however she gives a compelling performance ... Lewis Stringer, Frederick Horrey and Keith Shepherd are the most outstanding of the supporting cast and Valentine Dyall creates the tensest moments in Intruding Shadow." (Southend-on-Sea and County Pictorial, April 7, 1945)

"Dame Irene dominates [*She Slept Lightly*] as the courageous and cunning Lady Stanhope, and there is some fine work on the male side by vigorous Lewis Stringer as the Englishman, and Frederick Horrey as the German whilst Keith Shepherd is well cast as Pierre. In [*Intruding Shadow*] good work is done by Lewis Stringer, Barbara Douglas and Peggy Rush. Both thrillers are introduced by the voice of Valentine Dyall (as 'The Man in Black') and this helps to prepare the right atmosphere; but one felt that with such a general title as Appointment with Fear both plays might have been a little more horrific. (Cambridge Daily News, April 11, 1945)

"*Intruding Shadow* [is] written with a fine sense of suspense by John Dickson Carr ... Lewis Stringer has a big part in its success ... and Barbara Douglas has some emotional moments that are ably interpreted. [*She Slept Lightly* is] the best play of the evening, but we may be prejudiced by the fact that Dame Irene Vanbrugh plays the lead ... in the main it is Dame Irene's wonderful acting that tells. Her clarity of diction alone is a lesson to the others in how to make the best use of the spoken word but she has grace of carriage and that indefinable method of bringing power to her every scene that have such an electric effect on playgoers. Everything she does is imbued with a subtle charm even in her more tragic passages. She is strongly seconded by Lewis Stringer [and] Frederick Horrey ... Patrons will long remember the final scene with the vengeful woman creeping towards her helpless victim, knife in hand. Keith Shepherd lends power to Pierre." (*The Stage*, April 12, 1945)

"A successful radio feature is successfully translated to the stage ... [In *She Slept Lightly*, John Dickson Carr has] a chance to demonstrate his ability to create characters which, though conventional in their types, are well-drawn, and to create situations, which on the page seem stagey, are excellent from the theatrical point of view ... *Intruding Shadow* is written with some deftness though the characters never appear to touch reality ... Barbara Douglas and Keith Shepherd help to keep the suspense and the comedy at the right pitch." (*Croydon Advertiser*, April 27, 1945)

"*She Slept Lightly* ... is dominated by Dame Irene Vanbrugh, imperious as ever in the grand manner, she makes every word and gesture tell. Top marks for fine character acting go to Keith Shepherd. " (*Preston Herald*, May 8, 1945)

"Never can the sense of unity between players and audience have found better expression at Bath than in this dual production ... in [*Intruding Shadow*] the lighting effects are admirably devised and greatly enhance the dramatic value of the story even when, by an entertaining paradox, they consist of no lighting whatever ... Barbara Douglas plays convincingly [and] Namara Michael gives a good study of a dominating and over-anxious wife. June Whitfield instantly captures and consistently retains our sympathy as the girl spy in [*She Slept Lightly*]. Keith Shepherd presents two excellent studies [and] Lewis Stringer's tragic expression at a crucial moment in *She Slept Lightly* represents true art ... the standard of elocution is excellent." (Newspaper unknown, May 1945)

"You will get your money's worth in thrills ... if you don't experience delicious cold shudders up and down your spine and grip the arms of your chair — or you next door neighbour — with anticipatory horrors in your *Appointment with Fear* then you can ask for your money back. Lewis Stringer] gives excellent performances in both plays — as the romantic Captain Thorpe and as the beautifully sinister Richard Marlowe." (*Hull Daily Mail*, June 5, 1945)

"[*Intruding Shadow* is] a typical trick melodrama of the 'Who did it?' variety. Lewis Stringer's diction was good and there were two neat character studies by Robert Hey and Keith Shepherd, comedy being provided by Namara Michael ... [*She Slept Lightly*] was dealt with in a broader style of melodrama which Dame Irene Vanbrugh certainly got away with ... She is aided by Lewis Stringer [and] Keith Shepherd, who provides an impressive little cameo." (*Eastern Daily Press*, June 12, 1945)

"Lewis Stringer gives excellent performances in both plays, and Ethel Warwick admirably sustains the leading feminine role in *She Slept Lightly*." (*Scarborough Evening News & Daily Post*, June 26, 1945)

"Not so fearful as all that, [it] has the virtue of unusual entertainment, intriguing and therefore attention-compelling. In pitch darkness and with eerie sound effects, the audience becomes acquainted with a notebook recording some macabre goings on, gets a bit of the atmosphere, and is then eager to see how matters develop on the stage. The players, a competent team, contrive effectively to increase the tension, so that the two contrasting episodes – one, sudden death in a modern flat, and the other an intimate drama of the battle of Waterloo as the background, make their full point as swift pictures of the weird side of life ... in both places the diction of the players is exemplary, that of Lewis Stringer, who appears in both [plays], conspicuously so. Keith Shepherd provides two clever character studies and Ethel Warwick makes plausible the Lady Stanhope of the period piece ... the orchestra makes careful contributions, and includes an expert xylophone player." (*Bradford Telegraph & Argus*, July 31, 1945)

Thirteen to the Gallows

Thirteen to the Gallows by John Dickson Carr and Val Gielgud, and edited by Tony Medawar, is set in 11-point Baskerville Old Style and printed on sixty-pound Natures acid-free recycled paper. The cover illustration and design are by Deborah Miller. The first edition was printed in two forms: trade softcover, notch-bound; and 250 numbered copies sewn in cloth and signed by the editor. Each of the clothbound copies includes a separate pamphlet, *Inspector Silence Takes the Underground: A Radio Play* by John Dickson Carr.

Thirteen to the Gallows was printed and bound by Thomson-Shore, Inc., Dexter, Michigan and published in September 2008 by Crippen & Landru Publishers, Inc., Norfolk, Virginia.

CRIPPEN & LANDRU, PUBLISHERS

P. O. Box 9315
Norfolk, VA 23505
info@crippenlandru.com; toll-free 877 622-6656
www.crippenlandru.com

Crippen & Landru publishes first edition short-story collections by important detective and mystery writers. The following books are currently (September 2008) in print; see our website for full details:

REGULAR SERIES

Speak of the Devil by John Dickson Carr. 1994. Trade softcover. $15.00.

The McCone Files by Marcia Muller. 1995. Trade softcover, $19.00.

Diagnosis: Impossible, The Problems of Dr. Sam Hawthorne by Edward D. Hoch. 1996. Trade softcover, $19.00.

Who Killed Father Christmas? by Patricia Moyes. 1996. Signed, unnumbered cloth overrun copies, $30.00.

In Kensington Gardens Once by H.R.F. Keating. 1997. Trade softcover, $12.00.

Shoveling Smoke by Margaret Maron. 1997. Trade softcover, $19.00.

The Ripper of Storyville and Other Tales of Ben Snow by Edward D. Hoch. 1997. Trade softcover. $19.00.

Renowned Be Thy Grave by P.M. Carlson. 1998. Trade softcover, $16.00.

Carpenter and Quincannon by Bill Pronzini. 1998. Trade softcover, $16.00.

Famous Blue Raincoat by Ed Gorman. 1999. Signed, unnumbered cloth overrun copies, $30.00. Trade softcover, $17.00.

The Tragedy of Errors and Others by Ellery Queen. 1999. Trade softcover, $20.00.

McCone and Friends by Marcia Muller. 2000. Trade softcover, $19.00.

Challenge the Widow Maker by Clark Howard. 2000. Trade softcover, $16.00.

Fortune's World by Michael Collins. 2000. Trade softcover, $16.00.

The Velvet Touch: Nick Velvet Stories by Edward D.. Hoch. 2000. Trade softcover, 19.00.

Long Live the Dead: Tales from Black Mask by Hugh B. Cave. 2000. Trade softcover, $16.00.

Tales Out of School by Carolyn Wheat. 2000. Trade softcover, $16.00.

Stakeout on Page Street and Other DKA Files by Joe Gores. 2000. Trade softcover, $16.00.

The Celestial Buffet by Susan Dunlap. 2001. Trade softcover, $16.00.

Kisses of Death: A Nathan Heller Casebook by Max Allan Collins. 2001. Trade softcover, $19.00.

The Old Spies Club and Other Intrigues of Rand by Edward D. Hoch. 2001. Signed, unnumbered cloth overrun copies, $32.00. Trade softcover, $17.00.

Adam and Eve on a Raft by Ron Goulart. 2001. Signed, unnumbered cloth overrun copies, $32.00. Trade softcover, $17.00.

The Reluctant Detective by Michael Z. Lewin. 2001. Signed, numbered clothbound, $42.00. Trade softcover, $17.00.

Nine Sons by Wendy Hornsby. 2002. Trade softcover, $16.00.

The Curious Conspiracy by Michael Gilbert. 2002. Signed, numbered clothbound, $42.00. Trade softcover, $17.00.

The 13 Culprits by Georges Simenon, translated by Peter Schulman. 2002. Trade softcover, $16.00.

The Dark Snow by Brendan DuBois. 2002. Signed, unnumbered cloth overrun copies, $32.00.

Come Into My Parlor: Tales from Detective Fiction Weekly by Hugh B. Cave. 2002. Trade softcover, $17.00.

The Iron Angel and Other Tales of the Gypsy Sleuth by Edward D. Hoch. 2003. Signed, numbered clothbound, $42.00. Trade softcover, $17.00.

Cuddy – Plus One by Jeremiah Healy. 2003. Trade softcover, $18.00.

Problems Solved by Bill Pronzini and Barry N. Malzberg. 2003. Signed, numbered clothbound, $42.00. Trade softcover, $16.00.

A Killing Climate by Eric Wright. 2003. Trade softcover, $17.00.

Lucky Dip by Liza Cody. 2003. Signed, numbered clothbound, $42.00. Trade softcover, $17.00.

Kill the Umpire: The Calls of Ed Gorgon by Jon L. Breen. 2003. Trade softcover, $17.00.

Suitable for Hanging by Margaret Maron. 2004. Trade softcover, $19.00.

Murders and Other Confusions by Kathy Lynn Emerson. 2004. Signed, numbered clothbound, $42.00. Trade softcover, $19.00.

Byline: Mickey Spillane by Mickey Spillane, edited by Lynn Myers and Max Allan Collins. 2004. Trade softcover, $20.00.

The Confessions of Owen Keane by Terence Faherty. 2005. Signed, numbered clothbound, $42.00. Trade softcover, $17.00.

The Adventure of the Murdered Moths and Other Radio Mysteries by Ellery Queen. 2005. Numbered clothbound, $45.00. Trade softcover, $20.00.

Murder, Ancient and Modern by Edward Marston. 2005. Signed, numbered clothbound, $43.00. Trade softcover, $18.00.

More Things Impossible: The Second Casebook of Dr. Sam Hawthorne by Edward D. Hoch. 2006. Signed, numbered clothbound, $43.00. Trade softcover, $18.00.

Murder, 'Orrible Murder! by Amy Myers. 2006. Signed, numbered clothbound, $43.00. Trade softcover, $18.00.

The Verdict of Us All: Stories by the Detection Club for H.R.F. Keating, edited by Peter Lovesey. 2006. Numbered clothbound, $43.00. Trade softcover, $20.00.

The Archer Files: The Complete Short Stories of Lew Archer, Private Investigator, Including Newly-Discovered Case-Notes by Ross Macdonald, edited by Tom Nolan. 2007. Numbered clothbound, $45.00. Trade softcover, $25.00.

The Mankiller of Poojeegai and Other Mysteries by Walter Satterthwait. 2007. Signed, numbered clothbound, $43.00. Trade softcover, $17.00.

Quintet: The Cases of Chase and Delacroix by Richard A. Lupoff. 2008. Signed, numbered clothbound, $43.00. Trade softcover, $17.00.

Murder on the Short List by Peter Lovesey. 2008. Signed, numbered clothbound, $43.00. Trade softcover, $17.00.

Thirteen to the Gallows by John Dickson Carr and Val Gielgud. 2008. Signed, numbered clothbound, $43.00. Trade softcover, $20.00.

FORTHCOMING TITLES IN THE REGULAR SERIES

A Little Intelligence by Robert Silverberg and Randall Garrett writing as Robert Randall.

A Pocketful of Noses: Stories of One Ganelon or Another by James Powell.

Valentino: Film Detective by Loren D. Estleman.

Once Burned: The Collected Crime Stories by S.J. Rozan.

Funeral in the Fog and Other Simon Ark Tales by Edward D. Hoch.

Suspense – His and Hers by Barbara and Max Allan Collins.

Attitude and Other Stories of Suspense by Loren D. Estleman.

Hoch's Ladies by Edward D. Hoch.

CRIPPEN & LANDRU LOST CLASSICS

Crippen & Landru is proud to publish a series of *new* short-story collections by great authors who specialized in traditional mysteries. Each book collects stories from crumbling pages of old pulp, digest, and slick magazines, and most of the stories have been "lost" since their first publication. The following books are in print:

The Newtonian Egg and Other Cases of Rolf le Roux by Peter Godfrey, introduction by Ronald Godfrey. 2002. Trade softcover, $15.00.

Murder, Mystery and Malone by Craig Rice, edited by Jeffrey A. Marks. 2002. Trade softcover, $19.00.

The Sleuth of Baghdad: The Inspector Chafik Stories, by Charles B. Child. Cloth, $27.00. 2002. Trade softcover, $17.00.

Hildegarde Withers: Uncollected Riddles by Stuart Palmer, introduction by Mrs. Stuart Palmer. 2002. Trade softcover, $19.00.

The Spotted Cat and Other Mysteries from the Casebook of Inspector Cockrill by Christianna Brand, edited by Tony Medawar. 2002. Cloth, $29.00. Trade softcover, $19.00.

Marksman and Other Stories by William Campbell Gault, edited by Bill Pronzini; afterword by Shelley Gault. 2003. Trade softcover, $19.00.

Karmesin: The World's Greatest Criminal - Or Most Outrageous Liar by Gerald Kersh, edited by Paul Duncan. 2003. Cloth, $27.00. Trade softcover, $17.00.

The Complete Curious Mr. Tarrant by C. Daly King, introduction by Edward D. Hoch. Cloth, $29.00. 2003. Trade softcover, $19.00.

The Pleasant Assassin and Other Cases of Dr. Basil Willing by Helen McCloy, introduction by B.A. Pike. 2003. Cloth, $27.00. Trade softcover, $18.00.

Murder - All Kinds by William L. DeAndrea, introduction by Jane Haddam. 2003. Cloth, $29.00. Trade softcover, $19.00.

The Avenging Chance and Other Mysteries from Roger Sheringham's Casebook by Anthony Berkeley, edited by Tony Medawar and Arthur Robinson. 2004. Cloth, $29.00. Trade softcover, $19.00.

Banner Deadlines: The Impossible Files of Senator Brooks U. Banner by Joseph Commings, edited by Robert Adey; memoir by Edward D. Hoch. 2004. Cloth, $29.00. Trade softcover, $19.00.

The Danger Zone and Other Stories by Erle Stanley Gardner, edited by Bill Pronzini. 2004. Trade softcover, $19.00.

Dr. Poggioli: Criminologist by T.S. Stribling, edited by Arthur Vidro. Cloth, $29.00. 2004. Cloth, $29.00. Trade softcover, $19.00.

The Couple Next Door: Collected Short Mysteries by Margaret Millar, edited by Tom Nolan. 2004. Trade softcover, $19.00.

Sleuth's Alchemy: Cases of Mrs. Bradley and Others by Gladys Mitchell, edited by Nicholas Fuller. 2004. Trade softcover, $19.00.

Who Was Guilty? Two Dime Novels by Philip S. Warne/Howard W. Macy, edited by Marlena E. Bremseth. 2004. Cloth, $29.00. Trade softcover, $19.00.

Slot-Machine Kelly by Michael Collins, introduction by Robert J. Randisi. Cloth, $29.00. 2004. Trade softcover, $19.00.

The Evidence of the Sword by Rafael Sabatini, edited by Jesse F. Knight. 2006. Cloth, $29.00. Trade softcover, $19.00.

The Casebook of Sidney Zoom by Erle Stanley Gardner, edited by Bill Pronzini. 2006. Cloth, $29.00. Trade softcover, $19.00.

The Detections of Francis Quarles by Julian Symons, edited by John Cooper; afterword by Kathleen Symons. 2006. Cloth, $29.00. Trade softcover, $19.00.

The Trinity Cat and Other Mysteries by Ellis Peters (Edith Pargeter), edited by Martin Edwards and Sue Feder. 2006. Trade softcover, $19.00.

The Grandfather Rastin Mysteries by Lloyd Biggle, Jr., edited by Kenneth Lloyd Biggle and Donna Biggle Emerson. 2007. Cloth, $29.00. Trade softcover, $19.00.

Masquerade: Ten Crime Stories by Max Brand, edited by William F. Nolan. 2007. Cloth, $29.00. Trade softcover, $19.00.

Dead Yesterday and Other Mysteries by Mignon G. Eberhart, edited by Rick Cypert and Kirby McCauley. 2007. Cloth, $30.00. Trade softcover, $20.00.

The Battles of Jericho by Hugh Pentecost, introduction by S.T. Karnick. 2008. Cloth, $29.00. Trade softcover, $19.00.

FORTHCOMING LOST CLASSICS

The Minerva Club, The Department of Patterns and Other Stories by Victor Canning, edited by John Higgins.

The Casebook of Gregory Hood by Anthony Boucher and Denis Green, edited by Joe R. Christopher.

The Casebook of Jonas P. Jonas and Others by Elizabeth Ferrars, edited by John Cooper.

Ten Thousand Blunt Instruments by Philip Wylie, edited by Bill Pronzini.

The Exploits of the Patent Leather Kid by Erle Stanley Gardner, edited by Bill Pronzini.

Duel of Shadows, The Barnabas Hildreth Stories by Vincent Cornier, edited by Mike Ashley.

Author in Search of a Character, The Detections of Miss Phipps by Phyllis Bentley, edited by Marvin Lachman.

Murder at the Stork Club and Other Stories by Vera Caspary, edited by Barbara Emrys.

Dagobert: Detective of Old Vienna by Balduin Groller, translated by Thomas Riediker.

BETWEEN THE LINES

Edited by Donna Samworth

First published in Great Britain in 2012 by:
Forward Poetry
Remus House
Coltsfoot Drive
Peterborough
PE2 9BF
Telephone: 01733 890099
Website: www.forwardpoetry.co.uk

FOREWORD

In 2009, Poetry Rivals was launched. It was one of the biggest and most prestigious competitions ever held by Forward Poetry. Due to the popularity and success of this talent contest like no other, we have taken Poetry Rivals into 2012, where it has proven to be even bigger and better than previous years.

Poets of all ages and from all corners of the globe were invited to write a poem that showed true creative talent - a poem that would stand out from the rest.

We are proud to present the resulting anthology, an inspiring collection of verse carefully selected by our team of editors. Reflecting the vibrancy of the modern poetic world, it is brimming with imagination and diversity.

As well as encouraging creative expression, Poetry Rivals has also given writers a vital opportunity to showcase their work to the public, thus providing it with the wider audience it so richly deserves.

CONTENTS

83 ABBEY ROAD

I took a walk past our old house
Just the other day
And gazed upon the garden
Where children used to play.
The cherry tree we planted
Had grown so straight and tall
And the lovely crimson rambling rose
Still clambers up the wall.
The house looked sad and empty
The frames all cracked and worn
The windows dark and grimy
So lost and so forlorn
But I had a funny feeling
As I stood there for a while
That you would walk along the path
And greet me with a smile
You would put your arms around me
And life would be the same
Of course I knew the truth of it
That this was just a game
I could hear the sound of children
But then it was not so
For these were faded memories
Of a lifetime long ago.

Christine McCherry

HOW LONELY THE DAYS CAN BE

We said we would never
wish to be apart
that was when
you were close
to my heart

Now these days
you're so far away from me
and I know just how
lonely the days can be

We said we would never
wish to be apart
that was when
you were close
to my heart

Now these days
you're so far away from me
and I know
just how lonely
the days can be.

K Lake

MIRACLES COST MONEY

You said you could use a miracle,
So I lent you mine.
You returned it broken,
And my miracle was useless.
I cut it up and threw it away.
Saved for a new one.
But miracles are expensive,
And working is boring,
And boredom drives me insane.

I will live without a miracle, for I am too stubborn to work for it.

Lucy Coffey

POWER DRESSING

There is the man
in the pinstriped suit,
but nobody hears
what he's saying.

There is the man
in a purple frock,
it looks like
he could be praying.

There is the man
in a uniform
he's waving his hands
at the crowd.

There is the man
who is holding a gun,
we don't notice his clothes,
we just run . . .

Delia Hume

SPINSTER OF THIS PARISH

It's too late for love, I realise that.
My passion in youth was the open track.
The wide plains of India, the peaks of Nepal.
The Highlands of Thailand, I travelled them all.

My career came next, I was bold and forthright
But ambition I found was cold comfort at night.
Now here I am where I wanted to be.
Queen of the bees, the top of the tree.
I've conquered the corner where I belong.
I thought I had time, I was wrong

Yes I thought I'd find love, or love would find me.
But it soon became clear it wasn't to be.
Love waits for no one, the weak or the strong.
I thought I had time, I was wrong.

Maureen Reynolds

ELEPHANTS NEVER FORGET

We sat in the hotel lounge,
The maître d' explained,
'I'm sorry, ladies and gentlemen,
The elephants are here, again.'

The bull led his herd through reception
And out into the grounds:
The mums, the dads and the babies,
Who made happy elephant sounds.

'They come the same time every year,'
The MD explained to his guests.
'They won't do you any harm,
All the same, staying indoors is best.'

The bull thought, 'There's one thing
I don't understand,
Why they have to build hotels
On elephant land.'

The tourists they thought it exciting
To see these large beasts at close quarter.
They like to go out and join them,
But wonder if they oughta.

'We roamed this planet before you evolved,
Our ancestors taught us the routes.
Now we teach our sons and our daughters
The best places to find leaves and shoots.'

'They're enormous pests,' say the locals
'Trampling our crops and our plants.
And you should see the mess they make
When they do the elephants' dance.'

'We grub up the ground; we knock down dead trees,
We keep the plains tidy and clean.
Our dung is a compost for ivory palms,
We're enormous recycling machines!'

They stayed in the grounds a few days
Gorging on mangoes and fruit.
And when it was time to leave
The bull raised his trunk with a 'toot'.

4

With his family safely outside,
The bull turned around to the guests.
'We'll be back, same time next year,
Remember: elephants <u>never</u> forget!'

Evelyn Elliott-Clement

TIDY YOUR BEDROOM

Why is it that World War III
Breaks out if I ask you to make a cup of tea?
It's not hard to tidy your room
It's always someone else's job
Perhaps the Martians have decided to
Come down and stay instead of going to
Saturn we come to number 22.
I know, let's muck up the bedrooms
What fun it will be,
I'll leave dirty clothes, dirty plates
And crisp packets too,
CDs, DVDs and videos on the floor.

The bedrooms are a mess but no one's to blame.
Put your things away, I had to do it
Then it will be clean and tidy every day.
No one in the bedroom,
The Martians have come to stay and play
I know let's throw another DVD on the floor.
I love beings a Martians coming to stay,
Causing mischief, mayhem too
Getting people into trouble
Oh dear I hate a tidy bedroom
There's nothing to do
I know, I'll go and visit number 24.

P Lane

TIME TO MOVE ON

Move with the times
Don't look back, go forward
Don't live in the past, you can't change that
Now is the time not then
Look at who you are now
Not of who you was
Think of a new beginning
Not of the end
Then open your eyes, look around
You and start living
Old clutter ties you down and
Clutters the mind
Free yourself
Live for each day
Free your soul
Free your mind
Free your life
Freshen up, clear up and dust yourself down
See the light you just might
Memories are best kept in your heart
No in your mind
Don't let time pass you by,
Grab it, don't let it slip by
Get up and go, do those things
One at a time
Come out of the dark and into the light
We can't help what we've done, it's done
But we can make a fresh start today.
Good from bad, happy instead of sad.
Right from wrong, be proud, keep strong
You can do it now, prove it to yourself.
Love instead of hate
Remember the saying
Sticks and stones break my bones
Words never hurt me.

And to
Forgive our enemy for they know not
What they do.
We have to move on.
We have to have faith.
My saying is I can and I will.
Say my saying
It'll pull you through.

Georgie Ramsey

INTO THE TIME

Time is massive, it's weird and weary
Where does it belong? It's in a beyond
Time's a powerful glitch, 'has it a stitch?'
Time, does it rhyme?
I wonder, does speak, maybe it's a sign
The universe
What is time? Is at a loose end?
Or be very careful, it's bloody dangerous
Though, it can be amazing
But it's when you have to stop something earlier
Or moments ago, or years ago
It's hard, it could end up into smithereens
To encounter or evolve, something even more sinister,
Or a case of a déjà vu!
But though can be darker
No so calmer, or even the end of the universe itself, ouch
So into the time, vortex or timey loops
We build it up, make it, see it,
Jump through or under or inside it.
The holes of space,

Nothing left of us, but a trail of dust.

A dangerous game of cat and mouse
Time, beware, it's unique and eerie
So fascinating, painful and a struggle to keep alive.

It could be our last breath, or to dive into the last ever life
You've got left.

Shaine Sebastian Singer

STREET PEOPLE

(I wrote the poem 'Street People' in memory of my niece Kelly, much loved daughter of Jean and the late Barry Pearson, sister to Sean, niece and cousin. Kelly died on the streets in Soho, London on the 10th November 1999, aged 30, and is sadly missed.)

Friends all gone, families estranged.
The drunks, druggies, mentally ill and deranged.
The hopeless drunk with bottle in hand,
And then another until he can no longer stand
The desperate junkie in an endless quest,
Another fix needed, until then no rest.
Oblivion being so easy to achieve,
Nothing left in which to believe.
The mentally ill with invisible mates,
Constant voices and endless debates.
The old and deranged with memories fading fast,
Their only comfort of times long-gone past.
A different world to what we know,
Nowhere left for them to go.

We pass them by in the street,
Eyes averted so we don't have to meet.
The flotsam and jetsam of mankind,
The lonely lost with no ties to bind.
Shuffling baggage with vacant eyes,
No one hears their silent cries.
They may be people we knew a while ago,
What happened to make them sink so low?
Left to beg, borrow and steal to survive,
Maybe more dead than alive.
This is the so-called 'care in the community',
In this country of equal opportunity.
Millions given to overseas aid,
But our own social problems we choose to evade.

Does the soul depart when hope has gone
And the empty shell still lingers on?
Battered and broken beyond repair,
Or do distant memories linger there?
With fleeting moments of clarity,
Aware of their own disparity.
To still feel pain like you and me,
Maybe knowing what we think and see.
Comparing themselves and asking why?
Longing for the day when they finally die.

B Spencer-Moore

FRIENDSHIP

Friendship you cannot price
Closeness and helpfulness
Being really nice

A shoulder to cry on
Or someone to hug
Like a favourite teacup
Or a coffee mug

A friend that's a driver
Something I've never been
My gratitude to them
It has to be seen

Friendship is, at the end of the phone
When you're lonely and on your own
Friendship is having a listening ear
Whether your friends are far away or near

As you're my best friend
I've never regretted
Someone like you
Cannot be bettered.

Vince Elsbury

LIFE THESE DAYS!

Life these days can be hectic.
No money, no food, no electric.
I still have to sit down and accept it.
Nowhere to go, there's no exit.
I'm hating this recession,
It seems more like a depression,
It's like life is trying to teach me a lesson.
There's thousands of people in this same situation,
No beers, no laughing, no celebration.
Hard times we are facing,
It feel like our lives have been taken.
All I can say is never accept defeat
And use what God gave you, and that is your feet!
Words are strong, there's no need for a beat!
And forward this message on
Don't delete – sweet.

Dean Sherrington

THE CONCERT

I am going to have a concert
And I know it won't be free
But a night of country music
It is guaranteed to be

The artists are all local
The best there is about.
There will be plenty of hand clapping
And lots of sing-alongs and you will get a chance to shout
Why not bring your friends along

Now when the money's counted
And all have done their best
The artists have been paid
And a charity gets the rest.

Rosemary Dunbar

SHOPPING

A trip to town, a shopping spree,
A café table set for two
Where, over scones and cups of tea
We'd talk of all we planned to do.
We'd browse the stores, and then we'd stop
To luncheon, with a glass of wine.
We'd cross the square to window shop,
Then saunter on, your arm through mine.
The shopping malls and market halls
To us seemed like Aladdin's cave.
Abundant treasures filled their stalls
Persuading us to 'spend and save',
And bargains labelled 'two for one',
We'd by one just to get one free!
Quite needless, (but it seemed such fun).
Then, next your hand in mine would be
And homeward we would wend our way,
Aware of all the joys we'd had;
So mindful of a splendid day
When life was good and hearts were glad.

It's all still there; and I recall
The quiet tables where we met,
The busy shops, the bargain stall,
The market place, the square, and yet,
So much did I enjoy because of you
That, on my own, it holds no sparkle now.

John M Beazley

TORY STORY/LIB DEM PHLEGM

I condemn the government cuts
I condemn the government inflicted hurts
Rich boys who played with different toys
Rule over the weaker class
Bullingdon boys who are not aware of how they destroy
The ghost of Thatcher is alive and haunting us
Clegg and Cameron I hope you get sent down by the
return of socialism
God help the people of England, the poor, the disabled, the old.
Big society is the end of society.

John O'Shaughnessy

11

THE STYLE LIST

Vamp it up with pure indulgence
Be in bloom with back in time
In the post with animal magic
New in time with summer wine;
In the rap with big gem party,
Bit statement – Lisa Lashes is here
On your radar – body buffer
In the red with rouge brings cheer;
Feeling woof with human interest,
Make a splash with simply the best
Keep things cool with live block party
Seeing's believing – forget the rest
One of a kind – be a tough cookie
Glossy hair? Try new shine shield
Refreshing rest with gold shoe story
Camp in style with human field
Aim to boost your circulation
Mother denims straight up jeans
Make a simple tee for summer
Choke on yellow iced bogbeans!

Kenneth Berry

LOVE

Love;
in the today life.
It's everything.
If you find,
one precious
and genuine love.
Keep this love,
the life offer to you.
Because,
nothing, it's better
than you love.
Trust, immensely.
Believe with passion,
dedication and affection.
Love,
sincerely with your heart.

Antonio Signorelli

MOON FLOWERS

A magical place

An alien world

> Lines of vapour, green with blue
> Landscape swathed in every hue
> Pale moon sleeps in purple skies
> Unaware of peering eyes

A miniature world

All planned and perfect

> Nature will not change the scene
> What is now – and what has been
> Only Time has willing hours
> To change the face of pale moon flowers.

Anne Reeve

WHERE'S THE TRUTH, WHERE'S THE FACT?

I wouldn't wait for another soldier to die,
Keep them in paper and poppy and high,
Keep them so warm and so crisp and so dry,
Wrap them in wool, cuddle them 'til they cry.
Keep them in pain killers and government drugs.
Keep them in warmth and opium drugs,
Keep them so they are right in your face,
With tear gas, riot gear and policeman's mace.
I wouldn't wait 'til tomorrow to act,
Keep them in fiction and ignore the fact,
Keep them like fish in the ocean so warm
Wrap them from wind and the rain and the storm.
Keep them in WIFI and GPS,
Keep them tracked they couldn't care less,
Keep them in fear and right in their hole.
With terror, no rights and strict border control.

Rick Ferguson

NEW LIFE

Keep to schedule
Meet with time's grey bullet
Cloud peaking silently at bus stops of gruelling, non-entity life.
The shoal of painful fish equating and waiting to die
In solid, fumed, perfumed ditches of office space,
Fried in a corner next to the water cooler.
Brain on fire with life, while cockroaches scoot past on metal legs
Leaving them wistfully searching for small change
The smallest change; ensuring escape.
Slowly drifting in and out of temporary jobs
Post, ante, pre, before, never.
Left at home on the kitchen table, keys,
To another life; in an envelope
Inviting, beguiling, forgotten.

Karen Langley

GHOST 23.07.12

I wake up in the morning
I feel the moon and sun shine
On my pale white skin

Scatter, scatter, scatter, wash away

Look up at the stars
Look down at the reflection in the sea
See that girl, she is me

I am the girl who you sat by in class
I am the girl who had the funny looking glass
I am the person you never did recognise
I am a weary memory of a dream
I was that hit-and-run teen.

Natalie Gibbs

TRIPPING THROUGH SHADOWS

As Earth turned away from the sun into darkness
A sad summer's son – that ill-fated night
Fate then saw fit to rob me of life's gladness
Bodies moved slow, leaving twinkles in air
Lay, as I watched the wide canvas in spread
With cold-hearted glumness I wished for a hearth, then
Forethought and feeling returned to full flow
Excepting my tarry life barely missed step
It moved on at pace with an unearthly grace
Dancers all twirling, then lost in the mist
A mute in full song, still night journeyed on
Singing to villains with touch flashing bright
Here I moved too, then went crashing down
Silver light met the dark meat of my flesh
I drew myself up in the full sight of all
As drunkards made taunts from behind their hard noses
'Come one step, and two steps, a three steps then four
N***** you think you so mighty and tall?
Tall and mighty so you think you are Nig?
Come one step, and two steps, a three steps, then four'
As drunkards made taunts from behind their hard noses
I drew myself up in the full sight of all
Silver light met the dark meat of my flesh
Here I moved too, then went crashing down
Singing to villains with touch flashing bright
A mute in full song, still night journeyed on
Dancers all twirling, then lost in the mist
It moved on at pace with an unearthly grace
Excepting my tarry life barely missed stop
Forethought and feeling returned to full flow
With cold-hearted glumness I wished for a hearth, then
Lay, as I watched the wide canvas in spread
Bodies moved slow, leaving twinkles in air
Fate then saw fit to rob me of life's gladness
A sad summer's son, that ill-fated night
As Earth turned away from the sun into darkness.

Leslie Tetteh

15

GOING WALKIES

I'm Heidi the Westie and I've started to whine
Cos outside I see there's brilliant sunshine
When the weather's so nice I wish I could talk
Then I'd tell my parents it's time for my walk
Mam and Dad, there's no time to lose
On with your hats, coats and shoes
I jump into the car I like the ride
I'm hoping we're going to Finchale Riverside

Down the steep hill, away I go
These adults are really slow
They meet me at the riverside
It's rained a lot I hope they don't slide
They soon have worked up a bit of a sweat
I cannot believe it as I'm not tired yet
The end of the path is soon in sight
We spot some geese which have just taken flight

Two minutes rest I hear Dad say
Then we'll turn around and be on our way
As Mam turns to go she starts to slide
Down the riverbank on her backside
Dad puts out his hand to pull her up
The bank's so slippy she's finding it tough
After two more falls – we dare not laugh
It's third time lucky and she's back onto the path

The mud is so thick sticking onto her clothes
Leaving a path wherever she goes
I'm just thinking, Oh what a day
When we spot a lady coming our way
Just as she reaches us Mam stops her to say
It's dangerously slippy, please don't go that way
She can see Mam is muddy from head to toe
So decides that way she will not go

I hear Mam say, 'It must think I'm a tree'
As the lady's dog uses her leg for a pee
This makes the mud all sloppy and smelly
Causing bits to drop off into her wellies
The lady then said the dog was a stray
Just as it ran off without further delay
If Mam had known she'd have given it a rap,
Now she must get home and into the bath.

Dad can be a bit fuddy duddy
Doesn't want his car seats getting all muddy.
Mam has to sit on a mat in the car
Thank heavens we don't have to go very far.
Once home she strips off at the door
Her trousers can stand on their own on the floor.
Next time we walk we'll be giving Finchale a wide berth
As we don't want our Mam coming home covered in earth.

Margaret Robertson

SANDS OF TIME

Always the bud, never the flower in bloom
The lines in a chorus, never the tune
Always a chapter, never the book
Sometimes glimpsed, never looked . . .

Just a raindrop in a shower of rain
Another turn on that winding lane
A forgotten castle fallen in ruins
A star in the night sky, but never the moon

The distant memory of a forgotten dream
Another ripple on a running stream
The lost key that could have opened the door
That thing thrown away when it was needed no more . . .

A snowflake in a winter sky
A feather in your wing that helped you fly
The helping hand when you're down on your luck
Or that warm and needed hug

The word of compromise that ends a fight
The tender touch of a kiss goodnight
Just another line in a rhyme . . .
A single grain in the sands of time . . .

Barbara Rodgers

THE OLYMPIAN'S DREAM

Eyes closed. Stiff and posed.
Run fast. Forget slow.
Fleeting memories through my mind.
I will win. First place is mine.

Eyes still closed, the whistle blows.
And how about that, lo and behold,
I tear off the mark
People screaming in my ears,
Then it hits me – my worst fear.

Can I win it? Will I succeed?
Of course I will – I'm in the lead!

Speeding round corners, owning the track
All of a sudden, he's on my back!
He starts to overtake but I've got heart
So I keep flying like a dart.

It's him and me, neck and neck
I am put up to the ultimate test
Last lap and he's still not budged
So I have to put in one last nudge.

I forget everything, clear my mind
Just me on the track, no one behind
Think of my family, think of my friends
Then it's like a Godsend

I find new wings, go a bit faster
I am the king. I am the master.

Last bend, last turn
I reach, I burn
I run fast, I run quick
Now I feel a little sick
But I think I have won
I think of my son
I hope he's happy, I hope he's proud
Cos right then I shouted out loud
I crossed the finish line as bright as the sun.
'I'm Mo Farah and I have won!'

Nathan Morgans

TEARS IN HER EYES

In each and every corner of my heart
a mass of dead memory lies.
For so many years I have grown
aches and pains and seen its demise.
I can still drown in the onslaught
of heartrending tears in her eyes.

Time and again I ask myself.
Why did I have to vanish without a trace?
No clues, no signs and no love to show itself
and no cause to bring a smile on her face.
Must get back to the way we were
before the loss of old memories we share.

Gloom in my life ends with a spark of hope
and her heart beats with happy feelings.
Is there a challenge out there for me to cope?
No, there could never be any bargains or dealings.
How to evoke smiles on her face?
A quest is on night and day with all factors of interlace.

To soak away tears from her eyes
I have laid a table of resolve with love and peace.
All that is needed now to make her recognize
the safety of love for life and not on lease.
Above all she is mine as I am for her
for now in this world and thereafter.

Mojibur Rahman

HOME FROM HOME

The forlorn silhouette of someone's daughter
Perched on a bench wrapped in stench,
Abandoned in the abyss of plenty.

She looks at the passing parade of life
But sees no love, or an inviting smile.

Love is only a visionary moment from the
Recesses of yesteryear, a smile, only a faded
Sepia picture.

Tonight's embrace will only be corrugated
Sheets laid on concrete and granite in the sheltered
Opulence of diamond and tiara emporiums.

The day will come in sad reflective loneliness,
Weighed in carrier bags, wheeled around in trolleys.
An abandoned daughter, a forgotten wife, a mother jettisoned
In the river of forgetfulness and washed-up broken on the Shore of loneliness

Again and again, the curtain of night draws in and
The arches and doorways receive their guests,
Shadowy phantoms weaving-and-stitching through the
Fabric of everyday life but invisible to the eyes.

My heart wrenches, I wince from the pain of the shame,
A father, buried in the pit of sorrow, a son floating
Between space and time, and a husband adrift in
Shadowy despair.

I flinch because my conscience stings.
To see the ones without is a sin.

Ezekiel Headley

BEGIN AGAIN

Begin again
time to change.
Light the candle
remove the pain.

Open heart
peaceful face.
Life in motion,
changing pace.

Begin again
new memories made.
People, places,
pictures framed.

Daniella J Philbin

FOR MICHAEL 1934-2011

We used to want to see the spring coming together,
the shy levitation of snowdrops, narcissus massing together.

I will not tramp with you through the bluebells, listening to birdsong,
to the murderous cuckoo; beeches ankle-deep in blue, greening to birdsong.

I will not prune the thorny, fragrant roses with you, soaking in the sunshine,
heavy leaves of summer, angled shrubs blossoming in sunshine.

Nor will we pick our cankered apples ripening in autumn
flaming in scarlet, red and yellow, chilled leaves falling in autumn

I will stack the woodpile, shut the doors, drawing these curtains
against the cold, turn up the heat, watching snow curtain

the hard outside. You will not see the snow drifting silently
nor watch the stars, frost freezing, moon lighting silently.

By departing you've leached from the seasons' passing much of comfort,
without you leaves me to see this spring coming with little comfort.

Sue Cooper

WHORTLEBERRY PIE

I can taste it tart, sharp, satisfying,
with fresh cream from the earthenware jug;
we had it in summer holidays,
visiting Grandmother's mountain farm.

We went by pony and trap, up steep
rough roads with gorse and purple heather
where horned sheep and nimble goats grazed
and scattered wildly at the hoof sound.

We stopped halfway, 'Three miles,' said Father,
the pony drank from the mountain stream,
whilst we climbed the fence to the meadow.
Uphill to Grandmother's iron gates
a brown and white sheepdog came barking,
and she running arms outstretched welcoming;
she wore black with high-buttoned bosom
high-buttoned boots, grey hair in a bun.
'May we go and pick the whorts Grama?'
'They are best along the bottom ditch
take two milk gallons and don't be long.'

We groped with the dark purple berries
'mongst the leaves of shrubs shot and strong
we picked and ate, our mouth stained purple
'Lipstick,' said Tom so we looked at each other,
giggled and showed our tongue.
Grandmother had made the pie crust on
the wooden table, cleaned the berries,
then she put it in the bastable
on a crane over an open fire
'We'll have it for the tea,' she smiled
and shooed from the kitchen a brown hen.

Abina Russell

ALICE

Alice is pretty.
Alice is fun.
Alice has a smile
like a yummy iced bun.
Alice is saucy.
Alice has spunk.
Alice's bedroom
is littered with junk.
Alice has long legs.
Alice plays drums.
Alice is quite partial
to sweets and fruit gums.
Alice is gentle.
Alice can fight
when Alice's brother
is not always right.
Alice is lazy.
Alice is cool.
Alice does not always
like going to school.
Alice is trendy.
Alice likes clothes.
Alice looks in mirrors
in order to pose.
Alice can draw.
Alice is sweet.
Alice likes McDonald's
as a special treat.
Alice gives big hugs.
Alice is a guide.
Alice makes her gran
feel very warm inside!

Helen Dalgleish

LOVE

Love so difficult to put into words, it could be a touch, a look or even some special words.
The feelings I feel, are strong and true and on this day this is my promise to you.
I am here to support you through the good and the bad or even when you just feel sad.
I am here to protect us and our relationship too, because to hurt it would hurt me too.
I am here to help in whatever way I can, to guide you, to love you or just hold your hand.
I am here to receive you and to accept what you give,
Because without you I don't think I could live.
Our connection is special, it feel so right and I love how you hold my hand so tight.
It's those little things really that make one whole,
But if I had to break love down I'd say it's your soul.
You're kind, honest and true and this is why I am here today, because I love you.

Julie Gibbon

LAZY DAY

Lazy day inspire me,
You are silent and painted grey,
Your fleeting hours stolen
By somebody else's day.

I seek a burst of amber,
A splash of cyan-blue,
And satin cotton candy
Wrapping webs in morning dew.

Lazy day awake me,
You are sleeping it would seem,
Your fickle hues toying
With somebody else's dream.

I yearn for sculpts of umber,
Enveloped in shades of green,
And sways of scarlet sequins
Pinning sunbeams to a dappled screen

Lazy day invite me,
You are lonely
And full of sorrow
I will trade this day
For starlight,
And return again tomorrow.

R J V Horton

BOOKS AND BOOKSHOPS

Huge bookstore near Gordon Street,
Ornate friezes, fresh and neat.
An elegant cupola'd ceiling,
Reflects the probing way I'm feeling,
Thinking about modern ills,
Bar codes, electronics and bleeping tills.

Everything ascetic, massaged clean,
Virginal dust jackets glint and gleam,
This repository of the written word,
Its readers seen but rarely heard.
This textual tour de force,
A font of knowledge and its source.

People drift round groaning shelves,
Frightened to commit themselves.
All wearing deep and puzzled frowns,
Cat calendar or Robert CS Downs?
I can watch them from my post,
Like some supernatural suspended ghost.

From my eyrie in the roof,
Noticed by no one, quite aloof.
I survey ten billion words
On hamsters, tapirs, fish and birds
And pictures of every size and hue
Magenta, silver, grey and blue.

One emotion we all share,
Our love of books is ever there.
We love to view and touch and feel them,
To knead and stroke and almost peel them,
They are as flowers in our hands
Delicate angels on metal stands.

Crisp and fresh as winter's snow,
Diamond-white and all aglow.
Books and bookshops must succeed
The greatest pleasure is to read
And in a world where pleasure's died
A bookshop's where I come and hide.

Ron Hardwick

HER UNARRANGED MARRIAGE

My love's skin, paler than mine,
Yet not as soft.
He bare'th kindness so great,
And charms me all.
Kisses fondly and touches tender,
A keen ear has he.
Later nights in company with,
And when not, he's missed.
For comfort, teas and holding tight,
It cannot be flawed.
But stubborn is his tongue,
In ways most, perfect.
Yet troubled minds cause us quarrel,
Unsettled grounds.
For day of wed is not with thee,
Chosen, is tone deeper.
A suitor has been passed, arranged,
For exchange a dowry fee.
The coming nights are slower of pace,
And the day of sorrow is nigh.
Distances divide and tears will stream,
An answer has come to me.
A decision for all those concerned,
Is to run, smile, flee.
Hands tight, my chosen love takes hold,
And soon I becomes we.
Contact of culture, then run we did,
I never accept their plea.

Stuart Champion

WEDDING THE ROYAL WAY IN LONDON

The day – April 29 2011 – was a memorable day
When William and Catherine's nine-year encounter at St Andrews had its way.
See Kate this day coming as a common commoner from her commoners' domain
Before the demise of the delirious day, the Duchess of Cambridge to obtain.
See her in her flowing Sarah Burton immaculate white gown looking resplendent,
A rose periwinkle the gods to William have sent.
See William, in his Irish Guards colonel red tunic and behold another Arthur Wellesley.
And his best man and brother – Harry – in his black military attire a Montgomery's crony.
See the royal connections coming forth as formidable spectators to behold
The Queen in her splendid lemon-yellow suit leading the one thousand stronghold.
See the royals looking extraordinary in their gorgeous multicoloured chameleon dresses;
And the Middletons as magnificent as the blazing sun obliterating all commoners' appearances.
The day it was when Rowan Williams' proclamation decreed 'peace be still' to all criticism
And decisively dwarfed Kate's years of degrading derision in a daring jingoism.
The day it was that conclusively proved the triumph of love over aristocracy
And rubbished the conjectural hypothesis of marriage between only nobilities as crazy.
Doesn't love weigh higher in marriage than the primordial consideration of parity?
And will parity without love make successful marriage a reality?
Whereas parity in marriage without love is as worthless as withered weeds;
Love in marriage without parity is as worthy as gold beads.
To give fillip to love over parity at Westminster Abbey were 1,900 guests from diverse world cities
Notable guests that included royals, politicians, financial gurus, artists and celebrities.
And adding to the pomp and pageantry were five hundred thousand standby well-wishers;
Whose names in the Guinness Book could not have made better dancers.
How magnificent-looking the bride and groom were on their way to the palace!
How passionate the two kisses at the balcony of Buckingham Palace!
At the Abbey – Palace route, the crowd that tuned to the broadcast was marvellous;
Who could curtail the hubbub of over one million people in Union Jacks, gold and tiaras precious?
With William willingly undertaking to take under his roof his new found lily,
And Catherine the caterer understanding not to stand under but by Willy.
Full Success was indeed a special guest wishing the Duke and Duchess a marriage successful.
And perfect understanding was present to declare a conjugal relationship blissful.

Bode Babatunde

ME AND MY FOUR WALLS

Me and my four walls is what I've known
For the past four years
As I'm getting frail and old
Each day a drag
Watching the clock tick away
Seconds, minutes, hours each day
Watching daylight come through
The curtains in my room so blue
I say to myself today . . . I live too
I lie down back again
Thinking what can I do?
But every time I try
I can barely move
Struggling from chair to bed, and then to chair
I say to myself – at this age life's not fair
Worthless to anyone
It's just me . . . and my four walls
The phone I wait for it to ring a tone
Just so I could speak to someone at home
The television my other friend
The remote I press and then . . . that ends
Night has come, I just cry
Hoping someone might ask why?
Or maybe I should just die!
Because no one cares, they don't know
How it feels to be old and alone
They come, they see, and then they go
Relying on others not wanting to
But having no choice . . . it's what I do
I know I'm not wanted any more
But can't leave until he calls
Each night I ask, 'God take me please'
Happily I will leave this world and shut the door.

Nirmala Singh Bhaker

GENTLEMAN, RESIDING BELGRAVIA

'Gentleman, seventy, from Belgravia.'
Ooh! This could be my savior.
'Would like to meet a lady.'
Could it be me?
'Must be tall.' Yes! 'And slim.' Fuck!
But I like the sound of him.
Give or take a stone or three,
This could be me
'She'll be elegant.' Oh yes!
'And intelligent.' I guess?
Well, I'm not thick,
But he sounds a right prick.
'Tactile and attractive.'
I'll tell him I'm still active.
What? 'Not more than thirty-five.'
Saints alive!
On a dark night with the full slap
I'd never look that.
'Deeply sensual but refined.'
I've changed my mind.
What's he want, the old bugger?
A shag or a bag of sugar?

Dinah Smith

LOVE

Love is when you make friends with someone
Love is when you love someone
Love is when you kiss someone
Love is when you smile at someone so they smile back
Love is caring for someone so they care for you.

Abdul Shabaz-Miah

LISTEN! THOSE WHO HAVE EAR TO HEAR

The truth has been proclaimed
For two thousand years, the good news,
The gospel of Truth,
Hear! All who would listen.

Jesus, God's Son,
The way, the truth and the life.
Life to all who would listen.
Hear, let your heart rejoice.

Believe you are loved, know that love,
The love of the Father, our Creator,
The Creator of all we see.
Peace gained by Calvary.

Your ransom paid on the cross,
Enjoy that all-giving love,
Peace on your Earthly journey,
Hope in the resurrected Son.

So ears that are open; open
To God's good news for all,
Peace the world cannot give.
Only peace through His Son.

Hear – listen. Believe! Rejoice!

Ralph Watkins

FOUR YET ONE!

Four wondrous sons, four wondrous seasons.
Each very different but blending across with similar traits.

Spring . . . is new lambs gamboling and leaping, enjoying their youth.
Sunshine, daffodils waving in the breeze, entwining in the grassy meadows.
Fresh as the raindrops sparkling as they fall, making all they touch glisten.
Birdsong filling the air with joy and laughter,
Bringing an orchestral masterpiece of nature to life.

Summer . . . is brightness and long days, relaxing as the waves tenderly lap the shoreline.
Plants growing, blossoming, achieving their dreams – reaching upwards towards the sun.
Baby birds looking for reassurance as they take their first flight,
Spreading their wings and taking off into the world with a new confidence.

Autumn . . . is colourful russets and reds like a beautiful sunset.
Cool crisp mornings and warm comforting days.
Leaves floating delicately to the ground,
Twisting and turning being choreographed by the winds.
Animals gathering provisions for the long winter months ahead,
Preparing and thinking with a calm resourcefulness.

Winter . . . crisp, sharp, fresh, frosty mornings enlivening body and mind.
Icicles sparkling silently, reflecting their beauty.
Hibernation, warm and cosy like a huge welcoming hug.
Trees, lifeless and stark but standing strong and proud,
Knowing that their time to shine will once again be here.
Peaceful, quiet air not causing a fuss as Jack Frost wraps its fingers around.
Sometimes the beauty of winter is not seen, overlooked but it is there.

Sometimes the seasons cross and blend,
And surprise you with a parcel of summer in autumn or winter in spring.
Each season is unique and never the same.
Love them for their individuality and soulfulness as they take our world on its journey,
A year.
Just as each son brings his own uniqueness and spirit you will, at times, momentarily discover
snippets of one within the other,
Wholeness,
Family.

Karen Swann

31

ARE YOU WOUNDED?

Are you wounded and in despair, do you bleed?
Do you bleed inside where nobody can perceive?
Are you so hurt that on your hidden tears you do now feed?
Does each soul to you just seem to deceive?
Do you find no healing which you so much need?
In yourself you must believe
To no mortal need you go to for sympathy or plead

Do your memories hurt you and do they disturb your
peace of mind?
Do they make you weep in agony?
Do your tears make you go blind?
For they have been to you so execrable
Though you were wounded, they were not kind

But your wounds shouldn't make you disabled
You can heal your wounds through the healing of your mind
Though to do so presently seems inconceivable
Your wounds may have become so deep
That they would ever heal – of this you just cannot conceive
Blood may ooze from them even when you are fast asleep
But to their pain you should become insensitive
For life is for you to laugh in joy and not to weep
So to the hurt, please be less receptive

Time will heal you
You need not retort
To those souls who left you feeling nauseous
You need not seek justice from the society or from the court
Or let your face in misery contort

Every action has a reaction
So remain to your hurts gracious
A healing balm would soothe your wounds
If for it, you had sought
You would recover from the wounds caused by those
Who to you have been fallacious
This is a law of nature which need
Not to anybody be taught

Those who have hurt you will themselves be hurt
Such is the law of nature
For those whose soul is pure and those covered with dirt
To those who reside on the poles
And those who dwell on the equator
So muster up some strength soon
To heal your wounds; even though today they do so hurt.

Neelam Saraf

THE EMANCIPATION OF JAGO

Look into my eyes.
Can you see the image
Of you hurting me?
Those memories erased –
Breaking you.
Taking you
Into maelstrom of confusion.
It's your delusion.
Magic fakery that
Blew up in your crack'd mirror.
The signs that spelt out
Self-preservation and
Redemption cursed
In your veins.

Your deed is done –
Crime doesn't pay.
It remains dormant . . .
In your guilty bloody veins.
So lay to rest those evils
Step into the light and –
For here
We will
Stay.

Jagdeesh Sokhal

NO MORE RAIN

Ever feel like you are going backwards,
Down and down into an empty hole,
With nowhere to go and no one to hold,
With nowhere to hide?
Shadows lurking behind every corner,
Ready to suck you in.
Only the sun and occasional rain,
Falling down on me,
Ready to fall from my face.
I can't take back the clock,
So the rain falls in this empty space.
It's hard to know which road to take,
When the rain takes over.
Strangers staring from all directions and corners.
Unable to see right from wrong.
Is it better, is it worse?
I'm not in this alone, but there's no one around in this dark place.

But it doesn't have to be like this,
If it's worth having, let's fight for it.
Only down for a second,
Getting back up again and again.
You're not in this alone,
We're doing this together,
Fighting for what's worth having.
Quitting is not an option,
No matter how hard things get.

The sun is out,
And there is nowhere to hide.
Many open doors to run to.
No more rain falling down my face.
We've waited for the storm to pass,
And that is how we remember it.

But today is different,
It's brighter,
No more pretending.
The sun is out so no more rain on me.
With people helping at every corner,
Seeing right from wrong.
It's time to face it now,
I want to be happy and you need to know that.
Let's save the rain for another day.
For some questions are not supposed to be answered.

And for today,
Let's not quit when times are hard,
But fight for things that are worth having . . .

Becky Dunne

TIME

Time! Time! Time!
A four letter word that instructs,
An invincible item that decides,
A life changer,
that does not change itself,
The integral part of the world,

Time! Time! Time!
You amaze me with your enormous power,
You are money,
You are respect,
You are a life saver,
You are inevitable,

Time! Time! Time!
You are the unseen relative of every family,
your hand is needed in every home,
you are what makes a man,
like a jet, you are flighty in nature,
and you may never be caught once you are lost,

Time! Time! Time!
it takes a lot of focus and determination to walk with you,
you make and break things,
you are success and failure,
To know your worth, we must learn to appreciate you,
To know what you are capable of,
For us to have all the niceties you offer.

Saheed Abudu

DIAMOND JUBILEE FOR ELIZABETH II, OUR WONDERFUL QUEEN

Monday 4 June 2012 is a big day for our nation!
It is our Queen Elizabeth's Diamond Jubilee priceless station
It is more than a joyful day for every British family
Let us celebrate it, O you dear Islington's MP Emily!
Who says Queen Victoria was the only one
To have ultimately this unique and momentous honour?
To reign magnificently for so long a precious period of time
Or become the only one to present to us this grandiose offer
Which has adorned affably the beautiful Jubilee rhyme
Here she is our beloved Elizabeth the Second
After celebrating the silver one and another golden as a second
Her Majesty is marking with pride in every single lane
Her sixty years of a productive and a successful reign
For the ideal monarch she splendidly and significantly incarnates
Which reach the glory of the throne that defies every concern
To call everyone subsequently to the majestic bowing turn
Before the crown that always for British people its glamour illuminates
So let us light countless of beacons
Everywhere in the vast kingdom
Let Britain's flags flutter like pigeons
In this feast of love's referendum
Let us play the sublime music of Royal concerts
Throughout the dominion of Christendom
Let us enjoy our great festival of love's converts
Hence altogether animate this memorable occasion
And present our deepest gratitude and sincere congratulations
To Her Grandeur the head of our kingdom, to their Highnesses
And to all our adorable princes and glamorous princesses
In this splendid historical night
With the leaders and chiefs of knights
We renew our oaths of allegiances
To our respectful and glorious Queen
Our crown of the flourishing Royal states
Who give to our luck best chances

May God the Almighty bless the beloved Queen
May the Lord preserve who are behind the palace's gates
Wherever they may have to be seen
Rejoice as group, singles or as a couple!
Today is our festal opportunity so come to the church oh people!
To the synagogue, to the mosque and to the temple
Viva Britain and the British people!

Sidi Fawzi Seddiki

JOURNEY FROM IGNORANCE

Monopoly money lines my pockets with childish wealth.
In a dream, that sober thoughts have long surpassed.
Yet in my head,
A thousand reasons are daily explored,
As to my being.
And what will become of me?
As the age old trouble of life,
Pervades me from within,
Showing up my inability to live truly.
Round and round I go,
Unable to get off life's not so merry go round.
Content for a time to delude myself,
With the things I've idolised,
Chained together, yet alone and scared.
On and on I go,
Trudging my way through the trenches of uncertainty,
Just below life's well trodden path.
And the small voice, I'd been ignoring for so long.
Suddenly becomes amplified,
By my willingness to listen.
And as I look ahead,
I see where the roads cross,
And beyond that a light,
And I follow the light.

David Holmes

COUNTDOWN

He watches from the security of the bedroom
As he has done so many times since life began.
Frustration wells up inside, as pain and sorrow
Threaten to engulf him as he watches helplessly again.

The pleading and screaming stop abruptly.
Ear-hurting silence reigns through the flat,
Broken briefly by the slamming of the front door.
He remains in his crouched position to be sure it is safe,
The red numbers of the cheap digital clock
Counting down the remainder of life
With cold-blooded regularity.

Finally he deems it safe
To crawl across the dividing strip of carpet.
His movements are painfully slow but unwitnessed,
Intense concentration in the childish features.

A tentative finger reaches out
Towards the brown curls matted with blood.
A lifetime of struggle over,
She finally rests peacefully in death.
Her 22-year-old child sits by her broken side,
Unable to comprehend.

Ma . . . Ma?
His first and last word goes unheard in the quiet
Which hangs in the air like some pestilence
Carried on the wings of a deadly mosquito.

His glassy eyes now stare unseeingly at the poker
Lying by his mother's side.
Dried spittle adorns his chin,
As a fly crawls across his nose unhindered.
Death's stench has impregnated the air
Like a heavy eastern perfume,
Mother and son remain immobile
Lifelike waxworks in a macabre exhibit.

In his bedroom sanctuary, the red digits
Continue their impersonally regular countdown
To the end of time,
While the world goes on outside.

Clare Anne Thompson-Lewis

38

THE ELEPHANT IN THE ROOM

The elephant in the room is not a phrase which I like to use.
It means something so big that no one dares mention.
With years of bankers and politicians ripping us off
We are left to pick up the tab.

We are all in this together is what we're told,
But some of us more than others.
'Pay more for your pensions,' the millionaires in the cabinet tell us.
They don't mention that not so many years ago
They awarded themselves a 40% pay rise.

Doctors, nurses, teachers and public servants should only receive market rate.
The one bunch of public servants they seem to omit is themselves.
Can the country afford to pay them the gilt-edged pensions they receive?
Not a word is said.

Mary Foggin

HIDDEN IDENTITY

You know my name,
You know my face.
You know my home,
You know my race.
You know my eyes,
You know my tears.
But you don't know me,
Or my fears.
Not my hopes, or my dreams,
That hide when I'm awake.
My emotions are clear,
But not for you to take.
You don't know me and I don't know you,
So leave me alone, because this conversation is through.

Sian Lawson-Blake

NEARBY

The Gods within me cannot speak,

the angel's soft harps are still.

I cannot tell you of my love.

It is wrong to speak of such things,

I shouldn't love you.

But like a bee to a flower,

I linger nearby, waiting.

I shouldn't love you.

So I sit and watch you,

your smile, your laugh,

the soft curve of your lips.

I shouldn't love you.

But like a bee to a flower,

I'm instinctively drawn.

Always waiting, always lingering,

forever,

on and on.

Rhea Seren Phillips

I WALK ALONE

I walk alone,
Through darkness,
So alone
An empty pit,
Deep inside,
       So empty.

The snow blows,
    Swirling and twirling,
        Like tiny little dancers,
            Beauty and cold,
               All in one.

Fire roars at me,
  Flicking and spitting,
As pure and passionate,
As true love,
It kills me inside,
With every flicker.

I walk alone,
One day I know that,
     No longer will be,
     That one day will come,
But first I must wait,
       A day,
         A month,
           Maybe a lifetime,
             I'll never know.
        Until things change . . .
           I walk alone.

Lesley Acford

IF EVER

If ever I slip from your memory,
the tears from my eyes
yet unshed,
will fall listlessly down my cheek.

If you lose your love for me,
my heart will break
into thousands of shards.
But not before
giving most of it to you.

If you learn to laugh again
I will be happy for you,
in another realm
aside from the living.

If you sigh and glance at my picture
propped upon the mantelpiece,
and decide
that you,
once more,
can love again,
I will step back.

If in the future, your visits grow less frequent,
I will lie under the earth, content,
because as humans do,
they live on after tragedy strikes them.

I want to ask of you one more request.
Forgive me.
And then I will bother you no longer.
My pestering spirit will depart from you,
forever.
I cannot unshackle the manacles of guilt which
bind me to yourself.
My soul years for absolution.
Forgive me.

Despite your pleadings and promises,
despite your entreaties and eulogies,
my ears were deaf to them.
The rope was tight and fit snugly.
Forgive me.

And when you do love again,
forget me
and love unconditionally
like a mother
who loves her child.

For nothing hurts more than
to watch my love
love no other.

If ever I slip from your memory,
please, remember
the warmth of our past embrace
when you embrace another.

Kassandra Hangdaan

BARKING MAD

Speeches spouting change
From barking mad politicians
Parties making promises
Hoping we all will listen

Abolishing certain allowances
Lowering standards of living
Printing lots of money
To get the economy driven

Raising the retirement age
Shaking up the tax system
Ministers making cutbacks
While furthering their ambitions

Borrowing has gone too far
The country's debt has risen
The politicians can remedy this
With their life changing visions

Can the barking mad MPs
Lead us out of the recession
They could all be locked up
But will there be any policemen?

Craig Shuttleworth

STRANGE EMOTIONS

Possessed,
by an evil emotion,
which leaves me distraught,
hysterical and filled with agitation.

Controlled,
by a malevolent empathy,
succumbing to its craving desire,
leaving me without sympathy.

Occupied,
by a malicious sensation,
unnerving my whole existence,
condemning me to a lack of passion.
Dominated,
by a vile passion,
to fuck and devour without hesitation,
just to satisfy my lustful sensation.

Owned,
by a demonic indulgence,
blocking my mind from morality,
crushing me into a life with no substance.

Haunted,
by an infatuated obsession,
frequented with morbid beliefs,
without regard or consideration.

Influenced,
easily by eagerness,
portraying the best in life,
rewarded with nothing or less.

Held,
prisoner of crazed convictions,
infatuated and
surrendering to obsessive suspicions.

Alfred Vassallo

GOSSAMER WINGS

They lay scattered across the top of the hill,
some of them alone, seemingly wrapped up in their own cocoon of silence,
others in groups of two or three huddled together
as if the company would ease the burden of waiting.
Nothing stirred.
It was a very still day, warm with spring morning sun.
High above, a lark sang a derisory song
as if laughing and mocking.

Suddenly there appeared to be a change in the air.
Feeling this, one or two of them started to move
stretching their many coloured wings.
There was now an air of expectancy.
Then it happened,
the grass on the hill waved forward, teased by some unseen force.
It then moved back towards them as a warm thermic wind blew up the hill.

One by one they spread their beautifully coloured gossamer wings,
luxuriating in the warmth and feel of the sun .
First one, then in a sudden rush, they all left the confined prison of the hill
and 'ascended',
filling the sky with their sun dappled wings.

One or two had ventured higher than the lark,
now frightened back to the safety of her nest
no more the mocking one.
Others seemingly reluctant, to leave the bosom of the earth from which they had come,
flying apparently aimlessly up and down in front of the hill.

The high flyers, now drifting away like dandelion seeds,
chasing white fluffy clouds to unknown destinations.
Once again the air stilled,
those that were left began to flutter down,
landing once more on the hill,
some at the top, others halfway down,
the rest in disconsolate heaps at the bottom.

One thing they all had in common,
a warm glow in their hearts and a smile on their faces.
For these were no ordinary creatures,
had they not , for a short while, become one with the angels?
Ascending from their own world into a new dimension
whilst mere mortals below could only watch,
awe-struck in the knowledge that, yes, some people
really can 'FLY'.

NDP 'Paraglider' (Harry Damsell)

UP

Here's a question which an idle thought
Has prompted me to ask:
Isn't 'up' used often
In referring to a task?
I'm going to use a diff'rent rhythm now,
To illustrate.
If you can think of other signs
Of the phenomenon, that's great.

Horologists are winding up.
Bandagers are binding up.
Lotharios are eyeing up.
Strategists are weighing up.
'Night-owlers' are staying up.
Quarrymen are breaking up.
Divorcees are splitting up.
Prison guards are locking up.
Bunglers are 'cocking' up.
Corroded joints are seizing up,
And dental surgeons 'freezing' up.
Arteries are 'furring' up,
Incinerators burning up.
Investigators checking up.
Gardeners are planting up.
Phone-callers are ringing up,
After which they're hanging up.
Planners are drawing up.
Timber-mills are sawing up.
Seamstresses are sewing up,
And detonators blowing up.
Blockages are stopping up,
And circumstances cropping up.
Ice-skaters are slipping up.
Shopfitters are fitting up.
Pursuers are catching up.
Bank-robbers are holding up.
Bankrupt firms are folding up.
Hoarders are cluttering up.
Flatterers are 'buttering' up,
Support-recruiters 'drumming' up
(Cheer up; the end is coming up).
For the purpose of my summing up,
This format must be given up.

The above are some examples
Of how 'up' can be used,
And (more commonly, I think)
Of how it can be <u>mis</u>-used.
'Up' denotes ascent or height,
And surely, on reflection,
There often is no relevance
In the concept of direction.
If you analyse it, speech like this
Can frequently be seen
To be 'mixed up', or down, or sideways;
Do you understand what I mean?
I must arise (i.e. stand up,
or, better still, just 'stand' –
Is this rational analysis
Becoming out of hand?).
My time is up for sitting down.
(You can't sit <u>up,</u> can you?
Your bottom's horizontal,
Down where it was put by you.)
I concede it isn't crucial
Whether we say 'up' or 'down',
But ideally let's be rational.
Now I'll shut up, or down.

Anthony Hofler

THIS IS OUR QUEEN

Flags fluttering fitfully in the breeze
suddenly erupt into frenzied flapping,
voices on voices cheer and cheer
'Look! She's coming! She's here! She's here!'

Then, surprisingly, silence; out of her car,
she's standing before us and yes, we are
face to face with the Queen!
Not in all our wildest dreams
could we have foreseen . . .
She smiles, she's real, she takes our flowers,
she's so worth all the hours and hours
we slept on the pavement
waiting to see
our Queen, her Royal Majesty
and *she's talking to me!*

Did I curtsey? What did I say?
I can't remember; she walked away
to smile and speak to someone else
but she left a little piece of herself
with me!

Now she is my queen, my friend and she cares,
but how does she do it? She shares
herself with thousands worldwide
and yet remains mine.

I could tell of her gracious beauty,
her dedicated life of duty;

I could talk of constancy.
While scams and scandals swirl around
she, as always, stands her ground;

I could say for sixty years, all my life,
she has reigned supreme,
our queen;
but we all know the facts!

The only thing I want to say
is since that day
she stopped to chat
she has my heart.
And that's that!

Valerie Sutton

48

RETROSPECTIVE BULLIES

Necks outstretched like hissing geese we chased behind you,
taunting, teasing with all our might,
all too keen to please our senseless sense of fun,
and you were put to flight.

Over and over, again and again, we cackled
our mindless, mad-cap refrain, made up purely
for our own entertainment:
Loyce,-a-loyce,-the-toytoise/a-loyce-the-toytoise,
Loyce-a-loyce-a-loyce,-the-toytoise/a-loyce-the-toytoise;
But you were not amused by our tactless, tasteless tango.

Then, when you played your hopscotch game,
we'd grab your chain and run away,
giggling in pig ignorance, giggling away
as the dinner-ladies tutted; yet they always failed tell us
we were bullies.

But we didn't really see you,
you know, we hardly even looked,
we pair of silly schoolgirls, hooked blind on reckless rhythm,
dancing round like demons.

Yet although we had the rhyme, we really had no reason.
And we'd no idea at ten – it's true –
how deeply we'd be wounding you,
perhaps with wounds that wouldn't quickly mend.

So Lois, if it's not too late,
in retrospect, I want to say
I'm sorry we were horrid.

Eileen Caiger Gray

A CAT'S TALE

My body is weak and almost spent
My get up and go just upped and went
Just lazing, watching, waiting, sleeping
Sometimes I hear my mistress weeping

'More food,' she coaxes, 'try this nice cream'
Surely this must be every cat's dream
All this love and pampering just for me
But, weakness spoils my pleasure you see

It would be so nice to leap around
Checking out each mysterious sound
To go chasing birds and climbing trees
To be completely free of disease

I sleep and sleep and I hardly eat
I'm tired of all this fish and meat
Those tender morsels have no appeal
I'd quite like to try a different meal

I am suffering with incontinence
No wonder my mistress is so tense
With arthritic legs, and bladder weak
I'd apologise if I could speak

I can limp around from room to room
But I get so weary much too soon
I have a bedroom all of my own
I'm so protected and mustn't moan

But if only I had energy
To prowl around and simply be
Like other cats in the neighbourhood
Well that would really be so good

I'm imprisoned in this world of mine
Though some strays may find this quite divine
Yet the novelty would lose its fun
When they discovered they couldn't run

No more freedom roaming east or west
North or south or wherever seems best
No more meetings with other felines
No more romancing behind the vines

How sad it is being a lonely cat
Showered with love but what good is that
I'd much rather prowl here and there
Leaping on high walls without a care

Ahh! Here she comes my mistress dear
With words of love she tickles my ear
I feel a little more lively now
So I answer her, miaow! Miaow!

What's this she's got? A rubbery thing
With balls and bells which begin to ring
And a furry tunnel with holes inside
It looks a possible place to hide

Perhaps things aren't so bad after all
At least I move if only a crawl
This looks like a pleasant distraction
I think I'm ready for some action.

Wendy Godber

RIVALS

Earth, earth of sweet reprove, rejoice and low
to the worryburned brooks turn home – where waning woods,
burksome brown and ashed copsed, fungal grown, blurry
bordered; and in bobbins, green, great, gargantuan bare.
        In wormwood, greyed out green, alone I teach of fellow youth;
of newborn manners; locks and clumps, birds begone of maiden year;
where wind, in all its capricious bends, rings and doubled bluff
comes prairie over ocean lifts; enough, enough to make the seabard
swivel, cry-caw, leave, swoop, driven by a starry bubble,
to dive and dive, to beauty's bugle.
        Soft and golden-globed the buttered-berries plump, kernels burst
better broad; seared by waning leaf, whitewood, black braes that thrust
cold thumbs – ripe and lichen homecoming – what yonder bleakness breaks.
        The knave, bottled blue, double piebald dimpled true – sugar-skinned, O
darkling bird – nightgold, what better beauty been? What wonder? Lighting miles
too lovely for mountaintops to burden-bear; in dark, the whispers
of quieted dreamless sleep – awake! Awake upon a gallant face;
        tincture tiny, honeyed bonny head, your music blooms, heart, wayward be.
Watered down, the fetlock bobbing brook – a standing stone, perched,
blanched, double-sunned and weather folly – be stage restraint,
like warmer wedding gold.

Stacey Busuttil

I'M SORRY

I'm sorry I could never be the kind of daughter you wanted,
When you wanted A I chose B

C	D
E	F

We can carry on going through the rest of the alphabet,
However this is not what I solely wanted to say
I know that I'm responsible for the pain you feel today

I'm sorry

Please give me another chance,
I'll prove to you that I'm really worthy
But I can't make any promises

You see, you're always comparing me with other people's children
Him to her, her to him they're spotless in your eyes
It's like they're a God sent.
It was something I was unable to be, so I'm sorry.

I'm sorry for not being the way you wanted me to be.
You planned out my life,
But there was another plan for me.
The journey has been long and rough,
I've yet to learn so many things,
I've walked a few steps, your pulling me back
Out of fear you've sacrificed everything.

I'm sorry for all the lies I have told you,
Especially the ones that really hurt you,
You see it isn't easy finding a way through life.
I've suffered so much confusion, I needed time.
Precious time to express my mind

I'm sorry for being such a disappointment for you,
I've seen the tears that you secretly shed at night,
Praying vainly, in hope that I might change
But it's not in my hands.
It's in the hands of the writer of my destiny.
When it feels right I may come back,
But too much has happened, it's a messy story
A situation you wouldn't understand, so I'm sorry.

I'm sorry for never being able to express to you
How I feel.
You just wouldn't get it, ever if I tried
So I suffer in my silence like you do
In yours,
We wipe each other's tears, never saying a word
Because we know we're both beyond them.

I'm sorry, I'm sorry, I'm sorry
These words sound so hollow to me
I try to put some emotion behind it,
But fail because there is no heart in it,
I don't know what to say.
I'm struggling to express myself,
So I'll go back to those two words
I'm sorry

Kynaat Awan

LIFE

When you're young
you are carefree,
Oblivious to pain
you roam around freely,
Your ideas flourish
your thoughts cherished,
Then you grow up . . .
Money is priority!
It is used an many ways,
bills to pay,
food to buy,
Many problems come your way. . .
You learn to weigh them,
learn to deal with them,
learn to prioritise.
Then you become old . . .
The shine gone from the gold
and you are left out in the cold
all alone,
until the time comes to meet your Lord!

Bushra Latif

CONFESSION OF A SINGLE MAN/ONLINE DATING

I decided to try online dating,
Well, it's got to be better than waiting,
I know it sounds daft
And I bet that you laughed
But, you'll see, I'll be soon celebrating.
So, I open some sparkling wine
As I sign-up to 'dating' online
With questions a plenty
For my new online entry,
I drink, then I answer them fine.

I fill out a lengthy profile
It's detailed and takes quite a while
I give them my history,
No lies and no mystery
But then it sounds like I've no style?
So . . . let's change it . . .
I'm handsome, athletic
The girls find me strong and magnetic
I'm French and I'm single,
I'll make your flesh tingle . . .
No 'delete' . . .
That sounds pathetic!

Instead I write that . . .
I am deep into art,
I know Ruebens and Turner apart,
I love music and song
Poetry that's long,
So I'm not just some boring old fart.
Of course I don't look my age,
Not rich, but I earn a good wage,
Blonde hair with good looks
Love films, and of course books,
. . . it's their minds I would like to engage.

The woman I want, yes I'm sure,
Must be fun and in no way a bore,
Don't mind if she's flirty
Or wants to talk dirty,
Romantic, yes! Maybe much more!
Late thirties, quite small and petite,
Big boobs, but please not big feet,
Small bum and long hair
Either auburn or fair,

There, that's my 'wish-list' complete.

Now which dating site? Click . . . click . . .

Hmmm . . . 'Asian Babes' they sound my style
I could be on this site a while
At sixty a page
This could take an age
So I start up a 'favourites' file.
Oooh . . . now she's more my taste
(Breathe deep, don't do this in haste)
Firm breasts and curved hips
Brown eyes and full lips
Long legs, long hair and small waist.

In no time my 'favourites' are seven,
Four more, so now there's eleven.
All saying online
That they want to be mine,
Oh yes! I am in Asian heaven.
I email them all in one day
I want them to hear right away,
So they know from the start
My love's from the heart
And for their love I'm willing to pay.

Replies, they come in thick and fast
Each one costs me more than the last,
In such a short while
I've spent quite a pile
And I look at my statement aghast!
But these 'babes' they are longing for me
So the money I simply don't see,
I just keep on writing
It feels so exciting
Despite the exorbitant fee.

Do you know there are women out there
Who are up for a thrill, and a dare,
If you're willing to pay
They will go the whole way
Their soul and their flesh they will bare!
For who . . . well, for you.
It's true . . . here's what you do.
First thing . . . you must go online
No computer? Then come and use mine,
We'll pick you a site, make sure it feels right
You'll see, it will all turn out fine . . .

You'll see that in no time at all
These women will queue for a call
Like a film star on heat
They will all want your meat
Yes, whether you're large or your small.
So, you really can't help but succeed
As there's not enough men for their need,
Their hot and their waiting
These babes, online dating
You're food for their hunger, so feed!

And when you have chosen 'the one'
And you find all your money has gone
Don't give up the chase
Just keep up the pace
For he who's faint-hearted gets none.
And that's not an outcome for you
No, victory . . . for seeing it through,
Go get her, you stud
Nip her, right in her bud,
Go do what a man's gotta do!

Robin Martin-Oliver

SEA FRET

Chill; overlying
surf and wave formation's roar,
like pale icy floss,
softening the swish of oar
as survivors reach the shore.

Grey cover, like death
of those who failed to rise
above the wave-crest,
ne'er to see again the skies
o'er which the cloud scud flies.

As Death's harbingers,
the seagulls swoop down and screech.
Foaming wavelets flow
serpentine on sandy beach,
like wraiths beyond rescue's reach.

Jo Allen

THE INFANTRYMAN

Sign here son
This is for you
Join the forces
And fight for just causes
You don't want to kill
Prefer another thrill
You have no choice
Listen to the CO's. voice
Flying out to a distant shore
Armed to the teeth, training no more
Body armour, machine gun, grenade
Against IED's strictly home-made
Front line walking
Enemy stalking
Blinding flash, cacophony of sound
Searing pain, body hits ground
Technicolour dream
Distant scream
Fractured vision
Completed mission
Stretcher running, morphine calming
Mother dreaming
Death in a can
Or bionic man
God's choice son
Run boy run

Bill Wilson

SHELTER FOR A STRANGER

It was on Christmas Eve, I met him –
a forlorn figure, standing in
the gloomy street light with an air
of desolation, dense about him.
I'd all but passed him, but the helpless,
lost look in his eyes made me
to pause and then accost him.

'Hello, can I do anything for you?'
For sure he looked to be in need of help.
'I come from far-off place;' he said
in faltering tones, 'had some work to do;
now that it's dark, I wonder if
someone would lodge me for the night;
for I'm a stranger to this place.'

I looked at him.
His clothes looked old and worn,
threadbare though clean; he had a small,
cheap baggage in his hand.
My wife's frown at his sight flashed by
before my eyes; he wouldn't be welcome
in sophisticated hearths.
But there was a gentle, captivating
look in those bright eyes.
I resolved I'd just give it a try.
'Come . . .' I dragged.
'Call me David,' said he simply.
'There's our padre's house around the
corner; Sam Levite, a pious
man of God with deep concern for
welfare of the poor is sure to
find a place for you to stay.'
'Let me go alone and ask him,'
whispered David, as we neared the
parsonage; 'so I will know his
offer of a helping hand is
not dictated by your presence but the
offshoot of his Christian charity.'

So he went and knocked, which brought the
solemn parson to the door.
'My dear man,' said he, in reply
to the stranger's plea, 'it is now
Christmas Eve, and all of us are

pressed for time; I'm late now for the
Christmas Eve's fund-raising dinner
by our church committee for the
poor; I could have put you in the
parish hall to pass the night's chill hours;
but the bell will toll for midnight service
in some hours from now.' He paused a moment.
'I am sorry young man; may the good Lord
shelter you beneath His wings.'

The smile on David's face as he returned
was tinged with resignation sad,
as if he had expected it.
'O, come my David,' I consoled,
'be not disheartened; we will go
to Saul Compassion; he is very rich –
a most prolific contributor to
all worthy causes.'

With coloured lights that gaily winked
and glitt'ring throng and gleaming cars,
Saul's grounds and mansion throbbed with festive pulse
as David turned his timid steps towards
resplendent Saul surrounded by
his boist'rous guests; his tim'rous plea
provoked a loud retort.
'Are you mad, my little fellow,' thundered
Saul at cowering David, 'to come and ask for
lodging during Christmas festivities?'
Then as afterthought, 'I could have
lodged you in my outhouse; but my
kids – they wanted it to keep their
crib; but if you wait, my cook will
give you board when party's over.'

I winced for David at this crude outburst.
The anguish over David's visage struck
me deep, as my tormented brain
in vain pored over the next step.
To leave him to the mercy of
that foggy night was not in me;
and so, deciding then to brave my wife's
displeasure, took his hand.

Passing by the lowly hut of Hannah
Christina my mind recalled some
message to be passed on to that
poor widow who scraped a living

59

doing odd jobs in the nearby households.

Having told her, as I turned,
David stepped up quickly saying
'Mamma, I'm a stranger from a
far off place and leaving here tomorrow.
Could you lodge me for the night?'

'My son,' replied the simple matron,
'if you mind not this mud floor for your bed,
you're welcome; my own boy would be just
your age had he but lived; but four years back,
this very day he went to join his Maker.
So I fast on Christmas Eve at
Master's feet; but just a while if
you could wait, I'll make some
rice porridge for you.'

Then David turned and looked at me.
A strange glow radiated from
his face as if to say, some Christian
charity was still left on this earth.
I felt quite small before his gaze.
'You know,' I lamely muttered, 'you
can come and stay the night with me;
for you will have no comforts here.'

'I thrust myself on none;' he gently said,
'you offered me your place not as
a first choice but as last resort;
this woman having little, quite
willingly offered it to me.
Now I will go and sup with her
and she, with me.'*

As he spoke, David seemed to grow in
stature and his voice in timbre.
In awe I whispered, 'David, who are you?'
'David's my ancestral name,'** intoned his
voice, 'they call me Jesus.'

And he turned and crossed the hut's threshold
and vanished from my sight.

*Revelation 3.20: 'I stand at the door and knock: if
any man . . . open the door, I will come in to him, and
will sup with him, and he with me.'

**Reference to Jesus as the son of David

(Matt 25.43: 'I was a stranger and you took me not in')

(A narrative of what will most probably happen if Jesus were to visit man now, after 2000 years of Christianity.)

Dr Nithie Victor

EXCALIBUR

Take up the sword of truth, that of Excalibur and watch
As it tells the tale of times gone by, those of the myths
They call Camelot. Excalibur has powerful magic embedded
Inside it.

Just one touch and it will have you under its spell and in
No time at all you are transported back through a place of
Timelessness where the magic is everywhere, you can see it
And feel it all around you, it encompasses your entire being.

You are intoxicated by the power of such an enchanted place.
Is it, can it be real? Of course it can, just use the magic that is
Inside you to guide you on this mystical experience and see the
Truth for yourself.

If you choose to use the magic wisely, then stand back and be
Prepared to have your breath taken away, open up to the magic
And indulge your senses. Allow the enchantment of time to
Slowly dissolve away.

And here we are outside of time, on the other side of life, the cosmic heavens
Are opening right inside your reality. Feel the changes very subtle at first as they begin to
filter down. And my message to you is that I am returning and I give to you the gift of cosmic
consciousness. Remember my name, Excalibur.

Starchild

CHRISTMAS

She's sitting quietly all alone, in that dark cold Children's home
Can only be but six or seven, believes in fairies, God and Heaven
In her hands a teddy bear, now worn and torn with all that wear
That teddy means the world to 'she', no mum or dad like you and me

Outside a dark and dismal dawn, on this day our Lord was born
Her face pressed firmly to the glass, hoping that she won't be last
That Santa in his sack will bring, she wants no toys, just wants one thing
A mum and dad she badly needs, that warmth and love, but no one heeds
She turns a teardrop in her eye, she whispers, 'God, please let me die'
But in the corner, sack is empty, not like ours, filled with plenty
She prayed so hard but once again, Christmas Day just left her pain

He stumbles, bottle in his hand, from the shadows of our land
Another soul that no ones 'fond', 'cause he's a tramp, a Vagabond
Mum walked out when he was three, and left him to his Dads mercy
Who wanted him kept out of sight, now his son walks streets at night
Wrapping cardboard all around, whilst you and I in beds sleep sound
He sighs and hopes day 'be his last', then mind will rest and have no past

Young lover now all on his own, she left his heart without 'a home'
She told him she would never leave, but now warm heart and mind just grieve
And in his moments of despair, when he turns 'round and she's not there
A tear drop falls from 'smitten eye', a broken Heart heaves 'nother sigh
A life now lost its goal, direction, yearns for her to give affection
Every day a cross to bear, reminding him that she's not there

And as I write these words I weep, not for me will there be sleep
I see that child now growing old, she's got no feelings, so, so cold
All her crying was so absurd, 'they' walked away, 'they' never heard
Years of no one being there, has left this child, inside 'no care'
A 'damaged' child now she will be, will live her life in misery

I see a tramp, was so alone, who never, ever, had a home
He has no more, no need to hide, 'cause Christmas Eve, that night he died
In the gutter there he lay, whilst you and I rejoiced 'Lords day'

I see young lover sitting there, on his face an ice cold stare
Gun now pointing to his brain, calls her name, once more, again
Then just one instant lost in time, she at last, is free, his mind..

I think these folks of present, past, who wish their moments were their last
Who daily pray to him above, pleading, crying out for love
What kind of people can we be, to watch them suffer needlessly
After all, we're all the same, just all each have a different name

So Christmas Day when joy fills mind, and we all have a real good time
Lots of presents, lots of love, lots of joy from Him, above
Just think of these lost souls who roam, whose hearts will never find a home

Look upwards into God's blue sky, 'but for the Grace of God, go I . . .'

Peter John Edwards

LAST ONE LEFT

A thousand bandits rode in,
to that street in the West.
Where they burned down every house,
'til there was just one left.

Fires circled, and embers rained down,
The raiders approached the last building in town.
They quietly watched on, as a figure emerged,
but they couldn't believe it, it just seemed absurd.

An old lady stood small, a cane clutched in her hand,
An old lady determined to make her last stand,
This was her castle, disguised as a house,
The heart of a lion, in the body of a mouse.

The horde banded together, and began to walk nearer,
So the woman raised her cane to make herself clearer,
They stopped for a second, and she warmed up her throat,
And through clenched teeth, she suddenly spoke.

'I'd rather die here today, than give my house to the gutter,
And I will batten down every hatch
And secure every shutter.
Then put up a sign, to say to the rest,
You can't have this one
It's the last one left.'

Alex Cassidy

ASCENT OF MAN - A TRILOGY OF A POEM

Part I
When the early ape hurled
A stone at the fruit on a tree,
Or, to kill another animal out of fear,
Or, for turning it into food;
Two things happened at once,
The ape turned into Man of the species,
Different than the other animal species:

And invented the first machine,
And, climbed up on the first rung of the ladder
To heaven to ascend, to see the face of his Maker
The ancient watchmaker, who,
Created the machine of the universe

Much later, much later that Stratford bard,
Through his Hamlet pondered and wondered:
'What a piece of work is a man! How noble
In reason! How infinite in faculties, in form and moving
How express and admirable in action
How like an angel! In apprehension how like a God?
The Beauty of the world, the paragon of animals!'

Part II
True Greek God

Archimedes the 'Sandreckoner'
A son of Phidias the astronomer
The citizen of Syracuse, Sicily
But known as the Greek scientist

Discovered powers of levers
And created the giants cranes
That could lift the Roman ships
And drown them in the Sicilian bay
Or throw them many, many miles away

The inventor of the 'Archimedes' screw'
That still pumps out water in many villages
In present Egypt and many places in the world
He calculated the sand grains on a seashore
And invented the calculus and solved the theorems
That made easy to build buildings of all kinds

Archimedes you are the true Greek God
With thy levers, pulleys, spheres, spirals
Circles, parabola, cylinders, conoid, spheroid
And floating objects' measurements inside out
Science became the real empirical and principle
Not just on earth but in the wide, wide world
Of multifarious universe of stars, black holes and super nova!

Part III
Leonardo da Vinci

Leonardo da Vinci, what are you?
God! An angel! Or, divine human?
Man! Or, half man, half woman?
Are you yourself the mystic Mona Lisa?
Or, that, enigmatic smile on her face?

Are you an ultimate artist in the apex of art?
Creator of the zenithal the 'Last Supper'? Or,
Designer of the drawing of Vitruvian Man
Making art, science and philosophy wholesome
And father of Darwinstic humanism?

When you did the studies and the sketches
Of foetus in the womb, baby in making
Were you wanted to be a picture perfect artist?
Or, were you looking for the beginning of life?

Leonardo the Prince of Renaissance,
Your inquisitiveness in art and science
And inventions of the dykes and machines
Set man on the steps of the stairway to heaven
Is it the beginning or is it the end of Man?

Sasha Dee

BILBERRY PICKING ON THE WELSH MOUNTAINS

Up at dawn to beat the sun. Rival gangs they pass us
 all eager to start our day's work.
Several minds and all of one accord!

Large tins show our optimism, no time to stop until we reach the top,
and the mood holds all in its grasp.
The race has started!

Heights gained, some rest, not me as time means bilberries!
 Heads bob as we labour in the bushes
each to her own domain!

No trite exchange except to brag of better bushes found
and too intent to fill the tins
Who have become our masters!

Our heads are bowed as vow is made to fill our tins,
 while distant sounds tell that another 'catch' is found!
And we all rush to see!

Yells of anger as one is caught stealing from another's tin
Our tins have made us robbers!
Alas all honesty is lost!

Thieves (called cousins) found pinching from my patch,
My sister's tin I'll find to square the difference!
(Fighting means time, means bilberries!)

My sister screams, she's not so blind! No justice on this mountain!
A devil for a sister mind
Give me six cousins for this one!

'Same tart we'll share so who's losing?' I shout. Kith and Kin!
I'll stick to friends
At least they're of my choosing!

Friend Joan has a sister to help and this makes me very sore,
 and I'll make sure everybody knows
when we're weighing up the score!

And she has pop in her flask – not free tap like me,
 But of course her dad works down the mines
and he brings up gold you see!

What's that you say, 'Swap ham for home-made jam?'
 A grab is made before her mind is changed!
and off I go to show my gain!

Bilberries bartered for a bite, I warm to these again,
 my kin and kin, and think

you know where you are with your own!

They got their faults mind, but these I'll overlook,
at least they have free tap like me
our lunch just as prosaic!

Stomachs filled, we labour long until some shout, 'We're done!'
But I've not finished picking
and I'm sore with too much sun!

'Wait for me,' says I, and grab a hand (or three) of sister Pam's
and off I go unchallenged!
For so intent is she!

'First down is champ,' we shout, and race on with leaps and bounds
in eagerness to win
with thoughts of home and tea!

Our last lap gained, one slope to go, when Pam my headache for a sister
trips and falls
and starts bleating like a lamb!

We turn to see her tin roll and her arms are waving wild,
and the horror on her face
is still imprinted on my mind!

The tin bounces, rolls and eagerly gains ground,
and we make vain attempts to grab it
while we all grapple with the ground!

It out-manoeuvres our attempts to stop it, and on it rolls
while we throw some stones to halt
and the jubilant tin rolls on!

Now we are all involved yelling and throwing
While the lid comes off spilling contents
into sheep's truckles

In horror we see a day's work sacrificed to slope,
gazing mockingly out of truckles
daring us to tell the difference!

My sister wails accusingly, 'You could have saved for me!'
Such pain and sorrow!
What a funny sight to see!

A screaming sister shrieking after bilberries,
we all collapse in laughter,
for quite beside herself is she!

With such laughter poor Pam is quite nonplussed.
Still you think she would be pleased
that I'd stole, and saved so much!

But pleasures born of pain soon pass,
 and our tins seemed odiously full.
Our glee is lost to guilt!

No berries given to console of course
only sympathy, for we had to show our day's work
 back home for all to see!

But the rivalry's not finished on that day or all the week as mothers
 brags of pots of jam
made from our bilberries.

And we never tire of telling of Pam's horror on that slop!
While she relives her sorrow
to our unending glee!

Barbara Collar

GUESS WHO?

In life's bubbles, toils and troubles
I'm not here to stir things up,
I am with you all the way
Let's fight it till death, I say!
At birth I am there to register you
So that I can see, well, who is who.
I'm there as you wed your first wife,
Your second and third.
I will do what's best for you
That's my word.
Even when you think things are a-OK
I'll be here until your Judgement Day.
'Stop this folly, are you God?' he asks,
I reply, basking in his glee,
"No Sir, I'm your Solicitor
Now here's my fee!'

Michelle Dixon

BANKERS BONUS BONANZA!

To try, justify, mammoth handouts.
First, it is said, to spur on, the Bankers, making them perform better,
for the wider, economy.
Rather than an untouchable elite, whose mistakes they repeat.
Secondly, a way to keep, the bold, bright and best, of this rare breed.
Only arrogance and pomposity, to feed.
Such huge amounts, result in the loss of clarity.
Losing touch, with the value, of pounds and pence.
A catastrophic, series of events.
Large stakes, billions lost, still one takes.
Up in glass and steel, ivory towers.
Abuse of perverse powers.
Whilst the country braces itself.
For huge cuts, effecting health and wealth.
It will be as pernicious, as the wartime rationing of 1945.
As further towards extremes, they drive.
No compromise.
Only broken promises and further lies.
Meanwhile, the investment banker, continues to recklessly gamble.
So the figure, gets ever bigger, becoming a trigger . . .
To make them beyond the law,
The consequences no longer ignore.
Mergers and acquisition.
Damage and derision.
No amount of being able to 'Quantitatively ease'.
Will stop this disease.

The more they get, the more blasé.
As with our economy, roulette they play.
And the tax payer, is made to pay and pay.
Because the bankers are having a bonuses bonanza.

Tony Chestnut Brown

ODE TO THE SYCAMORE TREE

Zacchaeus was a little man,
To meet this 'Jesus' was his plan
Through his job he must have heard,
Who was in town – this 'Man of Words'

Zac was too short, So climbed a tree
He did this so that he could see
Above the crowds – curiosity ?

And Jesus saw this little man
Called out to him across the sand
Do you think He shook him by the hand?
And said, 'Zacchaeus, hey my man!'

With Jesus then he made a pact!
It changed his life – and that's a fact!
Started with that one small act,

Just in climbing up a tree –
Could be like that for you – and me
We'll claim responsibility

S'pose it's 'cause we have a choice
To listen to that 'still small voice'
Accept the challenge just like Zac
Choose to change and not look back because you're worth it!

Gilly Reville

TO THE DEPTH OF . . .

I have burst to tears, you passed indifferently.
I have got drunk by thousands of rivers.
And now I am touching this brightness.
I am touching, but I do not feel.
How it is to feel?
Tell me, how is it when someone tells you that he loves you?
I do not know.
You keep quiet.
I do not understand.
A volcano will explode
and we will not have a time to say something.
The art of dialogue – undiscovered for us.

Anna Siudak

VODKA AND TONIC

I apply more eyeliner
The morning after

To get that smudgy look
That tells you all that I had sex.

Friends take photos of us
Posed in pub bathroom mirrors.

One day I will be a mother, a wife.
For now I'm just myself.

Our names are not written down together
I am unmarried (even on Facebook)

I'm just a girl in a bar on a boat,
Walking home in heels.

Rachel H Scotland

MYSTIC

Beyond or because of
The look of dawns and rainbows
Hushed woodlands at dusk
Flowing water
Far space and stars
Is something else
Felt sometimes
But briefly
A blink. A shiver
An elusive scent in the mind
Meaning what? Perhaps nothing much
An obscure brain or sense event
An inner itch come and gone
Till next time
The mystic searches
But cannot quite find it
Not here
Though maybe elsewhere.

M G Sherlock

BETRAYAL

His eyes appeared distant, his body withdrawn
A lifeless disposition, he looked so forlorn
His expression was blank, so distant, and so cold
To me his eyes now appeared so very old
He turned away as if to stall and delay
Wanting to save the cruel words for another day.

But the words struck and punctured like bullets
It was as if someone had me by the gullet
Piercing, damaging and so harrowing the words feel
How could this ever be so real?
Yet one after another they kept on coming
I hope, I prayed that the bullets transpired to nothing.

The door slammed, the firing dwindled
The love that was once here; never to be rekindled
And as silence falls, I begin to sleep
But as soon as my eyes close, the tears they weep
Please God; just let me sleep.

I assess the damage the bullets created
Shrapnel and scars are evident within
How did I ever become so thin?
Wishing and hoping that help will appear
I just want to be taken far away for here
I helplessly search for answers and clues
Searching for the headline that may make the news.

Motionless and weak from a bleeding wound
I slump to the floor in the corner of the room
I hope and pray that the tears float away
But the tears they fall in an unrelenting way
I still believe that this is all just a bad dream
Hoping that somehow it will never be seen.

Desperation kicks in and panic takes over
I run and hide and dive for cover
If I can somehow avoid to be seen
Maybe this will all just be a bad dream.

Help arrives, salvation in sight
I breathe; I sigh and cling to the light
Noise and commotion all around
I almost can't stand the deafening sound.

I forget where I am, what has happened
I live in ignorance for one sweet second
For those few minutes its bliss and splendour
However I'm fully aware that soon I will have to surrender.

I wake up to another new day
Hoping that today I don't have to hope or pray
Yet the thoughts from yesterday are not far away
Soon they will be back to haunt and prey.

Miss Baker

SPARKY GETS SPAYED

He roamed the neighbourhood
And all the bitches looked good
Puppies were born
And they were his spawn
Dirty mongrels that couldn't be sold
All because Sparky was bold

One night the neighbours declared
Sparky needed to be impaired
But how shall we do it?
And who will pay?
They took him to the vets the next day
Poor Sparky got spayed
On his back he laid
He returned home
Without his bone

No more sparks for Sparky
But Sparky's fuse
Was randy and ready
Sparky's son became a pest
And still the bitches got no rest

The locals despaired
Stopping Sparky
Was going to be difficult
The mayor declared.

Sian Osborn

OH I WISH OTHERS HAD A CLUE

I have no arms or legs
At times I wish I was dead,
There is something deep inside my head.

I may smile each and every day
I don't want sympathy.
I still have a heart
Feelings and emotions too
Oh I just wish others had a clue.

I may not be able to run or jump
I may not be able to swim or paint.
Oh I wish others had a clue
What to say or do.

I may travel the world
So others may see I have a life
There are no limitations I set aside.

I didn't ask to be born this way
I didn't ask for arms or legs
Oh! Yes at times I do wish I was dead.

Take a moment to think about others less fortunate than yourselves,
Take a moment to think about love, feelings and emotions which are
Things that cannot be bought from a shop shelf.

Many people say I have a heart made of gold, this I often question why
Because why didn't God above just let me die.
It is then he whispers deeply in my ears,
'My child there is nothing in this life you should fear throughout your years.'
So keep that smile on your face with so much dignity and grace.

Anastasia Williams Owolabi

HEART

What to think
What to dream
Is it possible for any to become real

Why dream
Why cry
Shall I let love pass me by

An age is a number
A name is words

Love runs deeper
Through your veins
Through your soul

Can it be true
Is this love at all

Flowers may be a symbol
Holding hands to
But do any of these
Do they
Really
Come true

Where is romance

Surprise trips
Flowers
A kiss on the cheek

Where is love
Is it a fantasy

Rebecca Stinton

WHITE NOISE

White noise follows black light, scrambled thoughts racing by.
Good times and bad luck, rolling stones, chemical dust.
Drunken doorbells and chosen doors keep knocking wanting more.
Distorted screams, false ideals, light surrenders, sub-surreal.
Blinding passageways, bone dust beaches, flesh torn trees and seas retreating.
Crowded mushrooms explode from within, just causes, stinking sin.
Bubbles shrink and weather chimes, electrical bursts within pink slime.
Echoes sound, eerily profound, mashed up Plasticine invisible now!

Stefan Robinson

PAT GARRET AND BILLY THE KID

Adios Amigo
(Old friend)
Timber seasoned,
Even-handed,
Angry,
Man of land.
Man of the mind.
Wise councillor,
To this,
Wayward Youth.
Remained,
Noble in defeat.
Whilst I,
Bite bitter,
Into despair.
Yet,
You would not
See me beg,
For bread,
Or friendship.
Nor leave me,
Standing,
At the,
Gates of Hell,
Alone.

Stuart E Wright

WHAT HAS BECOME OF OUR WORLD

A fragile wind breezes my face,
Cold yet warm, perfect time, perfect place,

The sky so clear, with stars in abundance,
A vivid reminder of our mortal insignificance,

Isolated, my mind begins to contemplate and think,
With every thought it becomes easier to blink,

I question why? Where? and what?
Has life's philosophy been lost and forgot,

A contemporary view of a world gone by,
This time we live in is considered a lie,

Yet what is truth, but polite dishonesty,
For along with morals we have lost chivalry,

Men and women of yesteryear,
Fought to promote decency with lack of fear,

Their honour has been washed away,
Been set aside and let to lay,

The dawn of today is allowed to rise,
A dawn so bleak I sit and despise,

Those who frivolously bask in the ambience,
Unaware that they absorb this bedraggled essence,

Our only hope is an eclipse of angelic dreams,
A coalition and constellation of youth's innocent gleam,

So I ponder on, eyes feeling light,
Praying that this new moon restores life's might!

Adam Aboalkaz

HAVE YOU?

Have you ever seen the beauty
in a partner's childbirth pain
or felt her adoration
while dancing in the rain?

Have you ever watched her sleeping
as you gently stroked her skin
adoration in your fingertips
a love from deep within?

Have you ever suffered heartache
being parted for a day
counting down the seconds
you'd trade your soul away?

Have you ever separated
and suffered monstrous pain
every fibre in your body
yearns to hold her once again?

Have you ever watched a thunderstorm
in a lover's warm embrace
or caught a tear of happiness
running down her face?

Have you ever shared a sunset
then watched the stars above
the bubble that your living in
a bubble filled with love?

Have you ever heard contentment
in a lover's subtle sighs
two as one united
as you lay between her thighs

All these things well I have done
and oh so many more
a lucky, lucky, lucky man
with the woman I adore.

Glenn Merrilees

A TRUE VALENTINE RHYME

I thought I'd do a rhyme for you on this Valentine's Day
It saves me from buying a card that gets recycled anyway
To say how much I love you, words are not enough
Although it's not a sloppy rhyme full of slushy stuff

Instead I'll tell you all about what gets on my wick!
Like the way you turn your head to give your nose a pick
And fingernails in the car, lying on the floor
Studying your country maps that really is a bore

Jumping in your sleep and twitching all about
Nicking all the covers so I am left with nowt
Driving like a pensioner, your head just above the wheel
And if we want to have a kiss I have to crouch or kneel

Driving round the car park, trying to find a space
Taking you out shopping with 'that look' upon your face
The effects of just a couple of beers go right to your head
And worrying about our cash being in the red

But I wouldn't change you, not for a million years
I couldn't live without you; the thought reduces me to tears
So I've laid out all your clothes for you to wear tonight
As sometimes outfits you put on can give me quite a fright!

Tracey Watson

BROKEN

I am beaten. My heart will remain broken.
I exhale as my heart strings twist, pulling tort.
Aching. Screaming softly, I feel that I'm choking.
All breath escapes my sore chest at the thought.
I feel weak. My resolve since diminished.
Profound sadness will sear until I am finished.
Pain has become me, my heart torn asunder.
Picking up shards of a heart now left tattered.
With bleeding chest pieces, through meadows I wander.
Dead meadows of heather and memories now shattered.
Throat seizing up. Permit me hard spoken.
My throat clogged with pain from a heart badly broken.

Dean Vega

THE DAY AFTER THE RAIN

We'd had a row
And I came home.
You tried to call
I threw the phone.
The rain outside
Was lashing down.
My folks were driving
Out of town.
I sat alone
Curled in your chair.
I sat and cried,
It wasn't fair.
We were so young
We weren't in love.
Still the heavens
Opened up above.
I realised that
This was the end.

We drove each other
Round the bend.
I snatched a glass
And grabbed the booze,
A night with
Nothing left to lose.
I took a sip
And downed the rest.

I didn't feel
Exactly blessed.
I didn't feel,
In fact, at all.
And all I heard
Was the rain fall
The thunder crash
The lightning strike.
Then heard the buzzing
Of his bike.
I shook it off,
Was just the rain
Why would he come?
It was insane!
But then I heard it
Something more.
Three rappings on

Our stable door.
Looked at my watch
Said it was late.
Head banging
I was in such a state.
Opened the door
Slurred, 'What's the fuss?'
Froze still.
The moonlight
Glowed on us.
He took the helmet
In one hand.
I said I didn't understand.

He stepped inside
And took my waist.
I put one hand
Upon his face.
His leathers gleamed
His hair dripped wet.
Thought back
To the first night we met.
He said he couldn't take any more.
I turned away
To close the door,
And when I turned
He kissed my lips
With softness still,
Hands on my hips.
I pushed him off
I asked, 'Why now?'
Why after we'd just had a row?
He stood there silent
Intensely eyed.
I crumbled to the floor and cried.
He sat down
Took me in his arms.
He vowed to keep me safe from harm.
He vowed to hold me through the night.
He vowed to always be the light.
He promised me the world
And more.
He wiped my tears
And then I saw

What he was holding
In his fist,

The flower
From the first night we'd kissed.
The sun broke through
The windowed hall.
The phone rang
(You had tried to call)
He whispered gently
In my ear.
That I had nothing more to fear.
I stood up
Realised I was soaked
And that is when
I finally spoke.
I asked what he had
Come in aid of.
He said that he
Suddenly fell in love
And had to tell me straight away
Because it would be a new day
And he wanted it to start this way.

Olivia Sklenar

UNTITLED

Shall I play a pretty piece for thee
Upon my guitar, plucking strings
That resonate with such sweet harmony
Whilst mine novice heart softly sings
Along to a heavenly melody
As pure as fresh water springs?

Or perhaps I'll paint a picture?
With each stroke worth a thousand words,
Each word designed to describe a creature
As beauteous and rare as birds
Of paradise, such dazzling features
Which mine brush carefully disturbs.

My blistered fingertips stained with hues
Invented to rightly portray she.
She who I've failed to amuse
With my music, art and poetry.
Works created with nothing to lose
As she waits for a man that's not me.

Christopher Murray

82

BIRTH PAINS

The painful birth of motherhood
So few have really understood
Is but a shadow that foretells
The pain our parents knew so well
Of children singing out farewell

As to their freedom they rush out
With a merry, happy shout
'See you, Mom, Papa,' they call
Do they look back? Not at all
Headlong, heeding freedom's call.

While we stay behind, pretend
It's a new beginning, not an end
They have crossed a finish line
For the first time, we're left behind
Watching, waiting, marking time.

And *these* pains unlike birth pangs go
Not in waves, but slow, real slow
The first sharp stabs are weeks apart
When they forget to call, your heart
Then feel a spasm really sharp.

They carry on their merry way
We check our emails every day
Every text on our mobile
Is opened with expectant smile
Every call is answered while

For them it's, 'Can I call back please?'
Rattled off with smiles, with ease
While we hold back our tears today
Say, 'Sure, but don't forget, okay?'
And hold off for another day.

Until at last the birth pangs ease
They never really ever cease
Some day you know they'll have their own
And that's when you will know they've grown
By then you're really on your own
Not solitary, just alone.

Rohini Sunderam

NOTHING BUT YOU

A butterfly dancing her sweet tunes to me
and the world
if they care to hear her

She flutters her glitter
and pervades the air and my eyes too
with imagination beyond my usual capacity

I'm taken in to the mind's eye
the sweet soul
my breath gets sweeter
and my skin mellows in the dust of her heart
you've been here before haven't you?

She flies above
and beyond, of which she is queen
raising my awareness
shedding old skins

And in that moment
I feel so alive, engaged
starry-eyed
I did not deserve
you gave so much
in just a whisper

To my breath
with you
I am not dead

Danielle Masuccio

REGRETS OF A FALLEN SOUL

I stand at the end looking back . . .
seeing all that has gone before like shadows upon my mind . . .
alone in the dark my hands red with the mark of my guilt . . .
I stand there the madness of regret consuming me . . .
and I think of what could have been . . .

it's easy now with hindsight to choose a different path . . .
knowing what will be . . .
and yet it cannot be undone . . .
my choices cannot be unmade . . .
I did what I did and so I must pay . . .
it might not mean much to those I have wronged . . .
but I would make amends . . .
if I could . . .

pride caused me to fall . . .
and I have been falling ever since . . .
a sinner in the eyes of man and god I have become . . .
yet my heart did not want this to be . . .
how could I have done this . . .

I gaze upon my hands . . .
rubbing them as if to wash away my crime . . .
but I am not worthy of redemption now . . .

for proud and wilful was I . . .
so forgiveness is forever beyond my reach . . .
not that I deserve it . . .
I attempted to hide from what I had done
I tried to pass the responsibility . . .
to make others to blame for my choice . . .
and to free me from my sin . . .

in reality though I cannot escape . . .
my fate is deserved and eternal . . .
I will pay for my crimes . . .
in the heart of all men forever . . .

Peter Madden

LIFE'S ROBOTIC ROUTINE

We wake,
We yawn
We're born.

We crawl,
We walk,
We talk.

We go to school,
We're told to be nobody's fool.

We're told to keep our heads down and get a career,
We're told to constantly show courage and leadership without showing any fear.

We go through the daily routine of doing our nine to five,
We do a little overtime to help ends meet before we keel over and die.

We aim from the start to reach the top,
We just want loads of money because we don't know when to stop.

We argue, we fight, and we go to war,
We kill people that we don't know, without really knowing the reasons what for.

We come home and have our meals and maybe do a few light chores,
We sit and watch television like zombies unaware that we've become bores.

We enjoy the highs but struggle to deal with the lows,
We smoke and take pills to deal with our stress, while drinking beer to drown our woes.

We worry about meeting deadlines and whether if we'll keep our jobs,
We get annoyed at the have-nots getting everything, as in our eyes they're nothing but yobs.

We worry what people think and what they have to say,
We worry about the future instead of just living for today.

We eventually get to the point of asking ourselves what else is there,
We look out the window for hours on end as passers-by stop and stare.

We reflect briefly on what's done and what could have been,
We regret having to spend the rest of our days living the nightmare, instead of the dream.

Ronald Finn

THE BLACK GOWN WOMAN

The poor black gown woman stares through cold grey eyes,
For her world has been dimmed, by the black sin's tide,
And her hearing is impaired,
-With the cruel whispers of the mind,
She will never again find,
-Her pure innocence, washed away with the black sin's tide,

Her blackened heart is still as winter,
Though it does persist to beat,
Through the veins of her black gown,
-To her January cheek,

She shed her white robe freely,
And lost it to the ground,
-Covered in greed, shame and pity,
-All things profound,

Her fragile mind deceived her,
In impossible sugared thoughts,
-In a lost man she saw much deeper,
And paid the price, leading the lost,

Now her face hangs a tale,
And her skin is growing pale,
And the purity of her eyes,
A blackened memory of her hail,

Liam Jon O'Neill

3·1·2012 1.16AM, I COULDN'T FINISH MY WORK, SO I DECIDED THIS IS WHY . . .

Somewhere weird and warm, like a whore's womb we crawl.

Somewhere a devil of no stereotype dwells far too comfortable and sure.

A classy joint of high-pitched tremolo guitar and a slow beat in the back for the dazed to keep pace.

A glass of cool smooth water and a crisp strong tasting cloudy smoke to quench your quiet night.

Once a Trojan horse opened and out fell the midgets from a famous circus to laugh.

He went on sucking the teat from the large breast full of gin, out popped an olive with no pip and a smile.

The stars shine like gold teeth of rich card players and the waitresses like their big tips for serving their drinks.

Killers and pale white dolls with bloody red lipstick that could stain the moon from a distant kiss, all the girls claim to have dated Dillinger, but he just bedded them then beat them with his belt.

We are the generation of the damned and the doomed; we have no era just one year after another.

We count the times on one hand we have invented something new that we are proud of and that our children will re-live after we are long gone.

This world is stale and stinks up the galaxy.

Dimitrios Cofinas

SOLITARY CONFINEMENT

I'm trapped inside this blackness,
No cracks or corners to escape from,
All I hear is my heart,
Drumming an irregular beat,
And drips of rain crashing to the ground,
From the coldness above.
I pray for light to enter my darkness,
And cut through the warriors of death,
But as minutes turn to hours,
And hours become days,
I wonder if I'm dead or alive!

Sarah Seymour

88

SUMMER SONNET

How you shine
Day on day,
How you're mine
Just after May,
When you've come
Everything's bright,
When you've left
Gail's blow on at night.
You seem so calm,
You are always gentle,
You have such charm,
But never sentimental.
When I grow old, we'll still be together
Side by side in your hot sunny weather.

Caroline Cartmill

ENCHANTED BY DEATH

I aspired to be the moon
On a canvas teeming with stars
But now the canvas is dark and blurred
Or is it through my bloodshot eyes?
Enchanted by death I move
I walk alone by night
Will ever someone come along
To break the spell, tearing me apart?
Who rejoices my loneliness?
Who rejoices my plight?
A figment of imagination
Paranoia of someone pulling the strings,
Or is it just me without any inkling?
A caressing whisper, everything will be fine in a trice
I turn a deaf ear, because I know it's just a sweet lie
Seeping through my soul, darkness and spite
Enchanted by death, I move alone at night
Still holding to a thought, that there
Will be at the end of tunnel of death,
A warm, reassuring light

Akshaya

FROST

'Tis a sad face that haunts my windowpane.
Oft I see him, glance and then he's gone again.
Until one midnight, some romantic notion,
perchance to make him smile,
I loosed the latch, called out to him,
yet he, in hesitance, would not come in.
'Twas as if, though, I had let in the nightly chill,
the pane of glass stood there still.
I called again; I meant no ill.

So wake did I to sunshine streaming,
to find, in fruitless patience, I'd gone off dreaming.
But when I went about my window closing,
chanced I upon the glass
his breath, in spiral fashion froze,
and fancied I the imprint of a nose.
This lingering trace of presence while I had slept,
a constant vigil he had kept
and when dawn rose, away he'd crept.

Continued I for weeks in this routine:
arise and find he'd watched me dream
then approach the open window and inspect,
always the outer side,
the shining evidence of this lonesome sentry
for some enchantment surely blocked his entry.
If he, prevented by a charm unsaid
could not pass in so each time fled,
then I would go out to him instead.

Next night I discarded my dress, un-shoed my feet
and bare I went, my lover for to meet.
Closed eyes, I stood amongst the white
and felt his fingers find my skin.
My lips, he kissed, caressed me more
though never once his form I saw.
Dawn woke to see my bed bereft, my clothing tossed.
My mother, at first, she feared me lost.
She found my body, dead, entwined with frost.

Amy Crosby

THE DRAGON WHO HATES POETRY

The dragon who hates poetry is feared throughout the land.
This brutal beast won't back down until all poetry's banned.
So every bard's been bullied by his clamorous command;
'Forget your rhyming game!'
bellows the fiend of fire and flame.

There is no dragon scarier in any Earthly place.
His face looks like his bottom and his bottom like his face.
He'll sneeze out snot as big as rocks – you'd better clear some space –
(Splat!)
'Tremble at my name!'
demands the fiend of fire and flame.

Oh dragon flame! Oh dragon flame!
His face and bum, they look the same.
He rips raps raw, leaves limericks lame
and poets curse the day he came.

When lyric loving Lee tried turning song words into chants,
stopped writing them for people, only wrote them for his plants,
the dragon howled so horribly . . . Lee wet his underpants.
'*Your books I'll maul and maim*!'
he roared. Lee's words went up in flame.

Then Suzie Sue the farmer, she just felt so sad and blue.
To whisper verse in cattle's ears seemed a safe thing to do.
When dragon bawled she fainted, fell face-first into cow poo.
'*Just got yourself to blame!*'
chuckled the fiend of fire and flame.

Oh dragon flame! Oh dragon flame!
Leaves poets feeling fear and shame.
Is there nobody who can tame
this flagrant fiend of fire and flame?

Today, one rhymer stands up tall, calls out to any friend;
'*Our haiku, odes and sonnets 'til my death I will defend!*
Who here will join me now? Help bring this menace to an end?
Our feat will find us fame.
We'll beat this fiend of fire and flame.

Oh dragon flame! Oh dragon flame!
My rhyming comrades, I proclaim
we WILL succeed, earn high acclaim.
The poet's path we will reclaim!'

Dominic Berry

91

THE REVIVAL OF BIRAHINI, THE LONELY LOVER

Across India, upon canvases and within verse,
In songs distilled in the *natyashastra**,
Is captured love-lorn *birahini.*

In the ferment of separation from her lover,
She is tempestuous as a child,
Or sometimes aged beyond her years.

Her breath is frantic.
Her clothes are in disarray.
Her eyes cry rivers to hell.

They understood her illness well, the old artisans.
But behind this, is there no substance?
Is there no strength?

When the gears of industry pause and quieten,
When day's trials find solace in dusk's stillness,
Emotions bloom as lotuses and release fragrance upon the lake of thought.
Atmosphere heightens and gathers ranks amongst stray sentiments.

In my mind's eye, I revive *birahini* and her *sakhi*, her closest friend.
I am with them into the late hours of night.

I see her now in deep thought.
She is strong. She is rested. She is beautiful.
In *birahini*, new worlds are discovered and lost again.
One thought surfaces and sails towards the horizon of clarity:
And thus she speaks:

'Hidden in the deep recesses of my heart,
Lies that masculine being,
Whose gait bears the grace of a hundred tigers.
Whose smile bears the joy of a thousand rising suns.
Whose heart is infinite as the universe.'

'He is neither prophet nor messiah,
Neither scholar nor shaman,
He conjures no tricks.
He preaches no verse.
The world does not see him as special.
But to me, he is in himself, complete.'

Having felt the trance of your adoration, o *birahini*
I no longer fear for your life.
Shed your despair, and embrace the dawn of revival, *jagat janani***.
For you are the body and soul of the world.
In you is conceived the essence of life.

* Natyashastra: a classic Indian text on the practice of dance
** Jagat janani: means woman of the world literally. Here, it refers to the female creative force

Nandita Keshavan

ESTONIA - MUHU ISLAND - A STATEMENT

I walk upon a landscape's ghost
where wheel-ruts; hidden from the eye;
are booby traps for booted feet.
How curious to wade through flowery grass
where farm carts used to trundle in the past.

Remnants of pastures dwindle quickly,
under scrub, and scattered trees
which shroud this old land's history.

I walk upon a landscape's past
where others' feet have tramped before:
not all well-wishing to their hosts.
How curious to probe the alien minds
of those who claim their right to all they find.

Crumbling farmsteads yield to verdure.
Under their encroaching weeds,
their former lives are mysteries.

Freda Bunce

THE TARTED-UP BOOZER IN SHOREDITCH

We ditched our grubby little local
for a tarted-up boozer in Shoreditch.
A bar, a boozaaar, a poncy place
with Moroccan cushions
and leather bar stools, that swivel.

We ditched the familiar smell
of stale beer, and sodden bar towels,
for a molten-orange glowing counter top
with Bar written in neon lights
on top of a fish tank –
(home to five of the most miserable
marine creatures –
I had perhaps ever seen)
poor boozy bar fish –
taking it all in.

So we ditched the rabble and the riot
of our west-end local
for a bunch of moody indie kids
with shit haircuts,
rolling cigarettes and posing
as the singer/actor/part-time model

the girls in green Barbour coats
with bird nest hair,
sipping brown ale
when really they'd like a Bacardi Breezer
secretly –
(and I know this)

and everyone's so worldly
and messed-up and cool,
and they love it here because it's retro,
because it's 'old-school'

And they burn incense sticks
so you can barely tell your pint
from sandalwood –

and the girls look like boys
and the boys wear girls jeans
and it's all very 'scene'.

So we ditched our plump busty landlady
who sweats under bright lights
and breathes heavy as she pulls me a pint

we ditched her
for an indie-sindie barman
dressed in Grandad-style knitwear,
a dicky bow-tie
and Topshop's finest pair of thick black glasses
too big for his face –

'You look a bit like Jarvis Cocker mate –
and those are not prescription lenses
in those frames –
no no.'

He's mechanic and un-charming,
looks alarmed when I ask him:
'So what's your cheapest pint mate?'

He goes;
'No, like, sorry 'cause actually like
we like only do like
hurrrrr, bottles of beer
and they're all like . . .
4 pounds . . . '

So it's all very dark
and we take in the candle-lit ambience,
with random objects:
like a mannequin
and a moose head wearing a top hat
and lampshades like my nan had!

Drinking beer in a bar with no atmosphere –

and I look over at the DJ
and he's dropping beats
behind the smallest DJ booth
I have ever seen.

Next to the gents he's working the decks,
as though he was working the crowd at Creamfields,
and he is going 'absolutely mental . . .'
to a load of people, sat down.

So I begin to miss the local pub's jukebox mix
of punk, of folk, the occasional Irish,
the locals sing-song, soft soles
as they beat battered carpet
and I ditched it;

for Shoreditch!

Drinking in a place,
with no warmth,
no excitement
and distorted drum and base.

Not to mention perhaps the slipperiest floor
that I have ever walked across,
and I'm wearing high shoes yeah?
'Cause it's a little bit posh here,
so I kind of slide into the loos
where girls stare pretentious stares
and flick their hair
and look really posh.

And that's when we go and do some shots,
with indie boy Jarvis –
who is still, 'like, 100% deadpan . . .'

but he doesn't tell us his life story
like our old bloke in our local,
and I could spend a year here
trying to meet an old friend
or something humble
but we leave,
we leave 'cause it's shit.

I ramble home through the city drizzle,
street lights turn puddles jaundice-yellow
and I can breathe again.

Paraffin-blue lights cut through dark
and they make me jump,
so I climb onto the night bus
I take my shoes off

and we travel across this tourist town
to our grubby little local,
just around the corner,
where we know,
we are guaranteed,
to get a lock-in.

Laurie Bolger

GROWING A DREAM

Was it a dream?
No, it has to be real
having my children
because they are here
three decades have gone
in the blink of an eye
but I remember it well
their very first cry
holding them close
teaching them to talk
watching them crawl
teaching them to walk
Yet it seems like a dream
that I had last night
I see it so clearly
so vivid and bright
with the years rolling by
I miss it all so
cuddling my babies
watching them grow
soon perhaps,
they'll have a dream of their own
then I'll have grandchildren
and my dream will have grown.

Daphne Cornell

ELECTRIC BLUE

As sepia cascaded down,
a spirit flew, and flew,
a potion, a lotion drew,
drew, a tense love apart.

Seasoned by lemony sap,
upsurged with lavender balm,
magnetic it fused the dark,
dark, flowing mesmeric force.

Thumping, black swelling heart,
maroon skies, skin torn apart,
forbidden, just hidden form,
form burning with passion!

Blue room, electric power,
brought you to me, too soon
a flower lay blood-red raw,
raw, hair colour of straw.

Weekend tryst, a Cawdor
encounter, embedding our love,
velvet raven wings flew,
flew, shadowing the flame.

Aqua-marine merged gold leaf,
a crescendo of silver spray
conquered the canvas, there,
there, a picture of you.

Burnt wood embers died,
our bodies entwined, midst
forbidden fruit, curse forwarded,
forwarded, unwittingly by Eve?

Seasons of dappled shades,
sideways rain, brilliant white snow,
a present for you, brought tears,
tears, a bitter sweet end?

A union as intoxicating as
sweet wine, masqueraded
pretences, scented letters, lay,
lay, unopened, in dusty places.

Old prejudices still remained,
a single rose lay colourless
above a watery grave, goodbye,
goodbye, my electric blue . . .

Christine Evelyn Hawksworth

MY GOTHIC DREAM

My broken dreams are shattered on the floor,
You do not love the sinner in me no more.
I was your moonlight Cinderella,
You were my Gothic fella.
Under the veil of moonlight you said goodbye,
On a path way to Autumn you left me to die.
I wanted to be like you,
You wanted the same too.
But you abandoned me in the 12th hour,
Purple fairy dust has lost all its power.
A long way from my roots,
Despair down to my boots.
Like a black widow I was hollow hearted,
Like a dragonfly my heart departed.
No need to fear the reaper,
Exile is the greatest keeper.
So I bury you beneath my cold dark altar,
With a dragon reflection, I can not falter.
Papillon fill the skies,
Heaven's full of lies.
Leave me alone with my broken dreams,
And before the return to the sunrises beams.
Chain forever my love,
Like an angel from above.
A lonely beautiful death is all that awaits me,
Free my soul and let me run completely free.
Forever in my Gothic dream.

Beverley Price

CAN SOMEBODY THINK OF THE CHILDREN PLEASE!

Babies are a blessing no matter how they get here
Are we to ensure, then, that the conditions remain unclear
Because . . . things are not perfect and life is hard
And society doesn't stop and invisible forces are in charge
And we don't take stock or even take time
To really nurture ourselves, let alone a precious child
So . . . our babies having babies have been given license to survive
And the only thing to know is how much benefits 'they' will provide
And what other kinda freeness poverty will inspire
A generation of independents count like flames in a fire
Stories and witnesses helpless: *"I just don't know what to do!"*
Parents scared of their own spoilt brats like they didn't make the youth!
Reports repeat retorts of disdain, destruction and despair
And solutions aren't even the focus because our *'massas'* do not care
Depleted facilities, robust policing and no general sense is common
And intellects hold their tongues so as not to intimidate with intellectual jargon
Mob mentality driving life onwards, no real specific direction
And the hatred has polluted all minds, there's no discrimination with this infection
Frantic screams and squeals all at once into the atmosphere
Wild accusations, irrational statements breed the collective monster we call fear.
In our uninformed fright we find anything to justify the plethora of emotions and adrenaline
And continue to deny this result in our nature and blame and attribute it with the feminine

So I have a request, a heart-felt plea
I appeal to the best part of your humanity
To the place you go to learn, forgive and understand
For we have some work to do, every woman, every man
Can we please take a moment please to think of the children?
As it stands, we stand, it would seem, for chaos and confusion
These poor babes have no clue of the oblivion they are born into
Yet are blamed unashamedly for the decisions one makes in youth
I take this time to make my plea
Can someone think of the children, please?

The latest babysitter is no good, the service is detrimental
Parents take the role seriously, your guidance is essential
Kids getting bigger and basic speech they cannot handle
Little *zom-babies* turned beasts if your dare change the channel
Young mothers grinning proudly proclaiming, *'Dis child is too bad!*
Can't nobody speak to my child . . .' the sentiment is just sad
Tell-lie-vision occupying their developing thought space
You wonder why your under ten-year-olds struggle largely to communicate
Showered with gifts as standard like the misguided babe deserves it
If he breaks it in one of his many tantrums, money you don't have can replace it
Kids pacified once more you can re-join your peers to drink and be merry

Don't you care who your children are talking to?
Why does your six-year-old have a BlackBerry?
Left up to technology and the ever honest media, nobody's raising these babes any more
So when they stop being cute and use their bad attitude on you, your shock meets your heart on the floor

I remind you of my request from the very depths of me
And appeal once more to your humanity
To the place you go to learn, forgive and *overstand*
For we have some work to do, every woman, every man
Can we please take a moment please to think of the children?
As it stands, we stand, it would seem, for chaos and confusion
These poor babes have no clue of the oblivion they are born into
Yet are blamed unashamedly for the decisions one makes in youth
I take this time to make my plea
Can someone think of the children, please?

The biggest trouble I see in these my tender years
Is a common lack of male influence when we watch how children are reared
Even the term 'reared' I use extra lightly
Because they are being dragged up to be someone unsightly
So adulthood ensues and the law is applied
When these non-taught children age in-charge of their lives
Relationships are unpopular and the sexes cannot be friends
So child support comes as standard, benefits make amends
I should have some kids by now man or no man
Normality is to go fumbling through life without working a plan
I couldn't do that to a life, make one without being ready
So I'm wrong for wanting quality and life that's more steady

But can I take this time to re-make my request
Open your ears, or your hearts, whichever will give you this message the best
May the words resonate so you can firmly stand
For we have some work to do, every woman, every man
Can we please take a moment please to think of the children?
As it stands we stand it would seem for chaos and confusion
These poor babes have no clue of the oblivion they are born into
Yet are blamed unashamedly for the mistakes one makes in youth
I take this time to make my plea
Can someone think of the children, please?

The children are the future, blah blah youth, blah blah growth
Constant talks around the young, sentiments used by those who only care to boast
You are not a superhero for raising your babes alone
Nor having more than the average, so let's get off that tone
Babies are born with all the knowledge of the universe
Only to be dumbed down by our influence in societal commerce
Please refrain from projecting your fears and short comings

On the babes who come with messages of how better to run things
They don't deserve your insecurity and lacking discernment
Yet so many babes enter in through fleeting moments, no time is really spent
And stupid baby mamas never acknowledge their blatant idiocy
And pardon this image, but why does your four-year-old play casually with your *bitty*?
And these thugs who get to be fathers are either absent or in denial
And the answer to this mess is also known as *Jeremy Kyle*

So as if you didn't know I have a question
And if it's too much to grasp let me make it a suggestion
Because the state of affairs is too serious for TV
And my heart bleeds for the broken unit once called family
So can we please take a moment to think of our children?
They deserve some fresh air to this world of pollution
Every one of us cares and wants them to grow well
And avoid the state we have endured in this life of hell
Once more beautiful people, I make my plea
Can someone think of the children, please?

The story doesn't stop at the patter of tiny feet
For all of us were once there counting down in however many sleeps
And days were like seasons, with adventures galore
Then people stopped treating you like you were special any more
And the friends you made in school, in the world famous playground
Where friendships started and ended with thumbs up, or thumbs down
Now separated with age and ever massing inhibitions
Gone are the days when, avoiding the mud was the only mission
And we grew, got too big and too serious for fun
Now only feeling it in the lives of our little ones
So even we are the children who have had more time to play
But somehow we have distorted our joys through the day

So once more may I ask you to return with me
Because we are still the children, all of you, and definitely me
It's a community necessity, not just my plea
Let us really think of the children, please.

Maya Johnson-Hector

TREAD SOFTLY
(For my loved ones)

Tread softly when you come
As I have had it tough
Tread softly when you come
As I've not had enough

Tread softly when you come
My time has gone so fast
Tread softly when you come
My heart's still in the past

Soft arms to hold me warm
I've weathered lots of storms
Silk wings to pin me down
As I have been around

Will you wipe away my tears
And sweep away my fears
Will you fly me on the breeze
Let me keep my memories

Tread softly when you come
Don't hurt those I leave behind
Tread softly when you come
I'll leave my love for them to find

Will you dress me in gold
So I don't look so old
Will you ease away my lines
And dismiss my petty crimes

Are you coming as a dove
With messages of love
Will you give me love that's new
As I'm leaving quite a few

Tread softly when you come
Now my life on Earth is done
Speed me to love that's new
I'll put all my trust in you

Are you coming with the light
I won't fight you, I won't try
In the morning or the night
Now it's time for me to die
Tread softly when you come, we'll meet again loved ones, goodbye.

Mary Lockhart

A (NOT SO) BRIEF HISTORY OF MINE FROM BLACK HOLES TO CHEERIOS .

When I was a kid, I loved Sesame Street.
I'd sit and watch it every day of the week!
Grover would make me laugh with his comedy genius,
All those great Muppets had many things to teach us!

The count, in his Transylvanian tongue,
Would rhyme each number, one by one.

This seemed, to me, a clever thing to do,
Simply rhyming something, that's important to you.
John Lennon rhymed, what love is for you and me,
De La Soul rhymed why the magic number was 3!
Then Scroobius Pip rhymed the Periodic Table,

Now I'll have a turn, let's see if I'm able!

I have picked a subject of great abundance,
To see if I can give it, some style and some substance . . .

A star is born from a nebula,
From gas and particles formed over millennia.
They get pulled together by gravity's caress,
And once they clump, warm like a furnace.

So a star is basically a big ball of gas,
With hydrogen fusing helium, to help give it mass.
It's this fusion of the elementary,
That now shines upon the likes of you and me.
And for billions of years these stars hum,
The sweet refrain of equilibrium!
But eventually hydrogen's goose gets cooked,
So next in the chain is where we all get hooked!

Because up next is the formation,
Of the element carbon,
Which causes stuff to clump and harden.
Well, actually, it's not as simple as that,
But I won't bore you with that triple alpha tat!

Then when a star reaches old age,
It doesn't retire, or start smelling like sage!
If the star is big and dense enough,
The more it cooks and forms other stuff.

(Up to 92 stuffs, to be exact.
This isn't science fiction, it's all science fact!)

104

And once they're forming, the star is defiant,
Into growing itself, into a 'Red Giant'.
You can see this for yourself, in the night-time sky,
Glowing red, like a nocturnal eye.

Look up to Orion, to its top left, Betelgeuse waits to prove what happens next.
Eventually the star will start contracting,
This causes one hell of a nuclear reaction!
A chain of events impossible to halt,
It releases the elements locked in its vault.
An explosion so massive, it can be seen in the sky,
Billions of miles from the naked eye.

A supernova, not made from champagne,
And into the cosmos the elements rain.
92 different LEGO bricks forged,
In the star's burning belly they were cooked and stored!

And wouldn't you know it,
Or begin to conceive,
These elements are what make,
This planet with sea.

What makes the ground beneath our feet,
What makes the fruit we like to eat.
What makes the iron coursing our veins,
What makes the carbon from which we are made.

Because, if you're lucky enough,
As we certainly are,
From a star, you're not too near or too far!

That's when life as we all know it,
Forms and evolves to create a poet!
A poet who, in his own little way,
Has chosen to educate on this sunny day!

It takes 8½minutes for the light of the sun,
To reach our planet and touch everyone.
But it took us hundreds of thousands of years,
To realise what made us, into people and peers.

Love is the answer, so I believe,
But science too answers questions,
Too awesome to conceive.

Steve Collett

A FORM

A form's purpose should meander,
for form will unwillingly meander by purpose,
unless on purpose one wilfully admits in doing so.

What's four plus four
if we could change it
for the shape of

ten-

pin bowling I played without
a ball of course! For the charge
seemed much so they

rolled:

the coloured shoes
with the most jagged of bounces-
It seemed more savoury
to change the purpose of a

form

they asked me to fill
though I'd conjure towards
the exit-door and needle-

less

episode

arm in arms, mother always
took this seriously. A psychotic

of stand-up comedy stood lone
in the line of martyrs for
the evening watch then crazed

circles

were all we'd to walk
with crazed eyes and a

deep

swimming tongue for the free
man's meal. Watching the

cloud

of chalk seep over the brows.
No!
It's eight!
I knew better for spider's wouldn't
stage you and your lover a

picnic

area where I was designated
with a painted finger:
Only on this lawn!
Teacher too was

                                        wrong
way I turned once
and shoved to rotate by hostile
faces- I could only talk
                                        back
to back. I must now
imagine your laughter after
if I were there, if you were,
if what I said was
                                        funny
joke the others concluded
but it needed more attention on
                                        timing.
I thought I'd leave for the barred window
where the rejected novels of the
waiting room would paint my
                                        background
cold in the grey-floored
passages filled with murmurs,
chasing, instruction, detention and
                                        whistling
was the sound past
his hierarchical nasal hair of my
                                        conviction
I held onto for without
conviction there was no need
to say not ten, eight! And the
                                        knife
gnawed away biting
through my polyester pocket.
Time not ever harsher
than today mightily felt
                                        long;
about a seven inch blade
with five teeth at its tip
dressed in a silver line and equal
like precise perfect
                                        waves
mixed with giggles if again
the bitch had grasped
more words to
                                        say
would I be guilty?
For explain could the
                                        spam
be unfurled with the tin-opener?

Encoded with number sequences
without a thick breadth of organ-pink
all at the helm of the

              mouse

which scurried left to
right seeking refuge. It didn't feel
like home yet, I hadn't a broom.
The white arrow's back,

              breathing

without a throat to gasp.
Leathered sofas made
sounds when one considered
to find something that transcended
completely impassive.

              Ten!

It's ten for me. Fuck you
multiplied with a vehemently
executed

              kick

the stool. He nodded
as knots tightened.

              Understand?

My companion in circle walkers
hadn't the faculty to

              question

what's four plus four?
If I could change it
for the shape of

              ten

commandments or fallacies,
you should criticise.

Lakhveer Singh Azad

THE LOST VALLEY

The branches are all entwined as they are bound.
Stretched out and not making a sound.
They seem to be entangled like a rope.
Looking for the natural light of hope.

The foxglove flower with its pink petals shaped like
a bell.
That cannot be rung and does not tell.
The leaves with the rain dew.
All shiny and new.

The fir trees which are on display with spider
webs made of lace.
Don't look at all out of place.
The ivy that climbs and covers the bark
of the trees.
While the wind whistles through the breeze.

The elderflowers which are green and white
look like a hand that it held out.
The Lost Valley which you walk through.
Bringing in glorious colours which are bright
with plants being renewed.

The winter visitor who comes to our shore.
In the Lost Valley we are building an
artificial site to attract even more.
With his bright orange chest and his
feathers that are so blue with tiny
white flecks.
He drives into the water for his usual suspects.

For he is the King when it comes to fishing
and he doesn't need a net to haul in his catch.
And if a fisherman is near then he will have
met his match.

Angela Jory

LAUGHTER IS MY SUNSHINE

Laughter is my sunshine,
It keeps me warm and sane.
It makes my life more bearable,
Even when in rain.

So when the sky is grey and dull,
I let laughter tan my life.
Its rays adjust my focus,
And irons out all my strife.

It shines away my cobwebs,
And makes my future bright.
It helps to grow my spirit,
And gives me clearer sight.

It's the silver lining in my clouds.
Its power lifts my mood.
I don't know why or how it works,
But it's my daily 'Sunshine' food.

And when life gets me down,
I use laughter to lift my soul.
I find things to make me laugh,
To take back my mind's control.

I don't allow grey weather,
To darken up my mind.
I use laughter as my rainbow,
To bring colours to unwind.

A cheerful heart is good medicine,
For it melts away my pain.
And when I laugh at life and self,
There's an inner joy I gain.

Laughter oils the hinges in my life,
When I'm creaking under pressure.
It helps to lighten up my load,
And leaves me with a treasure.

A powerful weapon to behold,
When feeling weak and stressed.
It has such tremendous value,
Reminding me that I'm blessed.

So whatever makes me laugh,
And whatever makes me smile.
I'll seek these things to find,
A life that's more worthwhile!

Samantha Wallace

LLAMAS

Llamas never have been famous; don't know what their Latin name is.
Canis, Lupus even Rattus splash their Roman history at us.
Still the llama, large and lairy, often soft and rarely scary,
Even with her finest dairy has her name in tatters.

Less a goat and more a camel, smiles of yellowing enamel,
This is how I would describe the llama and her playful vibe.
Sure, I could say one more bit; that infamous thing, llama spit.
Perhaps it's merely llama wit amongst the llama tribe.

But others not quite so forgiving of the llama's way of living
See this sign as crude and rude and ponder ways to have her sued,
Although she's just a llama and that's just what llamas do.

Reputation all in tatters, who can say what really matters,
When llama hears the natters of her actions hissed and booed?

So on to facts less widely known to bring the llama's good name home,
Not knowing I was on such quest, but feeling I should try my best,
For creatures would if creatures could explain their traits misunderstood,
Replacing all the bad with good and not just done in jest.

In the moments after birth, baby llama's first on Earth,
Llama, with her little tongue, just cannot clean her babe from scum,
So instead she wakes him gently from his dreams, not accidentally,
But with love and care a plenty she will nuzzle and she'll hum.

As if she sings a lullaby unheard by man, but my, oh my!
The baby llama duly loves his mummy's humming truly,
Because he's just a llama and that's just what llamas do.

Reputation still so graceful as a full-grown takes the baby's place,
Until he spits, which hits your face and thus must build his name anew.

Alina Gregory

UNCONVENTIONAL FESTIVAL

My festival is us,
Full of lust,
Breaking my heart into two,
Just for you.
Foolish of me,
When all I can see,
Is me waiting in the wings.
Hurt by recent findings.
Best prepare this one woman show.
I press my lips to pen
My cathartic friend
My words fall onto page,
Shoot around the stage,
Aiming, for someone
Like fireworks firing off my tongue –
Caribbean colour filled
Like they do in Notting Hill.
Your words!
Yes, your words are the sticks
That causes hits upon my steel drum.
Is this how you get your fun?
As my heart rhythmically pounds
And then
Stops.
Until, you bring life to my lips
Tapping with finger tips
Your music
I queued hours for,
Chords I adore
Just for me, I'm unsure?

We're stuck in Glasto mud!
Raining passion begins to flood
Tent has collapsed
Under our relapse
Have I lost you in the crowd?

There you are
With poison nectar in your hand
Toasting this vision you understand.
I'll be your modern Venus from above
Bringing a Roman festival of love.

Where you feast on me
Whilst I lay starving,
Fasting like they do for Eid.
I want our Mecca to succeed.

I will walk in Pilgrim shoes
Across a stage just to prove
My festival is us
My festival is you,
Began so unconventional,
We're no longer two.

Natasha Wright

YESTERDAY

I remember yesterday.
The sky was blue, the sun was hot, the sea was calling me –
A beautiful summer's day.
On the beach I met a girl building sandcastles,
She asked, 'Would you like to play?'
And we did. Every day on the beach and in the sea.

Each year I met my friend on the beach to play.
Building sandcastles, collecting seashells, swimming in the sea –
Always a beautiful summer's day.
In-between the summers many letters we sent –
We shared our thoughts, our secrets, our dreams,
In touch, but miles apart our time was spent.

Thirty years past.
The sky was blue, the sun was hot, the sea was calling me –
A beautiful summer's day.
On the beach I met my friend and we watched two girls at play.
Building sandcastles, collecting seashells, swimming in the sea –
They were our daughters.

We remembered yesterday.

Karen James

A LITTLE WINDOW

You sit in a padded cell, they doubted your mind.
You have a little window, with which you stare out.
Out into a world of people, people so cold and distant.
They stared at you then, they didn't understand you.
Some laughed too hard, some eyed you with suspicion.
You sit everyday just staring, wondering what time it is.
Is time real in here anymore, when did you last see a nurse.
Or hold your purse, when did you last see a mirror.
Is your face the same, do you know your name.
You see a fly on the wall, wondering if it can talk.
It's been days since you spoke, the walls close in every day.
Stuck in this little cube, you're in here 24 hours a day.
You wonder how old you are, you can hear other patients.
Screaming loudly at the silence, but still you don't say anything.
You sit on your bed, your bed still unmade from previous days.
Your little bit of responsibility is too much, you saw God in your father.
But you hated God then and now, you killed your perceived God.
They sentenced you to life, a life of solitude and madness.
A plastic cup is all you own, placed atop a cardboard table.
Its frosty outside but you're not cold, you cut yourself to feel the pain.
A pain you enjoy on your own, you have cut marks a mile long.
You have no visitors or friends, you stare at bare white walls.
No pictures hang to soothe you mind, your hair once so beautifully long.
Is cut and burnt so short, your eyes don't shine like before.
Your skin is wrinkled but you're not old, your bed is your only seat.
The floor is solid marble stone, cold in the morning, warm at night.
Hour after hour you sit and stare, food is pushed through a hole in the door.
But it will lay uneaten like the rest, a fly looks at you disapprovingly.
You turn and stare right back, trying to stare the insect out.
Then you realise slowly, slowly, that the wall is totally bare.
Days, months and years have passed, everyday is the same for you.
The silence is all consuming, biting into every inch of your life.
A single tear runs down your face, you're a human statue of skin and bone.
Yet you never tire of being alone, you rarely sleep and never dream.
Your life never turned out as you wanted, you're a free person in your head.
You're a free bird who can fly away, up and away and past a little window.

Robbie Campbell

CROSSROAD

The book is near its end.
the flame all ready to puff –
I am standing at a crossroad,
and I know not where to stop.
But I fancy myself resolved
To make the best of the day;
So that when my time comes,
I may be ready for death.

Death is the frolicking water,
Of the lake I saw, the other day
Or the lady with cold hard eyes,
Embedded in her elevated face.
They are one and all to me.
Countenance, I hardly divide
But I long to know what to find
When my body is engulfed in flames,
Or eaten away by worms.
So that when my time comes,
I may be ready for death.

Sampriti Singha Roy

DESIRE

If life was a fairy tale
Then what would we do?
No good to balance the bad
Nothing to look forward to

We would be floating, lost
Our desires everywhere
Yet always fulfilled
From the thin of air

This is what makes us human
These wrongs and these rights
The bad making good, greater, and
Those things that keep us up at night

Lee Cameron

FISH

In my distant dream, I see you
My eyes don't want to open and let you go.
But the pain of betrayal rips my heart,
And, I stand in the water like a helpless fish.

The endless rain pours down on me.
I am drenched in our memories.
Is there no way to escape this painful love?
I wish this were my last dream.
I'm swimming against powerful tides,
I can't survive – I'm a helpless fish.

The moon is turning hazy, I can't see you.
Is this the power of true love?
I don't want to go on with this pathetic existence,
I don't want to live anymore like a helpless fish.

The tsunami of my turbulent emotions,
Is going to engulf me.
The shards of my painful past,
Overflow from my broken heart,
Leaving me only fleeting memories of our happiness.
I can't survive this love – I'm a helpless fish.

The gullible me and the sly you,
Was our love doomed from the start?
Don't leave me to be eaten alone.
In these mystifying depths, like a helpless fish.

It is courageous to live for a dead lover,
It is cowardly to pine for a cheater,
This coward continues to drag herself into the depths of the infinite ocean.
Like a fish that can't swim,
Like a dream that became a nightmare,
I flap fruitlessly, like a helpless fish.

Your hand as cold as ice, I never felt it,
Your fastidious personality that I forever tried to please,
I want to hate you but I remember your gentle words.
Lie to me that this is not the end.

In my distant dream, I see you.
I want to go on living but I'm half dead.
There can never be another you,
Someone else is not good enough for me.
Perhaps, we'll be together in the next lifetime?
For now, I'll continue living like a helpless fish.

Preethi Viswanathan

THE BEST OF BRIGHTNESS TO THE EAST TOMORROW

It has its own rhythm, peculiar to content.
A measured voice,
the phrasing, a rise and fall of cadences.

I think of those who wait and listen.
Edging further westwards while filling.
Pushing slowly northwards. Heavy seas?
Reserved for the West and Southern Straits.
For whom and by whose bidding?

Millibars increasing from five to seven.
Occasionally at first, good becoming moderate.

The mystery is enacted every night.
It is a recital I cannot resist,
rendered to the creak of timbers resisting winters' blasts.
It is a lullaby and I rejoice in a safe harbour.
Lows cannot reach me, highs elude me.
I set a medium course prolonged, sleep induced.

The best of brightness to the East tomorrow,
Perhaps gale later.

Barbara Turner

CLUBBING

Boys in the club, thinking they are it.
If only they realised their chat-up lines are shit.

Girl in the corner with a bright red mini skirt.
Truth is she is just a little flirt.

Man over there with tight blue jeans.
Mainly looks at fellas, we know what that means.

Two girls on the dance floor give each other a kiss.
Are they good friends or should I give them a miss.

You see all sorts when you go out at night.
Just hope it doesn't all end in a fight.

Giles Ayling

THE PUB

The pub is a place where you go to unwind and relax
To have a laugh and a joke or learn unusual facts
You may attend in company and exchange your news and views
You can choose to stand at the bar or maybe use the pews

A night out with your lovely wife is bound to include the pub
A pint of beer, a glass of wine and possibly some grub
You could, of course, be on your own – the pub still welcomes you
Allowing you to gather your thoughts then do what you have to do

Whether you are in a group, a pair or on your own
You get the feeling in the pub that you are not alone
You may get chatting to the staff if you feel inclined
They've probably heard it all before yet still they do not mind

You moan about this and groan about that then tell a silly joke
It's you they're talking about my friend – for 'there's nowt stranger than folk'.
All the things mentioned above I've done so many times
I've even read this poem out loud to make sure that it rhymes

Back to the title of this ode 'The Pub' is what it's called
I feel so much better now – my pint is being pulled
On my own or with my friends never doubt or fear
The truthful reason for my visit is something that's called beer

David Lowe

WITHOUT A CARE IN THE WORLD

Tiny fingers and tiny toes
A little mouth and a button nose
Born with fluffy duckling hair
And her tummy bare
Without a care in the world.
A mouth begins to learn to speak
Some say first words, I say it's a squeak
Her feet begin to patter round
Without a care in the world.
The mess, the screams, the finger paint
The creative moment that cannot wait
The camera that clicks at every memory
Without a care in the world.
The first day at school
The children trying to act cool
The innocence that overcrowds them all
Without a care in the world
The questions start coming for a mobile 'phone
And the innocent voice sets to an angry tone
The change begins to suddenly appear
Without a care in the world.
Next comes the boyfriends, the angry debates
The question of 'should I even retaliate?'
The harsh words that are spat without the hate
Without a care in the world.
With every care in the world one day,
She sits there, and lets her thoughts lay
The world seems to turn at last
The school days, the friends, they're all in the past
The loneliness of the world sets in,
The question of, 'will I ever win?'
The fear, the sadness, the independence grows
Where did the time go? Nobody knows
And before you know it, time's turned around
Born with little fingers and little toes
A tiny mouth and a button nose
She came out with fluffy duckling hair
And her tummy bare
Without a care in the world.

Caitie Bennion-Pedley

119

UNTITLED

Are you an angel sent from Heaven above
To quell the ghosts of my tortured past?
You have given me so much support,
And I hope a friendship that will last.
A smile that melts the strongest heart,
And a laugh that echoes in any room,
With eyes that lift my spirits when I'm down,
And a face that dispels the darkest gloom
I cannot describe beauty like yours
Each facet of your being and how you care,
From your delicate feet and your painted toes
To the scent and feel of your auburn hair.
You wove a spell I cannot break,
And strong feelings since we met.
My heart beats faster when you are near
And your love I never will forget.

Stephen Mortlock

AN ISLE OF HOPE

I cannot bear to witness the traumas of my history.
Through life's storms, I have faced the challenges and losses.
'Everything will be alright,' – 'rubbish' is what I say to that.
As I went into a whirlpool of self-destruction,
I was ready to become the ultimate deception.
Happiness. It's a handy cloak.

On the bow of my vessel I see the Hope that may be,
An Isle of Hope where these cloaks are no use to me
'Bring up the sails' I say! – 'We have Hope to discover!'
Yet, the storms keep brewing and the seas keep chewing
Away my memories, plunged into an abyss.
Happiness. It's taking anchor.

As I keep sailing towards the Isle of Hope,
I will keep fighting for a difference for my crew.
In this life I will not set anchor until I see the Hope
That waits for me. I may drown in the Sea of Sorrows
But I know Hope will lift me up on the voyage of life.
Happiness.
Engraved on my vessel.

Paul Phillips

120

CAVERNS

As I walk through the annals of my mind
through the passages that twist and wind
I walk deep into the darkness there, the one that hides thoughts of despair.

I remember the days when it was not like this.
When my desires were met, and the world was bliss.
Of wonderful things and the places I had been.
And the beautiful girl I loved and the things we had seen.

But once she had left the lights had gone out.
The laughter had vanished but so had the shouts.
Nothing remained in the dark annaled halls.
Nothing remained . . . no laughter or calls.

And now a stroll, broken tears on my face.
As something follows maintaining its pace.
But unlike me, it will not leave this place
For it was born in the shroud that I hate.

I dare not turn and gaze at its figure.
For I know why it spawned
I know that terrible trigger.

When my angel left, it crawled from the depths.
Under the caverns of my mind, in the darkness it slept.

But now it's awake and follows my tracks.
Thinking that I am too weak to fight back.
But I know that these caverns, in the end are mine.
And it shall stay that way till the end of time.

So when you walk down your own path.
Remember no matter how cold or how harsh.
That place is yours and yours alone.
And no foul entity may call it home.

So now you turn to face your monster spoken.
The thing that sprung up when your heart had been broken.
Yet steel your nerves and let it be known
That it shall be plunged back into the dark . . .
From whence it had awoken.

Thomas Roberts

'FOOSH'

The greatest thing I have ever learned
Is how to stay awake past bedtime;

(because as a woman,
          you know,
one must remain
independent
past her bedtime)

With shoulders squared and chest thrust out
And eyes stuck on the wall behind

          Your Eyes

are flecked
with the fleeting ghosts
and transparent markings
          we left
          when you
pressed your palms into mine;

and I can remember

          once,
           when I was distressed
           And you came to me and
draped me in your arms
& dropped them like pink-lace peach-y-hue
all down the length of my spine

                    --

          It is
Cold
& damp in here,
tangling at the borders of the sheets with you
          and there,
          within you,
I find myself stranded on one side
Of the thin white line
which runs between love and hate and
something to make us both behave a little bit silly

                    (a foolish thing to do;
                    it was, a fleeting fallacy –)

that leaves you
          white as
lilies bending,

122

      & ready as
frail lily flowers
      pretending
that they
      are more
      than love's ephemeral mayflies.

        --

I remember when you held me
And your heart pulsed out of itself
a wild thread
that wound between us
  charging the balance of my own
  into the stumbling of the many many,
and combining together our two rhythms
summoned the
off-beat sounds of *lub-dub* // *dub-a-dub* drumming.

        --

Your heart is cold,
        My love,
Cold as a cold fist clenching,
sour like breath staled from
coffee in the morning

      & the white powder capsules you used
to stave off the heavy insomnia
that clouds over you when
everything you've worked for
weighs heavy and buries itself
on top of you.

How many lifetimes might slip us by?

Living, as we do, off of softly-spoken dialects
in the starry-eyed hours when sleep hides from us
& the white-hot resin on your lips
leaves me sticky as apple pie.

The night-time makes
two glassy pools out of your eyes
      that
      show you
      to me
in the hours when the world is shrunk

and you and I
lie here,
only

Shattered to
slivers of fretful wakefulness
whilst we trade back-and-forth stories
of other lovers,
and of the-time
I ran aground atop of another man's thigh.

It is always in the darkness that we might promise
      to always
      be at one and always
      | ----- // | --;;,
      and always to care,
      to care deeply
      for one another

But now the night twists our words
to raindrops,
and presses eager ant bodies to wine.

Together we spur one another
on
 up
on
      to greater heights
of caffeine-cannibalisation;
that keep us alive
for a full twenty-four hours' worth,
of romantic pedantries,
of stale inter-intradepencies:
that heavy stench of I-love-you-always
and say-you-will-always-be
      mine;

and
I would love to tell you the truth,
    My Love,

but   forever
is such a long time.

I do not know death,
but spend nights
lying beside you
 like a magpie buried under

124

a snowshovel
until the dawn thaws our bodies
under heady heat & the sun's summer shine.

Your eyes are

 watching me,

They are
 yellow
 & they are watching me.

There they are
Out there
Out late
like a streetlamp caught
out, burning out,
after the starlight shines.

Darling dithering Insomniac:
Your tongue broken
and spirit shot through
in the early hours

I once gathered the world between us
and held it in my lap
 like
painted flowers

that are you;
(that they are pure as pure gold, as you);
and oh that
          there they are:

And
y'are, tired and dead,
I fear,
from another night
of
waiting too long for the sun to rise,

because every new morning we see in together,
is another night without saying goodbye.

Sarah Lee Lian Hand

BLEEDING RAINBOWS

The pen beckons full with red ink. It writes a story of disillusionment.
I look into the light reflecting from the shards of a smashed prism,
                                        bleeding rainbows,
And hallucinates history; soldiers raising arms, Romans in skirts, Greeks, Viking
Celts with severed heads attached to their belts, like talismans,
Dripping brains of saw dust, in their chipboard chariots.
                        Am I chasing smoke through two way mirrors?

Ananda Lowe

HIBISCUS; ROSE OF CHINA

A satisfying group of letters;
three vowels forcing the correct pronunciation.
The 'u' so rounded, so final.

'Otherwise known as . . .' (the label is handwritten).
'Blooms for one day only,' Withers, dies.
Does that mean tomorrow never comes?

Does the bush with one mighty sigh empty its lifeblood into waiting petals?
Does each thrusting, blushing bloom lie back on its stem,
gasping, climaxing?

I stand and hold the untidy, crimson straggle to my cheek
and scoop the sunshine from its centre to my palm.

Tonight, when all have left this Eden, ignorant of the rape committed
as doors closed on visitors,
will each petal take a last breath
and drift this way, that way, to the moss below?

What is this death worth to them who choose to spend their day elsewhere?
What will it mean to those who came and read the label?

'Tell me Rose of China,' I whisper, 'was it worth the effort?
Did coming when you did, make it all worthwhile?'

Nina Ford ·

MEMORY

What we remember seems to change
And darken round the edge.
Shapes and figures distort and fade
Our memory no longer holds truth.

Do we trust it? This reliance can
Cause fear and confusion.
Our memories become our enemy,
Blinding us from what we know.

The present, a gift.
The truth is no longer hidden in haze.

Laura Doherty

PILLS AND NEEDLES

Nobody's happy with what they were born
Their body's no temple, in their side it's a thorn
Syringes and knives, incisions and blades
Why not banish your greys with some bleached blonde shades?

Pills and needles, scalpels and files
Hair extensions that trail on for miles
Cheap plastic nails and streaky false tan
Stick-on eyelashes to impress your man

Surgery reverses the hands of time
Fillers and implants return you to your prime
Plump and youthful and glowing skin
Perfectly sculpted cheekbones and chin

Spend up your savings to whiten your teeth
Tattoo on make-up to hide what's beneath
Pay your surgeon with all that you own
A few nips and tucks and your body's been cloned

Lipo on the stomach to move fat to the bum
Regular Botox leaves your face smooth but numb
Thousands of pounds spent on vanity's name
Uniqueness is lost, they all look the same

Susan Thornberry

SPRING TIDE ON THE RIVER LYNHER

Now the Moon is Milk
And the sucking tide
Leaves lonely old boats
Asleep on the mud,
Through dull eyes peering
And salt shrouds sighing.

Then at sunset the sea
Springs up like a tune,
So they shake their old heads
And lift up their skirts
Dancing with mem'ries
Of lovers long dead.

There's an old lady
Who lives by the ford,
Gazes through curtains
At her ebbing stream,
Sighs at the quick and
The young and the strong.

At sunset she rises,
Closes her curtains,
Warms up some milk for
Her tea. Then she mounts
The stairs and lies with
That lover long dead.

Lies with that lover
As pale as the moon.

Keith Rossiter

ADVENTURERS OF THE VIVID BLUE

James is here,
Scruff of hair and grinning,
At my door
Knocking with small quick hand
'Playing out?'
Tasting adventure in the early morning air.
Up and into the day we already own.

Daring and half-admiring each other
In turn.
Sharing the ache of unripe summer fruit
Scrumped from neighbour's garden.
Knock knock ginger
And run and run,
Breathless and laughing in the peril of the moment.

We are cowboys
We are spacemen
Colour flashes in the long thicket,
Endless game hide-and-seek.
We are friends
With the minor confidences
Of children.

Late for tea, legs slowed,
Bikes across the quiet roads
Clutching this sprig of wonder we do not see,
Pedal into the darkening blue
Filled with the hollowness of sweets
And mirage passed
Back home . . . back home.

Kathy Parkhouse

TRUNCATED PROSE

Truncated prose with purpose fluttering
Stops by a jam jar open toed
''Tis yours fair buttercup', came the muttering
From the long grass by the road

The summer fly had grazed one ear
Its sound was so discreet
''Tis yours fair buttercup', to his rear
Did once again repeat

Truncated prose with purpose stuttering
Was now in some distress
''Tis yours fair buttercup', was spluttering
What got you in this mess?

Tony Stevenson

IT'S ALL ABOUT ME

It's all about me, what I do and what I am, it's all about me
Where I go and where I'm from
It's all about me, what I wear and what I say, it's all about me,
What I do every day.

It's all about me, my wealth, my health, my happiness.
It's all about me, my love, my children, my God no less.
My friends, my job, my football team I guess.
It's all about me, about what I see.

It's not about me, it's about you, me, we and us.
It's about love given without warning, without fuss.
Listening to those we love and trust and giving
The benefit of doubt to others.

It's all about me, it's all about you, about being caring,
About being true.
It's asking the question, who are we?
It's all about you, it's all about me.

Mark Wetherby

SECOND CHANCE

This isn't just a poem . . .
It's a test to see how strong your heart is

They say love only comes once . . .
That as soon as that love is forsaken
The heart of the beholder is then shaken

Friends and family are there to comfort you
But still your heart remains a cold blue
The fire and ambition you had has disappeared
Instead it is now replaced with hatred and fear . . .

Fear that your heart will stay alone forever
So you turn in on yourself and keep a distance from anyone whomsoever

But then you find that someone new
People like that someone you have seen very few
Slowly but surely that someone brings back that smile that you once knew
Your tendency to grow fond of everything that leaves that person's lips grew

But now you are confused whether this is true love . . .
That person does everything to make you feel higher than the clouds above

And now that someone grasps your hands in front of you . . .
That someone's eyes are piercing straight through yours looking deep into your soul . . .
And now that someone says the love that that someone has for you is well and true . . .

Now tell me, what would *you* do?

Javaad Junaid

I FORGOT

I simply can't remember when it started to begin.
Was it when I forgot to bring in the cat or take out the bin?
I can't tell you accurately, was it the twelfth of never,
It may have been yesterday, today or was it forever?
Which month are we in now
October, November or is it December?
I told you I put the car keys in a safe place,
But where, I simply cannot remember.
It's easy to forget, my psychiatrist said,
'It's just a state of mind.'
It was being in the supermarket
And unable to recall what I was there to find.
For the life of me I thought and thought and thought
And gave it a good try!
But confusion swirls around me as time goes by.
I know I have a bad habit, so my husband said,
When searching high and low for my glasses
I found them on my head!
Trying to keep up with birthdays and anniversaries
Is so very hard,
So I keep at home a stack of 'just in case'
Various gifts and cards.
I forget what people told me
If it doesn't interest me I know.
They say that's selective hearing
With people on the go.
Sometimes looking at my children
I hope their names I'll never forget.
It's a fear I have within me, that if I do I'll regret!
Whenever I see some faces, so familiar I feel stumped at times,
'Cause I can't put a name to them, I feel I commit a crime.
When my mate turns around to listen to me
In a nice way I look at her blankly
Because I forgot what I was about to say.
Maybe I should keep a diary,
Not that I'm a great note taker.
But I'll probably forget where I put it, pen to paper!
I forgot what I forget and forget what I forgot,
It happens so easily and it happens a lot!
This thing they call forgetfulness is so easy to do,
Don't be too hasty to judge others
Because it could happen to you!

Tahira Junaid

SO WHAT IF

So precious
are the moments
that we spend,
in each other's gaze

So soft
are your eyes
that sparkle
in the moonlight haze

So tender
are the times
that your body
is wrapped around mine

So sad
are the words
that you and
I seldom use

So
What if.

Stephen Mills

MEN

Men can be violent and men can be cruel
Men always say that they never went to school
Men always say things that make girls feel bad
And men are so proud of how many drinks that they've had
'Fourteen pints I've 'ad tonight and I don't mind telling ya luv
That I could fight with anyone if push really came to shove'
Preening themselves to make girls feel good
Never doing the right thing that they know that they should
Never being there when they're supposed to and always letting you fall down
When all the time before they said ya feet wouldn't even touch the ground
Men are the fixer and the 'don't worry ya pretty head'
And they only look forward to what they're gonna get in bed
Men only have two faults, I know this is true
It's everything they say and everything they do
But sometimes their timing is just like Big Ben
Good luck to you all when dealing with men.

Paul Clarkson

IN NORWAY

We sit on the bed,
us and a few kilos of snow.
We watch the room's corners.
Colourful snow, a syrup.

The place's full of framed photos.

In you the music
is like the speech of an obsessive guy –
phone covered by handkerchief.

My shorts are white and loose,
sunrays turn into rectangles.

Dust sits everywhere
as if chemistry books are being wiped
somewhere nearby.

It feels good,
sunrays stinging the earlobes.
Soften your lips, darling.

They told you,
a hundred years ago in this room
a scientific experiment was held.

Oftentimes to chase boredom away
we pretend to be scientists.

Evelina Porumb

GHOST

Bar room swathed like a wedding cake
Blinkingly enter only half awake
Smoke furls over warm drifts of air
Laughter as shrill as a battlefield flare

All your weakness in their parted lips
Inviting opportunities to be missed
Words like bubbles shine and burst on touch
Fearing those gazes that remember too much

Unable to steady the glass in your hand
Braced to bolt but unwilling to stand
Just a word or a fleeting smile
Your shameful desires redeemed worthwhile

Under halos of honey soft rings of gold
From dreams awakened there's no one to hold
So the taste in your mouth is all that remains
A bitterness surviving loves losses and gains

Like canine obedience to ultrasound
Or the scent of a truffle hiding underground
I haunt you like dry grit in your eye
Daddy-long-legs tickle of a lost crane fly

Condensation weeps like slow rain
Alcohol vapours smother the pain
You thought you saw me and rose to say
But the words and the vision had melted away

O C Keens-Soper

BUBLE ON THE BANDSTAND

Polished Lover Boy bought me
a bright, burnished Bublé CD
echoing smooth, smart stars
loving lyrics, voice, tone, bars –
soft steal of his poetry; our song,
how he'd just not met me – yet.

Gifted scratchy lingerie
lingered in long closed closets.
Fleeting meetings in Premier Inns
(tawdry and far from premier),
rolling round Folkington fields:
an affair – the secret revealed . . .

Tongue-tied, we solemnly trudged,
eerily empty Eastbourne bandstand –
only band was of thin, old gold –
as Bublé waited, breath bated,
a solo secret in car CD
for hushed husband and me.

We sat awhile on breezy blue,
white stripes, bare-back legs nylon – stuck,
wordlessly ceasing, woodenly creaking,
salt-nosed, watery-eyed
as mackarelled clouds washed past
beached summer's subdued sunset.

Bublé's coming to the Bandstand,
a late September one night stand,
many months on, a fitting tribute,
dead ringer for the star singer,
like Lover Boy – an unreal deal,
but a real-life bubble burster.

We won't be perched
on stretched blue stripes
with stretched blue hearts,
not wishing to remember,
come September,
the man I wished I'd never met.

Jilly Munro

136

DID YOU EVER LOSE A FRIEND YOU LOVE?

Here I am, staring at my past as I try to focus on my future,
This isn't a laugh, it's something I've gotta get used to.
Just conversed with my best friend she told me how her partner abused her,
I aspire to be more than that but at the same time I don't wanna lose her.
So instead, I made it clear to her that she can always confide in me,
And under no circumstance will she ever collide with me,
An actor/musician is what she desires to be,
But a soul partner above all else, is what is required for me.
She has an infectious smile I'm bemused, it takes courage the way she can do it,
And I know I can depend on her to ease my pain,
Because I know that she's been through it.
So it's vital that I be there for her in all forms to return the favour,
And no matter how big or small the problem is,
She needs to know that she express it to me,
Like ink written on a piece of paper.
I value our friendship in every aspect which is why I cannot put it in jeopardy,
She's always supportive and wants me to be the best I can be.
I put that into perspective as verbally I try to mend her battered heart
Whilst trying to be the best friend I can be
I had to step outside; the polluted but chilling air gave me the opportunity to think fluently,
And there's when I thought to myself 'there could never be a you and me'
But that's alright I guess, her personal life has nothing to do with me,
A best friend unfortunately is what I have to choose to be.

Ryan Sinclair

MISSED OPPORTUNITY

You are the most amazing woman I have ever met,
that's one thing I will never forget.
To me, you are the woman I should 20 years ago have met,
I wish I did, oh, we would have been wed.
Children, we would have had some,
for they would have brought us so much fun.
Life right now, is so right,
I can't wait until you are my wife,
one day soon, Mandy my dear,
I will make sure our life is full of cheer.

Siman Preston

DRIVING THE FLAMENCO SUNSET · DUENDE

Shivering in paradise, knowing it does not matter where I am
But who I'm with
That all the soft sunlight that I had longed for
Had no warmth to give
The blue seas all around were just an empty ocean after all
The purple sunlit mountains trapped me like a prison wall

A dark bar in Birmingham I thought you would leave me;
It was not your plan
I should have run right then into the bright lit streets
But I stayed in your hands
Then every southern perfumed day I longed for your dark face
Pink moon nights I counted off 'til back to our own space

I have heard that Flamenco artists feel an emotion
Like a state of grace
Somewhere between ecstasy and desperation
I have been in that place
They call it Duende* and it cannot be described in words
So I won't even try; I just know that desperation hurts

So warm, was that strange time in England when we
Pretended to be free
When we had been together it felt like something
Of the ecstasy
Flamenco music in my car and the sunset like deep song in my face
Driving west away from you still I was in that state of grace

Now I am in as lonely a place as ever I have been
You're in my mind
I've forgotten how to dream and that's frightening to me
Like going slowly blind
Driving that Flamenco sunset in dusky colours of a dream-like land
As fleeting as Duende, I could not hold it in my hand.

Duende is almost impossible to define. 'The duende is not in the throat: the duende surges up, inside, from the soles of the feet.' 'A mysterious force that everyone feels and no philosopher has explained.' So, then, the duende is a force not a labour, a struggle not a thought. 'All that has dark sounds has duende.' - Garcia Lorca.

June Palmer

HOPE

I wish I knew the 'Meaning of Life'
to see beyond this pain and strife;
To draw back the curtain of darkness
which falls – *not* just at night;
And discover a world full of joy and light!

Deep down I believe that there is
much in this life for me;
I believe that love, the Universe and
nature will all help set me free.

And so to be true to myself
must *surely* be my goal.
For only then will fear leave my heart
and joy fill my soul.
And so with faith by my side,
my path for life *I will* find:
For already, waiting there for me,
Is *my peace of mind.*

Androulla Pieri

I HAVE NO ROOM

I have no room
for me
in myself

so I'm staying
with someone else

to find my place
on the little piece
of space
belonging
not to me

Piotr Gabryelski

FRIEND OR BREADWIN

The letter 'r' signifies pleasure or pain
Say it hard; say it slow and you will see my claim
The only letter in friend, that keeps it sane
For without that 'r'
It's turned to fiend
Which turns the whole situation to an ugly scene
Friends is not my favourite but Breadwin is
Friend has an end, which is a hit or miss
Breadwin signifies that both can win
Two in harmony with bread between, I mean,
Break bread with a breadwin and both has won
Keep your breadwins close, because friends are long.
Win with a breadwin, the word 'in' denotes,
Outlook is inward, filled with notes
Brings warm hues of red that breadwin taunts
Derived from brethren, the lungs exalt.
A play on good words and deeds, no pause
Movements like water fluidity soars
You can learn from a breadwin, if you listen with cause,
As there is an ear, in this word and not much is lost,
Friend or breadwin
Now you understand
Friend or breadwin
Which one's in your clan
Friend or breadwin
Only you can plan
Friend or breadwin
Choose well and stand.

Leone M Nangle

PERDITUS

Sea of mystery washing over me
always complaining won't let me be
crack of the whip a taste of the salt
the seeds in the ground waiting to grow

Land of spies spray dirt over you
always learning but don't have a clue
like blood to the hound
rabbit in lights
the rope that binds me
and hangs me from heights

Frayed at the roots
torn at the top
bruised from the game
avoided the shot
thorn in my mind
thoughts on my side
like you are the pray with no place to hide

The black clouds are coming chasing the sun
time is unravelling
coming undone
salt in the wound
the web has been spun
empty chamber is what's left in my gun.

Charles Donald

THE HAUNTING

I think I'm being haunted, by a yoghurt,
It could be peach,
It hovers at my bedside just out of reach.

You must think I'm idiotic
Working myself up to a state of hysteria
Spooked by a probiotic,
I'm sure it's friendly bacteria.

It might be easy to dismiss as trivia
This paranormal activia
But I'm taking no chances,
I've bolted the door, changed every lock
To save me from this culture shock.

I've called a priest to pray, to say a mass
To exorcise this L Casea Immunitas
And I think it's worked, the lachrymose lactose it seems has
Taken flight and crossed over into the Muller light.

My rest was short-lived, my slumbers soon disturbed
By an eerie phantasm, that sprayed me with a curdled ectoplasm
And now I'm haunted night and day
By the wailing of a ghostly fromage frais.

It's all my own fault
That will teach me to dabble with the Yakult.

Kevin McMahon

AN IMMORTAL HEART ON THE BEACH

The clouds are orange.
The sun is soon going down.
The birds are flying.
Ricky and Lara,
The sunset's warmth bathes their skin.
These two share one heart.
It is immortal.
Their footsteps won't disappear.
The beach is their home.

Laraine Smith

MY GUARDIAN

Love can be such an extravagant thing,
A process which usually succumbs to a ring.
The fights over the days that crumble,
Sudden loss of that feeling, we mumble.
One in three result in departure, sorrow,
What about the children, what will they think tomorrow?

The heartache that roams this planet,
But love draws many in like a magnet.
To either pursue or to let go,
The true meaning, very few actually know.
My guardian is my love,
The wings of an angel, fell from above.
A defender of heart and being,
They always enquire how I am feeling.
His gentle touch caressing my lips,
The Tetley Tea he drinks, slowly sips.
A watchful gaze from his eyes I see
Yet with two worlds that collide; let us be?
And so I end this on a positive note . . .
Here I fly to a new planet, watch me float.

Megan Manners

BEFORE THE END

If we'd have known in advance
Just what was in store
Would we play that game,
Would we risk our all?

It was all too easy,
I ensnared you with my charm and captivated you with my words,
You made the world honour your beauty and weep at your grace

People would look longingly at us and what we represented,
The living embodiment of happiness, of greatness
Even a life less ordinary

But today we sit, barely able to hold each other's gaze,
Are we hurt or scared
Neither of us know how to behave,
Do we even know what we had and what we've lost . . .

Mark Prime

FREE DOWNLOADS!

They've altered my application
activated my archives
booted my browser
buried my broadband
book-marked my bits
connected my console

captured my cartridge
clicked on my cookies
commandeered my curser
dropped down my devices
delved in my downloads
documented my data

dragged out my driver
displayed my desktop
erased my errata
encrypted my emails
fancied my favourites
fumbled my floppy

fragmented my fonts
fire walled my folders
gorged on my gigabytes
grouped up my game ports
hijacked my hardware
hacked at my hyperlink

hung out my homepage
hosted my hard drive
inserted my icon
interrupted my intranet
jellied my java
jumpered my jack-plug

keystroked my kernel
kneaded my knick-knacks
logged on my laptop
labelled my language
massaged my poor mouse
merged with my modem

minimised my monitor
muddled my memory
memorised my moniker
negated my network
networked my nonsense
opened my outputs

outsourced my options
plagiarised my process
programmed my printer
punctured my popups
partitioned my password
queried my qwerty

questioned my query
quoted my quandary
raided my right-click
recycled my registry
selected my software
sampled my startup

serviced my smartdrive
scheduled my scanner
sentenced my shortcuts
trepassed my trackball
trojaned my toolbar
uncovered my uploads

underlined my undo
violated my version
vetoed my vectors
vented my volumes
wormed in my window
winkled my wizard

x-rated my excerpts
yawned at my yarns
zeroed my zip-drive.

Seamus Harrington

RESURRECTING - SAC-OWER-EOUS CHILD

The realms of resurrection buried,
Excavating bloody beliefs of slavery,
Decimating riots in a blink,
Rejuvenating imagery primed energy.

Shrillness of voice overpowering the silence,
Tears bursting eyes insane,
Holiness captured and tortured,
Bodies are in colossal pain.

Daemons dancing in chaos of secularity,
Dungeons blasted by uncanny cloud,
A shrine struggling to rise above the regime,
Insisting to conquer sacredness stout.

Freeness exhilarating inside obscurity,
Comatose creatures are honing existence
Yet a miniature annoying death,
Courageously battling with paranormal stance.

Enacting with mischievous precedent,
Shielding the human race from the ultimate
Slaughtering designed platform for resurrection,
It's time to dance the dance of devastation to elevate.

The architect of this lighteous hope is a child
A child who preserves the invasion of Godly surmise,
The power of thousand stars unite to exterminate,
Rest in peace darkness in scintillating demise.

Spiky mind crafted absolute revolution,
Where noises will be concealed inside silence,
A sun will rise from west signalling victory,
Lord's dance of destruction will certify the resurgence

This child will craft a world of peace,
Mists and shams destroyed in remuneration of brighter sky,
Darkness will deliver the light,
Entire universe will be enlightened with child deify

That sacred powerful courageous child destine,
To end pain, darkness, daemons and rise as divine.

Diwakar Pokhriyal

LIFE

Life is not what you make it
Things happen, but you have to take it
Simple measures are made to ensure you have a better life.
But! who is the one who comes through when life takes a turn for the worst?
You instigate parts of it, you probably hate.
Give life a shot and see where it gets you.
Carry on regardless and the strength will shine through you
Take each day at a time and breathe a sigh of relief
Don't make a mockery of what you have,
Go forth share your hopes, dreams and like a boa constrictor,
Weave in and out.
You might be surprised what you get out of life,
Because around the corner is a very long road,
Helping you every step of the way.
When you think you can't make it, but you certainly will,
Disguise yourself as someone who can
Punch the air around you and shout out
'Life, life, here I am'. This is more than money can buy.
It's free for as long as you want it, so go ahead, dream that dream,
Run that mile,
Have your say with a smile.
Be content with what you have,
Share your ideas and grab a chance
To express your feelings in words on paper like I have done.
This is my way of living life to the full.

Susan Rigby

LOVE AND FAITH

Shaking hands touch, unsure eyes meet,
A pair that were once one, complete,
A couple that were once so in love,
But parted when push came to shove,
A pair that are now hurt and broken,
Saying things never to be spoken,
Hurling all sorts of abuse and insults,
Not thinking about their results,
He wants to sort out his lifestyle,
While she wishes to reconcile,
Yet he only wants what is best,
And this is his ultimate test,
His test of faith, and of belief,
And he just passes on the grief,
Ev'ry night he sits hoping and praying,
That it's the right things he is saying,
Getting the guidance from above,
About how to fix this broken love,
But he stays strong, with his faith,
Cos that is where he feels he's safe,
Standing by God; forever and always,
Cos that's how he'll live out his days.

Ben Smith

SLEEP WELL

Sleep well, you who I love so well
The time takes on the tone of night
Compels to draw the curtain tight
It needn't know the place we dwell.
Your breath, as all fades to twilight,
Shall in time exhale the morning dew;
The nightingale sings in its flight
Let its song be my lullaby to you.

Sleep well, you who I love so well
The old fireplace still glows gold
The licking fires seeped into the stone,
Scattering its warmth upon us.
Tonight the slouched willow rises
To see the stars we dote upon,
For heavens hold many surprises
None of them from us withdrawn.

Sleep well, you who I love so well
Thoughts hush our parting lips
Guard against words, but a kiss
To seal into memory all that is.
For the night is young: let the dreams
Not carry you far from my heart,
I'll hold tight, till the morning deems
It time for the night to depart.

Ligita Kneitaite

MANCHESTER'S BURNING (AND BANKSY'S GETTIN' PAID)

Old man shivers in his living room (while Banksy's gettin' paid!).
Sally Army's filled each room (and Banksy's gettin' paid!).
In Hulme the kids are kicking cans (yet Banksy's gettin' paid!).
Sure-Start centres, closing down ('cause Banksy's gettin' paid!).

Contributions, work age upped (while Banksy's gettin' paid!).
Wages down and facing further cuts (and Banksy's gettin' paid!).
Food, fuel, public houses taxed (yet Banksy's gets his pay!).
Overdraft, credit cards, loans are maxed ('cause Banksy's gettin' paid!).

NHS staff pay capped low (while Banksy's gettin' paid!).
Teacher's heavy workload grows (and Banksy's gettin' paid!).
Single parent, part-time work (will Banksy's pay your way?)
Repossessed your pride, bills darkly lurk (and Banksy's upped the rate).

A nation built on credit cards (while Banksy got his pay!).
Rising fees make student life so hard (and Banksy's paid!).
Streets in flames and strewn with loot (yet Banksy's booty's paid!).
Livelihoods lost, disaffected youth (and Banksy still gets paid!).

Is this a time to riot? Manchester's burning (while Banksy's gettin' paid!).
This ain't protest, just cops 'n' robbers warring (and Banksy's gettin' paid!).
Opportunity sucked from every town.
Independents started to drown.
Stake peaceful pickets through the cold-heart financier clowns.
Let's bring these thieving vampires down!
(So Banksy don't get paid!).

Alexander Cooke

BEAUTIFUL DISASTER

Within my fitful slumber I stir uneasily, a desolate sigh escapes, I grieve the destruction I have wrought.

Eyes twitching beneath weeping lids, self loathing and derision chasing through my every thought.

My hand with a fierce misplaced yearning reaches across the bed.

It clutches at the sorrow filled emptiness of regret then drops forlornly all energy from my limbs has fled.

I twist the sheets within my clawed hands, as I choke on a guilt-ridden scream.

You were my only solace, beautifully pure and flawless, now you remain that way only in my disillusioned dreams.

I was once as you were my heart un-mutilated, pure and undiluted.

Now shattered into unaccountable pieces jagged and putrid.

I walk my debilitating path now companionless, diminished with no reason to remain standing tall.

I peer out at you within the jeering crowd, from beneath haunting devastated eyes and know with a sense of depraved clarity that you like they eagerly await my fall.

I raise my chin pride and regret war within my gaze, as I fight to fold your eyes with my own

I beg and plead forgiveness for what you have become, I thought that the insecurities, demons and taints were mine alone.

A single silver tear grudgingly rolls down my cheek as I gasp my breathing becoming uneven and faster.

I finally fall to one knee avoiding your gaze and whispering you were and always will be my own beautiful disaster.

Laura Gough

ROCK STAR TOO

Unable to mend, or defend herself from herself,
She befriended life on a drug fuelled bender.
An insidious, hideous, idiocy, ingressed and possessed
When she needed a rest from the banality of sanity.

Her reality and morality became skewed
When she pursued lewd acts for crack.
She was infatuated, degradated.
Segregated from the community by an immunity from feeling or dealing with emotion.
An alien notion.
For her devotion lay elsewhere.

In the glazed haze of her addled stare,
You could see the reflection of her favourite pipe.
A pathetic, synthetic, chemical life.
Matrimony in a complicit visit,
A sacrament that does not limit the exquisite orgy of ecstasy,
Which takes the place
Of the space
Where her life should be.

David Lodo

UNTITLED

I am a water baptised Christian
In this creation that is affected by corruption,
But I believe and do what I know
That I should to trust God the Father.
I am born from my dad and mom
Who are from the Caribbean
And I was born in Balham,
And I was in Jamaica for a while.
I went to schools as a pupil both primary and secondary,
Grammar and comprehensive.
I attend church liberty meetings every Sunday,
And I do charity mosaic jobs from Monday through to Friday.
I am recovered so I do not feel hurt now
After being in hospital because I was head injured
In the year, 1988
That caused me to be autisically eye-sighted
And other badly hurt body feelings.

Andrew Richard Lennon

WHEN THE SUN RISES
(To Omilos Eksirpireton Greece, and participants of the 10th annual seminar, with love)

You will find joy
In the mid morning glory
When the path of light
Un-blind its eyes
Of the darkened gory

You will find rhythm
In the holy sieve
When the weary heart
Finds the anthem of peace
Beyond the oceans of stars

You will find cleansing
In the purest sea
When the dreadful stink
Charm thy godly body
Of past,
To healing of dance,
In the whispers now

You will find love
In the comfort bosom
When the silent air
Bore delight
In the groovy night
And magical spice
Of rainbow colours

You will find hope
Someday;
Somehow;
You will find rest
In the brightest sun.

Michael Kwaku Kesse Somuah

FOR SOPHIA

How long have I been blind, Sophia?
To the city's devil breath that is baking my back.
To the horror of the fiends I find nestled in the wooden cracks.
To the broken arm, to the broken gut,
to the stalled engine and the broken foot.

How long have I been blind, Sophia?
To carry this pig carcass on my back.
Filling our teacups with rose petals and ash.
To the ten a penny scenesters picking at the threads.
Sharing our cigarettes with rag men and fish heads.

How long have I been blind, Sophia?
To my chipped tooth, my bleeding gums and my horse's hoof.
Blowing on thistles and shouting from roof tops.
The kneecaps of churly men shatter,
through ritual eyes, we watched them fall.

How long have I been blind, Sophia?
To the jangle man at my gate,
to the spit of your cigarette,
to dip of your bones,
and the never-ending chorus of our telephones.

How long have I been blind, Sophia?
You green phosphorus rag!
You brown-eyed gun!
You melting clock!
You carcinogen smile!

How long have I been blind, Sophia?
To lady Italy,
to lady China,
to lady Russia,
to lady Bristol,
to lady London,
to lady Leeds,
to lady Newport Station,
to lady river, swan and spider.

How long have I been blind, Sophia?
To the curtain of smoke.
To the ghosts of headless birds.
To rain wandering and a sea of worms.
To the herd of clouds that pass silently over our heads.

How long have I been blind, Sophia?
To the burning Malachim at the end of your bed.
To pink rose vomitous.
To the unused fireplace in your room
and the mattress on your floor,
where together we slept.

How long have I been blind, Sophia?
To these conversations before France
of feathers, faith and jealousy.
The remnants of cigarettes
and your grandmother's headscarf.
The remnants of green and blue
and of possible disease.
The unfinished list we created
with our incandescent fruit smiles.
Your first return and the horrible immediacy of your farewell.

How long have I been blind, Sophia?
To the doorstep of your new home
where we offended the neighbours with our pleasantries.
In Wales you were always barefoot.
In London you slept under the shelter of a neon light.
I didn't even know you were going to Switzerland!
I hated you in Switzerland!

How long have I been blind, Sophia?
To this foul wonderment.
To the wall of gutless poets and writers,
waving their fists at the sky
and howling at the milky rose of temptation.
I am a blistering shock of light!

How long have I been blind, Sophia?
To the belt of creation,
the terror of absence,
the fermenting cup,
the recreation of animal
and my flawed attempt at living.

How long have I been blind, Sophia?
I courted the beast of repetition,
contemplating my triumphant return to sanity,
my grotesque lack of empathy,
and my always inevitable re-admittance into reality.

How long have I been blind, Sophia?
To the kitchen sink,
to my shirt sleeves that are stained yellow.
To the erratic toll of church bells that decorate the drawl of the extractor fan,
and to the red door we had both grown so fond of.

Damien Knightley

LION FISH

Lion fish is gliding through
Sun-drenched waters, crystal blue
Atop each spine toxicity
The splendid savage of the sea

Swims through kelp of emerald green
Lion fish rests, in wait, unseen
Gradually begins to dive
Waiting for prey to arrive

School of fry in silver glances
Tease the light with graceful dances
Into the seaweed drift and flow
Unaware what lies below

Outlines move silhouette-like
Lion fish prepares to strike
Breaking cover at full dash
Skewers silver with a flash

All around the lion's form
Twinkling scales in snow globe storm
Sinking slowly to the bottom
One more victim, soon forgotten

D Jones

UNTITLED

As the sun sets over the town and mountain tops.
As the tide comes in on the beach.
I feel your hand in mine.
Your presence beside me.
Comforting me.
I am home.

Through the shadows and darkness.
Into the warmth and light.
I feel your hand in mine.
Your touch on my skin.
Reassuring me.
I am loved.

From the life-giving mountains.
To the barren cities.
I feel your hand in mine.
Your kiss on my cheek.
Protecting me.
I am safe.

From my body to yours
From your body to mine.
Our minds open.
Our bodies exposed.
Loving me.
I am free.

Sophie Crockett

TINGRITH AND THE TREE

Hello, my name is Tingrith,
Said the tiger to the tree,
I think you have a lot to fear,
From stripy cats like me.

That's rubbish, said the ancient oak,
You're not a real big cat,
Those metal sides are void of fur,
And your brass tail's too fat.

Well, why should I believe a tree?
The cat said with a scowl,
I've never heard of talking plants,
You make me want to growl.

At least I'm not a robot,
Replied the grinning oak,
You're just a simple old machine,
A sprocket-fuelled joke.

The tiger felt a stab of pain,
He knew he was alive,
He could walk and talk so well,
He knew he'd always thrive.

I know I am a real big cat,
The tiger said out loud,
I can do some awesome things,
I'm very well endowed.

What a silly metal brain,
The tree said with a smile,
You're just here to serve your man,
Relaxing is my style.

I do not slave for anyone,
You're just a lowly seed,
The tiger growled and scratched the bark,
You're nothing but a weed!

The tree was getting angry,
His face showed great disdain,
He'd been insulted by machine,
A beast without a brain!

I think you are quite vile,
Said the old oak to the cat,
Just go away and catch a mouse,
Or curl up on the mat!

At least I am more use than you,
Said Tingrith with a grin,
You cannot move a single branch,
You have no hair or skin.

You are made of metal,
The old oak said with glee,
Just look at all your painted stripes
No skin or hair to see!

I make food from the sun,
And sprout out from the soil,
At least I'm made of Earthly stuff,
Instead of silver foil!

But you can't even move a limb,
Said Tingrith growing tense,
Your silly branches never flinch,
You're just stuck in suspense.

The poor old oak was helpless,
He knew he could not move,
But he was growing from the ground,
Surely he could prove . . .

Just then the master came outside,
He saw his metal pet,
His ancient oak looked very sad,
Was Tingrith now a threat?

Now what is going on out here?
The old man said to both,
Tingrith you are not to speak,
You swore that silence oath.

Your talking has upset my tree,
I speak with him each day,
I'm really glad he's robot too,
I like them best that way!

Annabelle Walker

REDVOLUTION

Lately, more than usual
I've been feeling slightly tense.
To put it less politely
I've lately been incensed.
It's been coming for a while
Rising up in angry bile
My rage.
It's something that just won't behave
No matter how I try
Sometime soon someone will die.
But why?
What has caused this wrath and fury?
Well, I'll tell you, it is purely this . . .
If one more moron on the lash
Laughing as he takes a slash
Shouts out
'Oi ginger, want to play?'
'I swear I'm going to make him pay!'
If one more joker thinks that he
Wants to take a piece of me
Bring it on . . . I'm ready.
Ever since I can remember
Ever since a childish member
Of the human race
In every place
At every time
I have heard the same old boring lines.
Ever since through playground tears
I listened to their evil jeers
Carrot top
Or ginger cow
I'm still not quite sure I know how
I've lasted until now
Without committing homicide.
Ginger minger hurt my pride
And brought me close to suicide.
Ginger bimbo
Ginger geek
Ginger four-eyed weirdo, freak.
Ginger biscuit
Ginger bruise
Ginger nut
And ginger pubes.

'Gingers shrivel if it's too bright
So they can't go out in daylight'

Even fat kids hate the gingers
Even kids with extra fingers
Even he-shes
Even hos
Even freaks with webby toes.
You've never seen such vile oppression
As that of those whose hair is Titian
So now my rage knows no permission
I am cruising for a fight
Gingers of the world unite
And stand up for your ginger rights.
Crush this snarling vicious squall
So one day we could rule them all.
Stand up against this tyranny
This thinly veiled conspiracy to keep us down
To drown the sound of our uprising
Don't give into their mollifying
Frankly freakin' patronising
'Gingers are pretty in their own unique way'
Fascist propaganda!
Don't panda to their little minds
But batter their pathetic lines with cold hard stares,
Remember gingers come in pairs
So when he comes in for the lean
Shout our loud 'recessive gene'
And cross your legs.
We don't need them
We need each other
Ginger child of ginger mother
We don't need monthly bottled care
To frizz out our natural flair
But raise our fists high in the air
Death to all the ones who stare
Those who tried to keep us down
But laughing never saw the frown
That sealed their fate and raised our crown
Finally our proper place
The mighty ginger master race!

Lettie McKie

MY MOON

I have a moon.
When I throw it in the air,
It lands in my hand
Thump.
In the light it glistens lilac, golden, sky
Blue.
In the dark it is heavy and small,
Cratered.
The moon sits in the night, glowing
From within.
I cherish it, keep it safe
Safe
From thieves. You want my moon,
Don't you?
It smoulders quietly, then flashes suddenly.
I keep it safe.
My moon.

Fionnuala Munro

CORAL LOVER

'Envelop me,' she gently said
as she took me to her watery bed.

Prawn-pink and naked, I waited
while you
in your spiny splendour teased
and touched me with your tentacles.

Others watched and flexed their muscles
while I joked like a clown fish,
afraid to make waves.

Turtle-skinned and tongue-tied,
you stroked me
with your soft
sea-fingers.

I clammed up.

Victoria Cole

162

TORCH

I carry this torch, for you are the one,
I fell apart, when you broke my heart.

You made me cry, but I could not see,
The pain you suffered, when you lied to me.

My torch, is lit for only you,
My heart was broken, but now fulfilled.

The trust is growing, the past is going.

Your promise you made, on our wedding day,
The one that, I made to,
Remember that day, remember that thought,

That was the day . . . I lit my torch.

You are my valentine, you are my life,
How beautiful you are, my lovely wife.

Christopher Hardy

AUTUMN AT FLATFORD

Our two sons were at our front door, carrying their lunch boxes for an afternoon out,
we soon travelled into the Constable countryside with sheep, goats and horses roaming about.
We walked down the country lane to the old house at Valley Farm,
inside, we stood by a spinner and an open fire, all nice and warm.

This building has its original staircase uncovered by a dog chasing a mouse,
after the rain, the outer limestone walls had become cream, all around the house.
At the mill, we saw a reflection of Willy Lott's cottage clearly,
and close by, we could see the view of John Constable's painting 'The Hay Wain' perfectly.

Lunchtime at the Dry Dock, we sat next to a young girl using pastels at her leisure,
and Taylor was eager to copy and create his own sketch with great pleasure.
A man was also painting his scene looking over to Flatford Bridge,
whilst Ashton fed the ducks and swans carefully standing on the ridge.

Some walkers strolled along the winding path to Manningtree,
whilst others went the opposite way to Dedham and its church amongst the trees.
Our boys had their wellies and ran through the large puddles with a great smile,
a mild November afternoon spent in this wonderful place for a while.

Adrian Bullard

163

BANK JOKE

Our banks are one big joke,
as they give us an unfair yoke,
the yoke of charges is one of their jokes,
how I wish they would go up in smoke.

Boom, bust, bailout, is the cry of the banks,
bonus, bonus, bonus, is the song of the bankers,
bankers demand a yearly bonus on time,
whether it's boom, bust or bailout time.

Governments are easily sucked in,
by the banks and bankers who draw them in,
who tell them that the economy is dim,
for them to satisfy their banking whim.

If banks do not get their greedy way,
then they will make the needy pay,
save with us and get no interest,
borrow from us and you'll pay a high price,
like it or lump it, this is today's yeast,
of today's banking beast.

Miss payments on your home loan and
Banks will make you pay a hundred fold,
any more missed payments that come from you,
then banks will take your house from you.

The banks can't fall,
so they always have a ball,
if they do start falling,
the government goes calling,
then they'll agree to take tax payers' hard-earned cash,
to prop up their weak, plundered bank stash.

Banks say,
(take our credit card and live our life and
make us money all of your life,
as you'll be paying sky high interest all of your life,
just for that small taste of our greedy banking life.

We should be jailed,
but we always get bailed,
so there's no chance of us ever getting nailed and
we blame each other to avoid the gutter,
so we can live our life like a nutter.

We gamble your money on stock exchange,
then we tell you that your money has changed,
we charge you interest on your own savings,
while along we are making billions.

If our government ever runs out of cash,
then we'll just go crying for the European Central Bank's stash,
with their policy of supporting the banks,
we always take their money and we never say thanks.

We would hate to lose our bonus pay,
'cause we would lose our easy pay,
so we the bankers would just rue the day,
if we ever lost out on our huge bonus pay.

If you're ever a penny short in your account,
for a direct debit of any amount,
then we'll charge you a huge amount,
even if you can't afford to pay such an amount.

Is this legal you will say,
of course it is, we will say,
as our friends in government told us to say,
they legalised our charges for them to stay.

There's no hope of ever getting justice,
But you can try if you must 'as,
the whole system is also our friend,
so you, my friend, will lose your case, in the end.

So, by hook or by crook,
we bankers will always get our loot,
even though we deserve the boot,
for gambling and squandering your hardworking loot,
truthfully we say to you,
we just don't give a hoot).

So, here's a (trainee) poet's advice for anyone with ears to listen,
(don't take a sip from a banker's cup,
as you're drinking from a devil's cup,
one sip is all it takes,
for you to be in debt forever,
to poisoned banking snakes.

Just pray to your god,
that you will not be bought,
by corrupt men of useless thought,
Just stay in the black and out of the red,
as this stops your money from going dead.

Being in the black is banking out of harm's way,
because the banks can't take your money in any form of way,
so by banking this way all your days,
should make you feel a little bit happier every day,
knowing that you're banking the fee, free way).

Desmond Flynn

TRAVELLING MINDS

Catching the early train on a Sunday autumn morning,
Soaring to new heights as we gaze at the dawning,
Each alternate breath interrupted with a yawning,
Akin to the sound of white water roaring.

The resonant tone is set,
For the overture is debt,
The karma comes back round;
But the mountain wears no frown

A brand new day bright, crisp and clear,
Over-casting shadows on our doubts and fears,
As we set on a journey of hopes and dreams,
Open countryside opens the mind's eye pristine.

Now that this picture grows clearer,
Like fog lifts the morning dew,
Progressive notions draw nearer,
Night becomes day and all is new.

We have travelled fourfold along this dusty trail,
Passing through nook and cranny, mountaintop and dale,
In hope of redeeming our own holy grail,
Prescient visions capture undertakings we entail.

Upon a seat of stars,
The constellation's sparkle,
A silhouette of Mars,
May set the tone and marvel.

Parrying both the vision and the voice,
Bearing solitude with metaphoric psalms,
Each of us in our own little space,
Chanting mantras to keep us calm.

Matthew Western

A PRESCRIPTION FOR PAIN

Look what you have done
You have created a prescription for creating pain
Do you really want to drive me insane?
Yes we all have a right to some individual fun
But this is way out of line
You have gone and crossed the line
How do we go back to the trust?
When the trust is gone what is there to rely on
Our love was more than enough for the two of us
But you have gone and done wrong
What do we do now, what can be regain
In this prescription you have created for pain

It was wrong, so badly wrong
I love you but the song in my heart has died
Overcome with weakness you lost what made you strong
The pain I cannot hide, has risen to extreme high
Forgive and forget; how does one start?
In irreplaceable pieces you have broken my heart
I believe in you as night follows day
My complete trust I gave to you
Then you rock my world like a foundation made of clay
Can love weather this, can love be renewed?
I am wounded in my heart and mind
Can we find the way back for us to be; this time?

A prescription for creating pain
And how the pain hurts; like I have never hurt before
My heart feels like winter rain
Cold and dismal and so unsure
I love you, it is hard not to love you; I have loved you for so long
And I still believe that we truly belong
But this insincere act has taken away something precious
Something that had only belonged to us
Where have we gone wrong that you should deceive me so?
Do you not want this anymore?
I really want to know
Because on us I cannot close love's door
Talk to me, this wound is so deep
Now for all the wrong reasons; I get so little sleep

Delores Anderson

FOR ADDICTS

Don't despair at loneliness
Desolation and gloom
Or think you're any less a person
For staying in your room

As long as there's a window
And even if there's not
You're still here in the world

As Odysseus was
And all the great adventurers
Leaders and archetypes of strength
Who resisted temptation
And have been around for centuries
In schoolrooms and universities
Stimulating grey matter and debate
Inspiring new philosophies
From the ancient timeless

But you've as much right to be here
As them or anybody else
In the lively, living places
Like cafés, libraries, colleges
Galleries, supermarkets
Sports arenas
Planes, trains and automobiles
And at sea with your intrepid crew

And maybe one day
Your story will inspire people
In schoolrooms and universities

The one who was curious

Lured by sirens
Seduced by nymphs
And swept away by hideous monsters
During the tempest

And however bare
Your empty cell may seem to be
Remember that all those people
In the lively, living places

Return to the same emptiness
Where there's just themselves
And no jobs, no money
No chocolate, no religion

168

No music, no drugs, no alcohol
No books, no family, no friends
No battleship, no crew

Some are joyful here
Some ill at ease
But there's no shame in either

And if your tormentor weakens you
And you start to feel you'll never cope
And you churn with fear
It's then you need to tell yourself
That this is your life force
And your single ember of hope

Anne-Louise Lowrey

TORN APART

Hardly talk anymore
It's hard and it hurts
But it's been so long now
And the arrangement still doesn't work
8 years between us
But we were like twins
We laughed and had fun
But it started to end
People get involved
This broke us up
I want to be there for you
If anything troubles your mind
If you ever get hurt
Or ever need to talk
But 4 hours once a week
And 1 weekend every 3
Has torn us apart
And has now made me realise
That you are so important to me
It feels like we aren't brother and sister
But by our parents we are
We try to get on now
But still argue a lot
However you're my little bro
And my love for you will never stop.

Jade Piggott

JOURNEY TO WHO I AM

Next time
Next time someone asks me who I am
I'll tell them

I'll tell them that
I'm – an amazing God like specimen painstakingly crafted in God's own image
And I'll mean every single word of it

For far too long all I felt was invisible
I didn't like myself
Couldn't recognise myself
So every time I stepped out confidence was lacking
And questions were abounding

Looking around me didn't help
It just made me wonder
Why my face wasn't spotless
Why I wasn't taller
Why my boobs didn't grow quicker
My hips weren't wider
My waist not smaller
My teeth not whiter
My stomach not flatter
My grades not higher
My swag not flyer
This could go on forever
Basically the world made me wonder

And every time I stepped out confidence was lacking
And questions were abounding
I just wanted to be invisible

With teenage years came cross continental migration
And that didn't help matters
You see this new culture was such a frustration
My new peers – I couldn't understand a fraction
With so much opportunity
Their dreams somehow never achieved conception
Morality was missing in action
Fun was identifiable by a chain of regrettable actions
They existed just to be the centre of attraction
And I to them was just a side distraction
My name – they mangled beyond recognition
My accent – they ripped to shreds with no contrition
My feelings they crushed with no emotion
And I couldn't find myself in all of their commotion

So I felt invisible
Wanted reality to match my emotion
Felt invisible craved a confidence that only comes with true self definition

So I set out to find myself

At first, I moulded myself into the image of their perfection
And when they said I was beautiful, I guess I was
I lived for those moments when showering me with compliments;
I saw glimmers of that confidence that person I so badly craved to be

I didn't know who I was so I sold whatever that was at a high price
Just so I could hear someone say you are beautiful
Choosing to forget that when he said I was beautiful he wasn't giving me an upgrade
He simply acknowledged what God made.

I became almost all their expectations
Only to find that the new me – wasn't matching my expectations
I didn't know who I was
But I had to be – I was I had to be worth more than that

With that realisation I took my first step on the road to who I am
Saw a sign defining bondage as allowing *my* self worth
To be determined by others' subjective limitations
So I looked for a standard that wasn't subject to permutations
Salvation freed me from self-imposed incarceration
My self worth can only be defined by the Creator not his creations
I opened Psalm 139 and found my true definition
It wasn't linked to my profession
Or my current situation
It didn't fluctuate with emotion
In fact it made me rise out of depression

I opened it and it said
I am fearfully and wonderfully made
And with that discovery history was made

Beauty is in the eye of the beholder
So if for some reason you don't behold mine
It doesn't dismantle what God made
My confidence has totally been remade
And my value, it's not man-made
I know who I am so I can embrace what I am
I'm 5 foot 4 of intelligent, beautiful awkward awesomeness
Who is fearfully and wonderfully made

On those days when I wake up daring to forget what God has made
When the confidence of yesterday has somehow been mislaid
I react with purpose until my misgivings are allayed
Repeating to myself in the mirror of life

I am not invisible; I am not worthless (x2)
I am 5 foot 4 of intelligent, beautiful awkward awesomeness
I am weirdly, wonderfully, fearfully and awesomely made
And I dare you to prove different.

Because this is who I am.
An amazing God like specimen painstakingly crafted in God's own image
This is who I am.

Tolu 'Poetic Echos' Agbelusi

UNTITLED

Words cannot express just what I hold for you.
And from the very first time I kissed you I knew my love was true.

All my love I thought was set in stone
me and you forever,
one and one equals whole.

Those precious moments will forever be close to my heart.
I thought our love was till death do us part.

I've tried so many times to try and express just how I'm feeling.
My mouth speaks no words but my heart takes the beating.

All I feel is one broken shell.
The day those words entered your mind, my body went to hell.

You see I'm trying to say I love you – because I know it's all so true.
But darling you've proper crushed me I just don't know what to do.
I want to hold and kiss you
just want to be your boo
But the day you shattered my heart
A piece of me left you.

I try so hard to forget.
But the promises I've heard all before.
Time after time I keep telling myself I just can't do this anymore.

I love you so much it hurts. It hurts even just to breathe.
The tears I've cried it's hard to explain. But I'll just tell you I could just barely see.
No matter how much pain I feel or just how much it kills.
No amount of alcohol will numb me nor does the pills.

Karen Anderson

BECAUSE I LOVE YOU . . .

The mist had come, and the sun was gone
my love was lost, and I was alone.
Too weak to move, I just stood there,
too afraid to believe, what just happened here.

There she was, in front of me,
so near, yet so far from me.
I stared into her dazzling blue eyes,
they were looking back at me.
I remembered, they were full of love,
but now she is gone,
and it feels they never belonged to me.
I always thought her heart was mine,
and now it seems, she never had enough time.
Thinking about her makes my heartbeats slow,
I don't think I'm ready to let her go.

There she was, I saw her again
one more day passed, I kept waiting for her in the rain.
I looked at her, with desire in my heart
I knew I will cease to exist, if we were to part.
I wanted her to be mine, I craved for her
but she was too divine, to be my girl.
My heart was true, and my love was pure
and for all I knew, it had no cure.
One day she saw me, and blinked her eyes
and I felt my heart, crossing the skies.
Deep down I knew, it was too good to be true
but still I promise, I will never stop loving you.

Mohit Gupta

HATE CRIME

These words are so painfully strong,
Why can't we all just get along?
Every single day in the papers, or on TV,
Someone is dead; could have been you or me.
The world has become such a violent place,
Now it's all no meaning, we are still all the same,
But many cowardly people play the hate crime game.
We all have abilities and disabilities and issues to raise,

We all do things in our own special ways.

This terror needs to stop, this hated needs to end,
Peace needs to be brought out, the world we shall mend.

Hate crimes are not good for the upcoming years,
The new year isn't for tears, but rather cheers,
The clock strikes midnight ending a year of fear
So now is the time to down your beer.
We forget the bad times and remember the good
Do you know what's happening in your neighbourhood?
These crimes we see and hear, are not right,
Forget the dark and stand in the light,
It doesn't matter how old you are,
Make a note to change and do not leave a scar,
It does not take a dollar or coin,
So, don't make it hard, and just join,
Leave the hatred and racism behind
Start all over and be kind.

Our speech is free
So are our dreams
Until it's too late and we hear the loud screams.
Could we do anything to prevent it?
Do you think the people meant it?

If that person *only* had a mentor
They could report it to a 3rd Party Reporting Centre
If only they knew before it was too late
That they had been a victim of hate
No crime isn't too small to report
I know you can feel rather fraught
All the paperwork to be filled out
All I want to do is shout.

We are all the same on the inside
Except we don't want to hide
Why should we hide because of hate crime?
None of us have the time.

Still life goes on around us all
No one stops to think

Hate crime is all around us
And that's what I think stinks.

Kate Green

STORM THE BASTILLE

Storm the Bastille, Lenin Marx
Anti-imperial might
Just get lost along the way
With another bright idea

Freedom rings, wait the day
For a taste of things to come
Out of touch, out of mind
To face the real world

February sings a mutiny cry
Echoes in the ranks be the last one
On the front to face a fight with no arms
Bitter is the taste a new uprising

Shadow on the reign, fall on Louis
The window will decide the new republic
Falling on the blade cutting changes
Marie Antoinette allez the sun king tricolore.

St Petersburg is out of touch
Change is on the way
October sting feel the bite
And leave the cold outside.

Jason Hingston

THEY NEVER TOLD US . . .

Baby, they never told us about sex
Never told us the truth of it
They took it for themselves
And gave it back to us
Shrouded, torn and fumbling blind
Baby, they never told us about sex

Our cultures never told us about sex
They shipped it off to Hollywood
Built altars to it
On our TVs, our billboards, our movie screens

They airbrushed it
Dressed it up
Made it untouchable
Perfect lovers making perfect love in perfect worlds
That none of us recognised

You know the score:
Beautiful man spies beautiful woman
In a launderette
Beautiful man gives eyes of sex to beautiful woman
Beautiful woman looks back
Mouths 'yes'
As she drops her laundry basket

Cut to room with bed
Candle lit

Slow motion shots of tops ripped off
And flying through the air in the shape of swans
Beautiful woman hums Cindy Lauper songs
Beautiful man's torso is distinctly bronze

Beautiful man cartwheels on to bed with significant grace
Beautiful woman's hair stays perfect in place
As she backflips off headboard
And lands in beautiful man's embrace

Sex starts straight away
Skipping small talk
Skipping awkward phase
Skipping contraception and foreplay

Stopping only for beautiful woman
To whisper, 'Wait'
Before hitting stereo play
And falling backwards slowly
To the sound of Marvin Gaye

Cut to perfect double orgasm
And harmonised groans
Beautiful woman screams, 'Take me home'
Someone somewhere plays a saxophone
Marvin continues to moan

Cut to the lighting of cigarettes
As friendly debate on personal political leanings starts
Beautiful woman blows smoke rings
That looks remarkably like hearts

Marvin croons, 'We're all sensitive people'
Beautiful man looks to camera
Winks
Says, 'Wait till you see the sequel!'
The credits roll
And we're left empty and thinking,
Where did we go wrong?

Baby, they never told us about sex

Our schools never told us about sex
They gave us textbooks and diagrams and sex ed
Gave us the mechanics of the body
But missed the landscapes of the soul

They filled our young minds with methods
Told us 'go and explore'
Pushed us through the door as adults
We thought we knew it all
They never told us
That holding the soul of another
Trembling in your arms
You're as vulnerable as a child and utterly disarmed

They gave us the addresses of the clinics
Taught us the names of the diseases
Showed us ways of protection
But never how to guard against the weeping
The rejection
The insecurity
The doubts
They never told us that when you join with another
You touch their spirit
And light fires together that can never be put out

Baby, they never told us about sex

Our churches never told us about sex
They locked it away
Silenced its name
Gave it over to taboo
And deleted it from their scriptures

Its absence made it shameful
And our urges confused
And so we removed our desires from any mention of God

They never told us that God is a lover
Whose passions are storms
Whose desire is the rainclouds
And whose groans are the dawns
That sex is a painting
And He is the artist
And the strokes of His brush are the longings we'd die for

Baby, they never told us about sex

They sent us out blind and hungry
With ideals in our lusts
Made sex into a stage
And put the spotlight on us
Filled us to bursting with a need to impress
In the way we perform
The way we undress
How we beat our score and our personal best

We turned our beds into competition
Our flesh a fleeting mission
We made prowess our idol
And left each other bleeding
Turned lovers into rivals
Until it was just about
Me . . .

Baby, they never told us about sex

They never told us about love
How love is a journey
And journeys take heart
That the hope of the ending
Outlives the passions of the start
Never told us about the miles
You have to walk with another
Before you can even hope to call yourself their lover

They never told us that the battles and mistakes
Bring you closer together
That the hurt and the pain
Make the touch more tender
That the groans touch forever
When you let the other win
And that love takes you places
Lust has never been

That sex is desire
And desire is love's dawn
And love is two spirits
Disappearing to one
To come undone in the melodies
Of eternity's song
Of baby
Darling
Darling
Yes
Baby
Yes
Yes
Yes

Sh'maya

MY SPACE

This is *my* space
Space for me
Space to breathe
Space to be

To rest, recover
Re-energise
To grow, to flower
Self-actualise

To mediate
Away from strife
And contemplate
Another life

This is *my* space
Space for me
To think, be still,
Be free, be me.

Robert Barker

UPDATING MY STATUS . . .

Jenny is 'single', her status has changed,
so a girlie night out is quickly arranged.

I log on to find an event invite,
we're getting together on Friday night.

Kelly's accepted, three have said maybe,
Deb's can't come, she's expecting a baby.

'Don't tell Emma,' I'm warned by Yvonne,
'Jenny hates her so she can't come.'

'Don't update your status and mention the date
cos Bev's not invited and neither is Kate.'

Fran's status is cryptic, 'just popping to town',
for those six invited it means, we'll meet at The Crown.

Lisa takes pictures, we pull faces and smile;
'I'm gonna put this one as my profile.'

'No you can't,' yells Yvonne, but it's too late,
the picture is up, we'll just have to wait.

That familiar beep; it's Bev on chat,
'I've seen that picture, where are you at?'

'Err, I walked past The Crown and saw Denise,
it was a last minute thing according to Lise.'

I don't get a reply and can tell she's upset,
'She'll message Kate now and tell her I bet.'

I realise our lives are for all to see,
the peril of virtual reality.

Deliberate statuses written to hurt,
some with good news, others dish out the dirt.

Friends getting married, that's lovely to hear
and to catch up with loved ones who don't live near.

But I really don't care Brian's going to the gym
I was with him at first school and never liked him.

Becky can't decide which sandwich to choose,
do I really log on to hear this news?

I leave my friends, feeling somewhat deflated.
It's time, I think, to become de-activated.

Jayne Drewery

181

FORWARD POETRY INFORMATION

We hope you have enjoyed reading this book - and that you will continue to enjoy it in the coming years.

If you like reading and writing poetry drop us a line, or give us a call, and we'll send you a free information pack.

Alternatively if you would like to order further copies of this book or any of our other titles, then please give us a call or log onto our website at www.forwardpoetry.co.uk.

Forward Poetry Information
Remus House
Coltsfoot Drive
Peterborough
PE2 9BF
(01733) 890099